It Had to Be You

by

Mike Owens

It Had to Be You

Cover Art by *Jennifer Greeff*

The Wild Rose Press, Inc.
PO Box 708
Adams Basin, NY 14410-0708
Visit us at www.thewildrosepress.com

Publishing History
First Edition, 2022
Trade Paperback ISBN 978-1-5092-4086-9
Digital ISBN 978-1-5092-4087-6

Published in the United States of America

Are you all right? I came to check on you."

He jumped at the sound of her voice. Her head and bare shoulders were above the gunnels. He looked behind her, where ripples should mark the path of her swim, but saw none.

"How did you get here?" In other words, how had she made it from the shoreline to his boat, over two hundred feet, without leaving any trace on the surface?

"How do you think?"

"You didn't swim, did you?"

"Not exactly." She hoisted herself over the side of the boat. Sometimes she wore a bathing suit, sometimes she didn't, tonight she didn't, and she was luminous, brighter than the moon. She must have been visible from some distance, radiant and naked as she was.

"I'm cold. You have to get me warm."

He wrapped his arms around her, and she folded into him every nook and cranny of his body. He ran his fingers through her hair…perfectly dry. How in hell?

Even dragging his fingertips across the surface of the water left a trail of ripples, but she'd left no trace. "Can you fly?" he asked, and he got the answer he should have expected.

"Not exactly."

Praise for Mike Owens

"A magical romance that will keep you wondering from beginning to end."

~Lauran Strait, President, Hampton Roads Writers

~*~

"Michael Owens has done it again—this time in *IT HAD TO BE YOU*, a page-turner where a man runs away from one life and falls into a wild adventure that challenges what it means to come home. You're in for quite a ride…"

~Michael Jon Khandelwal, Executive Director,
The Muse Writers Center (Norfolk, VA)

Acknowledgments

Many thanks to the readers and writers
at Hampton Roads Writers and at The Muse
and special thanks to Patrick Clark
for reading the complete manuscript.

Chapter One

Charlie had a big one, a lot bigger than Phil's, and he never missed a chance to rub it in. "Hey, neighbor, did that thing come with training wheels?" the bastard yelled, just before shifting his faster, more powerful, and most important of all, bigger riding mower into high gear then tearing off across the lawn, leaving a very pissed off Phil Claussen sitting atop his own modest mower in a cloud of exhaust and grass clippings.

Phil waved and smiled at Charlie, adding a brisk "Good morning." And a softer, "Go fuck yourself."

Seven years now, Phil, his wife, MaryBeth, and daughter, Addie, had made their home in Wakefield, North Carolina, a small, idyllic town nestled in by the Albemarle Sound, close enough to be considered coastal, but not so close that they had to deal with summertime beach crowds. The first four years or so had been all he could ask for, not perfect, mind you, but smooth enough that he considered himself a lucky guy, that is, until two years ago when Charlie Hughes, newly retired vinyl siding salesman, moved in next door and declared lawn mowing to be an Olympic sport with bragging rights awarded to the winner.

"You ought to trade up and get yourself a real man's mowing machine," Charlie said just after he'd walked over and introduced himself. Phil had never linked his manhood with his mowing machine, but Charlie certainly did, and they would have that same conversation at every neighborhood barbecue for the whole mowing season. It was just grass, for God's sake, and it shouldn't bother him, but it did because, deep down, Phil was as competitive as the next guy, and Charlie, with his persistent needling, pushed his buttons.

Two lovely spring weekends ruined already as he'd watched Charlie tearing around his yard like some crazed Indy 500 driver, pausing only to smirk while Phil dawdled along on his own more modest mower, adequate, sure, but a distant second in the neighborhood mowing competition. A more patient man would have been content puttering along on his five-horsepower lawn machine while fantasizing that Charlie, as he raced around his yard like a madman, might sustain a small sun stroke causing him to lose control of his mower, which would then veer out into the path of an oncoming waste management truck. Problem solved in one glorious crash. But Phil couldn't depend on the fickle finger of fate landing on Charlie. It might just as easily point in his own direction. So, he needed a plan with satisfaction guaranteed, and soon.

He had two choices, go bigger or strangle Charlie. Bigger sounded better, although killing Charlie had some appeal. If you wanted to stay in the game, you had to have the right equipment, in other words, a mowing machine bigger and faster than Charlie's. So, the last Wednesday in April, Phil did the mature, reasonable thing, the only thing a guy could do. He marched into the showroom, Lawn and Garden Tools of Wakefield, NC, and thumped on the cowling of the gleaming blue lawn tractor sitting right up front by the window—tractor, mind you, not just a mower.

"She's a real beauty, sir." The salesman wore a blue tie the same shade as the mower. "Why don't you climb aboard, see how it feels. Mind you, it's even better when you fire it up, but of course, we can't do that inside. Take it from me; she purrs like a kitten, a very big kitten." The salesman laughed and clapped Phil on the shoulder like he'd just shared some big inside joke. "This is an all-terrain mower. If your lot is rough, full of hills and valleys, no problem, this baby handles them easy as pie. And you have a huge forty-eight-inch mowing deck, so you'll have plenty of time left over for weekend golf or fishing. This machine will mow, tow, and mulch and do everything but fetch your morning coffee."

"She's a beauty, all right," Phil said, "but that's a pretty hefty price tag." All told, over four times as much as he'd paid for his current mower.

"I know it sounds like a lot of money for a lawn tractor, but we like to think of this as a generational machine, one that you'll pass down to your children and grandchildren, too. With this machine, the Claussen family will never have to worry about yard work again."

Phil climbed aboard and nestled down into the spacious seat atop twenty-five horsepower of grass-shredding power, and that's all it took. The decision was made. The price, the size of the mower, the fact that his own lawn measured only 60 X 150 feet, just details. "Oh, yeah," was all he said.

He dismounted, circled the most beautiful mowing machine he'd ever seen. He kicked the tires, big tires, lawn tractor tires, kick 'em all day long and never leave a mark, reared back with his hands in his pockets, like a man who knows what he's looking for and has just found it. *We're talking destiny here.* Yeah, Peerless, best brand you could buy. Now, won't that be something, him cruising by on a rig that dwarfed Charlie's, running rings around the Hughes model while the bastard sat there with brown stains forming on the seat of his pants. *How do you like it now, Mr. Charles Hughes? You and your little toy mower. Eat my grass clippings.*

"We'll get this baby delivered tomorrow. That sound okay?" The salesman glowed as he filled out the paperwork, no doubt, a big commission his for the taking. "Of course, you'll be wanting the extended warranty. We highly recommend it."

"Of course." It seemed a bit odd, an extended warranty for such a reliable machine, but Phil asked no questions; he was far beyond that point, floating, as he was, up by the ceiling of the showroom, dreaming his dream, a tractor of his very own. He could hardly wait to see Charlie's face.

"And you'll probably want the cart and attachment, very handy for towing stuff around your yard."

"Oh, sure," Sounded logical enough. "Do I get a hat too?" Phil asked. He wouldn't be much of a Peerless man without a blue hat bearing the official logo.

"I'll get you one right now." The salesman trotted across the showroom and returned with a couple of hats. "Here's one for your wife too," he said, still beaming.

A hat for MaryBeth? Great, but the first hitch in his

plan now emerged. It would take a lot more than a hat, even one with an official logo, to placate his wife. He'd never discussed the great riding mower dispute with her, and more than likely, she wouldn't understand the finer points of the contest. In particular, she wouldn't get the ones that had just driven him to lay out a large chunk of cash for an industrial-sized mowing machine that blew a big hole in the family budget.

"Five thousand dollars. Charlie, what in hell were you thinking?" And she would probably point out that their own small patch of grass required only minimal time and effort to mow. She wouldn't understand the psychological damage done by continually coming in second place behind Charlie's riding mower.

"What about Addie's college fund? Did you even consider that? Don't you ever think about anybody but yourself?" By this point, her rant would come from a red face with steam coming out of her ears. Thanks to Charlie Hughes and his damned mower, Phil had just dropped a large shiny blue turd in the domestic punch bowl.

His hands shook as he drove away from the dealership, considering this new dilemma, facing a far more formidable adversary than Charlie Hughes. An enraged MaryBeth—and she would definitely be enraged—could hurt him in ways Charlie never dreamed of, and worst of all, he'd deserve everything she dished out. He wished he'd gone with plan A—strangle Charlie and be done with it all. Phil could almost hear the popping sound as his bubble burst, so he did the only reasonable thing; he stopped for a beer.

Sean's Bar and Grill, they knew him here, not that he was a regular—he wasn't—once a week at most, just that the owner, Sean Billups, despite being so near-sighted he could qualify as handicapped, had a knack for linking names and drinking habits. By the time you'd dropped in a couple of times, Sean knew your name, what you drank, and how much. He knew whether you were a one or two-beer man, like Phil, or whether you were likely to occupy the barstool until closing time. He recognized any departure from usual habits, spotted trouble before it got started.

Before Phil even asked, Sean set a frosty draft in front of him. "Hot out?" he asked.

"Oh, yeah. Gonna get even hotter, I hear," Phil answered with the standard reply, the same one he'd heard and used for years now. To get along in a small town, you had to speak the language. Any other response, no matter how creative, would draw suspicious looks from any local who heard it.

Then Phil committed his own blunder: "I bought a new mower," he said without being asked. Some topics, such as weather, fishing news, scores from the high school athletic teams were innocuous entries that didn't require a response. But purchase of a new lawnmower required an explanation, making Phil sorry he'd brought it up in the first place.

"Oh, yeah, what did you get?" asked Sean.

"Peerless," Phil said softly, hoping the topic would fade and be forgotten quickly.

But that was not to be because Sean announced in a loud voice, "Peerless, you must have come into some money." Several heads turned in Phil's direction with expressions that were less than kindly.

"You probably have a big yard to mow," Sean said.

"No, just that my old mower keeps breaking down,

and I wanted a new one," Phil said. So, he now found himself in a preview of the discussion he would have with MaryBeth, facing questions for which he had no solid answers.

He sipped some of the foam off the head of his beer, searching desperately for a plan to justify his new toy, and what do you know, why, there was an idea already…heat. It wouldn't do to spend a lot of time out mowing the lawn in hot weather. It was unhealthy, and he wasn't getting any younger. His new mower would cut his sun exposure way down, decrease the risk of skin cancer. Could he write it off as a medical expense? Probably not, but at least he could try the argument on MaryBeth.

And his allergies, he'd forgotten all about them, how he spent the spring months wolfing down prescription-grade antihistamines, had already started his seasonal regimen. Simple enough, cut down on the mowing time, cut down on the exposure to all those seasonal irritants that left him teary-eyed and sniffling like a girl whose prom date failed to show, and maybe avoid the medication-induced catatonia that had him bumping into large, immovable objects.

Damn, he was on a roll. "Another cold one over here, Sean." The bar was the best idea he'd had all day. He did some of his best thinking on a barstool. All he needed was one more piece to tie his whole argument together, and if he sat there long enough, he could for sure come up with a plausible plan to justify the mower. After she heard him out, MaryBeth would be congratulating him instead of calling him an idiot, although she didn't seem to need much of an excuse to call him an idiot.

But after the second beer, he was no further along, still stuck at square one and going nowhere fast. The sun exposure angle sounded good, and the allergy issue helped, but when he added up the total, he was still far short of a sound argument for his tractor. He needed a big idea, a solid idea, something without any cracks. He needed another beer. And another beer.

"You gonna be okay?" Sean stood in front of Phil, wiping the bar with a ragged towel, a concerned look on his face. Other customers had drifted in, and most of the spaces at the bar were now filled by men, each of whom looked down lovingly at his cold glass of beer, except for the one guy who had ordered coffee. The seats on either side of him remained vacant.

"Huh?" The outlines of Sean's face were a little less sharp than earlier, as if Phil, like the bartender, was developing a visual impairment.

"Driving, I mean. You've had four since you came in, and unless you had an early lunch, I doubt you've eaten anything. Drinking on an empty stomach is bad news, especially on a hot day." This was Sean's equivalent of a cease and desist order.

Four? How could that be? Seemed like he just got started, but Sean had cut him off politely. "Oh, hell. I'm fine." Phil paid up, got up to leave, caught his foot in the chair rung, and fell straight backward, right into the lady walking behind him.

Coins, coins, all over the floor. From the corner of his eye, he read the label on the large jar the lady must have been carrying, *DONATIONS FOR WAKEFIELD'S HOMELESS*. He wasn't even aware that Wakefield had homeless. Now their nickels, dimes, and quarters were scattered all over the barroom floor. A lot of hungry homeless in town because Phil Claussen, in spite of the warnings clearly written on the bottle, had augmented his medication with alcohol.

Phil and the donations collector landed on the floor in a tangle. Somehow her skirt wound up draped over his head, baring her from the waist down. She looked way too old to be wearing a bright red thong, but these days you never knew.

"You drunken lout." The enraged and exposed woman struck him in the head with a purse that must have contained a brick, possibly a couple of them. The blow, along with the beer and the drugs, scrambled his brain.

He struggled to get to his feet, but her left leg was locked around his neck choking him. He bit down. She screamed. Phil rolled off to the side, and she crawled after him, pummeling him with her fists. "You sorry bastard."

Laughter erupted from the tables around the bar. "Cat fight," someone yelled.

"You're half right," came the response. "Five bucks says she kicks his ass."

Phil crawled beneath a table. The woman knelt beside a chair, swinging her leaden purse at his head.

He couldn't get away. *Bam, bam, bam.* How did you fight a woman with a purse full of bricks? This wasn't in the manual. It seemed to go on forever. Finally, strong hands grabbed his feet and pulled him from beneath the table. They seized his arms and lifted him off the floor. He lurched forward, not trying to get away, just needing to sit down because the room was spinning, and nausea washed over him in waves. A brawny forearm locked around his throat.

"Just settle down, buddy. You're already in enough trouble. You don't want to add resisting arrest to the list."

Resisting arrest? He'd just had the shit pounded out of him, and now he was resisting arrest? What the hell was going on?

When the cop eased his grip, Phil threw up. Most of it landed on the lady who was still screaming in his face.

"You piece of shit," she yelled, then sank her knee into his groin.

The room went black, and he slumped back into the arms of the cop.

****

"Where am I?" His mouth tasted like he'd gorged on kitty litter, not all of it fresh. When he tried to sit up, things exploded in his head. By his own estimate, he must be close to death. Why not go the few remaining steps, have it over with? How much worse could it be?

"Phil, can you talk?" MaryBeth sat beside his gurney. He couldn't see her face but could make a pretty good guess about her expression. "What happened?" Hers was not a happy voice.

"I don't remember." He touched his forehead.

"Don't do that." She jerked his hand away. "You have stitches there."

"Stitches? Where'd I get stitches?"

"There are cuts all over your head. Here, here and a couple more right here. Probably hurts pretty bad, huh?"

"Yeah, like maybe the local baseball team used it for batting practice. What happened to my head?"

"She hit you with her purse, that's what they said,

that lady you got into a fight with."

"I didn't fight with anybody." He hadn't thrown a punch, not even one. How could that be called a fight?

"Apparently, you did. They say she even tried to come in here to get at you. God, I hope it wasn't somebody I know. This sort of thing could ruin us."

"Ruin us? I feel ruined, for damned sure. What is this?" He couldn't raise his left hand.

"Handcuffs. You're under arrest." She spat out the words like she was trying to expel a bug she'd swallowed.

"What the hell?" His memories of the past few hours were still jumbled, and the more he heard, the worse it got.

"Phil, they said you got into a bar fight, drunk and disorderly. You know better than drinking when you're taking medications. This is going to look just awful in the papers."

"Don't tell me. I don't want to know. I want to go home." Yeah, home where he could murder Charlie Hughes, who was responsible for this shit storm in the first place. Then he would fill the bathtub with water and drown himself, or at least try.

"Not tonight. They're going to put you in the medical wing at the county jail when you're stabilized. You'll have a bail hearing sometime tomorrow. I can get you out then." Whether she really wanted him back home was another matter, drunk, disorderly, not exactly a suitable spouse. She kept glancing over her shoulder, apparently afraid of being recognized.

Not that he could blame her, not after his grand performance. "Oh, God. Please tell me this is all a bad dream."

"Nope. It's for real. Look, I have to get home to Addie, prepare her. You'll probably make the evening news."

She scurried away and didn't look back. Yeah, she was pissed, humiliated, too. How embarrassing was it to visit your husband when he was drunk, beaten up, and handcuffed to a gurney?

The doctor, or so his nametag said, a pudgy dark-haired man who still sported a few pimples, pulled back the curtain and stood next to Phil. He must have eaten onions for lunch, and the overpowering aroma caused Phil's stomach to start a weird corkscrewing motion. The aromatic physician pointed a little light into Phil's right eye. The beam felt like a nail driven through his eye socket.

"Hold still," the doctor said.

"It hurts."

"It's gonna hurt worse later. You're in line for one hell of a hangover."

"What? I only had a few beers; not like I drank a case all by myself."

The doctor scratched his beardless chin like he might actually believe Phil. "You taking any medications I need to know about?"

"Just some pills for my allergies; they're prescription."

"Antihistamines? Man, you can't drink when you're taking antihistamines. Don't you know that?" The expression on the doctor's face suggested he thought he was having a conversation with a first-class idiot.

"Yeah, my wife just reminded me. Can you give me something for this headache?"

"Too risky. You might have sustained a slight concussion, so we have to be careful with your meds. I guess we should keep you overnight for observation. That lady whacked you pretty hard. How the hell did you get her so riled up?"

"It was just a stupid accident. She went hysterical over nothing." So, he'd be spending the night in the hospital? Sounded a lot better than jail. "Thanks, Doctor. I do feel woozy."

"I don't doubt that. I'll have them take you upstairs, get you admitted."

"How about this?" Phil tugged against the handcuffs.

"I'll ask the cops if they'll take them off. Otherwise, they stay."

"But I'm not a criminal."

"That's between you and the cops." The doctor walked away, taking his onion scent with him.

They took him to a private room at the end of the hall. Just outside his door, a uniformed officer dozed in a chair propped against the wall. They'd taken the handcuffs off but obviously weren't taking any chances of him escaping, hardened criminal that he might be. Couldn't very well have him running around loose in the community.

Phil stared at the ceiling, trying to take stock of his situation. In the space of a couple of hours, he'd managed to totally screw up his life, and he'd taken his family right along with him. All because of a damned lawnmower, which really was Charlie's fault, not that anybody would believe him. And maybe mixing beer and allergy pills wasn't too smart, but he never would have done it if fucking Charlie hadn't started up with his fucking mower.

Now he was in serious trouble. He'd never been arrested before. Aside from a couple of traffic tickets, he'd never run afoul of the law. Maybe that would count for something. But even if he was able to get off, he was still in deep shit. Once word of his escapades got out, there would be some serious damage control to be done. Jail time—if that's what he got—would close a lot of doors, his job being one of them; felons didn't get to teach school. Could a felon walk into a bank and negotiate a car loan? Not without a gun.

And the smelly brown stuff he'd stirred up would splatter all over MaryBeth and Addie, as well. He could only imagine what his wife was telling their daughter. *Daddy got drunk and busted up a bar*. No, she'd come up with a more sanitized version, and hopefully, she'd leave out the part about the lady beating the hell out of him. Jesus, his head hurt.

The nurse came in to take his blood pressure. "How does your head feel?" she asked.

"Like I got run over by a truck. Can I get something to eat?"

"I can give you some juice. The doctor doesn't want you eating solids tonight."

"But I haven't eaten since, since breakfast." The beer didn't count.

"I'm just doing what the doctor ordered. Don't make any trouble now." She wagged a finger at him. "There's an officer right outside."

Don't make trouble? What did she think he was? A career criminal? He was a member of the Rotary Club. He had friends in town or used to. How many of them would he still have after this? How many of

MaryBeth's pals would still associate with her after her hubby got thrown in the slammer? Banned from her bridge club? Seemed likely.

And his poor daughter, there were still six weeks left in the school year, and she'd have to get through it with everybody knowing her dad, a teacher, no less, had a charge of drunk and disorderly beside his name, and equally bad, brawling with an old lady...worse still, he lost the fight. Better he should have died in the fray, sparing his family the shame and humiliation he'd dropped on them. Without a doubt, it was the worst day of his life.

Chapter Two

Phil woke when the first rays of sunlight cut through the blinds in his room, each beam drilling into his eyeballs. MaryBeth sat beside his bed, maybe considering smothering him with his own pillow, the quickest solution to a nasty problem, then she could at least recoup a few points via the bereaved widow theme. "When did you get here?" he asked.

"I brought you some clean clothes," she said. "I threw out your others. The way they smelled, I didn't dare take them home. How does your head feel?"

"A little better. God, I'm so hungry I could eat the swill they serve at the school cafeteria."

"They were bringing up breakfast trays on the elevator, so I guess they'll feed you soon. I would have brought something from home, but the nurse said not to bother."

"How did Addie take this?"

"Let's wait until you've eaten. Then we'll talk." She had a folded newspaper under her purse. It was too soon for his offense to have made the local paper, but the way his luck was running, he probably would make the front page, photo included. Just the sort of stuff small-town readers loved, *Teacher jailed after drunken bar brawl.* The kind of headline any daughter would be proud of.

"MaryBeth, I can't begin to tell you how sorry I am

about all this, but please, tell me something. I need to know what I'm up against."

An aide brought in a breakfast tray and sat it beside his bed.

"Eat first. I'm going down to the cafeteria to get something." She left a small pile of clothing on the stand beside his bed then rushed off as though she could hardly wait to get out of his room. He couldn't blame her. Hopefully, there was a toothbrush somewhere in the stack of stuff she left because his mouth tasted like something had crawled inside and died.

A beefy cop—did they come in any other size?—walked in and hitched up his belt. "What's this?" He pointed to the pile of clothes.

"My wife brought me some things to wear. My other stuff was pretty messed up."

"You won't need 'em. They're bringing something over from the jail."

"You don't mean one of those orange monkey suits." The only way to make it worse would be to parade him down Main Street in handcuffs while the residents threw rotten vegetables. No, a bar brawl wasn't something he wanted on his permanent resume, but the whole bit, handcuffs, jail uniforms all seemed a bit over the top. They were treating him like Public Enemy Number One.

"You got it." The cop grinned. "Standard procedure."

Just like on TV, except this was for real, Phil Claussen, formerly upstanding citizen, would be led around in an orange jumpsuit. In addition to Phil's own rather quiet neighborhood, the Wakefield PD covered two adjoining regions where low-level criminal activity was not uncommon. Most of the behavioral problems Phil encountered among his students came from these areas. Unfortunately for Phil, there was no way he could be distinguished from the other miscreants the cops faced every day. He couldn't very well protest, "I'm from the suburbs, the good part of town." For now, he was just another law-breaker, and the prevailing powers had apparently decided that a crook ought to look like a crook. Whatever happened to innocent until proven guilty, or was it the other way around?

"For heavens' sake, man, why can't I wear my own clothes?" Bad enough he'd be trundled out of the hospital dressed up like some lowlife; with his luck, the cop would probably put the cuffs back on, too.

"You're in custody, so you'll wear what prisoners wear. You got a problem with that?" The cop looked as if it would make his day if Phil objected, especially if things got physical.

"Let's go, then," Phil said. He didn't want to face his poor wife, not after all the grief he'd brought down on her.

"Ain't you hungry?"

Phil looked at the breakfast tray and shook his head. "Not anymore."

"You don't mind if I eat it then?"

"Help yourself."

By the time the cop had polished off Phil's breakfast, a guard from the city jail arrived with his outfit. Bad enough that it was bright orange, it also had *PRISONER* in big white letters, front and back. They stood on either side of Phil while he put it on.

"Nice fit," the cop said as Phil fumbled with the

drawstring on the trousers. "Very becoming, sir."

Phil wanted, in the worst possible way, to smack the smirk off the cop's face, but that would only make his situation worse.

"What about his shoelaces?" the guard asked.

"We'll confiscate them when we get him to the jail. Stick out your hands," he said to Phil.

He cuffed Phil, then attached the cuffs to a chain that he passed around his waist. As they led him out, Phil asked the nurse, "Please, tell my wife." He shuffled down the hall with his head hung low. He was wrong. Yesterday was only the second worst day of his life. Surely, today was the worst.

****

He rode to the jail in the back seat of a police cruiser. They took the scenic route, right through the middle of town. Phil kept his head tucked down low. It was almost a relief when they reached the jail and pulled him out of the car, then through a door he never imagined he'd go through. The farther inside the jail he got, the worse it smelled, a thoroughly repulsive mix of urine, unwashed bodies, and other things he couldn't identify and didn't want to. They stopped in front of a wire mesh cage.

The man on the inside chewed on the stub of an unlit cigar. "Name," he said.

"Me?"

"You see anybody else here in an orange suit, dimwit?"

"Claussen, Philip Claussen."

"Spell that last name."

Phil spelled it out slowly like he was talking to a child, his school voice, in other words.

The man in the cage looked up and growled. "You're gonna make friends fast, asshole. Shoelaces."

"Huh?"

"Shoelaces. Christ, how dumb are you? Somebody still have to tie your shoelaces for you?"

Phil knelt down but couldn't reach his shoes since his hands were manacled to his waist. He looked up at the cop and shook his head.

After the cop unhooked his cuffs from the waist chain, Phil surrendered his shoelaces and shuffled off down the hall between two officers, one of them almost a foot taller than the other. Both of the men were on the beefy side, and both seemed to be the type who enjoyed the suffering of others, especially if they were the ones inflicting that suffering.

"You're going to the medical wing," one of them said. "Deluxe accommodations."

The stench rose, and Phil's stomach roiled. They passed through a heavy metal door, and the noise hit him like a gust of wind, sounding like a professional hockey game where the fans were yelling for blood and getting it. Was he walking into the middle of a riot? "What's going on back there?" he asked.

"Sounds like the boys are having a little fun." The taller cop chuckled.

"Shouldn't you check it out? Somebody might be hurt." Phil tried to slow down, but the cops dragged him onward.

"Where do you think you are, boy? Some kind of rest home?"

"But I thought the medical unit would be quieter."

Both cops broke into laughter. "It *is* quieter," one said. "You should hear the main unit. You wanta go over there, take a little tour?"

"No, no. I just didn't expect it to be so noisy."

"Don't worry if it's noisy. When it gets quiet, that's when you worry."

They stopped in front of a large cell. Phil counted eight men, at least three of whom were clearly ill. One was bent over vomiting into a stainless-steel commode sitting in plain view just off the center of the room. "You're leaving me here?"

"Think of it as your new home, and these are your new neighbors. We certainly hope you'll find these accommodations to your liking, sir." Both cops laughed, and after the shorter one unlocked Phil's handcuffs, the other opened the door and shoved him inside. Most of the noise had come from a small group of five men huddled off to one side. When Phil staggered into the room, it got very quiet.

"Careful of this one," the cop said to no one in particular. "Bad actor, busted up a bar, beat up an old lady." He laughed as he slammed the door behind him.

Like throwing a piece of fresh meat to a pack of hungry wolves. Phil sat on the floor, his back to the wall, while the others eyed him like some alien life form. He looked back down the long, empty corridor. Shut off as he was, he could yell his head off, and nobody would hear him, not that anybody cared in the first place. He stared at the floor.

"You missed breakfast. You're lucky." The man who spoke had a scar running along his forehead, ending behind a patch over his left eye. "Look what it did to poor Smitty." He pointed to the man heaving into the commode.

As hungry as he was, Phil was glad he hadn't eaten

anything; somewhere between the cage where he left his shoelaces and his cell, he'd have lost it for sure.

"What's your name, punk?" Big guy. Muscles bulging out all over his orange suit. Bald head. Letters tattooed on his knuckles, the kind of guy that made you thankful there were jails, so long as you weren't inside with him.

"Phil."

The big man took a few steps toward him, then stopped in the middle of the room, ground his huge fist into his palm. "Tough guy, huh? You figure you could bust me up?" The giant took another step.

Phil shook his head. "They said I got a concussion. I get in another fight, it might kill me."

The giant eased off into a corner. Apparently, the thought of a murder rap was enough to sidetrack his plans of pounding on Phil.

****

They came for him sometime around lunch, the same two cops who'd brought him in earlier. He had no way of knowing the exact time; they'd taken his watch along with his shoelaces. "Hope you've had a pleasant morning, sir," the shorter cop said, dripping sarcasm and seeming disappointed that Phil had no new sites that required suturing. They half-dragged him along, one walking faster than the other so that Phil had to shuffle along sideways in his unlaced shoes to keep up.

They pushed him into an open room containing six small tables, chairs on either side. "That's your lawyer." The taller of his escorts pointed to a whippet-thin, well-dressed woman, Marcia Bishop, who Phil knew from her role as president of the local PTA. He also knew that, in addition to a busy law practice, she was a mother of three children as well as a constant feature in local races and ran in the Boston Marathon two years before. He'd tried a few practice runs with her but couldn't keep up at all.

Her eyes grew wide as she looked at the ruin he'd become. "Oh, my God, Phil."

Phil shuffled over and held out a manacled hand. "Hello, Marcia. It's good to see you, just sorry it had to be like this."

"You look like somebody's been teeing up golf balls and hitting them off your poor head." She took his hand in both of hers.

"Where is MaryBeth?" Phil asked, glad that his wife wasn't around to see him in such a pathetic state.

"Regular visiting hours aren't until this afternoon. They let counsel in earlier. Have a seat."

"When can you get me out of here?" Phil asked. He was close enough to catch the subtle aroma of perfume, a vast improvement over the jail cell reek.

"Your hearing is later today. MaryBeth can post bond then, or better still, maybe we'll get lucky with the judge. We have some other things to discuss first," Marcia said.

"Such as?"

"Such as how an upstanding citizen like yourself got into such a mess. Now, tell me the story and don't leave anything out. We have a real problem here and have to proceed carefully."

"I didn't really do anything. I tripped, then I collided with a lady, we fell down, and she went hysterical. Just look at my head."

"Details, Phil, I need to know exactly what happened."

He couldn't bear to look her in the face as he told her the whole sordid tale of beer, antihistamines, a misstep on a barstool, the collision, then the brawl on the barroom floor. He made no mention of the big blue riding mower that triggered the whole sequence of events or of his plans to murder Charlie when he got out of jail.

When he'd finished, Marcia sat shaking her head. "You know, in my line of work, I hear a lot of amazing stories, but yours takes the cake. Talk about being in the wrong place at the wrong time, and it's worse than you think. When you fell off the barstool, you just happened to land on the mayor's sister. She came to the bar to pick up donations for the homeless. They collect them in a big jar down at the end of the bar. Guess you've never noticed."

"Mayor's sister?"

"Right. She says you attacked her. She's pressing charges. This could be trouble, big trouble." The attorney's pained expression, eyebrows meeting in the center of her forehead, might have been the one she served up for condemned men, a forewarning that they should expect the worst.

"But the people at the bar, they saw what happened. Ask them. I never attacked anybody."

"You know Mayor Tidwell?" Marcia asked.

"Heard the name but never met the man."

"You know he's been re-elected four times?"

"No." Phil's aversion to all things political rose up to kick him in the butt. Why couldn't he have cultivated some associations with the local movers and shakers?

"He's a very powerful man. Anybody who crosses him pays a price. I've already talked to the bartender, and he clammed right up. Tidwell could have his alcohol license pulled in a heartbeat, shut him right down, so he's saying nothing at all."

"What does that mean?" He asked the question, but he already knew the answer.

"It means you're on your own as far as witnesses are concerned, your word against hers. It counts for something that you've never been in trouble before, but the mayor's sister is out for blood...yours. First, I'll need to find out what she wants you charged with, assault and battery at the very least."

"She's claiming assault? Look at my head. And the doc at the hospital said I got a concussion. If anybody got assaulted, it was me."

"I can't disagree with you there. Hopefully, the judge will see it the same way. It's almost two-thirty," Marcia said. "They'll be taking you over to the courthouse shortly. I'll meet you there. We should be able to get you out then."

"Can I change? I want to wear my own clothes. I hate this damned orange outfit."

"Since you're still in custody, they'll probably make you wear what you have on. The judge has this weird rule about prisoners looking like prisoners right up to the time they're released."

She sat for a moment, tapping her pen on her tablet.

"You look like you want to say something else," Phil said.

"Just this, Phil, I've known you for several years now. I can think of any number of men who might get into a mess like this, and it wouldn't surprise me in the least. But not you. You're one of the good guys. My kids say you're the best teacher in the entire school. So, was all this just one crazy coincidence, or was it something else? What am I missing here?"

"I don't know," he said. "I just don't know. I wish I could point a finger somewhere else, but this was all my doing. Mind you, it was all incredibly stupid, but it was me, start to finish. And I dumped a huge load of garbage on my poor family. I have no idea how I can ever make it up to MaryBeth and Addie. They don't deserve any of this."

****

The Peery County Courthouse, complete with four white columns that framed the entrance to the red brick two-story building, sat back off the street, and visitors strolled up a wide paved lane to reach the front entrance. Phil and his shackled, orange-clad cohorts were not allowed to sully this pristine view; they were delivered in a van and dropped off at a less visible back entrance. Their brief trek in fresh air was a welcome change, but even that limited exposure to the prevalent spring pine pollen dusting almost every surface outdoors brought on Phil's sniffles.

The courtroom was stuffy and slightly aromatic like someone forgot to remove the dirty laundry. MaryBeth was already there, seated off to the side, several rows back from the front, wearing her black suit and, as best Phil could tell, no makeup. All she needed was a paper bag over her head to achieve complete anonymity. But he could hardly blame her. He could only guess how she felt watching her husband parade along handcuffed with a group of prisoners. Thank God she hadn't brought Addie. *Look, sweetheart, there's your daddy. Doesn't he look cute in orange?* She waved, sort of a timid half-wave like she was brushing a stray strand of hair from her face as if she didn't want anyone to know she was waving at him.

In the second row behind his attorney sat Phil's antagonist, the lady who carried a brick in her handbag. She'd cleaned his vomit off her and changed her clothes, but she looked just as angry as she had in the bar. She turned and pointed him out to her friends as he shuffled along. The looks he got would stop an onrushing train.

Phil slouched into a chair, aiming for invisibility, like his wife.

The bailiff called out his name, "Case number 304, the people vs. Philip Claussen, charged with assault, drunk and disorderly." Marcia tugged Phil to his feet. "Don't say anything unless the judge asks you a direct question, understand? And try to look a little contrite. It might help."

Looking contrite would be easy enough if he decided to go that way, but he was nobody's goddam penitent, and if punishment was to be meted out, he would take it like a man. He drew himself up straight and stood at attention, military style.

The judge was a walrus, or at least so closely resembled one that he could probably lie on a beach among other walruses and not draw undue attention. Only his horn-rimmed glasses might give him away. The dome of his skull reflected the overhead lights, redirecting beams whenever he turned his head. The only hair visible above his collar was a white handlebar mustache with curled tips and shaggy eyebrows that stuck out almost as far as his mustache. Yep, a walrus, for sure.

"Mr. Claussen." The walrus spoke, then he paused, apparently hoping Phil would begin to squirm under the heat of his gaze...not going to happen. Phil stared straight ahead at a point just past the judge's right shoulder.

"Your behavior of April 25 was shameful. You caused physical injury and humiliation to one of our distinguished citizens in the course of her volunteer work helping out less fortunate members of our community. You made a public spectacle of yourself." Then he launched into a rambling twenty-minute reprimand on how disappointing it was to have a role model, a high school teacher, appearing before him on such disgraceful charges. Phil tuned out during most of the judge's rant. He didn't need to hear shit about community standards; he upheld them as well as the next guy, better than most, usually.

"In your favor, you served with distinction in the U. S. Army." The judge then counted off a number of medals, most of which Phil couldn't remember ever receiving. And where in hell had the judge come up with that information? Phil kept his medals stuffed in a shoebox in his closet, so he couldn't figure how his military history became public domain.

"What I cannot understand, Mr. Claussen, is why a man with such a distinguished military career, who has been a model citizen until now, suddenly goes off the rails in such a disgraceful fashion. Can you enlighten me, Mr. Claussen? Tell me why this happened."

"No excuse, your honor. I deeply regret the pain and suffering I caused to members of the community and to my own family." He would fall on his sword if he had one.

"No excuse indeed," said the judge. "This court fines you one thousand dollars, Mr. Claussen. I warn you, never appear before me again, and, son, don't disgrace the uniform. You hear me?"

"Yes, your honor." He would have remained standing at attention if his attorney hadn't grabbed his elbow and pulled him toward the aisle.

"Let's go," Marcia said. "It worked."

"What worked?"

"The military angle. The judge is strongly pro-military. Has a nephew at West Point. I was able to show him your service records, which were quite impressive, just before we came in. I've used that tactic in a couple of other cases, and the judge has been lenient every time."

"Where did you get my service records?"

"From MaryBeth. I asked her if you had served, and she gave me a box full of your medals. Saved the day, if you ask me. I'm a little surprised the judge let you off so lightly. He could have nailed you to the courthouse wall."

"So, I can go home now?"

"First, you have to go back to the jail and pick up your stuff. Then you're a free man, so long as you stay out of trouble, and for God's sakes, avoid the mayor's sister."

Phil extended his hand. "Thanks, you really came through for me. Defending me didn't win you any points with the mayor or his sister."

"Don't worry about that. I'm tougher than I look," she said. "Honestly, I never liked her much anyway. You, on the other hand, are an asset to our community, and I'm glad I could keep you out of jail. Just promise me you'll never do anything like this again."

"Promise." He could only hope for the best since he really couldn't figure out why he'd pulled such a stupid stunt in the first place.

He had to wait until three other cases were concluded before they could be loaded into the van for the trip back to the jail. Somehow, he'd missed MaryBeth's exit from the courtroom. Hopefully, she would pick him up at the jail, or maybe not. In what he assumed was her current state of mind, she might make him walk home. No wonder, who wanted to ride around with a jailbird anyway?

****

Back at the jail, he retrieved his belongings and changed into the clean clothes MaryBeth had brought. He'd never really appreciated shoelaces until now as he replaced his own. As he walked past the desk sergeant, the same man who'd given him so much crap when he was brought in, Phil might have raised his middle finger, just a little.

The Claussen family car looked empty at first glance, but MaryBeth was waiting inside, hunched down in her seat, hiding her face as best she could.

"Where did you go?" he asked. "I thought you'd wait for me." He was hardly in his seat before she peeled away from the curb.

"Thanks a lot, Phil. That was the most humiliating experience I've ever had."

"I didn't enjoy it much myself." He struggled into his seat belt.

"I just hope they didn't see me."

"Who?"

"One of the women sitting with the woman you

attacked, I know her. We're on a school committee together—Addie's School. It was bad enough that she had to see you like that. I just hope she didn't connect us."

"I'm sorry, MaryBeth. This must be awful for you."

"You were in the morning papers. Addie wouldn't go to school today. She was afraid the other kids would laugh at her, and she was probably right. You have made a royal mess of our lives."

"I'll make it up to Addie somehow, you too. Thanks for setting things up with Marcia. She saved my butt, I guess." But whether his butt was worth saving was another matter entirely.

Chapter Three

They said nothing more during the drive home.
Phil's stomach reminded him that he had last eaten
solid food sometime yesterday, but now didn't seem the
right time to mention it. When MaryBeth pulled into the
driveway, there it sat, the source of all his trouble, all
gleaming and blue, its rear tires larger than those on the
family car. "You want to explain this?" she asked.

"My mower." He'd forgotten all about it. It looked
even more immense in his driveway than it had in the
showroom, more like a military assault vehicle than a
suburban lawn care product.

MaryBeth glared through the windshield, eyes
wide, nostrils flaring, knuckles white as she gripped the
steering wheel. "Did you buy this before or after you
started drinking?"

"I'm sorry," he said.

"Sorry doesn't cut it, Phil. You'd better straighten
this mess out and quick." She stepped out of the car,
taking a wide route around the mower as if it might be
the source of some deadly toxin.

"I don't know if they'll take it back."

"I don't care what you do or how you do it; just get
rid of it." She stomped off toward the house.

"Hey, jailbird." Charlie Hughes walked across the
lawn and parked his backside on the Volvo fender.
"What's this I hear about some old lady beating the

crap out of you after you knocked over her walker?"

"Knock it off, Charlie. I'm not in the mood."

"Come on, man, you're a celebrity. You're the only jailbird in the neighborhood." Charlie rubbed his hands together, clearly enjoying himself.

"Hey, what the hell is this?" Charlie's eyes bulged when he spotted Phil's new mower, doubtless realizing that he'd just been dropped to second place in the neighborhood mower derby. "Peerless, damn."

Charlie didn't need to know the mower was now a flashpoint in the Claussen household, and Phil wasn't about to disillusion him. Let the bastard sweat. This mess was all his fault in the first place.

He turned around to face Phil. "How much?" he asked.

"Go home, Charlie."

Phil ran his hand along the smooth, shiny fender of the mower, how he wanted to fire it up, play with his new toy, but what might otherwise have been a joyous occasion had turned into a complete calamity. So, he walked away, leaving the big Peerless in the driveway. Maybe, if he had magical powers, he could snap his fingers and make it all go away—mower included, maybe Charlie too—but that wasn't going to happen.

He took stock of his situation, then did the only thing a guy in his situation could do—run, make a strategic retreat to the basement, his little hideout. He'd finished off a small section at the bottom of the staircase several years before, dark paneling, shoddy carpet, just a bit on the aromatic side, like putting a bunch of old tennis shoes in a plastic bag and inhaling the aroma. He loved it. MaryBeth called it his cave, probably joked about it to her friends, but at the moment, a cave seemed like a damned good place to be.

He made his way over to the old leather recliner, a survivor from his bachelor days. MaryBeth had banned it from the upstairs. "Either the basement or the dump," she'd said. Okay, so the leather was scuffed and cracked, and it smelled, well, not exactly like a bouquet of roses, but now it creaked under his weight as if saying, "Welcome home." He patted the armrest, an old friend.

He didn't like to think this way, but as a man who didn't believe in coincidences, it almost seemed as if the universe had conspired to make April 25 *kick-the-crap-out-of-Phil-Claussen-Day.* He'd played right into it by doing something irreversibly and inexplicably stupid…Phil Claussen, major league fuckup.

"Phil, are you down there?" MaryBeth's voice cut through the silence like a siren, making his head throb again because the worst thing about hangover headache was the guilt, which he had in abundance.

"Yeah."

"Well, come on up here. Addie's waiting, and we have to talk."

"Just a minute." Maybe she would give up and go away, yeah, maybe on a cold day in hell.

"Now, Phil, right this minute. You have some explaining to do."

He might be able to handle MaryBeth's full-on frontal assault, which he fully deserved, but Addie was up there too, and she was a different story altogether, Addie with her big brown eyes, and, God forbid, maybe a tear would fall, and that would break him into tiny pieces.

He pushed himself up out of the recliner. He took a

few steps toward the staircase that led up to the kitchen where his inquisition awaited, then, with no conscious intention on his part, his feet turned and walked through the side door that led out into the backyard. He had no choice but to follow along. What else could a guy do?

His feet led him around the garage to the lawn tractor, and they climbed aboard. He wiggled his toes. "Okay, now what?" His feet said nothing, so he just sat and waited and watched the sun set in the cleft between two maple trees in his backyard. What a sight, the rays funneled into a glowing wedge by the early spring foliage. Was this why his feet had brought him here, to witness this magical event?

The curtains parted, and MaryBeth's angry face appeared. She shook her head. In a moment, she was right out there in the driveway. "Phil Claussen, you come inside this minute. What if the neighbors see you out here sitting on that mower? It's almost dark."

Yeah, what would the neighbors think after your husband had taken a swan dive into an empty pool? What indeed? For that matter, who cared? A guy could sit on his new mower any time he wanted, right?

She crept around the mower, not approaching any closer than ten feet. "Are you drunk again?"

"Don't think so."

"Dammit, Phil, you're ruining everything we've worked for." Leave it to MaryBeth to put a global spin on his troubles, but she was right, and he knew it. She stomped back inside, leaving a vapor trail behind her.

Phil sat for a while longer. His wife, in her own instinctive way, was trying to protect the family unit. She was the she-bear shielding the den and cub-bear Addie from the ravages of a meandering, worthless man-bear who would, as she put it, ruin everything. He was the lightning rod for all their troubles. The brown smelly stuff he attracted that rained down on him fell on his wife and daughter as well and would continue so long as he was around. He saw only one solution.

That night, after MaryBeth had gone to bed—thank heavens she was a sound sleeper—he loaded two bags with clothes and toiletries and stashed them in his den. The next morning, he was the first customer at the Peerless dealership. The young salesman who'd sold him the lawnmower was just getting situated at his desk.

"Mr. Claussen, how are you liking your new mower?"

"Take it back." Phil slapped the keys and his blue Peerless cap down on the man's desk.

"Why, Mr. Claussen, we can't very well do that, not after you've signed a contract and we've made delivery."

"Take it back." Phil raised his voice several decibels.

"But, Mr. Claussen…"

"*Take it back.*" People walking past the dealership paused to check out the cause of the commotion inside.

Now the manager ran out of his office, took one look at Phil—a berserk man with a head full of stitches could draw a crowd in a hurry—and said "Take it back. Give him back his money."

Phase one of his plan was complete. Then he drove across town to the RV dealership and traded in his Toyota and the refund from his mower for a two-year-old RV—two bedrooms, a bath with a shower, flush toilet, complete kitchen including a microwave oven.

"She's practically new," said the salesman who'd followed him around the lot for the past twenty minutes. "Maybe I shouldn't say this, but the fellow who bought it new got divorced a few months later, said it hardly left his driveway, so he sold it back to us. That's why we can make you such a great deal on it."

Imagine that, Phil thought, an RV figuring in a marital breakup. He didn't bother informing the salesman of his own domestic troubles.

By the time he got home, MaryBeth was up and about and apparently stunned when he pulled the behemoth into their driveway. She stood there, wide-eyed as if she'd just seen the ocean for the first time. There was no explanation he could offer that might possibly account for what he'd done other than saying, "I'm doing this for you and Addie. It's all for the best. You'll see." He ran inside the house like a scared rabbit, grabbed his two bags, then tossed them into the RV.

As he climbed in behind the wheel, they both stared at him in disbelief, Addie from the living room window and MaryBeth standing on the lawn. How he wanted to grab them both, hold them close while he explained that this was the only way, and they were better off without him. With him out of the picture, she and Addie would have a chance at a normal life without having to constantly explain his police record.

He took a deep breath, waved and backed his shiny new vehicle out of the driveway, knocked over Charlie's mailbox, and drove away. He stuck up his middle finger as he drove past Charlie's house.

****

Rapture can burst like a soap bubble. Phil's did just

that, even before he passed the Welcome to Wakefield sign that faced the opposite direction. He held the steering wheel in a death grip, fearing that at any moment, his resolve would fail, and he would turn back. *I love my wife, I love my daughter, I love our life in Wakefield, so what the fuck am I doing here?* The same question kept popping into his head, bringing more and more second thoughts about his choices. He tried not to think about all the entanglements, the strands that still bound him, personal, professional, social, to his community. He left them all trailing behind him, like the limp streamers from a parade float that got caught in the rain. *Don't think, just drive.*

He approached the on-ramp for I-40, the interstate that ran almost straight east and west across the country. What he needed now was distance, putting himself at a place too far away to even think about turning back, so he tried to slip into the mindset of a long-distance truck driver, always looking ahead, never backward.

He looped around Raleigh in the early afternoon and Winston-Salem an hour and a half later. He was aiming for the outskirts of Asheville and the mountains and made it just past six o'clock.

He stopped at the first pancake house he saw and loaded up on carbohydrates and coffee, a Belgian waffle, scrambled eggs, and sausage patties that doused his hunger pangs completely. Comfort food, that's what he needed, and that's what he got.

When the waitress came by to refill his coffee, she leaned across the counter. "Look, I won't tell anybody, I promise, but you're that actor guy, George Clooney, aren't you? I won't say a word to anybody."

"Sorry." He shook his head. He didn't know whether a big tip was her aim, but he was more than generous. Then, fortified against most of the untoward possibilities he could think of, he walked out into an early spring evening and found himself rubbing his arms to fight off the chill in the air. He spotted a Ready-Mart just across the street where he loaded up on staples...beer, bread, coffee, milk, paper plates and cups, and, for emergencies, a family pack of chocolate-covered peanuts .

His next immediate need was a campsite big enough to accommodate the RV. He had no intention of tackling the mountain range at night, driving something as cumbersome as his new RV. He passed up a couple of sites that had neon lights strung out across the entrance. He was looking for something much more low-key, which he found five miles farther along.

"You're lucky, got the last available spot," said the elderly attendant as he took Phil's twenty bucks. Lucky? If he were lucky, he wouldn't be here in the first place.

Backing the big rig into the campsite was an adventure, requiring three tries, during which he almost knocked over the outdoor grill. He wished he'd paid more attention as the RV salesman went over the various features of his new home, but his fight-or-flight instincts had been running at full power during the demonstration, and most of the technical details floated right past him.

The electrical hookup was simple enough or would have been had he listened when the process was explained earlier, and it didn't help that he was attempting to make the connection in darkness. The electrical cable was coiled so tightly that as soon as he plugged in one end, either to the RV or to the outlet by the campsite, the other end pulled loose. He decided that the potential risk of messing it up—electrocution—outweighed any possible gain, so he gave up and tossed the cable back into the RV. He had more success with the water hook-up but still managed to soak his pants before he made the connection to the RV's hose. What the salesman had called the "poop pipe," the drain for the flush toilet, Phil left for another time.

His next top priority was a long, hot shower to wash away not only the grime he'd accumulated after a day's driving, but also to help with the transition into his new life, but there would be no transition tonight. There were six other campers waiting in line, so instead, he took a stroll around the campground. The other RV travelers were a chatty group, but when he tired of answering the same question, "Where's your wife?" he headed back to his own campsite.

He pulled a chair, still wrapped in cellophane, from the storage compartment under the RV and popped the top on a beer. So far, so good, no major catastrophes. He'd made it through the first day and managed to resist the almost constant urge to turn around and head back. But it was for the best, right? Maybe the brown cloud that hung over him had followed him along, sparing his family.

That night, with the windows open and a cool breeze blowing through the RV, he slept much better than he expected or deserved…no nightmares, no assaults by crazed campground killers, no dreams of giant blue lawnmowers chasing after him. Just before he drifted off, he said a little prayer for the health and happiness of his wife and daughter, hoping he had done the right thing for them.

The next morning dawned fresh and bright and full of hope that the most difficult part of his trek was over, and Phil, up early even without the assistance of an alarm clock, sat outside by his RV and took in the spectacle, the morning sun burning through a thin haze of cloud cover.

He strolled around the campground, his nose following the pungent aroma of freshly brewed coffee, when, out of the corner of his eye, he glimpsed the rapidly moving form of what he first thought might be a small deer but turned out to be a leggy Weimaraner, mouth open in a toothy grin and stubby tail wagging furiously.

Without a second thought, Phil dropped to his knees and held out his hands. In an instant, the wiggling dog was in his arms, licking his chin. Phil enjoyed the first good laugh he'd had since he fled Wakefield.

"Oh, I'm so sorry about that. Molly, come back here." An alarmed female voice came from a somewhat stocky body that hurried over toward him, her smile equally welcoming as her dog's.

"No problem at all," Phil said. "Glad to meet you, Molly." He rose and extended his hand. "Name's Phil. Beautiful dog you have here."

"I'm Alice. Molly's not like this with most people, but when she sees someone she likes—and she clearly likes you—she's off and running."

"The feeling is entirely mutual," Phil said.

"I just made fresh coffee. Molly and I will be pleased if you'll join us."

"I wouldn't want to impose," he said.

"Not a bit. I always say any friend of Molly's is a friend of mine as well."

He followed her over to where a travel trailer with fold-out sides sat beside a late model red SUV. The surface of her picnic table was covered in plastic containers, a large aluminum cooler, and, best of all, a two-burner camp stove, one burner of which warmed a pot of coffee. She poured them each a cup.

"Looks like you've been here a few days," Phil said.

"Yes, when I find a place I like, I tend to stay put, sometimes for a week or so. It beats towing this trailer all over the country. Besides, Molly seems to like it that way."

The dog hadn't left Phil's side.

"She has a real crush on you," Alice said. "You passed the character test with flying colors."

"The what?"

"Molly has what I consider to be the most acute bullshit detector on the planet. If anybody is less than one hundred percent genuine, she'll have nothing to do with them. When she went running over to you, greeted you like a long-lost friend, I knew you were the real deal."

"She might have made a mistake this time." Clearly, the dog had a higher opinion of him than he had himself.

"Molly doesn't make mistakes."

A hush fell over the campsite. The road noise faded into a distant background hum, and even the birdsongs seemed muted. Up to this point, he'd been holding the fragments of his life together by a thread, a thread that broke when the dog put her paw on his knee and looked into his face, no, his soul, with big dark eyes that seemed to know far too much.

"Molly and I are good listeners," Alice said.

"I did something bad," he said, "bad and stupid. I hurt the people I love most in this world, then I ran away. So, sorry, Molly, you blew it this time. You made friends with a creep."

Alice came around the table, sat beside him, put her arm around his shoulders. Now he sat caught between two pairs of eyes, one large and dark and supposedly possessing uncanny powers of assessment, the other, light gray in color with smile wrinkles radiating from the edges.

"I told you before, Molly doesn't make mistakes, and I have a pretty good batting average myself. You're searching for something," she said.

"But what? I have no idea."

Now she laughed softly, a sound like wind chimes in a light breeze. "You'll know it when you see it. You're not running away as much as you're running toward something else. You might be needed someplace you've never even heard of, and it might be closer than you think. Take that from a very smart dog and an old lady who's been around the block a few times." That said, she kissed him softly on the cheek, then went inside her camper, Molly following closely behind her.

Searching? Running toward something? Out of all the parts of his life that made no sense, this idea went to the top of the list. Phil sat for a moment longer, trying to process this new prediction about his future, a much more positive outlook than he held himself, even if he had no idea what Alice was talking about. He knew now his only path was forward, so that's what he did.

Back at his own campsite, he unhooked the water supply to his RV, then checked out the other connections. He could foresee the day when he left something—water, electric, or poop pipe—hooked up to the campsite and drove off with a line of spare parts dragging along behind, not to mention a very pissed off campground attendant. Satisfied that he was clear for takeoff, he climbed in and fired her up. His chocolate-covered peanuts, while tasty enough, didn't cut it for breakfast, so he drove back to the pancake house for a refill before hitting the road.

The interstate took him through Asheville, NC, and along the way, he spotted the turnoff for the Biltmore Estate, adding that to his list of places to visit in the future, if he had a future. On the west side of Asheville, he skirted the Pisgah National Forest, passing a road sign for Lake Junaluska. You could look for a long, long time and not find a prettier mountain lake. The previous summer, late July, Addie had attended a church camp there, and, after a few days of mewling homesickness with daily calls home and pleas to come to her rescue, she settled in and loved it. Maybe he could make this trip again with her someday, something to hope for.

A little farther west, I-40 took a jog northward across the eastern end of the Great Smokey Mountain National Park. The mountains appeared to be awakening after their winter sleep showing patchy greenery, and a few early rhododendrons bloomed among the pines. He exited the interstate long enough to visit one of the viewing overlooks. He got out of the RV and walked over to the stone rampart that ran along the edge of the overlook. The late morning air was still brisk, and it would be weeks yet before the foliage show hit full stride, but the view now was certainly worth attending to. Perhaps another trip, another time for sightseeing, not now. There was safety in distance, so he climbed back aboard and continued his flight.

By late afternoon he was drawing near to Knoxville, Tennessee, and pulled into a burger joint. He had to park the RV in a vacant lot across the street. He could foresee the day when his home on wheels would become a damned nuisance.

It seemed to take forever to cross Tennessee, shaped as it was like a rectangle that had been stepped on. He stopped for the night and reached Memphis by his third day on the road.

Crossing Arkansas took two days. Even though he'd never set foot in the state, driving across it left him none the wiser, hermetically sealed as he was in his RV. Aside from snippets of conversation at gas stations, he spoke to no one for three whole days.

He'd never had any burning desire to see Oklahoma and the Great Plains, but that's where the highway folks had laid out I-40, so that's where he went. Seemed like he'd just passed the state line when the oil rigs began popping up like giant insects from a sci-fi movie. From then on, it was either oil rigs or cattle; he preferred the cattle. He passed the sign for Muskogee, hummed a few bars of the song, and kept on driving. Same with Oklahoma City, maybe some other time.

In spite of his tinted windshield, in spite of his sunglasses, the afternoon sun was boring a hole in his brain, so he left the Interstate and turned north toward a little town called Kingfisher. His campsite map book indicated there should be a few suitable locations for him to spend the night. Soon he began to wonder whether his map book might have deceived him. He'd been driving for the better part of an hour and, except for the ancient gas station with a sleeping dog and a few rusted pickup trucks, had seen no sign of human habitation. Had he driven right past Kingfisher? This bothered him less than he expected. He could, if necessary, simply pull off the road and set up housekeeping for the night since he was completely mobile and self-sufficient.

Chapter Four

Yeah, pretty smooth sailing, until the hairs on the back of his neck began to prickle, then the prickle became an itch requiring vigorous scratching, then she popped up on the roadside. Not she, exactly, not at first. At a distance, she looked like a blur, then like a stick figure, then as he got closer, a rather startling picture emerged, that of a youngish blonde woman wearing very brief cutoff denim shorts and a yellow tank top that left her midriff bare, and no shoes. Her outfit might do nicely enough for the beach but seemed both inappropriate and inadequate for a roadside in the middle of nowhere.

The smart move would be eyes on the road, just keep on driving, but old reliable, responsible adult Phil Claussen—not the same guy who, on a whim, went out and bought giant blue riding mowers—intervened, and better judgment be damned, he slowed down. He couldn't very well ignore her, wish her somewhere else. She was right there on the side of the road with her thumb stuck out, well, not really stuck out, more like her fist resting on her hip with the thumb wagging only an inch or so like she didn't really care one way or the other whether he stopped or not, but in spite of all the warning lights going off in his head, she was his responsibility, for now.

He stopped a few feet past her and rolled the

window down halfway. "Need a ride?" he asked, half hoping she'd just wave him along like maybe she was waiting for someone else.

No such luck. She opened the door and climbed into the front seat. "Thanks."

The warning lights in Phil's head flashed even brighter. With his record of recent mishaps, he could protest to the high heavens that he was just trying to lend a helping hand, but he wouldn't stand a chance, alone with an unattached, defenseless woman. All she had to do was say the wrong word to the wrong people, and they would put him under the jail without a second thought. He tried not to stare at her—*Just drive, numbnuts, watch the road*—but he might just as well have been talking to a street sign.

Worst of all, she probably knew he was looking. This was a girl/woman who was used to being stared at. "Going far?" he asked, trying to release some of the tension in his neck and his back and everywhere else.

"Just up the road." Soft, sultry voice, she'd just driven another nail into his coffin. Besides, if "just up the road" was anything like the last fifty miles or so, they would still be in the middle of nowhere. What the hell would he do then?

He whiled away a few awkward moments thinking about his wife, or was it ex-wife? What would she say if she knew he was roaming around the countryside with a beautiful, near-naked companion? Better still, what if Charlie could see him now? For sure, his former asshole neighbor would crap in his grass-stained pants. Phil drew some small comfort from that thought.

But soon enough, he became uncomfortable with the silence in the RV. Before, when he'd been alone, no problem, but he wasn't used to being so close to someone and not having some sort of conversation. Didn't seem civilized, and one thing he was, was civilized, regardless of what MaryBeth and the Wakefield Police Force might say.

"You don't talk much," he said.

"Don't start anything."

"I was just trying to be friendly."

"You better not try any funny stuff,' she said. "I'm a cop."

She turned away quickly as he glanced over at her, but not so quickly that he didn't see just the barest hint of a grin. What the hell? Was she playing him, stringing him along in some weird game where she stood by the road barely dressed, guessing the next guy to drive by would not be a serial killer?

"Yeah? Where's your ID? Cops are supposed to carry ID."

"My purse got stolen."

"They stole your shoes, too?" Her toenails, when he caught a glance at them, were painted bright pink, not chipped or broken, and from the careful steps she'd taken to get to his door, this girl wasn't used to going barefoot.

"I lost them."

"What about a weapon? Cops are supposed to be armed, right?" Although where she might conceal a weapon in her scanty outfit was baffling.

"Don't get any ideas. I have backup following along behind us. If you try anything, they'll be all over you." Her voice was anything but threatening, sounding more like she was on the brink of laughing outright.

"I hate to tell you, but there hasn't been a car

behind us for the last fifteen, twenty minutes. It's so flat I can see for miles, and there's nothing there. You don't suppose they got lost? Maybe had some engine trouble, a flat tire?" Yeah, two could play her silly game.

"I'm warning you, try any funny stuff, and you'll be sorry." Again, sounding more like mirth than threat.

"Oh, maybe your backup is in a helicopter, like, right overhead? Except it must be a real quiet chopper, maybe one of them stealth types, no noise at all."

"Shut up." Terse words, more like a dare, *continue at your own risk.*

The angle of the late afternoon sun still blinded him, and his sunglasses were only moderately effective. He couldn't say much about the countryside now because he was concentrating on just keeping his rig on the road. It didn't get any easier when he first caught her scent...lilac, a stranded woman who smelled of lilacs. What next?

He caught her staring straight at him, a little smile at the corners of her mouth, playful, and absolutely fearless, like she knew something important that he hadn't figured out yet. If he'd been keeping score during their little exchange, she'd be way ahead, and he didn't even know the name of the game.

"You can let me out up here," she said after a prolonged silence.

"What?" He looked to either side of the road, nothing, a few strands of barbed wire, occasional tumbleweeds, but little else. "But we're still in the middle of nowhere. What are you going to do? What if nobody else comes by?"

"Not your problem, just stop and let me out."

"But it gets dark real quick out here, and cold, too.

Not to mention the coyotes." Where did that come from, he wondered? He'd never seen a live coyote in his life.

"You're just trying to scare me. Coyotes are little farts. I'm not afraid of them."

"No, there are some bigger ones now. I read about them, coywolves, they're called. The coyotes bred with wolves, made them bigger and more aggressive, and they hunt in packs. You need to think about that."

"It doesn't matter."

"Come on, let me give you a jacket or a blanket or something. You'll freeze when the sun goes down." It was almost like a challenge. Was he, Phil Claussen, ex-jailbird, a decent guy or just another loser?

"Why should you care? You don't even know me. For all you know, I might have killed somebody."

"No way, you don't even have a weapon."

"I know karate."

"I don't believe you." It had taken him a while to catch up, but he finally knew that this verbal sparring was just a game with her. But leaving her on the side of the road barely dressed was not an option. "Look, at least let me drive you to someplace you won't freeze to death or starve."

Now, sniffling, quiet at first, then more pronounced. Slowly, like an oncoming tide, she reached the crying stage. So the tears came down for a few minutes, but it didn't seem to him that she was in any real emotional distress, more like she was testing him, just part of the game?

"What did I do now?" he asked. If he lived ten lifetimes, he would never understand how women could turn the waterworks on and off at will.

"It's been a while since anybody did anything nice for me unless they wanted something in return. Are you expecting me to do something for you? Is that what you're thinking?"

"No way, I guarantee it. Even if you offered, I wouldn't take you up on it. I don't take advantage of people like that."

"What, you don't find me attractive?"

Again, there was that brief flit of a grin, so brief he wondered whether he'd really seen it. Even though his shirt collar was open, it suddenly felt tight, like something was closing around his neck, something moist. "Yeah, but that's not the point." No, the point was abandoning someone on the side of the road in the middle of nowhere, something he would not do.

"Oh, you mean, because you're married."

"Right, that's it…married." Earlier, he'd thought about chunking his wedding band out the window. His marriage was probably history, right? Now he was glad he still had the ring. It didn't afford him much protection, but something was better than nothing.

"That doesn't stop most guys," she said. "You really must be different."

"Yeah, that's me, a real Boy Scout."

She laughed, for the first time, what a beautiful laugh. How long since he'd heard a woman's happy laugh? The smile spread across his face before he had time to stop it.

"No, I didn't mean it that way. It's just good to know that there are still a few nice guys out there." She folded her legs up on the seat and rested her chin on her knees, a posture that he didn't think possible. "What happened to your head, all the stitches, I mean."

"I got into a fight, got my ass kicked." She didn't need to know a woman did the kicking.

Only a few rays of sunlight played in the clouds above the distant line of hills when they pulled into the small town that appeared to be closing down for the evening. "This must be Kingfisher," he said.

Right at the first crossing street sat the smallest shopping center he'd ever seen. You could stick four of these into the monstrosity near his hometown. And the parking lot was at least half full. Where did all these shoppers come from? He hadn't passed a single house for miles.

"We need to get you something to wear," he said. He tugged out his wallet and passed her three twenties. "I don't know if that's enough."

She held the bills in her hand for a moment, as if he'd given her a golden key or something, and, for the second time that afternoon, she sniffled. "Thank you. You're not coming along?"

"No, for sure you don't need me to help you buy clothes."

"How will I know if I look okay?" Even in the darkening cab of the RV, the smile she flashed at him was full of deviltry.

"I'm sure whatever you pick out will look great." His open collar got even tighter. And things didn't improve as he watched her walk across the parking lot…no, walk was not the word. She prowled like a big cat. Nobody walked like that naturally. She had something in mind, and the possibilities that ran through his mind were the type that got guys like him hanging by the neck from a limb of an oak tree.

Just before she stepped onto the entrance, she half-turned, gave him one last look, a little glance over her shoulder. Was that a wink? From that distance, he couldn't tell. He hoped it was, and he hoped just as strongly that it wasn't. He began to feel like he was drowning.

He climbed out of the RV to stretch his legs. No telling how long before she came back, if she came back at all. Just as likely, she would take his money and slip out a back door, leaving him standing there like the fool he was. Maybe this was something she did every day, always relying on another sucker to pick her up and give her a few bucks, a new twist on panhandling.

He took a couple of laps around the RV, checking for any damages done on the road, but, except for a thick layer of dust, it looked the same as when he'd first begun his trek. He leaned against the RV's door, his shiny new toy, twenty-one feet of freedom on wheels…still, only a temporary solution. He understood that. Oh, it would be fun for a while, the freedom of the open road, adventure around every corner, every man's fantasy. For all he knew, many women might share that same fantasy. Maybe MaryBeth herself had entertained similar thoughts.

But running away was not a permanent solution. Sooner or later, he'd have to start looking ahead, making plans, but not yet.

As he watched the darkness settle in beyond the lights in the parking lot, he thought perhaps he'd seen the last of his traveling companion, but he wasn't that lucky. Barely twenty minutes had passed when she sauntered back out to the RV.

"I'm all set," she said, holding up a surprisingly large bag of what he hoped was fairly conservative clothing, and shoes, too. "Can I change in the back of your trailer?"

He opened the side door, and she bounced up the steps like she couldn't wait to get into her new duds. "I'll just wait out here," he said. He stared down at his feet, anywhere but directly at her.

This girl was fast. In no time at all, she paraded down the two steps and did a little pirouette in front of him. "What do you think?"

Sensible, was what he thought, although sensible on her looked very good indeed. A dark blue sweatshirt and pants, and a pair of white sneakers. He stopped himself just as he began to speculate about what else she might have purchased, new underwear, for instance, no business of his, for sure. "Very nice," he said and realized immediately that he should have chosen a more flattering word. *Nice* sounded pretty lame, and the frown on her face told him as much.

"And I got a toothbrush and a few other things." Again, that devilish smile, or was he reading too much into it? Maybe she smiled the exact same way at her uncles or her cat. "I have fifteen bucks and change left over. Can I treat you to a cheeseburger?" She held up one of the sales tags, still attached to the sweatshirt, for him to see.

"You sure got a lot for the money," he said.

"I'm a smart shopper, and a lot of this stuff was on sale."

"Great." What else could he say?

The déjà vu moment was upon him before he had time to head it off. A couple of years ago, his daughter Addie kept bringing home shopping bags, and even he, with his limited knowledge of girls' stuff and prices,

55

could see the disconnect. Her usual explanation, "It was all on sale," didn't hold water. Then he looked inside one of the bags, found it stuffed with high-priced items, all of which still had sales tags attached.

"MaryBeth, I'm afraid our daughter is shoplifting." That was his second mistake.

"Oh, for heavens' sake, Phil, all girls do. Don't make such a big deal out of it."

"Did you do it?" he asked his wife.

"How dare you ask me that." End of discussion.

Then, a week later, his daughter was driven home in a squad car...shoplifting. She shared the back seat with two of her friends. At least MaryBeth had been right about that...apparently, all girls do it. And some of them get caught.

Now he had to wonder about his traveling companion...smart shopper or thief? Not much he could do about it now, and besides, he was hungry.

Parking spots at the Burger Barn were not designed to accommodate a rig the size of his, so he sat idling on the roadside while she went inside to buy burgers. When she returned, she set the bag of food between them. "Here, try the fries. They're tastier when they're hot."

"Delicious," he said as he munched on a couple. "My map says there's a campground just up the road. Want to drive on up there where we'll have more room?"

"Gosh, you sure are organized, maps and everything."

Organized? Not hardly. If she knew the truth, how he'd run away from his former life with only a direction in mind, no specific destination, organized would probably not be the word she chose.

And underneath it all lay the very uncomfortable possibility that his current situation wasn't all accidental, that perhaps some of it might have occurred by intent, that he had sabotaged himself and his former life, like lighting the fuse, then stepping in front of the cannon. All well and good to blame it on some cosmic conspiracy, but in the end, he was the one holding the match.

Now the mouth-watering aroma of burgers filled the cab of the RV. She held the bag on her lap, feeding him fries a couple at a time while he drove, and before long, they'd finished off all of them.

"I guess we were both hungry," she said. "But we still have the burgers." Then she began humming, some bouncy little tune that he didn't recognize. Probably one of those new songs that his daughter might like, but which was wasted on him. "Turn on the radio if you like," he said.

"What, you don't like my singing?"

"Your singing is just fine." Was she really and truly offended or just winding him up? He couldn't tell with this girl.

"But you don't like it."

"You sure have a way of twisting words around. All I meant was if you wanted to listen to something, in particular, feel free."

But she laughed, that magical bubbling sound, like clear water capering through a rocky creek bed. "Just trying to get a rise out of you."

Yeah, like she really had to try.

Chapter Five

The sign, SUNSET CAMPGROUND, was lit intermittently by a flickering bulb, although there was still sufficient light to make it out without the strobe effect. About fifty yards up the road, Phil pulled up by what he assumed to be the office, a small cabin-type structure with a sagging roof and warped siding, leaving large gaps that couldn't possibly block a cold wind. An even more dilapidated structure with a half-moon cut into the door connected the cabin by a path to what appeared to be well-worn…an outhouse? Still in use? Any passer-by who stopped and asked to use the facilities was in for a bit of a shock.

"Twenty bucks for the night." The gaunt man he found inside never stopped looking at the TV. "Sign the book."

When Phil signed the ledger, adding his name to a list of unreadable entries, he noticed the man's blue cap had a Peerless logo. Yeah, he remembered Peerless, best damned tractor you can buy, only, he would probably never find out, seeing as how his went from the dealership to his driveway and straight back to the dealership, and along the way torpedoed his marriage without ever being fired up. Who'd have ever thought riding mowers could be so dangerous?

"Showers and toilet faculties included," the gaunt TV addict said. "How many of you?"

"Just the two of us."

"No kids?"

Phil shook his head.

"That's good," Mr. Gaunt Man said. "Kids get a little too noisy for me. Pick any site you want. They're all available except for a couple up the road there. And there's firewood by the shower building if you want it. Have to carry it yourself, though."

The area was quiet, flat, and had the same view he'd seen all day. The campsites all looked the same too, so he pulled into the first spot just off the path. A picnic table sat alongside the cleared edge of the site, and there was a fire pit built with a circle of stones in the center.

His traveling companion was out the door, stretching her arms over her head before Phil even turned the engine off. "I'd really love a quick shower before we eat," she said.

"The guy said there's showers and a bathroom in the building over there. There's a shower in the RV, but the hot water doesn't last very long."

"The outdoor shower sounds like more fun. Will you walk over with me?" she asked. "You've got me scared a coyote might jump out at me."

Seemed a little far-fetched, but since he was the one who'd brought up the coyote bit in the first place, he grabbed towels and a flashlight to check out the facilities, and she followed him down the path. The restrooms looked clean enough, and he checked out the shower stalls. Okay too. "Looks fine to me," he said and set the towels on the bench just inside the enclosure. "I'll leave the flashlight for you."

"Thanks, hey, what should I call you?" she asked.

She started to unzip her top, and he turned on his heel.

"Phil, everybody calls me Phil." He was about to ask her name—seemed only fair—but when he turned back around, she was half undressed. Introductions would have to wait.

He grabbed a load of firewood to take back to the campsite. The wood, mostly pine, was dry and flamed right up, releasing a spicy aroma along with more heat than he needed yet. The evening air was cool but not so chilly as to require a roaring fire. He knelt by the firepit and separated the embers with a stick.

Moments later, she sauntered back up the path, looking bright and pink like freshly scrubbed fruit. Something luminous about her caused the lump in his throat to come back with a vengeance. She backed up to the fire and rubbed her backside. When she took a deep breath of the "wonderful fresh air," he found he could hardly breathe at all. This could not go on; a guy could only take so much. "I still don't know your name," he said.

"Feed me first," she said. "Then we can get into all that personal stuff. I'll get the burgers if you'll pull over a bench from the picnic table."

"There's a couple of chairs in this locker underneath," he said. In fact, after several days on the road, he hadn't really checked out all of the features on his new mobile home. Three of the chairs in the locker were still wrapped in cellophane, as was a fold-out cot. And there were still other items stored farther underneath, but it was too dark to make them out.

As the flame danced in the fire pit, they pulled their chairs alongside. "You know, I forgot, I have cold beer in the refrigerator."

"Thank God, I would kill for a beer," she said. "This is really neat," she said later as they sat by the fire having burgers and beer. "I never dreamed the day would turn out so nice. I'm so glad you finally came along."

Phil sloshed a bit of beer on his shirt. "What do you mean...finally?"

"I mean, you kept me waiting for a long time."

"I kept you waiting? What are you talking about? There's no way you could have known it would be me driving by. Could have been anybody."

Now she laughed softly, a melodic sound that so reminded him of a stream flowing over and around stones. "It had to be you, Phil. Can't you see that?"

"No way, it was pure chance that I decided to drive down this particular road. I could just as easily have headed in the opposite direction or stayed on the interstate."

"Unless it was meant to be anyway, like maybe it all happened so you could come out here and rescue me from the coyotes." Her gaze locked on him, so he couldn't look away if he wanted to.

"You're making a joke out of it."

"Am I? Think about it. Sometimes things happen, and we don't find out why until later." She finished her burger and folded the wrapper into a neat little square. "Now, you're tired and I'm tired, so where do I sleep?"

"Bedroom on the left, just past the kitchen. There's blankets on the shelf by the bed." He didn't give it a second thought, like he'd been planning for her to stay with him all along, and so had she.

As she walked past his chair, she leaned over and kissed him on the cheek. "Thanks for taking care of me,

61

and I'm sorry for your trouble back home, but I'm glad you're finally here."

"No problem." Her reality was becoming entangled with his own, so that he wasn't sure which way was up. What did she mean about everything that had happened being part of some big plan, supposed to happen, like his own decisions didn't make any difference? What if he'd tried that explanation on the judge back in the Wakefield courthouse? He'd probably still be in jail instead of driving around the countryside rescuing half-naked women. He doused the embers of the campfire, then went inside where his bed lay empty and waiting for him, and he fell dead asleep as soon as his head hit the pillow.

****

Coffee...unmistakable, borne along by a cool breeze that coursed through his RV. Had he forgotten to close the windows, or had someone just opened them? He pulled on his trousers and padded down the hallway, where he found the source of the intoxicating aroma in the pot sitting on the galley stove. His new traveling companion, still nameless, was sitting outside in one of his lawn chairs sipping from her own cup. He watched her through the window for a moment, trying to get a read on her, but came up empty, just as before. She had switched back to the shorts she wore the day before but still wore the dark blue top. Damn, the girl had great legs.

When he ran his hand over his chin, he was surprised at the stubble of whiskers. A glance in the bathroom mirror confirmed what he'd dreaded; with no one to care one way or the other how he looked, he'd begun to let things slip. A shave, a quick shower, and a change of clothes later, he poured himself a cup of coffee and went out to join her.

"You clean up real nice," she said. "I tried to be quiet, so I wouldn't wake you."

A fresh cup of coffee and a big smile from a pretty woman…there were worse ways to begin a new day.

"How long have you been up?" he asked, rather surprised at himself for having slept so soundly and so late in the morning.

"I'm an early riser, like to watch the sun come up when I get the chance."

The stale odor of the previous night's campfire mingled with the tart aroma of pine trees and coffee. When the breeze shifted to the west, it brought a faint smell of livestock, dung, large bodies foraging, a big change from the sea breezes he was used to in Wakefield. There were more birdsongs this morning than usual, or maybe they'd been there all along, and he'd just failed to notice.

"You seem to be in a good mood," she said. "Pleasant dreams last night?"

"You might say that. Aside from coffee, I don't have much in the way of breakfast," he said.

"Yeah, I noticed your cupboards were pretty bare." Her laughter was the frosting on the cake of his new morning.

"I guess we can stop someplace along the road to eat. Maybe find someplace to do some grocery shopping too."

"Okay, but first, you have to take me for a walk."

They left their cups, his only half-finished, on the picnic table, and she led him down the path past the other empty sites. When they reached the bathroom, he paused. "Need to make a quick stop," he said.

"You can manage without me?" she asked, that same playful grin flitting across her face.

When he'd finished, he made a noisy show of washing his hands, then joined her farther up the path. The trail formed a circle with individual sites on either side, but his was the only camping vehicle present.

She linked her arm through his, casual, all perfectly natural, and they walked together, shoulders rubbing, sometimes hips bumping, leaving Phil in a state somewhat like ecstasy.

"I could get to like this camping bit," she said.

"You've never done it before?"

"Not like this, not with all the comforts of home like you have."

The more he thought about it, the more reasonable the idea seemed, being footloose and fancy-free, needing nothing more than a place to park for the night. Of course, he had his own very specific reasons for being out on the road, but he had no idea what hers might be. "So, why not?" he asked.

"Too busy most of the time," she said.

"Working, you mean?"

"Yeah."

"What kind of work do you do?"

"Different things."

"What kind of a job is that, exactly?" he asked.

"Come on, Phil, there you go with the questions again. You have to learn to enjoy the moment. Besides, it's time for you to feed me again."

Sometimes talking to her was like playing ping pong, back and forth but getting nowhere fast. But he was beginning to like the game.

The morning sun was well up into a clear blue sky by the time they had all the gear stowed away and pulled away from the campsite. He found the lighter traffic on the state road much more to his liking and made a mental note to stay off the interstate with its steady crush of eighteen-wheelers.

They found a pancake house sitting between a drug store and a movie theater with no other buildings in sight. "Who is there around here to watch movies?" he asked.

"You'd be surprised."

"But we're in the middle of nowhere," he said.

"It's not nowhere. It's Oklahoma."

"Oh, yeah, right."

A bit later, gorged on carbohydrates and coffee—he would have to watch the carbs—they went back outside into a blinding sun that left them both blinking. A small crowd of six, all elderly men, had gathered around the RV. Where had they come from?

"Nice rig," one of them said when Phil approached.

"Thanks, almost new, still getting used to her." Phil spoke without thinking, assuming the guy was referring to the RV, even though he was checking out Phil's blonde friend as well.

The small group of onlookers dispersed without further comment, and in a moment, it was as if they'd never been there at all.

They climbed back into the RV where Phil had himself a quiet chuckle as he pulled back onto the road.

"What's funny?" she asked.

"Nothing, I wasn't laughing."

"You most certainly were. You think it's funny, calling me your nice new rig, about how you're still getting used to me? That's your idea of a joke, is it?" She poked him in the ribs.

"No, no, I was just talking to the guy, couldn't very well ignore him, could I?"

"No more pancakes for you, my friend...new rig indeed."

He glanced over; she was smiling. The earth was once again spinning smoothly in the proper orbit. Wakefield seemed a million miles away.

Now well beyond Kingfisher, they were back out into open country, a large herd of cattle grazing off to the west, otherwise, except for the occasional cluster of oil rigs, empty plain with nothing else in sight.

"Oh, look," she said. "There's a coyote." She pointed to a rather small gray blur of a beast racing along parallel to the road as if it was trying to outrun the RV. "See, I told you they were little farts, nothing like that half-wolf half-coyote thing you were talking about. You made that up just to scare me, didn't you?"

"No, I swear, I saw something about them on TV. I never realized coyotes were so fast," he said.

"Have to be. Some people hunt them, you know. The slow ones get picked off pretty quick."

"I didn't know that." But he knew the principle, didn't he? The fast ones survive, and the slower ones get picked off. Lately, he was just trying to avoid getting picked off himself.

The coyote veered off away from the road and soon was out of sight. It was just him and his blonde friend cruising along with no place in particular to go.

He was comfortable being with her. He no longer felt the need to fill up the quiet spaces with meaningless conversation. In spite of the fact that she was still a big mystery to him, and he had a million questions about her, whatever happened was okay, and if nothing at all happened, that would be okay too.

"Still headed west?" she'd asked.

"Reckon so. Haven't given it all that much thought." Although he had an uneasy feeling that she knew where he was going before he did.

"Okay if I tag along with you?" she asked.

"Sure." Right now, having her alongside him was just about the best thing he could think of.

Less than an hour beyond Kingfisher, she became agitated, twisting in her seat.

"There it is. OMG, I just knew it."

"What? Another coyote? Where?"

They were entering the outskirts of another small town, a few clapboard houses with siding that needed paint followed by the beginnings of a modest business district a bit further on, when she began waving her arms and pointing.

"No, don't slow down here. Drive on up to the cross street and make a right. Then, pull over somewhere and let me out."

"What's going on?" He looked for a road sign but saw nothing. In fact, when he'd checked his map earlier that morning, he saw no town of any kind indicated before Enid, farther to the north.

"My car, the little blue coupe, parked right back there at the gas station. The bastard."

"What bastard? Would you please tell me what's happening?"

"Harry, my ex, I had to stop by the road to pee. I couldn't wait. Anyway, the bastard drove off and left me squatting there with my pants around my ankles."

"He just drove away and left you out in the middle of nowhere? Took your car?" So, she had an ex. Not such a big deal, was it? In all likelihood, he would become one himself as soon as MaryBeth realized she and Addie were better off without him.

"Not exactly, well, technically it's his car, but he owes me. So I'm taking it back, that is, if he was dumb enough to leave the keys inside like he usually does." She was halfway out the door before he came to a full stop.

"That's it, then? I guess I won't be seeing you again?"

No answer. By then, she had cut between two squat buildings on her way back to the gas station. Should he wait or just drive on? If she was able to retrieve the car, she'd probably be long gone. On the other hand, if she got into a fracas with Harry, the bastard, she might need some help. Phil might not know how to defend himself in a fight with a woman and a purse, but guys were another matter.

The cross street proved to be a dead end, so he had to back the RV out again before he could return to the gas station. But the lot was empty…no little blue coupe, no blonde friend. He drove up and down the main street a couple of times but found no trace of her. He stopped at the gas pump and filled the RV's tank. *How could she just run off like that?*

A very disappointed Phil went inside to pay the gas station attendant, slowing at the door to step over a sleeping black and tan hound dog that showed no signs of life as he passed. "Okay, if I leave the RV parked over in the corner of the lot for a while?" he asked. "Need to stretch my legs a bit."

"Sure." The attendant showed only slightly more life than the dog. "You're the only customer today anyway."

Phil locked his vehicle, then walked up and down the streets where he'd just driven. He peeked into alleys and vacant areas, even ventured into a few backyards. He found no blonde girl in a blue coupe, but what he saw was even more surprising. This nameless town, too small to appear on his road map, was not the typical shanty-town he'd been driving through since he left the Interstate. The streets were conspicuously clean, and the storefronts along Main Street were so well-maintained they looked as if a maintenance crew had been through in the past couple of days.

There was a barbershop with an old-fashioned spiral barber pole out front, right next to a tobacco store with an honest-to-God cigar store Indian beside the front door. Phil peeked in the front window of an ice cream parlor where the counter man, who back in the day might have been called a soda jerk, wearing a black bow tie along with his white shirt, was serving up a gorgeous banana split to a rather hefty patron who held a large spoon in her right hand.

Reflected in that same window, he saw across the street, something he'd only seen before during a road trip with MaryBeth and Addie through Amish country in Pennsylvania…two women wearing old-fashioned bonnets. He took a step back and did a slow turn, taking in the whole street. It was like stepping back in time. The appearance of a horse-and-buggy combination would not have surprised him in the least.

But as exotic as the town might appear, he hadn't found what he was searching for. She was gone. His grand adventure was over. His feet and his heart were heavy as he climbed back into the RV. The usual happy growl of the engine struck a more mournful note as he fired it up.

The front seats of the RV now seemed a vast and empty space and, for the first time since he'd started his trip, Phil was lonely. He scratched himself in an intimate area that had been off limits when she was around while he considered his reacquired single status.

His supply of groceries was seriously deficient, and, since his blonde friend had headed off for parts unknown, he'd be shopping for himself, probably the saddest obligation of a single guy and the reason he avoided it when he could.

He drove to the edge of the small town to a market with a parking lot big enough to accommodate his RV. The sign out front said Herb's Groceries and Hardware, a combination Phil would have to see to believe. But, as advertised, a wide center aisle divided the market into hardware on the left side and groceries on the right. He browsed through the hardware section where nuts, bolts, nails, and tools of every imaginable kind were either set off in individual bins or hanging from the wall. Nothing was bound up in the clear plastic wrap he was so used to seeing. If you wanted a half-pound of roofing nails, there was a scale by the aisle…weigh it out yourself then put it into a paper bag, not plastic.

The grocery section was less impressive. The selection wasn't great, but he didn't plan to spend a lot of time cooking. Fortunately, the frozen foods section had an abundance of TV dinners, which would fit perfectly in his small microwave oven, and their cooler was well-stocked with beer, one of life's essential food groups, especially for a single guy.

He took one long look over his shoulder before he pulled away, still hoping for a glimpse of her, but the little blue coupe was gone, and so was she. So, that was that. His adventure with the blonde hitchhiker might make a great story to share with the guys someday, assuming he would have friends sometime in the future.

Once again, he was headed west, alone. When the time came, he would change directions, just looking for an opening, a way through, no real plan, no destination in mind, nothing more than getting around obstacles, all the while keeping an eye peeled for a blue coupe driven by a blonde with sparkling blue eyes.

Yeah, life at its most basic, that was Phil Claussen once again, gasoline, food, beer, and a place to sleep. What else did a guy need? Out of that brief list, he lacked only a place to sleep, and now he was on the lookout for another campsite. He would be knocking off early in the afternoon, but what the hell? Not like he was on a schedule. He might even drive back and spend more time browsing through that antique hardware store.

Chapter Six

Back in his military days, he'd had a friend who had grown up in Oklahoma, the same general area through which Phil was traveling. "What's it like?" Phil had asked.

"Nothing much." And that was all his friend said.

Phil drove through the next few miles of nothing much before he saw the campground sign. At first glance, this campground looked like the others, table-flat with a horizon that seemed to go on forever, but the area had an abundance of pine trees and shrubbery. Off to the northwest, the haze of the late afternoon sun layered over areas of undulation, so there must be hills nearby, and, from the darker areas of green, now turned grayish so late in the day, maybe hardwoods in addition to the ever-present scrub pines.

Phil parked alongside the entrance, and moments later, a bald, older guy shuffled out to the RV. Was this a kind of final common pathway for the elderly in the Midwest, caretaker of a campground? The last three he'd seen, including the current fireball, looked as if they'd been cast from the same mold, like some sort of weird sci-fi scheme, cloning campsite attendants.

When the man got close enough, Phil could make out his blue eyes, quite similar to another set of blue eyes that had dazzled him so recently. Without saying anything, the fellow walked all the way around the RV, then stopped in front of Phil and looked him over too.

"NC plates," he said as if he'd made some startling discovery. The old guy wore leather deck shoes that didn't appear to have undergone heavy use, certainly not farm labor. His slacks were creased, not razor-sharp, just enough to show they'd had proper care.

"Huh? Oh, yeah, started out in Wakefield, North Carolina, right on the coast," Phil said.

"Never been there. Reckon it's pretty, all that open water. Won't find much of that around here, not like you're used to anyway."

"I'm enjoying the change of scenery," Phil said.

The man made direct eye contact with Phil, then looked away, as if in an instant he'd seen what he wanted to see. "Nice rig," he said, nodding toward the RV.

"Yeah, just getting used to it." The comment lodged in Phil's throat, remembering the recent humorous exchange involving his blonde hitchhiker, but then, most of the conversations he'd struck up along the road started off with some comment about the RV. No problem, things had to begin somewhere.

"Reckon you'll be staying a while?" the old man asked.

"Not sure yet, don't really have a schedule. Say, what's the name of the town I just drove through? It's not listed on my map."

"Clayton, that's its name. Don't know how it came to be called that. Don't even know if it deserves to be called a town, really just a village, a few shops, enough to supply the basics. Pancake House has good food, and the steakhouses ain't bad either. They're about the same, all three of them."

"Three steakhouses?" Phil asked. Seemed a bit much for a town that hardly sounded big enough to have its own zip code.

"Yeah, this is beef country. Steak for breakfast, lunch, and dinner."

"Seafood?"

"If you mean catfish, yeah. Get it any way you want, so long as it's fried. Drug store gets the newspapers every day. You want something else sent in, they can usually get it for you.

"We got a courthouse and a sheriff, Barnhill's the name. Best lawyer in town is named Newton if you need one. You go browse around a bit, you'll see." He made no mention of the bizarre appearance of the village, but perhaps it didn't seem so bizarre to him as it had to Phil.

"What's the name of this campground?" Phil asked.

"Birchbark Campground, I'm Sy Birch. I own the place. Try to keep it up as best I can. You see anything that ain't right, you let me know, and I'll take care of it."

"Say, you haven't by chance seen a blonde lady driving a blue coupe, have you?"

The old guy cocked his head to one side, raised an eyebrow. "A blue coupe now, you say?"

"Right, have you seen her?" Phil's hopes soared. Maybe she lived around here. Maybe this guy knew her. Maybe his blue eyes…family, even?

"What's her name?"

And just like that, the lights twinkled, then went dim. "I don't know."

The old fellow looked away, chuckled. "Sounds

familiar," he said. "If I see anybody looks like that, I'll tell her you're looking for her. But I don't know your name yet."

Phil stuck out his hand. "Phil Claussen." The hand that grasped his was softer than he expected, not one used to hard manual labor but still firm and genuine.

"Glad to have you, Mr. Claussen. Hope you'll be with us for a while. Let me know if you need anything. I live right down at the end of the road. There's a pond on down the path. Folks catch an occasional bass, clean enough to swim in, too. No lifeguard, though."

The fellow walked away having said nothing about payment, and the way the old guy had checked him out seemed more like an interview than a casual chat. He seemed to know something about Phil's mystery woman, so maybe he was getting closer to the source of the mystery. Still, best not get his hopes up; watching them crash back to the ground was no fun.

Phil drove the RV past several vacant campsites, finally stopping at one hidden from the road. Tomorrow maybe he would go for a walk. He'd had his butt stuck in the driver's seat for almost a week with no exercise, and it felt as if it was getting bigger…turning into a lardass, perfect. For the evening, he just took a tour around the campground. He was becoming used to the countryside smells, so different from that of seaside Wakefield. Here the piquant aroma of scrub pines was ever present. The usual pungent aroma of livestock was absent, leaving fresh, clean air that Phil inhaled without reservation.

He was the campground's only occupant, except for an owl that he heard but could not see. Unless things picked up during the summer months, this place couldn't be producing much revenue for Mr. Sy Birch.

By the time he got back to his campsite, the light had begun to fade, so he grabbed an armful of firewood along with some smaller stuff for kindling from the stack beside the shower stalls and formed a little pyramid in the small circle of stones beside his RV. He tugged on a light jacket as his campfire flared up to warm him just as the sun began to slip away, taking both its light and heat along. He retrieved a chair from his storage compartment and a cold beer from his refrigerator. A campfire and a cold beer, things could be worse. But it wasn't enough. He had all the ingredients for a relaxing evening, but still, it wasn't enough, and he knew exactly what was lacking.

He missed her, whoever she was, wherever she was. A day and a half spent together hardly seemed long enough to form a real relationship, and he still didn't know her name, but he wouldn't soon forget her smile, her sparkling blue eyes, her happy laugh, that faint smell of lilacs. Yeah, he missed her. He crossed his legs in front of the fire and got lost in thoughts about scenarios that never would happen.

He woke with a start. Must have drifted off, but he couldn't have been out for long because his fire was still burning brightly. The silver luxury sedan that pulled alongside his RV looked new; he couldn't be sure. But the voice, he knew that instantly.

"Hi, did you miss me?" She skipped from the car to his chair and planted a vigorous kiss on his cheek. "You didn't answer me," she said.

"Huh? What?"

"Are you glad to see me or not?"

"Oh, yeah, sure." As he stood, his chair tilted, and,

had she not grabbed his arm, he would have fallen flat on his face.

"Easy now. How many beers have you had?"

"Just that one and I didn't even finish it," he said as the contents of the can he'd just dropped flooded out onto the ground. "What in the world are you doing here?"

She maintained her grip on his arm. "Looking for you, silly."

"How did you find me?" he asked.

She laughed. "It was easy. Men are predictable, and you are even more predictable than most. When I spotted the campfire, I knew. Now, how do you like my new outfit?" She twirled in front of him. The white outfit fit her like a second skin, and the zipper in front was opened far enough to display enough cleavage to make him dizzy. The psychedelic effect of the wavering light from the campfire as it danced across her body completed his meltdown. "Wow," he mumbled, and that was the best he could come up with, at least until he could breathe properly.

"Wow?" she said. "That's all after I went to the trouble of getting dressed up for you? I guess it will have to do."

"Sorry." He still mumbled, and the harder he tried, the worse it got.

She rescued him with her happy laugh and another kiss on the cheek. "You're so cute when you're flustered. Now, sit down so I don't have to worry about you falling." She moved about with ease and confidence as if this evening reunion had been planned all along.

So, he sat. He looked at the campfire, looked at the

rim of sky still light above the trees, looked at his feet, anywhere but the vision in white that undulated in front of him. Maybe, somewhere in an alternate universe, this sort of display wouldn't cause much commotion, but he, Phil Claussen, modest middle class for as far back as he could remember, was overwhelmed. This was like overdosing on chocolate cake and ice cream, way too rich for the likes of him.

"You have a different car," he said.

"Yeah, I traded up."

"You traded that little blue coupe for a luxury model?" If true, this would be the most one-sided deal since the Dutch screwed the Native Americans out of Manhattan for a bag of glass beads.

"Not exactly. Now stop asking so many questions and help me get things ready. I hope you haven't eaten because I have a surprise for dinner. Do you have a table? We can have a picnic here by the fire."

"Yeah, I think there's one under here." Sure enough, the storage compartment under the RV that held the chairs had a foldout table as well. Phil popped the table legs out and moved it around until he found a level spot.

"Great," she said. "Now, help me get this cooler out of the trunk."

Phil lugged a large red cooler from the car over to the table. "What's inside?" he asked.

"That's your surprise." From somewhere, she produced a small can of cooking fuel—it was like a magic show where she pulled items out of thin air— which she lit after placing it in the center of the table.

"You're cooking?" he asked.

"That's for melting the butter."

"Melting butter?"

"Of course, silly, you can't very well have lobster without melted butter. I thought you knew that."

"Lobster? We're having lobster?"

"You know, you don't have to repeat everything I say." She cut two sticks of butter in half and placed them in a small pot over the Sterno flame. "Okay, we're about ready. We still need several large plates, four at least, knives, forks, and a couple of large serving spoons. While you're getting that stuff, I'll get the champagne glasses out of the car."

He almost parroted *champagne glasses*. He caught himself just in time, but the look on his face must have said just as much.

"You don't have any," she said. "I checked before." She fished around in the cooler and brought forth a chilled bottle of champagne with a French label. "Careful with the cork. You can't very well drive with only one eye."

So, they sat down to a feast, the likes of which Phil hadn't seen in a long time. His salivary glands kicked into overdrive. After his brief chat with Sy Birch, he'd written off the possibility of any exotic seafood dishes, and now she'd turned up with lobster. Watching her arrange the items was even more like watching a magic act, trying to figure out where things came from and guessing wrong every time.

"Are you warm enough?" he asked. The garment she wore didn't look capable of conserving body heat or designed to.

"Perfect," she said.

When he mangled his lobster trying to retrieve the succulent meat, she pulled over his plate, split the beast open, and then cracked open the claws, leaving everything laid out for him. And she made it look so easy, as if she'd done it hundreds of times before. "There now," she said, "you won't chop off a finger trying to get at the goodies."

Between the succulent lobster and the champagne, his taste buds were dancing for joy. "This lobster was cooked fresh," he said. "Where did you ever find fresh lobster?"

"Nothing but the best for you, sweetie."

"But…."

Oh, well, the details could wait for later. After a rather frenzied bout of eating, Phil leaned back in his chair. "That was magnificent. Thank you."

"Glad you enjoyed it. Be careful when you stand up. I doubt you're used to champagne."

She was right, of course. Champagne and its after-effects were not part of the daily fare in the Claussen household. He had to concentrate on staying upright, giggling in spite of himself. He tossed a couple of small logs on the campfire. "I'll bag up the lobster shells. There's a latched garbage can just down the trail. Otherwise, the raccoons will scatter them all over."

By the time he got back, the aroma of coffee wafted out of the RV's kitchen. A few moments later, she brought two steaming mugs out to the table.

"More plates?" he said as she set out small dishes, forks, and one large knife.

"I have one more surprise for you." From the trunk of the new car, she brought a cake box, opened it, and placed on the table a chocolate cake that had *Happy Birthday, Annette* in white lettering.

"Well, well, I finally learn your name. Happy

Birthday, Annette."

She smiled and shook her head.

"But this is you, Annette, right?"

"Not exactly."

"You mean, this is someone else's cake?"

"No, it's my cake, but Annette isn't my name. I'm sure it's a delicious cake, though." She hacked off a hefty slice and slid it over to him. "Try it. I know you'll like it."

The champagne bubbles were still bouncing around in his brain, and even more intoxicating was the beauty in the white body glove sitting across from him, smiling, whoever she was. Mesmerized, hypnotized, pulverized…whatever the process, the result was the same. Phil didn't know which end was up and didn't care. He only hoped this crazy ride would last a bit longer.

"Please, help me out here. Who are you?"

"Phil Claussen, so many questions, you're going to spoil the party." She cut off a small piece of cake and held it in front of his lips. "Here, one bite for me."

"How do you know my last name?" he asked.

"You must have told me."

"I don't think so."

"Well, it says so, right on your driver's license, Phil Claussen, thirty-four years old, six feet one inch tall, one hundred and eight-five pounds, brown eyes, brown hair. That's you. There's even a photograph, but I must say, it doesn't do you justice. You should make them do it over again."

"You looked in my wallet?"

"Of course. A girl can't very well go riding across the country with a total stranger, can she? And I know my safety is important to you, right? And we're sleeping together too, remember? Now, eat your cake before your coffee gets cold."

Sometimes you win, sometimes you lose, and sometimes you just plain give up. Phil just plain gave up. "Good cake," he said.

Later, after all was stacked away and the fire was burning low, she headed toward the silver sedan once again. "I know just the thing to top off the evening." She returned with a squat bottle and two brandy glasses. "A little brandy," she said. "And you know, you should upgrade your stock of drinking glasses, and your liquor cabinet is seriously deficient too. If you want to catch a girl's eye, you're going to have to do better than just beer."

"Yeah, okay." What else could he say? Life could not in any possible way be better than at this moment. Phil Claussen was a very happy man.

He dreamed about her several times during the night. One very erotic fantasy involving a zipper and a large scoop of chocolate cream frosting from Annette's birthday cake left him sweaty, panting, and in possession of a formidable erection that made a tent in the sheet that covered him. "Settle down," he said to the penis tent. "Nothing happening here, so you're just wasting your time."

He thought he was still dreaming the next morning when he felt her touch on his shoulder. But there she was, as real as anything, her face only inches from his, her blue eyes sparkling as if they were backlit, her faint scent of lilacs seeping into his skin. She hovered there for a moment while his brain circuitry switched off, leaving her as the single entity left on the planet.

"I have to leave early," she said. "Coffee's on the stove." She kissed him, on the lips this time, then she was gone before he could ask where she was going, when she would return, would she return at all?

As soon as she kissed him, the lines that encircled Phil's reality got all blurry again. If he was still dreaming, he did not want to disrupt the magic, so he lay very still, waiting for the touch of her lips to reappear, but she was well and truly gone.

He took a cup of coffee with him as he strolled along the narrow lane past the showers on down to a small pond with the morning mist hanging just above the surface. The trail was neatly filled in with small gravel, such as might be seen in a state park or some other outfit with a fat budget and plenty of hired help. The night before, when he'd taken a stop in the bathroom, he'd marveled at how spic and span the facility was. The owner, Sy Birch, if that was really his name, must run a tight ship.

The pond looked inviting enough, and he considered for a moment taking a quick dip but lacking any swimming attire, it would have to be a bare-assed plunge, and he didn't want to find out the hard way that the locals frowned upon nudity, particularly in a thirty-four-year-old man.

A snake, black with yellow stripes, slithered beneath the log where he was about to sit, so he remained standing. Off to his right, a large bird startled him, croaking like one of the herons that stalked along the shoreline of the Albemarle Sound, only Phil couldn't imagine what it might be doing so far inland. He couldn't see it clearly, but the bird apparently didn't like the idea of sharing the morning tranquility with anyone or anything.

He emptied the now cold contents of his coffee cup beside the path and checked out the pines across the pond and their identical upside-down reflection in the glassy surface of the water. The picture would be perfect if his new blonde friend were standing closely beside him. The memory of the kiss she'd given him before leaving still lingered, but, like the images of the trees, was now only a reflection; he wanted the real thing.

Chapter Seven

The family he'd left behind in Wakefield would have been up for at least an hour by now. Addie was probably off to school, hopefully without any further embarrassment from her father's antics, and MaryBeth would have settled into her desk at the real estate office. Her boss, slimy Larry Lemmings, would have dropped by, patted her on the shoulder, and they would have made plans for lunch. Phil suspected that sometimes they made other arrangements, too, like a noontime tryst at the Coastal Inn a few miles down the county road. But he couldn't prove anything, and now it wouldn't matter. Who would blame her for seeking comfort after her worthless husband had abandoned her and her daughter?

Just over seven years ago, Phil, fresh out of the military, had taken a teaching job at Wakefield High. He met MaryBeth at a social for new faculty members. She was there with a recently divorced school administrator who introduced her as his favorite real estate agent. Newly hired and very nervous, Phil stumbled and spilled his drink on her when they were introduced.

He was surprised when she called the next day and asked where she should send the bill for having her dress cleaned. He apologized again and gave her his address. An hour or so later, she showed up at his door.

"Don't bother about the dress," she said, "but you owe me a drink." She spent the rest of the day with him, then the night as well, and two months later, they were man and wife. Addie, then six, was a bonus, a daughter from a previous marriage that had ended in divorce. MaryBeth refused to divulge all the details of that breakup, only that it involved infidelity, her husband's. She apparently made out with a nice cash settlement too, but never shared the specifics with Phil.

It took Phil some time to figure out his role in the marriage: MaryBeth wanted a husband. Being a single mother was inconvenient, and Phil was a convenience, not unlike a new kitchen appliance that saved time and effort. Having a husband seemed to make life easier for her.

His main source of regret about the arrangement was Addie. He wished they could have been closer, but MaryBeth always found a way to make sure he was on the outside looking in. For their entire married life, he always seemed to be at least a step behind, maybe more. He didn't learn that MaryBeth's father had been a serial philanderer until soon after their sixth anniversary. And whatever heartbreak MaryBeth's mother had endured, she was sure to have shared with MaryBeth, who would have shared it with Addie, wisdom passed down through the generations. Men are shits. Case closed.

So MaryBeth probably felt that she had to protect Addie from men, all of whom were worthless philandering scum, Phil included. If she knew about his new blonde friend, she would feel quite vindicated...worthless scum, all of them.

When he got back to the RV, he found Sy Birch

waiting for him. Sy had a big smile, apparently happy about something. "Been down to check out the pond?" he asked.

"Yeah." Phil was glad now he'd decided against going for a swim.

"Not much to it, clean, though. You ever want to do any fishing, there's a bigger lake close by. I got a little skiff. Take you out any time you want to go. Bass jump right in the boat."

"I just might take you up on that," Phil said.

"What did you think about our little village? Probably not quite what you expected, huh?"

"You're right about that." How could he say the village looked like it belonged in the previous century without the risk of insulting the old man? "Looks as if things don't change much around here."

Sy chuckled. "No, they don't. Most of us like it that way. Kind of like to know how you feel about it, especially when you get to know some of the people. Real nice folks around here. I got a truck you can use if you want to take another look around. Be easier than driving that big rig."

"I appreciate that," Phil said. "I'll let you know." He hadn't been there even forty-eight hours, and touring Clayton, Oklahoma was not high on his list of priorities. Still, he wondered why Sy was making such a big deal of it.

"I figured, being from a small town like Wakefield, Clayton might suit you if you're interested."

"I thought you said you'd never been to Wakefield," Phil said.

"Right, looked it up on that Google computer thing. Amazing what you can find out there."

Amazing for sure, and if Phil had ever guessed that he would be scrutinized, investigated, and recruited as seemed to be the case, he might never have stopped here in the first place.

"By the way, I think somebody took down your road sign," Phil said.

Sy chuckled again, that soft laugh that suggested he was in on some joke shared by locals only. "Never put one up," he said. "No need, really. Them who's looking for Clayton will find it, no trouble, them that ain't, they'll pass right on by and never even know they missed it."

Sy took a couple of steps toward the path when he stopped, turned, and retraced those steps. "Say, you ever find that blonde lady you were looking for?"

"Huh?" Phil had forgotten to mention his blonde friend, but Sy obviously had not.

"You know, the one driving the blue coupe?"

"Oh, yeah, she turned up." It probably would have been less complicated if he'd lied, said he'd never seen her again, because he had no intention of describing the fantastic evening he'd had with her, but honesty was the default choice for Phil, so he 'fessed right up.

"Figured she would," Sy said. "Probably not driving that little blue car, was she?"

Phil shook his head.

"Figured that one too. Didn't get her name either, did you?"

"No, how did you know that? Do you know her?"

"Not exactly." By now, Sy was walking back down the pathway. He waved over his shoulder without turning around. "Good luck, and let me know if you need the truck."

As Phil watched him walk away, the little similarities between Sy and his blonde friend began to add up, the way they both tilted their heads to the left as they spoke, how they stood, right hand perched on a hip, the blue eyes. No, Sy didn't smell of lilacs, and his laugh sounded more like the croak of the bird that had startled Phil earlier down by the pond, but there was enough to make for more than a random association. And as usual, Phil was in the dark, everybody in on the joke but him.

He made a late breakfast of coffee, potato salad left over from the night before, and a piece of Annette's birthday cake. He couldn't shake the image of someone—Annette—still in a funk over her missing cake, but that was just another problem he could do nothing about. As he was cleaning up, he heard an unusual sound, raindrops tapping on the roof of his RV. This, unless his memory was failing, would be the first rainy day since he'd set out on the road, and since he had no one to talk to but himself, would be a perfect day to settle in with a good book.

Before his personal catastrophe, he'd begun re-reading some of the works of Thomas Hardy in preparation for his teaching duties later in the year, which now would never happen. *Jude the Obscure* lay on top of the stack he'd managed to grab as he ran out the door in Wakefield, and that's where he started. The story line, including infidelity, had gotten Hardy jammed up at the time—to be sure, extramarital affairs took place in the late nineteenth century, but writing about the topic was shocking and unacceptable. To Phil, it all seemed quite tame in view of current mores, his included. All in all, not nearly so entrancing as his new blonde friend, but far less complicated.

By the time he'd read through two chapters, the rain had stopped, so he went outside for some fresh air. This time, feeling adventurous, he walked around the loop of the campground path in the opposite direction. The birds had started up with their singing, and the cloud formation that had brought the shower was a distant smudge on the horizon.

The logical extension to such a leisurely morning was another cup of coffee or an afternoon nap. After a few moments of consideration, during which he snipped off another small piece of Annette's delicious chocolate birthday cake, he decided on the nap. He stopped by the door to what he'd begun to think of as blondie's bedroom. In fact, he hadn't even entered the room since she'd taken up occasional residence. The warmth left by her body would be long gone, of course, but her smell? Would her pillow still hold faint traces of the floral aroma he'd caught in the early morning as she'd kissed him goodbye?

The sheets were tucked in tight, military fashion. No, he wouldn't lie down there. He could never remake the bed as she had done, and if she returned, she would know instantly he'd been there. Instead, he raised the pillow to his face and took a deep breath. Yes. There it was, rather, there she was. The scent left him dizzy. He wanted her back, but he still didn't even know her name.

****

His mystery woman didn't reappear that day, or the next, or the next, and the disheartening possibility that he'd seen the last of her reared its ugly head once again. Where had she gone? What was she doing? Who was she?

Phil wondered, what if he happened to blunder into some parallel universe that included other more rational versions of Phil Claussen, and he happened to meet one of them on the street. The other version of himself would grab Phil by the shoulders, shake him several times, maybe even slap him. "Wake up, you fool. Don't you see what's going on? You don't know the first thing about this woman, and you're letting her lead you around like the village idiot."

True, perhaps, but the rational alternative Phil Claussen would not have seen her blue eyes sparkle or her golden locks glow in the morning sun. He would wait as long as it took.

Besides, he was running low on groceries again—junk food seemed to disappear quickly, and the rest of Annette's birthday cake had simply vanished—and hoping the-girl-with-no-name would drive up with a trunk full of lobster and champagne wearing one of those painted-on outfits made for a nice fantasy but did nothing to dampen his hunger pangs. Tomorrow, rain or shine, he would hit the road.

And he would have done just that except for another luxury line auto, this one dark green parked next to his RV the next morning. He hadn't heard her drive up, and he found her curled up asleep in the back seat of the car. She had a black leather jacket pulled over her, but from the amount of bare flesh on display, she must have been naked beneath it.

Nope, leering at someone sleeping nude wouldn't do, too much like peeking through someone's bedroom window, but as he turned to walk away, the rear door opened just a crack.

"Morning, Phil, say could you get me a blanket or something to cover up with?"

"Sure." He returned with the blanket from her bed and turned his back while she wrapped it around herself. He waited, hoping for some explanation. In the ordinary world, the world where he lived, things like this didn't happen.

"That's better," she said as she stepped out bundled up like an emerging chrysalis and, once again, shoeless. "But I don't have any spare clothes here. Do you have anything that might fit me, at least until I can buy something or maybe bring some things over?"

"You've been driving around naked?"

"No, silly. I had my jacket. What kind of girl do you think I am?"

"No shoes, either?" he asked.

"I must have lost them. It's hard to run in heels, you know."

Why was she running in heels in the first place? What happened to her clothes? He never got to ask because she moved close beside him and kissed him on the cheek, resolving issues without real answers. "Most of my clothes are hanging in that little closet next to the bedroom in the back, and the rest are in the suitcase," he said. "I didn't have a lot of time to pack but help yourself."

She hopped into the RV, and he turned to walk away, all sorts of possible scenarios running through his head, some erotic, some dangerous, all bizarre, and screaming for an explanation. He'd only gone a few steps before he heard laughter coming from his bedroom. "Is something wrong?" he yelled through the door.

More giggles. "Oh, Phil, you actually wear this stuff? I mean, ties? You brought ties on a camping trip?"

"At least I don't drive around bare assed."

Full bore laughter now. Then something hit the floor.

"You okay?" he asked.

"I'm fine. Honest to God, Phil, you are the funniest man I've ever met."

Him? Funny? As if her own behavior were perfectly normal.

She emerged moments later wearing his tan cargo shorts that hung below her knees. She had cinched them to her waist with a knotted tie, blue with yellow stripes, one of his favorites. The T-shirt she'd selected would have been enough to cover her completely, except that she'd tucked it into the shorts. She wore brown flip-flops that she must have stashed in the RV on an earlier visit. "Don't you dare laugh," she said. "They're your clothes, remember?"

But he couldn't help himself, neither could she. "Just for that, you have to buy me breakfast," she said.

"The guy who runs the campground says there's a little coffee shop about a mile up the road." Phil didn't mention Sy by name, hoping she would pick up on it; she did not. Whatever she knew, she was keeping to herself.

"We can walk, right?" she asked.

"Sure, if you don't mind walking in those flip flops. Why not take the sedan?"

"I need to keep it off the road."

"Don't tell me, that car's not stolen, is it?"

"Not exactly. Now stop asking so many questions.

I'm hungry, and that's all you need to know right now."

Yep, Phil Claussen, village idiot, with a luxury automobile, probably hot, parked next to his RV. How would he explain that if the sheriff came snooping around? "Not exactly" wasn't going to get him very far.

She held his hand as they walked along, the sedan becoming a distant memory, and, in spite of the questions swirling around in his brain, he felt happier than he could remember. She pointed things out to him, in an otherwise barren landscape, tiny wildflowers he would never have seen, the names of trees—to him, they were all scrub pines, and several birds he hadn't noticed. "Where'd you learn about this?" he asked.

"I grew up here, remember?" He couldn't recall her ever mentioning that fact, but then she gave his hand an extra little squeeze, and the tingle ran all the way down to his toes. When he chuckled in spite of himself, she turned on him.

"Why are you laughing?"

"No reason, just happy," he said.

"You better not be laughing at my clothes because if you are, I'll take them off right here. I swear."

"No, nothing like that. You look fine." He had no doubt she'd do what she said. "You might bring over a few things to keep in the RV, just in case."

"You mean move in with you?" Now she took his hand in both of hers, and he was lost, completely and totally lacking in decision-making ability. Gobsmacked, a slang term that fit perfectly. Any delusion he had about being in control of the situation flew right across the prairie like a cloud chased by the wind. "You sure don't waste any time," she said.

"Just thinking ahead," he said. "That would be

better than you driving around with nothing on."

"Okay, I'll bring some stuff over. Might be fun, living with you."

He wasn't sure, had moving in been his idea or hers? Either way, the prospect put a little extra zip in his step.

****

The sign above the entrance to the diner said Charlie's Place. It was small, four booths along the wall, each with a small jukebox, four tables, and six seats at the bar. The coin-fed juke boxes at the tables made him feel as if he'd traveled backward in time, just as he'd felt in the hardware store, back to when drive-in movie theaters dotted the landscape and carhops on roller-skates delivered burgers and milkshakes right to your car.

As soon as they entered, she jumped a step ahead of him. "Do you hear that?"

"The song? Some guy singing?"

"Yeah, that some guy singing is Hank Williams, my all-time favorite."

"Really? I never would have figured you for a country-western fan," he said.

"I'm not, really, but Hank is special. Let's get one of the booths. They have more of his records. He lived a hard life, died when he was only twenty-nine, and the sadness comes right through in his music," she said. "Makes me want to cry. Don't you think he's just the greatest ever?" Dani leaned in toward the little record player with its yellowed cover so dense as to make the song titles difficult to see. "Well?" she asked again, a challenge as much as a question.

"Hank is good, real good. I like Hank," Phil said.

"But what?" Her eyes narrowed, a little fire around the edges.

"But nothing, I didn't say but anything."

"You didn't have to. I can see it in your eyes. So, let's have it."

"It's not a big deal. I'm just more of a Willie Nelson fan myself." He knew he shouldn't have said it. The signs saying danger, quicksand were clearly posted, but he'd stepped right into it, violating a personal preference for one country-western singer over another.

"Willie Nelson?" Her voice was shrill. Some of the other patrons looked toward their booth. "You think Willie Nelson is better than Hank Williams?" She lurched back against the partition between hers and the booth on the other side. A head in the other booth bobbed forward.

"Dang it, Dani, you made me spill soup on my shirt."

"Gosh, I'm sorry, Herb, but this man provoked me. He claims Willie Nelson is better than Hank Williams."

"I never said that. Who's Herb?" Phil asked.

"An old friend or used to be. He's right in the next booth, and what are you grinning about?" she asked.

"I finally learned your name, Dani, right?"

"Yes, short for Danielle. I was going to tell you anyway.

"What's your last name?" he asked.

"We have to get something straight before we get into that personal stuff.

"Yeah, Willie is the man," Herb said softly.

"I heard that, Herb. There's gonna be more than soup on your shirt if you're not careful, and why are you having soup for breakfast anyway?" she said, voice still a few decibels above normal. Phil was relieved that poor Herb, whoever he was, had blundered into the fray, deflecting some of the intensity away from himself.

A large body walked over from behind the counter, heavy enough to make all the floorboards creak. The body had forearms of the Popeye variety, that is to say, huge. "Dani, sweetheart, can't you hold it down just a bit. It's way too early to start trouble."

"I'm sorry, Leroy, but maybe you can settle an argument for us."

"We're not having an argument," Phil said.

The forearms went into a defensive position. "No way I'm getting into the middle of this. Just a little peace and quiet. That's all I'm asking. Let the other folks enjoy their breakfasts."

Phil took a chance. If it worked, he was golden. If it flopped, he might sustain even greater injury than being beaten about the head with a purse. Besides, he was really hungry. He reached across and took her hands, holding them tightly. "Look, why can't we do this? Let's agree they're both great singers and just enjoy them as they are? That's what you're always telling me, right? Just take things as they are and enjoy life as it is."

"Okay, then, but this isn't over. You know that, don't you?"

"Yeah, but let's eat before all the food gets cold."

Phil guessed the breakfast they consumed—eggs, bacon, hotcakes, and candied apple slices—should last them the rest of the day. Along with the meal, he got an ongoing update on the short, unhappy life of Hank

Williams. No, it wasn't over, and he would never mention Willie Nelson again.

Every time he looked at her, listened to her, she became a different person, like watching a chameleon change in front of his eyes without knowing why or how. Any hope he had of understanding this woman was fading fast if it had ever existed at all, but it didn't matter, did it? The important thing was, they were together. The details could come later, or whenever.

"You're rubbing your stitches," she said.

"They're starting to itch."

"I think they're ready to come out. It's been about ten days, right?"

"How do you know that?"

"You got stitched up on the twenty-fifth of April, and today's the fifth of May, ten days."

How on earth did she know about that? He'd told her next to nothing about the calamity in Wakefield that sent him fleeing town in the RV, but somehow, she knew chapter and verse. It didn't seem fair, this weird telepathic ability she seemed to possess.

"You had trouble back home," she said.

"I left a big mess back there, my job, my marriage. I should go back, straighten things out, but I'm not looking forward to it." It was a continuation of the brief discussion they'd had before, sitting by the campfire, about making bad decisions. That had ended badly for him when she suggested maybe it was all meant to happen in the first place, and his own decision had very little to do with it. She'd lost him right there.

She moved across and sat beside him, looped her arm through his. "Wait just a bit. Let things settle down. You have more friends there than you think, so you won't be alone, and you have friends here too. Remember that. Now, let's get back and take those stitches out," she said.

"You're going to do it?"

"Sure, I've done it before, and anyway, it's not rocket science."

****

The hike back to the RV was just as pleasant as the one a short while earlier. He had a full breakfast to work off, and his new roommate-to-be was alongside him, holding his hand. Any man who asked for more needed his head examined and not just about stitches.

The actual prospect of suture removal was another matter. He remembered very little of the sewing-up process in the hospital and was less than enthusiastic about her taking them out in the RV. Would she be sawing away at the threads with a Swiss army knife?

She placed him in a chair by the table in the dining area, directly in line with the light from the window. She must have caught on to his anxiety, and she patted his shoulder. "Don't worry, it won't hurt a bit." Why was he not surprised when she produced her own suture removal kit from the shelf above her bed in the RV and when the entire process took only about ten painless minutes?

"There," she said. "Now, just a little Vaseline to soften the scabs, then they'll come right off. By the time your hair grows back in, you won't even know they were ever there. Although I kind of like the bad boy look. You just need to pick your fights more carefully. Stay away from old ladies with rocks in their purses," she said.

"I'm not even going to ask how you knew about

the purse," he said. "You wouldn't tell me anyway, right?"

"Not exactly. Now, I'm going to pick up some of my things to move over here. You do still want me to stay with you, don't you?"

Her blue eyes danced in front of him, and he wasn't sure whether his feet were touching the floor and didn't care. "Yeah, sure."

"That wasn't very convincing," she said.

Sometimes he got it right, like now, taking her in his arms and kissing her.

"Much better," she said. "Now I believe you."

"I thought you didn't want to drive the big sedan."

"I know a back road."

"Where do you live? Do you want me to come with you?"

"No more questions now. I'll be back soon. Can you stay out of trouble for a while?"

Trouble? The question struck him as altogether ironic, with his world flipped upside down, the person responsible for the flip now asking him to stay out of trouble, in other words, no more flips. "I'll do my best," he said.

Left on his own, he had chores to fill up the afternoon, the first being a bath for the RV. The wise designers of his vehicle had placed a mop and a bucket in the locker underneath, alongside the chairs, table, and a few other items he hadn't yet taken out for inspection. He found a hose in there, too, and attached it to the faucet mounted on top of a pipe that extended up from the ground a short distance from the picnic table that he'd almost run over when he first parked the RV. He made short work of the front, back, and sides of the RV, restoring much of its showroom luster. The roof, however, was out of reach.

As if by magic, Sy Birch ambled down the path toward the campsite, an aluminum stepladder on his shoulder. He was still some thirty yards from the RV when he began coughing so violently that he had to stop and prop himself on the ladder. Phil rushed out to meet him. "You okay?" he asked.

"Yeah, just a little coughing spell. Catches up with me sometimes. Thought you might need this," he said, extending the ladder to Phil.

"Much appreciated," Phil said. "How about we have a beer first?"

"Now you're talking."

And talk they did, well past the first beer and on into the second. Phil became aware that Sy, as he'd done during their earlier talk, was guiding the conversation, which came to be more than just a friendly chat. Now Sy was asking questions about his work in Wakefield, community organizations, his military background, and other personal items. Several times fits of coughing interrupted Sy's questions, although not so severely as before. Phil tolerated the mild interrogation, partly because he had nothing better to do—he could wash the RV any time—and partly because he'd taken a liking to the old man.

Also, there was the possibility that Sy would fill in some of the many blank spaces in Phil's own database on the blonde sprite who flitted in and out of his life, leaving him confused and always wanting more. A brief lull in the conversation seemed to offer Phil his chance.

"She came back," he said, shamefaced that he still could not call her by name.

"Figured she would," Sy said.

"You know her pretty well, do you?" Phil asked.

"Since she was a kid. She's a special girl," Sy said. "You be good to her." He stood, stretched, and took a few steps. "Keep the ladder as long as you like." So much for the heart-to-heart talk. Hell, Phil didn't need anybody to tell him she was special. He'd figured that out for himself. What he'd wanted was her name, and a little background information wouldn't hurt, either.

But Sy was on his way, taking whatever information he had with him, walking slowly, stopping a few times when his cough reappeared. Apparently, Phil had missed the mark in his initial assessment of Sy as a hale and hearty elder; this man had health problems, and how that might or might not fit into the current equation, he had no idea.

Chapter Eight

He finished washing the RV and stashed Sy's ladder in the locker, lest some light-fingered passerby claim it for his own. A couple of beers, a brief chat, and a chore completed, all that he needed now to complete his afternoon was a nap, next on his list.

He opened the windows in the RV then stretched out on his bed. Where was she now, and what was she doing? The car she drove was hot, had to be, and, if so, she was the cutest car thief he was ever likely to meet. Those were his last thoughts as he fell asleep.

When he woke, the light outside had begun to fade, and a few fireflies had started an early light show. He lurched off the bed. He was turning into a slug, nothing but eat and sleep, and speaking of eating, he headed toward the kitchen. He found a short note taped to the refrigerator door. "I've gone for a swim in the pond. Come and join me and bring the wine."

He hadn't heard her come in, but the sedan was there, barely visible in its little nest of pines, and there were two small suitcases on her bed, so they were now officially roommates. He checked the refrigerator, *Pinot Gris*, a chilled white he hadn't had before. He pulled the cork and grabbed a couple of glasses. He didn't plan to go swimming but guessed a beach towel might come in handy, so he tucked one under his arm.

The pond was shrouded in mist, and at first, he

didn't see her. Then, slowly, she emerged, flowing through the water toward him, head, shoulders, torso, hips, and beyond, all perfectly and beautifully bare and glistening. He would have spoken if he'd been able, but whether from muscle paralysis or failure of his brain to send out the necessary message, he remained mute, once again, gobsmacked.

"What's the matter, Phil? You act like you've never seen a naked girl."

He managed a sound, more like a grunt than a word.

"What's that supposed to mean?" She stood at the water's edge, hands on her hips, rivulets of water trickling down a body that made time stand still.

He unfolded the towel and wrapped it around her.

"Umm, that feels nice and cozy. You brought the wine, too. Good boy."

If he'd possessed a tail, it would have been wagging furiously.

They sat in a sandy spot, and she poured wine for the two of them. "This is beautiful." She clinked her glass gently against his. "I guess I should apologize, coming out of the water at you like that."

He cleared his throat twice. "I was almost afraid to touch you. You didn't look real, standing there in the mist. Like, if I touched you, you'd disappear."

"Well, maybe you do have a romantic side after all."

"Is that what you call it? I thought I was just being stupid, like some dumb kid the first time he tries to ask a girl out."

She scooted over so their hips were touching. "I'll bet you were totally sweet."

"Nope, just stupid."

****

An hour or so later, total darkness now, they sat opposite one another at the small foldout dining table. She was still wrapped in the beach towel.

"Tomorrow, I have to go to Oklahoma City, ditch the sedan."

"That's a long drive," he said.

"No problem, it's just business, and I'm used to it."

"And you have to promise to stop driving around naked."

She patted his hand like you might a wayward puppy that's just peed on the new oriental carpet. "Phil, I brought some clothes over, so I'll hardly be running around naked. Now don't go getting possessive on me. We have a good thing here. Don't mess it up, okay? Just be patient with me."

She went into her bedroom and closed the door. The next morning, she was gone, and the towel was hanging from the hook on the door.

We have a good thing here. What the hell was that supposed to mean? He headed for the door. His circuits were overloaded. He had to get out, walk, run, anything to let off steam. He ran, slowly, for a mile or so before his lungs sent him a message about exploding if he kept it up, so he walked back, pulled his chair alongside the RV, and waited. So much of his life now turned on the comings and goings of his companion. He twisted in his chair each time he heard a car pass on the highway, hoping….

****

The next morning shortly past ten, Sy ambled— some folks walked, Sy ambled, a slow-rolling motion

105

that seemed to be going nowhere fast—down the path, slouch hat pushed back on his forehead, a couple of fishing rods in one hand and a rusted tackle box in the other. All he had to do was wave them in Phil's direction, and the message came through loud and clear. A few moments later, they were standing by the skiff, a small wooden affair that looked as old as Sy himself. Phil could only hope it was seaworthy, but since they'd only be cruising around the pond, it probably didn't matter. If it sank, he could swim to shore. He hoped Sy could do the same.

They pushed off and drifted, nudged along by a light breeze. Sy didn't bother with the oar, and, figuring Sy knew where he wanted to go, Phil left it alone as well. The old man raised his face to the morning sun and smiled. For a while, neither of them spoke, as if talking would break up the purity of it all, blue sky, the pond surface ruffled by the breeze, and silence.

Sy spoke first, and even in the so-very-quiet morning, Phil still had to listen closely to catch his soft voice.

"Mighty peaceful back here," Sy said.

Phil nodded, having not much else to add to what was so obvious.

"Man could do all right for himself here, easy living."

Phil nodded again, still in the obvious category.

"You ought to think about it."

"Me?" Phil feeling stupid because he was the only other person in the boat. A nervous laugh, then, "I don't know the first thing about running a campground."

"Not much to it, that's the best part. Just keep things tidy. Mostly free time for you, plenty of time for fishing."

Sy's suggestions seemed casual enough, but there was almost a sense of urgency in his voice as if time were short. And Phil wasn't at all sure what the old man was putting on the table. Was this a job offer of some sort? If Sy was trying to sell him a campground, he was in for a big disappointment because the main attraction in Clayton, OK, was not the easy life of a campground attendant. The big deal locally, for Phil, had driven off in a sleek green vehicle, and waiting for her return was what kept his RV anchored in Sy's Birchbark Campground.

"Just something to think about while we're fishing." With that, Sy took up his pole, attached a red and white bobber to the line, then tied on the smallest hook Phil had ever seen. He lowered the line over the side without baiting the tiny hook. "Pass me a beer, will you?"

When Phil handed over the beer, Sy pushed the tackle box over with his foot. "Help yourself."

To Phil, whose fishing expeditions in coastal waters involved quasi-scientific assessments of fish species and their habits, tides, water temperatures, salinity…you name it. Sy's lackadaisical approach to such a vital quest bordered on heresy. Fishing was serious business, not some hit-or-miss recreational activity. His fishing buddies in Wakefield would have thrown him right out of the boat for showing such lack of respect.

He rummaged through the tackle box and came up with a serviceable spinner bait, hooks a bit dull, but one did not criticize tackle that was freely lent. Within fifteen minutes or so, while Sy leaned back, eyes closed, face bathed in sunlight, Phil had hauled in several fat large-mouths.

"Nice fish," Sy said, looking over the first one.

"You keep them?" Phil asked.

Sy shook his head. "Too much trouble." Then resumed his morning meditation.

As morning turned into early afternoon, and Phil continued boating bass, Sy covered his face with his hat and lay back in the skiff, his head resting on the stern.

The old bastard, Phil watched Sy snooze undisturbed, his line hanging limp over the side of the boat. All morning long, Phil had hauled in fish, removed the hook, released the fish, then did the same thing all over again.

Only now, tired, sweaty, reeking of fish and truly yearning for a cold one, did the wisdom of fishing with a small, unbaited hook become apparent. Leaving himself with almost zero chance of hooking a fish would have spared him a lot of unnecessary effort, allowing more time for the only boating activity more important than fishing, drinking cold beer. What he'd thought of before as futility on Sy's part, maybe even senility—forgetting to bait your hook, after all—now seemed infinitely wise.

Yes, the old man had taught him a lesson, even though he wasn't sure yet what it might be. As they drifted back to shore, Sy obviously refreshed from his nap, Phil just as obviously tired and smelly from his pointless labors, the old man grinned at him, "Fella could settle in here, get real comfortable." Maybe if the old guy made that remark about quiet and peaceful once again, Phil would toss him into the pond.

Phil stretched the line out from the bow cleat and

looped it around the trunk of a pine tree. They made the short hike back to the RV, Phil carrying the rods and tackle box. When he tried to return them to Sy, the old man said, "Hang onto them. You might need them sometime." It was as if he'd already made a commitment to stay on.

So, this was more than two guys out fishing in a boat. Sy, like Dani, seemed to have a barely hidden agenda. Everything he said or did had a subtext, and Phil got the uneasy feeling that his days of freedom on the open road might be coming to an end.

Phil gave himself a thorough scrubbing until his hands no longer smelled of fish, fixed a late lunch, and settled back to wait. Now, where the hell was blondie, his mystery woman? Now it wasn't so much a question of whether she would come back, but when.

In the midafternoon heat, four days since her departure, he heard her pull down the drive, this time in yet another new silver luxury model with the sales sticker still attached to the rear window. As she'd done with its predecessor, she pulled the new model off the trail where it sat hidden by the trees.

Their reunion was different this time. She fell into his arms. "I'm so glad to see you." Her hair was mussed a bit, and there appeared to be a small bruise beneath her left eye. She wore a red sweatshirt with NEBRASKA lettered across the front, jeans with the knees worn through, and tattered sneakers. Not a very flattering outfit, but at least she was covered, and he was thankful for that. She leaned on his free arm as they walked to the RV.

"What can I bring you?" he asked.

"Beer, please."

In between sips, she leaned back with her eyes closed.

"You look tired," he said. He knew he should let her rest, but he hadn't talked to her for what seemed like forever, and he longed for the sound of her voice.

"Pooped," she said. "That one was a little close."

"What was a little close?"

"Oh, nothing. I'm just mumbling." Her words trailed off into a whisper.

He caught the beer just before it slipped from her hand. Her head lolled back in the chair, and she snored softly.

"You're going to have a sore neck if you sleep like that. Let's get you inside." He had to carry her to bed. He slipped off her sneakers and spread a blanket over her. The peaceful look on her sleeping face seemed to him to be as beautiful as anything he'd ever seen. He leaned over and kissed her forehead, and she smiled in her sleep, hopefully thinking about him.

While she was sleeping, he called home to MaryBeth again. He'd called earlier, around lunchtime, but got no answer. Either she wasn't taking his calls or, more likely, she was down at the local motel doing the wild thing with the Lemmings bastard. Probably they were on a first-name basis with the staff. Maybe they had their own special room, kept a change of clothes in the closet.

She answered his second call, just barely. "Where the hell are you?"

"Oklahoma."

"Did you say Oklahoma?"

"It's just past Arkansas, right between Kansas and Texas."

"I know where it is, idiot. Why are you there?"

"I thought we could both benefit from a little space."

"Halfway across the damned country? Phil, if you know what's good for you, you'll get your sorry ass back here. And I mean quick."

"How's Addie?"

"How do you think?

"You suppose I might speak to her?"

"Don't even think about it. Did you hear what I said?"

"I heard. You sure you want me back there?"

"No, I'm not. It wouldn't kill me if I never saw you again. But there's stuff we have to straighten out. Your attorney came by last week, Winthrop, it said on her card."

"Who?" He had an attorney? News to him.

"Winthrop, I just told you. Cute little blonde. You're not screwing around with her, are you? Damn you, Phil, you've destroyed this family, and just so you know, I'm filing for divorce. You can talk that over with your bitch attorney." She hung up before he could respond to the verbal broadside she'd just launched at him.

He'd destroyed the family? No, no, no, he left to spare the family, not to destroy it. And MaryBeth was filing for divorce? How could that be so soon? He'd been away for just over a month. Her finger must have been on the divorce trigger all along, and he'd just given her a reason to fire away.

And the cute little blonde attorney, that could only be…but it couldn't be *her,* not Dani, because she was in Oklahoma City dealing cars that might very well be hot, or so she said. And she'd never said her name was Winthrop. All he'd gotten from her so far was a first name, Dani, and he wasn't even sure about that. More questions added to a list that was too damned long to begin with.

From what MaryBeth had said, he would, in all likelihood, soon become a divorced man. The bridges that might have led him back to his old hometown were, if not burned down altogether, were certainly ablaze.

He needed another shower to clear his head after the round with MaryBeth, and since he'd used up all the hot water in the RV, this one would have to be at the campground showers. Something about an outdoor shower, nothing above but trees and sky and tranquility, and he could sure use a hefty dose of tranquility right about now. He took his own good time soaking before he finally turned off the water and began to towel off. He made his way back up the path and was back at the RV when Dani caught up with him just outside the door. Once again, he got the escalated version of her greeting, a vigorous hug, and a light kiss on the lips.

"I was afraid you'd run away and left me," she said.

"Just went for a shower."

"You smell nice. I probably don't. Can you wait long enough for me to shower too?"

"Sure, where else would I go?"

"Of course, you could join me." She winked at him.

"That might take a while," he said.

"I'm counting on it."

"Besides, I'm really hungry."

"I must be losing it," she said. "Can't even compete with a cheeseburger."

She came back from her shower wrapped in the beach towel, and, from the way things moved around beneath it, nothing else."

"Don't look yet," she said. "I'm not finished."

Getting finished took her almost forty-five minutes, and his appetite was into overdrive. Now all he could think of was engaging in mortal combat with a sizzling hunk of beef, at least, until he was confronted with a beautiful woman who was, as she'd promised, finished.

A bright floral sundress clinging to her shoulders by spaghetti straps, light on the makeup, which she didn't need anyway, not with those lethal blue eyes. A blink or two from those babies could boil water. Low heels raised the top of her head to the level of his shoulders. From that point on, everything was pretty much the same. She smiled, did her little pirouette. He tried to say something witty, appreciative, but couldn't because the sock he must have swallowed again was stuck solidly in his throat.

A little tap on his cheek with her palm. "You're supposed to tell me how pretty I look." He tried really hard, but the sock wouldn't budge. Maybe there was something wrong with his vocal cords, cancer, some neurological condition.

"Phil?"

He nodded. "Uh huh."

She moved closer, so close that the faint aroma of lilacs got into his head and turned everything to mush. "You obviously weren't trained very well. I'm going to have to work on you. I did all of this for you, you know."

113

"Okay," he mumbled. If she'd said she was going to pull out his fingernails, that would have been okay too.

She slipped on a light jacket. "First, we need another car."

"But we have the new car and the RV. Soon we'll need our own parking lot."

"No, the new one's not for keeps. In fact, I'm going to get rid of it this evening. A guy I know has a nice little sedan, low mileage, and I can get it at a good price."

"What guy?" His hands got clammy as he considered the possibility, no, probability, that he was becoming involved in something illegal.

"Now you have that worried look again. This is all above board. Trust me."

Perhaps, had he been capable of logical thought, he might have objected. But she was so close, almost touching him, and there was no hope for him. One person, if it was the right person, could fill your life right up so there was room for nothing else, and having that experience even once was almost more than a guy could hope for.

"You'll drive, won't you?" she asked.

"Yeah, not often I get the chance to drive a new car like this. I see you haven't taken the sticker off yet."

"Right, so no speeding, and don't run any red lights."

"How far?"

"Fifteen miles or so, Taylorsville. They'll still be open when we get there."

The smooth power of the vehicle proved so seductive that, on the first straight stretch of road, Phil lost track of his speed, the only indication being the rapid rate at which fence posts flew by.

"Phil, watch it, okay? That cop we passed must have been asleep, but we might not be so lucky next time."

"We passed a cop?"

"Off to the right, down in a little wash. They hide down there sometimes. Believe me, that would make his day, writing out a ticket for a foreign car."

"I should have asked about this earlier, but you do have the registration for this vehicle, right?"

"Not exactly."

"Oh, my God."

"That's why you have to be careful. Remember, you're driving."

"But you're an attorney, right? So, you could probably get me off." He'd been wondering how to ask if she was the Winthrop attorney who had visited MaryBeth and probably lit the firestorm that had fallen on him.

"Who told you that?" She twisted in the seat until she was facing him.

"I called MaryBeth earlier in the afternoon, and she said an attorney named Winthrop came by claiming to represent me. That must have been you, right?"

"Maybe, I do have a law degree," she said.

"You never told me your last name is Winthrop," he said.

"That's because Winthrop is not my name. I just use that from time to time. I had some business cards made up with the name, just in case."

"In case of what?"

"You never know what might happen. Best to be

prepared."

"Well, give this a little thought; MaryBeth said she's filing for divorce."

"Really? So soon? You've only been away for a month or so."

"Yeah, it makes me think maybe she had something going on before I left, and I just gave her an excuse to file."

"Could be, just let me go over the papers when you get them," she said.

****

The sign said Taylorsville, and beneath looked to be a three-digit number that Phil guessed was the population. It had been scratched through and rewritten three times, each new number smaller than the previous one. "How much farther?" he asked.

"This is it. Pull over at the garage on the right."

Phil had never seen a padlock quite as large as the one holding the garage doors closed. Whatever was inside was being held securely. Dani directed him along a drive to the rear of the building, where a short fireplug of a man with a shaved head held open a gate and motioned Phil through.

"Wait here," she said. "I'll be right back."

He wasn't leaving the car, not because she said so, but because of the pair of snarling pit bulls that had taken up station right outside his door. Even in the heat, he kept his window up. Those four-legged bastards looked mean and hungry.

In a moment, she was back, waving for him to join her.

"I can't," he yelled. "The dogs."

"For crying out loud." She marched over to the

dogs, gave one a sharp kick in the ass, and wound up for a try at the other. But by then, both animals had run off yelping into the dark recesses of the lot.

"I wish you wouldn't be so mean to my dogs," fireplug man said.

"Then teach them some manners," she said. "Come on, Phil."

Chapter Nine

The small, closed room reeked of motor oil, sweat, and the half-eaten pepperoni pizza lying on the corner of the desk.

"Earl, this is Phil."

The man she introduced as Earl was a larger version of the fireplug man outside, with hair. Since most noses aren't naturally bent in three different directions, Phil guessed that Earl's had met with blunt force more than once.

"You have my money?" she asked.

Earl slid a thick envelope, complete with greasy fingerprints, across to her. She picked up the envelope and handed it over to Phil. "You ain't gonna count it?" Earl asked.

"It's all there because you know I'll be back if it isn't. Now, where's my car?"

"Parked over by the fence. Louie will bring it round."

"No, I'll get it. I don't want his sweaty backside in my car. Gas tank full?"

"Sure."

"It better be. Come on, Phil."

"Christ," Phil muttered.

"You say something?" she asked.

"No, nothing." But he was thinking, two pit bulls and one big ugly dude, and she put the fear of God in all of them, including the fireplug man. And he had an envelope full of money in his hand. "What am I supposed to do with this?" he asked.

"I'll take it. How do you like the sedan?" she asked as Phil slid in behind the wheel.

"Liked the new one a lot better," he said.

"Yeah, me too, but this one's paid for. Now, how about some dinner? I'll bet you're hungry, right? Turn left at the intersection, and about a mile or so, you'll see the place on the left."

He followed her driving directions, and, all by itself, surrounded by a dirt parking lot that was almost full, sat Big Ben's Barbecue.

"We're here," she said, so excited her voice rose to a squeaky pitch. "Not so much from the outside, I know, but just wait."

"There's a neon cow on the roof," he said.

"Of course, silly, where do you think barbecue comes from? And that's a steer, not a cow. Don't let anybody hear you call it a cow."

"Smells like the place is on fire," he said as they walked across the parking lot.

"That's the mesquite smoke for the barbecue. What did you expect, charcoal? Honestly, Phil, I thought you'd know better."

The inside was spacious, maybe twenty small tables, many unoccupied, because most of the crowd lined up at the take-out window. Dani's entrance caused a bit of a stir among the male patrons, and many of them exchanged greetings from a distance.

"You're scaring off my friends," she said to Phil.

"Excuse me, but I never said a word."

She tugged him toward a table by the far wall.

"What do you think so far?" she asked.

"Smells great."

"Just you wait."

A few moments later, a large blonde woman wearing a red apron bustled up to their table, lugging a pitcher of iced tea in one hand and a couple of plastic mugs in the other. "Hello, sweetheart, I thought you'd forgotten about us," she said. "And who is this handsome man?"

"Margaret, this is Phil," Dani said.

Dani got a kiss on the cheek, and Phil got a lascivious wink. "The works?" Margaret asked.

Dani nodded with enthusiasm that made Phil wonder about "the works."

"No beer?" Phil asked after Margaret left.

"Just iced tea," Dani said. "They lost their liquor license a few years ago, too many fights."

"I don't suppose you caused any of them." He spoke softly, like thinking out loud, guessing she wouldn't hear him above the din of many conversations, but she did.

"Phil Claussen, what a rotten thing to say after I've been so nice to you."

"Just a joke," he said. The last thing he needed was another confrontation with an angry woman. At least she wasn't carrying a purse.

"Well, it wasn't funny. Don't do it again, or I might have to get rough with you."

The vehemence of her objection made him think maybe he'd guessed right, after all.

Margaret saved the day by returning in no time with plates laden with beef ribs and sides of coleslaw and macaroni and cheese. Barbecue, Phil knew, was a dish prepared ahead of time, and service required little more than arranging it on a plate. But there was a catch; barbecue, as strictly defined in Phil's mind, was pork, not beef, and seasoned with vinegar sauce, not catsup. In the eastern part of the state he'd just fled, North Carolina, this preference of sauce could lead to vigorous if not violent arguments. He saw at once that alcohol was not the inciting factor in fights at Big Ben's; it was the sauce slathered over the ribs, which, being beef, were all wrong in the first place.

"Dig in," Dani said.

Phil hoisted a rib to his mouth and bit in. "Not bad," he said.

"Not bad? What do you mean, not bad? This is the best."

Dare he mention that beef topped with catsup was nothing more than a hamburger in a party dress? Might he allude to eastern North Carolina, the official birthplace of genuine pork barbecue, chopped or pulled, smoked for hours over hickory coals, where the large rib on which he now gnawed would be passed over to the family dog? Not likely. He'd already run afoul of Dani's favorites when, during breakfast at Charlie's Place, he'd expressed a preference for Willie Nelson's songs over those of Hank Williams. He'd learned his lesson then and there.

When Dani asked again how he liked the barbecue, he had an answer right at hand.

"Outstanding, best I've ever tasted," said a wise man.

Sometime later, stuffed with a meal that he'd enjoyed even though it wasn't as advertised, real barbecue, they drove back to the campground. Dani pulled the thick envelope from her jacket pocket and emptied a stack of cash onto the RV table.

"Damn, that's a lot of money to be carrying around," Phil said.

"Should be about twenty thousand," she said. "If it's not, I'm going back to see Earl. And I need your signature here on the registration form."

"Why me?"

"Because I bought it in your name. It works out better that way."

So far, he'd gone along with the program, no questions asked. He'd looked the other way when things got weird because, well, because of her. Now, pen in hand, he hesitated. There was his name typed in the registration box, just waiting for his signature. Might just as well make up a rubber stamp with Philip Claussen on it, then she wouldn't need him at all.

"Is something wrong?" she asked.

"No, guess not."

When he reached down to sign the form, she took his hand in both of hers. "Phil, look at me. No, not down at the table, look at me." She pushed her chair aside and crawled onto his lap. There were those blue eyes, just inches away. He couldn't look away, even if he wanted to, because she cradled his face in her hands, not that he wanted to, not really.

Her breath was like an exotic spice, elusive at first, then everywhere and everything. She breathed for both of them, and in spite of having a beautiful woman on his lap, their noses practically touching, his feeling was more that of intoxication than arousal.

Maybe she was a witch.

Maybe he didn't care.

"Listen to me," she said.

He thought there was a touch of desperation in her voice. "I know I get a little weird at times, but I would never, ever do anything to hurt you. You have to believe me. Phil? You mean so much to me, more than you know."

He thought for a moment he wouldn't be able to speak, but finally, the words came. "What I believe is, if a woman like you comes along just once in a guy's lifetime, then he should consider himself incredibly lucky. And here you are, right now, and I can't believe how lucky I am. That's about all I have to say."

She leaned forward so their foreheads touched. He caught the glimmer of a tear rolling down her cheek. "Hold me," she said.

She snaked her arms around his neck, and they clung to one another so tightly there was no space left between them, physically or emotionally. He held her that way until the tension left her body. Then he helped her to bed, even helped her undress, down to her bra and panties, before he tucked her in bed.

When he started to step away, she said, "Wait."

She pulled him down to her and kissed him long and hard. No friendly peck this time; this kiss was for real. "I want you," she whispered.

"I want you too, but we agreed, remember?" Of all the dumb agreements he'd ever made, this one was right at the top of the list.

"I know, no hanky-panky until your divorce is final. Well, I've waited this long for you, so I guess I can wait a little longer. But I'm warning you, as soon as those papers come through, I'm going to be all over you." A slight chuckle, and just as quickly, she fell asleep.

"I'm counting on it," he whispered back to his sleeping goddess, then kissed her on the forehead.

She'd left the stack of cash along with the registration form on the table. Phil signed the registration form and put everything back into the envelope. The thought of thousands of dollars lying around gave him chills, which gave him an idea. He stashed the envelope in the refrigerator.

The next morning, she was up and gone before he got out of bed. He found a note stuck to the door of the refrigerator. "Nice try, but it was the first place I looked. Love and kisses, D."

Chapter Ten

"Sometimes we sound like an old married couple." Dani made this observation after a spirited discussion bordering on argument about who would get the use of what had become the family car that Tuesday morning. Phil wanted to drive to the trading post for newspapers and some groceries, while Dani insisted she needed the car to get to work, wherever and whatever work was.

The RV didn't figure into the transportation equation. Short trips in the big rig were completely impractical, and besides, this was home base for both of them. By now, Dani had more clothes stashed in the RV than he had.

But such small squabbles could portend trouble in its early stages, with more to follow. Phil had had first-hand experience with this sort of exchange as he had watched his marriage to MaryBeth deteriorate into a series of skirmishes, becoming more deadly each year until he'd finally sunk the entire operation with a great blue Peerless lawn tractor.

"I didn't mean that in a bad way," she said. "I love what we have here, and I think we'd make a really cute old married couple."

"You think so?" he asked.

"So long as you keep your hair and don't put on weight."

"Okay, so how about I drive you to work, then I'll

go to the market, and I'll pick you up later in the afternoon." He guessed she wouldn't like the arrangement because it would give him an idea of where she went and what she did when she left in the morning. He guessed right—she shook her pretty head—but he didn't push it.

"Here, you take it." He handed her the keys. "My stuff can wait."

"Thanks."

He thought he could read in her eyes how she knew he was taking the first step in a compromise solution for the sake of the relationship. "This means a lot to me," she said, and she gave him another kiss to prove it.

So he wound up hiking to the market and back again. He felt good about himself. He could behave like a mature adult when he wanted to, not like some stupid jerk who would go off and buy an oversized lawnmower for no good reason. Yeah, Phil Claussen, grownup. He liked the sound of that. Maybe there was hope for him after all.

That evening, after she returned, her hair looking like she'd had a close encounter with a leaf blower, and, without insisting on an explanation—although he certainly would have preferred one—he grilled ribeye steaks and plied her with a nice cabernet that he'd bought earlier. He scored major points with that arrangement. Phil Claussen, thoughtful adult male—a rare beast if ever there was one. Still, he wondered about her hair.

After dinner, she cleaned the dishes and announced she was going to bed early. He got a kiss but no explanation.

The next morning, she dropped the car keys in the

middle of the table. "Milly is all yours." She'd begun calling the car Milly, and since Phil could think of nothing better, he played along.

"Earl is driving me around in his truck today."

Right on cue, Earl's truck pulled down the drive, a mammoth vehicle with a steel girder in place of a bumper. The big rig looked capable of pushing over trees and maybe RVs too.

Dani stared through the window at the truck, shaking her head. "No, no, no, no," she said.

The two of them had barely cleared the door of the RV when a young woman bounded out of the truck and ran up to Dani, locking her in a firm embrace. "Sis, long time no see. You are hard to track down. Been avoiding me?"

"How did you find me?" Dani asked. She seemed less than enthusiastic about the arrival of her sister.

"Hey, I have my ways. And who is this handsome hunk over here?" She skipped over to Phil and seized his arm with both hands. "Now I see why you've been hiding out in the woods."

"We're not hiding, Angie. This just happens to be convenient."

"Convenient for what? No, don't tell me, I can guess. Aren't you going to introduce me?"

"Phil, this is my sister, Angie."

Angie's hair was a bit longer, and her tan a bit darker, but everything else, identical.

"You're twins?" Phil asked.

"No, just sisters," Angie said. "Actually, I'm two years younger."

"You are two years older." Dani's look would have ignited a campfire.

"Maybe, I forget sometimes. People always say I look younger, and that's what counts, right?" She looked up into Phil's face as if she dared him to disagree with her.

In all the weeks he'd known her, Phil had never seen Dani so ruffled, but she was ruffled now, and then some, flushed, breathing rapidly, fists clenched. Worst of all, he was caught in the middle. He was the Christmas toy that the sisters tore apart because they both wanted to play with it, only to find that neither of them cared about it after they'd ripped it to shreds.

He got a look at Earl, standing safely off to one side. The big man's mouth was spread into a wide grin. Meanwhile, his own arm was becoming numb due to Angie's surprisingly strong grip.

"Listen, I don't know what kind of crap she's been feeding you, but I can tell you stories about this girl that will curl your hair," Angie said, and Phil would indeed like to hear some of those stories, anything to fill in the background on this mystery woman who had become such an important part of his life. But the situation was deteriorating rapidly, and he'd seen what women could do when it came to open warfare—they kicked your ass, and with Angie holding his arm so tightly, short of dragging her along, he saw no means of escape.

"Earl said he was driving you to work, sis. Why don't you two run along, and I'll stay here and get acquainted with Phil." Once again, Angie looked up at him with smiling eyes that held fire but lacked any warmth whatever.

"Absolutely not. That's not going to happen," Dani said.

"See, she doesn't trust me, her own sister." Angie

laughed. She was probably ahead in the point score, but that didn't mean she would win the war.

And when the war came, Phil wanted to be far, far away. If necessary, he would crawl beneath the RV and hide out there until the coast was clear. But then inspiration saved him.

"Hey, Earl, I got cold beer. Why don't we grab a couple and go down to the pond, so these ladies can get reacquainted."

"Damn good idea," Earl said.

As they walked along the path, Earl clapped a gigantic paw on Phil's shoulder. "Scared you, huh, those girls?"

"Hell, yeah."

"Scared me too."

They crept away like furtive animals.

The pond lay like an upturned mirror, exactly reflecting the few passing clouds and rimmed with the images of surrounding pines. Tranquility and beer, not a bad combination. Nature provided the tranquil bit, and Phil brought a six-pack. He and Earl each downed their first cans in a long single gulp, a true contest of manhood, followed by a prolonged period of belching. "I needed that," Phil said as he passed another one over to Earl. "How do you think we can get out of this? We can't hide out here all afternoon. We'll run out of beer before long."

"We won't have to. I've watched them together for years. They'll growl at one another for a while, then, before you know it, they're best friends again, giggling like little girls. So, how in the world did you wind up here in Clayton?" Earl asked. "Not many people have ever heard of the place."

"I'm still trying to figure that out. I just pulled off the Interstate to take a break, drove down the county road, and found Dani. Next thing, I wound up in Sy's campground, been here about three months now. Never intended to come here in the first place, much less stay. It just turned out that way."

"Wouldn't have anything to do with Dani, would it? Staying here, I mean," Earl said.

"I've never met anybody like her. You know, it took me a couple of weeks just to find out her name."

Earl laughed and farted, both at once.

"How'd you do that at the same time?" Phil was impressed by what seemed a difficult if not impossible feat.

"Practice, lots of practice," Earl said. "So, she strung you along for a few weeks."

"Yeah, pissed me off at first, the way she seemed to know so much about me, and I knew next to nothing about her. I thought about leaving several times, climb into the RV, turn the key, and drive away, but I couldn't do it."

"Sounds like she's got you hooked good and proper."

Shortly, just as Earl predicted, the sound of giggling preceded the girls as they walked down the trail arm in arm.

"See," Earl said. "What did I tell you?"

"We got it all worked out," Angie said. "Dani—she drew the name out like it was a big joke, which it probably was, to everybody but Phil—and I will take the truck, and you boys can take the afternoon off."

"But how...?" Earl clearly doubted their ability to do whatever needed doing.

"We'll stop by the garage and pick up the dogs," Dani said. "Nobody's going to mess with us."

"Nobody in their right mind," Earl said.

"I know just the thing," Phil said. "First, I have to make a beer run. We are seriously deficient. I have Sy's fishing gear, and he said we could borrow his boat any time. Anyway, by the time the girls get back, we'll catch enough for a good old-fashioned fish fry." As quickly as he'd caught fish when he was out with Sy, they'd have plenty in no time at all.

"More likely, we'll have a couple of drunks passed out in a boat full of beer cans," Dani said. "We'd better pick up some food on the way back."

****

If the fish don't bite, you can't catch them; some sage in Wakefield had passed that on to him years before, so, in a way, it wasn't their fault, not exactly, as Dani would say. Phil had planned for this contingency with a cooler full of beer, believing, as he did, in the ultimate perverseness of the universe.

Phil's plan required that the fish not disturb them by biting, thus requiring that they be caught, handled, and stashed somewhere while he and Earl would be obligated to catch other fish, stealing time from the other more important activity…drinking beer.

The fish in the pond cooperated by refusing to nibble at any bait Phil or Earl tossed to them. So, the outing turned into a drinking contest that ended in a dead heat, two semi-conscious males in a boat, no fish. Sometime later in the afternoon, Phil heard female voices, confusing because they'd taken no women on board when he and Earl set out.

"This is a new bra. If it gets ruined in this muddy

water, somebody's going to pay for it. At least you had the good sense to take yours off, but then, you always were up for skinny dipping, as I recall." Giggles. Wet bodies climbing around in the boat, dripping on them.

"That's the idea, splash them, see if that will wake them up."

Earl groaned; Phil cursed while the splashing and giggling continued.

"We got us a couple of nasty drunks here."

At that moment, Phil had his second bad idea, to crawl out of the boat, get away from all the noise and commotion, which was giving him a headache.

"Oh, no, Phil Claussen, you're not going anywhere."

A body landed on top of him, not at all unpleasant since the body was wet, cool, and didn't seem to be wearing any clothes.

"Where did you think you were going?" the naked body asked.

"Work, I gotta get to work. I'm late." Which was ridiculous since he didn't have a job, but he wasn't thinking clearly at the moment.

Now the girlish giggles escalated into real howls of laughter, which made Phil's head throb even more violently.

"Keep it down, Angie. We're pretty much naked, remember? Don't want to draw a crowd."

"Ha, I can remember when something like that wouldn't have bothered you a bit."

"Shut up and row the boat."

There followed a period during which his memory failed him. He was in a different location without any idea of how he got there. Had he walked up the trail?

Doubtful. Crawled? Or had they dragged him from the pond to the RV? Somehow they'd stretched him out on one of the two camp cots from the RV. More amazing, because he weighed half again as much as Phil, they'd managed to get Earl onto the other one.

"You have to drink something, Phil," Dani said. "Iced tea, unsweetened, just the way you like it."

At the other cot, he heard Angie urging Earl to do the same.

"I guess food is out of the question," Dani said.

"Arrogh." More of a groan than a word, but it was the best Phil could do under the circumstances.

"You see, I can't always tell what you mean by that funny word. Sometimes you mean yes, sometimes no. Just nod your head," Dani said.

So he did, and instantly the hand grenade that was lurking right behind his eyes exploded. No, he would not move again, ever. And if he died, so what?

"You having any luck?" Dani asked her sister.

"Not much," Angie said. "We're in for a lively evening with these two. You want to go catch a movie or something?"

"We should probably stay with them, make sure they survive."

"If Earl doesn't make it, I got dibs on his truck," Angie said.

"I almost forgot, I have a nice bottle of white wine in the fridge, and we won't have to share it with them. Should go well with the chicken."

Chicken? They'd brought back chicken? The thought of wine made Phil's stomach convulse like it was trying to escape from his abdominal cavity, but fried chicken, he could handle some of that, after he was fully conscious, of course.

Sometime later, it was dark, or perhaps he'd died. No, he heard voices. Angels? No, not angels, because angels didn't tell dirty jokes.

Later still, softer voices now.

"So, he's your special guy." Angie's voice? He couldn't be sure.

"Yeah, he's really nice when he's sober. I've never seen him shit faced like this before. Wonder what set him off?" Dani's voice this time.

"What does he think about your little business venture?"

"He doesn't. I haven't told him much about it," Dani said.

Phil's ears went on high alert, finally a chance to get some inside information on Dani's mysterious auto-switching business. *Come on, girls, let it all out. Nobody around to listen. Me? I'm dead drunk. Won't remember a thing I hear.*

"How long have you been together?" Angie asked.

"Two months and three days."

"Wow, you've got it right down to the day. I'm guessing he's great in the sack, right?"

No answer.

"Two months, and you haven't done it yet? No way. Sister, dear, this sounds serious. When were you going to tell me about him, after the wedding?"

"Officially, he's still married," Dani said.

"Oh, no, not a married man. You never learn, do you?"

"He's getting divorced. His wife's attorney sent the divorce papers, and he signed them and sent them back. That was three, four weeks ago. Haven't heard from them since. As soon as he has the documents, he's free and clear."

"That doesn't mean you can't have sex, out here in the woods, all nice and private with that gorgeous hunk of man."

"He wants to wait until he's really single. He's funny about that."

"A real Boy Scout, huh, that's even worse than married," Angie said.

At that precise, critical moment, someone farted, loud enough to produce an echo and probably cause ripples in the pond, Earl, he hoped.

"At least one of them is still alive," Dani said.

Both girls howled, and one of them, Angie, he thought, fell out of her chair.

Another thunderous fart. More laughter, but this time in a deep bass note.

"Earl, that was disgusting."

"How'd you know it was me?"

"You're the only human I know of who can do that."

Phil raised up off his aching shoulder. "What was that noise?"

"Glad to see you're still alive," Dani said. "That was just Earl passing gas."

"No, it sounded like a gunshot."

"I heard it too," Earl said. "From over there." He pointed back toward the direction of Sy Birch's cabin.

A second, then a third shot, this time heard by all.

Chapter Eleven

"Handgun," Phil said, his stupor lifting quickly as it always did at the sound of gunfire.

"Uncle Sy," both girls whispered at the same time.

"Sy is your uncle?" Phil asked. "I never even knew you were related. Why didn't you say something?"

No answer from either of them. Just another mystery for Phil to add to what was becoming a very long list. "I'm going to check it out." Phil was off his cot and staggering down the trail. "You coming?"

"Wait a minute," Earl said. "Me and Dani should take the truck and leave before the sheriff turns up."

"Why?" Phil asked.

Dani took his arm and pulled him aside. "It's better this way, for us and for you too."

"Does it have something to do with the new cars you've been parking in the woods, behind my RV?"

"Not exactly…well, yeah, maybe."

He held both her shoulders firmly. She could not help but look straight at him. "Dani, are you a car thief?"

"Heavens, no. Look, I'll tell you all about it later, but we have to hurry now. Can you handle a gun?"

"Yeah, learned a little in the Army." He'd learned all about loading and unloading a weapon safely, but his poor marksmanship was legendary. She didn't need to know that, of course. He was entitled to a few secrets of his own.

"Great, stash this in the RV." She handed him a 9mm semiautomatic, the slide opened on an empty chamber.

"Where have you been keeping this?" Phil asked, "and why do you have it in the first place?"

"For protection. Just hang onto it for now. Put it somewhere out of sight, but not like you're hiding it. I'm going to take the money out of the refrigerator. If the cops find it there, you'll have a lot of explaining to do."

"Protection from what, and why would the cops look in my refrigerator?"

"It's what they do. Just nosy. I'll explain the rest later."

"Maybe I should leave, too," Phil said.

"No, that would look suspicious. Angie, you stay here with Phil. If anybody asks about my clothes in the RV, tell them they belong to you."

The truck's taillights flickered as they drove off down the bumpy road. Phil was left holding a gun, a bagful of money, and a few dozen new questions that needed answers that he probably wouldn't get. "I'm going over to check out Sy's place," he said. "You don't have to come."

"I'm coming with you. I don't want to stay here by myself, and I have to see if Uncle Sy is okay. Where are you going now?"

"To get my flashlight." The beam was weak and flickered between poor light and none at all.

"You need new batteries," Angie said.

"No shit."

As much as he would like to see exactly where he

was going, the flashlight would be a dead giveaway to anybody lurking around Sy's cabin and wouldn't provide much illumination anyway, so he switched it off, and they walked in darkness, quietly. They stopped before they crossed the open road, waiting, listening, but heard nothing.

The door to the cabin stood wide open, and the interior lights shone through. Phil had been inside visiting with Sy a few times but never ventured beyond the front room where Sy, now slumped in a recliner, a blood-stained newspaper in his lap, an entry wound in each side of his chest and one between his eyes. Gray goo, resembling oatmeal mixed with blood, was splattered across the headrest of the recliner.

When Phil got a closer look, it seemed as if Sy's mouth was curled upward in a smile. He'd seen a number of corpses during his days of active duty, but none of them smiling.

He motioned for Angie to stay back. "Don't come inside," he said.

Angie had been whimpering on the way over, and that whimper now evolved into coarse sobbing. She was trying to talk through the crying jag, but all he could make out was "Poor Uncle Sy."

He held her for a while until her sobbing began to subside. "I should call the sheriff," he said.

But before he could do that, a state trooper and the county sheriff arrived within minutes of each other. The trooper's flashers were on, but the sheriff's were not. How had they found out so quickly? Only fifteen, maybe twenty minutes had elapsed since the first shot, and it made no sense that the two cars could have arrived so promptly, unless the shots he'd heard weren't connected to Sy's death at all. Otherwise, the sheriff and the state police must have been called before the shots were even fired, which made even less sense. Who announced a murder in advance, especially to law enforcement?

The two officials squared off and had a brief argument about whose jurisdiction was whose before they even went inside.

"Who found the body?" the sheriff called out, even though he was looking straight at Phil when he said it.

"That would be me, Phil Claussen. My RV is parked at one of the campsites. I came over as soon as I heard the gunshot."

"How many shots?" The state trooper, all crisp in his unwrinkled uniform, stood behind the sheriff, writing Phil's responses down on a notepad.

"Three," Phil said. Which the trooper could easily have found out by counting the holes in the body.

"You touch anything?" the sheriff asked.

"Not a thing. Haven't been past the door."

"And who are you?" The trooper looked at Angie as if she'd suddenly dropped off a cloud.

"I'm Angie, Mr. Claussen's—I mean—Phil's friend."

She left out any mention that Sy was her uncle if indeed he was. Phil was beyond taking anything for granted at this point. There were just too many loose ends hanging to take anybody's spoken word as the absolute truth.

"I know her." The sheriff stepped over to the chair and knelt by the victim. "Well, Sy, they finally got to you. Always figured they would, sooner or later."

"What are you talking about?" the trooper asked.

"You know this man?"

"Yeah, Seymour Birch. Known him for years. I reckon we'll call this an armed robbery with fatal wounds to the victim. Poor old Sy. You folks can go back to your RV."

"How can you say it's a robbery?" The trooper was practically bouncing on his toes. "There's no sign of forced entry, no sign that anything was taken. And he was shot at close range." He produced a penlight from his pocket. "See, powder burns on the chest wounds. And on top of that, you're letting our only suspects walk away."

"Suspects? Who said we were suspects?" Phil said. "All I did was discover the body, and right off, I'm a suspect?"

"Okay, everybody needs to settle down here." The sheriff took the trooper by the arm and led him away from the doorway, but Phil could still pick up most of their conversation.

"Best thing you can do," the sheriff said, "is to go tell your boss that, when you got here, the sheriff's department had already started up an investigation, and you offered to help, and they said they appreciated your offer, but that they could handle it. You get all that?"

The trooper mumbled something Phil couldn't catch.

But he heard what the sheriff said. "You're real close to stepping into a big mess that, believe me, you don't want any part of. Do yourself a big favor and leave while you can."

Phil was beginning to understand why Dani and Earl had taken off. Now, seeing a state trooper warned off, this looked to be a bad situation, and he had blundered right into the middle of it.

"And I'll need your driver's license." The sheriff prodded Phil in the chest with his thumb. "You hear me? I want your license."

"Why?" Phil asked.

"Because I'll want to talk to you and your lady friend tomorrow, and I want to make sure you don't run off. Now, license, or you can spend the night in our jail."

"On what charges?" Phil asked.

"I'll come up with something. It's a lot easier than you might think. And if you piss me off, I'll make it a couple of nights. Meanwhile, we'll strip your RV down to the rivets. Sure hope we don't find any drugs inside, but you never know."

Phil surrendered his license. He kept a mental list of people he would punch out if he ever had the chance, and the sheriff had just made the top of that list.

And he'd thought the day he woke up in jail with his head full of stitches had to be the worst day of his life, but ever since then, it seemed like he'd been on a long, downhill slide that couldn't end up well.

All the way back to the RV, Angie clung to him like she might drown if she let go. They sat in his tiny kitchen, and he draped a blanket over her shoulders. "Doesn't the sheriff know you were related to Sy?" he asked.

"He knows, but the state trooper doesn't need to know."

"Why not?" Phil asked. "You want to tell me about it, seeing as how I'm stuck right in the middle of it now?"

"It's complicated." After that, she said no more,

141

and it didn't seem quite fair to press her so soon after Sy's death. So, as usual, he was left hanging. Just great, he thought, being mysterious must be a family trait with the Birch sisters.

"I'll put the chicken in the refrigerator," Angie said. "Unless you want some tonight."

"No, not hungry." Seeing a pleasant old man shot full of holes hardly encouraged an appetite.

"Where do I sleep?" she asked.

"Dani sleeps there, first bedroom on the left."

"Oh, then you don't…?"

"Sleep together? No. I'll be in back if you need anything."

"She told me you were holding out on her, but I didn't believe her. I guess she was telling the truth," Angie said.

****

Two things woke him up the next morning, the smell of coffee and a tapping at the RV door. Coffee was almost always a good thing. A knock at the door could go either way.

By the time he got dressed and went to the kitchen, Angie had already let the sheriff in, and they were both at the table drinking coffee. The sheriff slid Phil's license across the table. "Here's your license, Mr. Claussen. Sorry if I was a little abrupt last night. Sy, Seymour, was an old friend. I hated to see him done up like that."

"Looked like he was almost expecting it, just sitting there," Phil said.

"Maybe he was, but I'm not gonna say any more about that. How long you been camped out here?"

"About two months now. I've been paying his

142

weekly rate."

"He had a little over one hundred dollars in his cash box. I guess that was yours."

"I paid him last week," Phil said. That alone should take him off the list of suspects. If he'd robbed Seymour Birch, he certainly would have taken his own payment back.

"Did you see much of him, aside from paying the rent?" the sheriff asked.

"We had a few beers together, sometimes here, sometimes at his house. Went fishing a few times. A real nice fellow. I'm going to miss him." Phil didn't have to fake any feelings of regret; his were genuine. He and the old man had connected; something that didn't happen every day, and on those rare occasions when it did, was special.

"Have you seen anybody suspicious around?"

"Suspicious? No. It's really quiet back here. I was wondering, though, you didn't seem surprised when you saw him, like you almost expected it to happen."

The sheriff looked as though he started to say something, then changed his mind. He took a couple of steps then stopped at the door. "Sy ever mention oil?"

"Just that he hated the sight of oil rigs," Phil said.

"Yeah, that sounds like Sy," the sheriff said. "One thing that would really get him stirred up was having oil rigs messing up his view, and that's part of the problem. If I find out anything, I'll let you know. Thanks for the coffee."

Phil didn't know how much insight into their current situation Angie might have, but the look on her face said she had better say something. "What the hell is going on here, Angie? A sweet old man gets shot full

143

of holes, and everybody seems to take it right in stride. And Dani and Earl take off before they even find out what happened. Talk to me."

"Look, Dani will make this right," she said. "She didn't just run off and leave you hanging."

"What would you call it, then? Why did they take off like that?"

Angie stared at the table, furrows forming across her forehead. When she looked up, the furrows were gone. "How about some nice fried chicken for breakfast? I'll warm it up in the microwave."

****

After they polished off the fried chicken, Phil and Angie spent the morning edging around both of the elephants in the room: the unsolved murder of a friend and relative and the continued absence of Dani and Earl.

By the middle of the afternoon, when they were both beginning to foam at the mouth, Phil grabbed the keys to the car. "I have to make a trip to the market," he said. "Do you want to wait here in case Dani and Earl come back?"

"No, I want to come with you. I'll go crazy hanging around here by myself."

They drove up to the trading post to check out the newspapers and what passed for fresh vegetables. Angie picked through the various bins of green edibles, all of which somehow looked alike.

"Gosh, you eat this? No wonder you're so grouchy." She kept her face turned away, and he couldn't tell if she was joking.

"Grouchy? Me? Who said I was grouchy?" He picked out a few zucchini.

"That's probably from last year's batch," she said.

"No matter, squash lasts forever."

Phil made his usual run on the refrigerated compartment that held his favorite frozen TV dinners, then grabbed a half gallon of ice cream in case things really got difficult. A hefty helping of Rocky Road had gotten him through a number of tough situations in the past, so he took an extra carton just in case.

They continued their little dance on into the afternoon, waiting for the two fugitives, Dani and Earl, to return. Angie played her own little game, like when she walked out of the bedroom topless, her T-shirt in her hand. "Oh, Phil, I thought you were outside." She covered herself but was damned slow in doing so and did only a partial job at that.

He did his part by letting his gaze linger on her body before turning away.

"They're just breasts, Phil. Nothing you haven't seen before."

"Yeah, right."

****

Evening darkness began to settle in with no sign of Earl's truck.

"What would you like for dinner?" Angie asked.

"Ice cream."

"I'll be happy to fix you something else. I'm a fairly decent cook."

"Ice cream," he said again and retrieved one of the cartons from the freezer. He didn't bother with a bowl, just grabbed a spoon and dug in.

Angie looked deflated, like he'd just denied her the chance to make up some lost ground, but the situation called for desperate measures, and that meant Rocky

Road. "There's another carton in the freezer if you want some," he said.

She shook her head and made coffee instead.

Phil had made a sizeable dent in the ice cream carton before he realized it wasn't doing anything to lift his spirits, so he returned it to the freezer. "I think I'll take a walk," he said.

Angie was on her feet in a second. "I'll get my sweater. Should we bring a flashlight? Maybe some water in case we get thirsty?"

"No, just me." He should have realized that telling her that he needed some alone time would unleash a barrage of questions. Why hadn't he had the good sense to sneak out when she wasn't looking?

"What's wrong, Phil? What did I do?"

"You didn't do anything. I'll be back in a few minutes."

"It's about my breasts, isn't it? They're too small. You don't like them."

"Your breasts are fine, both of them. No more talk about breasts, and for heaven's sake, don't tell your sister I saw yours."

"Please, don't run off like this. Can't we talk?"

Can't we talk? He'd be a damned fool to pick up on that one. Like grabbing a snake by the tail and figuring you wouldn't get bit because the head was at the other end. Besides, there had been plenty of time to talk already, and Phil was none the wiser.

"But what if Dani comes back? I can't very well tell her you're walking around in the dark. She'll give me hell."

He hurried out the door before she came up with some more plausible objections. "Be right back." If a dose of Rocky Road didn't do the trick, a walk on a pleasant evening was the next best thing. The new moon gave off little light, leaving the entire celestial stage to the stars, which did not disappoint but didn't provide him with any answers either. Another quarter mile, perhaps, and he turned and headed back.

Chapter Twelve

He'd left the main road and was halfway down the drive to the RV when he heard a scream. For most of his walk, he'd been suffering from his awkward placement of the 9mm Dani had given him. He'd had no reason for tucking it into the waistband of his trousers other than not knowing where else to put it, but having it now seemed like a very good idea, even if he had little chance of hitting anything he shot at.

He covered the short distance to the RV on the fly. On his way to the door, he had to circle around a huge, black Town Car that looked almost as big as Earl's truck. He reached the door just as Angie came flying out. She smacked into him, and they both went down in a heap of thrashing arms and legs.

"Run, Phil," she said, a ridiculous suggestion due to their entanglement, which was not unlike the predicament he'd gotten into with the mayor's sister in the bar in Wakefield months before. Hopefully, this one would have a better outcome. He struggled to his feet as two hefty men charged through the door of the RV.

"Who the fuck are you?" large man number one yelled at him.

"Since you're in my RV, the polite thing would be for you to introduce yourself first," Phil said as he regained his footing. He was pretty sure where this was headed and figured Angie was safer on the ground for the time being, so that's where he left her.

"Fuck you." With that, the large man launched a large fist at his head.

It seemed that most of the large guys Phil had met recently, beginning with the goon in the Peery County Jail in Wakefield, wanted to punch his head off, and, if not for his extensive training in hand-to-hand combat, he would probably be lying comatose somewhere with severe brain injury. Maybe he couldn't shoot for beans, but he could mix it up with the best of them.

With a quick nod of thanks to the instructor who had taught him to handle situations like this, he slipped the punch, straightened out, then smashed his elbow into the man's face. The impact was unsettling, as the man's nose and possibly other facial bones cracked beneath the blow.

The second big guy took aim and sent another right-handed missile at him. The punch would have done serious damage to his head had it connected, but when the punch met with nothing but air, the momentum pulled the man forward and left him in a vulnerable position. Phil drove his knee into the man's groin, lifting him off the ground. The sound the big guy made upon impact with his knee was scarcely human, but this didn't stop Angie, who, as soon as the big guy landed, began kicking at any exposed surface.

"Damn, Angie, I leave you alone for half an hour and look what happens. Are you okay?"

Angie nodded while she continued kicking the fallen man.

Phil felt some small degree of sympathy for the poor bastard, curled up around what had to be the most painful set of balls on the planet. He pulled Angie away.

"Who are those assholes? You know them?"

She shook her head. "Wish I was wearing heels. I could puncture his fucking lung."

When he finally got a look at her face in the light from the RV's door, both of her cheeks were reddened and beginning to swell. The boys had slapped her around.

"Why in hell were they beating on you like that? What if I hadn't come back when I did?"

"I don't even want to think about it." She took another kick at the fetal figure on the ground.

Headlights bouncing down the road. Cops? Not likely. More bad guys seemed much more like it. He pulled the handgun from his waistband and chambered a round. He held the weapon close to his thigh, hoping he wouldn't have to use it.

The new vehicle couldn't get past the Town Car, but its occupants could. Dani and Earl were on them in seconds. Dani embraced her sister while Earl checked out the two victims on the ground.

"Man, what the hell happened here?" Earl knelt by one man, his flashlight illuminating the facial changes left by Phil's elbow.

He flipped on the safety, then eased the weapon back into its former position of concealment. "A little disagreement," Phil said.

"Remind me never to disagree with you." Earl walked over to the other guy who was still whimpering, cuddling his balls. "Him too?"

"The same. I haven't called the cops yet."

"Don't," Earl said. "I got a better idea."

After the girls went back inside the RV, Earl

moved his truck off the trail far enough for the Town Car to get by. Then he backed the car closer to the RV. Before he got out, he popped open the trunk.

"Shit, man, don't do this," the man with the busted face said.

"Either you go peaceable, or I'll turn him loose on you again." He nodded toward Phil.

The guy crawled into the trunk with barely enough space for him alone.

"Don't spit blood on the carpet," Earl said. "Your boss won't like that."

He grabbed the other whimpering figure by the collar of his jacket and dragged him toward the vehicle. The guy braced his hands on the bumper and refused to go farther.

Earl gave him a vicious slap. "Listen, Sunshine, you might think your balls can't hurt any worse than they do now but think about how it's going to feel when we cut 'em off." He made a snipping motion with two fingers.

Somehow, two large men got loaded in a trunk; just looking at them packed in so tightly made Phil's stomach roil.

"I'll drive my truck," Earl said. "You follow me in the Town Car. I'll stop in front of a junkyard a few miles east. Just kill the engine and leave the keys in the ignition."

"Leave the guys in the trunk?"

"Somebody will let them out eventually."

On the drive back, Earl pulled in at the trading post. "We're gonna need more beer. It might be a long night."

"What the hell's going on around here, Earl?" Phil

asked when they were back in the truck. "Poor old Sy gets shot to death, then two goons come to my RV and slap Angie around. I don't want to think what might have happened if I hadn't come back when I did."

"Sy had enemies. Some people didn't like the way he did things. The oil people and developers wanted his land in the worst possible way, like millions and millions of bucks. Even some of the locals wanted to see it dug up, oil wells sprouting up, new housing, new jobs, but that would be the end of Clayton. It would get swallowed right up, and Sy loved his little town. His place was the only thing keeping them out."

"What about Angie? Are the girls in danger?"

"I expect when they get a look at what happened to the two guys they sent out to your RV, they'll think twice before they try anything else, for a while, at least."

"I don't like this, Earl, cold-blooded murder, beating women. I don't like this one bit."

****

Space was tight around the dining table in the RV. Earl insisted they leave a clear lane to the refrigerator that contained their beer. Phil was poised above a seat across from Dani, but she waved him over beside her. "I want you close by me," she said.

He watched the three of them exchange glances like he was still on the outside looking in, which he was, but not for much longer.

"I need to give this back to you." He pulled the handgun from his waistband, popped out the full clip, and ejected the round from the chamber, then slid it all over to Dani, who slid it right back again.

"Please, Phil, keep it. Much better to have it and

not need it than to need it and not have it."

"Maybe, but you still haven't told me why I need a gun."

"You mean you had that gun when those goons were slapping me around?" Angie's voice was shrill.

"I'm glad I didn't have to use it. You cross a line when you shoot somebody. It gets messy, and there might be a body to dispose of." Not to mention that the likelihood of him hitting whatever he intended to shoot was less than hitting something he'd never intended to shoot in the first place.

"If you'd come back a little later, the body you'd have to dispose of might have been mine," Angie said. Her face had continued to swell, and her look suggested she held him personally responsible for it. Phil pulled the gun out of her reach.

"I'm going to look like a porcupine tomorrow," she said.

"I have some frozen peas in the freezer if you want to try them."

"How about I stick my whole head in the freezer," Angie said. "Anything to keep my face from swelling up like a balloon."

"You won't fit."

"How come you were out walking around in the dark anyhow?" Earl said.

"Just needed to do it." He figured that if they wanted answers, they were going to have to provide some of their own first. "Now, who are those guys, and why were they beating up on Angie?"

"First things first," Earl said. "We gotta eat." He pulled two bags of nacho chips from a plastic bag."

"Wow, all we need are candles and soft music."

Dani's smile looked forced like she was trying to exhibit a merriment she really didn't feel.

"Yeah, nothing cheap about these two," Angie said.

Earl took a long swig from his beer can and followed it up with a loud, prolonged belch.

"Perfect," Angie said. "Just perfect."

"I declare this meeting officially in order," Earl said.

"Good," Phil said. "I'll start, and if I don't get some straight answers, I just might finish it too."

"Phil, what do you mean?" Dani's eyes were wider than he'd ever see them.

"I mean, this thing we're all sitting in is on wheels, and I might decide it's time I fired it up and moved on."

"Oh, God, Phil, no." She grabbed his arm and pulled it to her chest.

"Hear me out. There's some really weird shit going on. I've been here a little over two months now. It was three weeks before I even knew your name. I still don't know where you live. You bring new cars here, park them, then take them away. I don't know where they come from, how you got them, or where you take them."

"I can explain, Phil." Dani's voice was shrill, almost desperate.

"Let me finish. A man I'd grown very fond of, and an uncle to two of you, gets shot to death, and everybody seems to take it in stride like it was expected. And as soon as we hear shots, you two take off in your truck. I come back tonight to find two goons in my RV, and they both try to bust my head. As usual, I have no idea why.

"So, somebody start talking, or, I have my keys in my pocket, and tomorrow I'll be heading out, looking for someplace where people don't treat me like the village idiot or try to fracture my skull."

The inside of the RV went completely quiet. Earl stopped chewing his chips. Phil scanned the faces around him and found everyone looking at the table.

Earl stood with some effort. "You and Dani need to sort this out. Angie and me, we'll just be in the way."

"No, sit. Everybody stays." A small crowd was his last line of defense. If left alone with Dani, she would pull that little trick where she wound herself around him, turned her blue eyes on high beam, and drew him so close their noses touched. Then he would be lost, his ability to think clearly would be gone.

"The first thing I want to know is why you two took off in your truck after Sy got shot. I mean, Sy was your relative, right?" He didn't need to add that when the shit hit the fan, friends and relatives didn't usually run the other way.

"Yes, and we loved him to death. He practically raised both of us. We left because of a work thing," Dani said. "We're in the repo business, Sy's business, actually. One night we made a mistake, well, really, I made it, but it was an honest mistake, one anybody could make. I mean, whoever would think there would be two black sedans parked side by side like that. Well, one was dark green, but it looked black in the dark. So, I repossessed the wrong car, and the sheriff got involved because the owner claimed we stole it. He was kinda pissed, and Uncle Sy had to smooth things over. If the sheriff saw Earl and me here, things might become complicated. So, we left."

"So, you're repo? Really?"

"We reclaim property for its owners when people stop paying for it. I know what you're thinking, but it's not the same as stealing, not at all." She slid closer to Phil so their hips were touching.

"Sy has been running the business for years, and all three of us are involved, but Dani does most of the actual repossession work. She don't look like repo, does she?" Earl said. "That's why she's so good at it. They usually don't catch on until it's too late."

Earl passed him another beer. Phil was surprised to find he'd finished the first one so fast.

"The main reason is, she's a genius with cars. If it's got an engine and wheels, she'll get it up and running," Earl said. "The ignition system hasn't been invented that she can't bypass."

"Uncle Sy taught me." Dani smiled up at Phil, like a kid proud of some trick she was better at than anybody else.

"What about the goons that beat up on Angie? And why do I have a gun in my pants?"

"Competition," Earl said. "There's money to be made in repo, and money draws attention. Some of the people aren't as nice as we are, but you know that already."

"And then there's Uncle Sy's property with all that oil underneath. A lot of people want to get their hands on it. That might be what got Uncle Sy killed," Dani said.

"I heard about that," Phil said. "I just never thought somebody would shoot him over it."

"It was no secret. Lots of people knew about it, and lots of people wanted to get their hands on it, but Uncle

Sy would never allow any drilling on his land. He liked Clayton just the way it was, and oil rigs would ruin it all, so, no drilling."

"If lots of people knew about it, why keep me in the dark for two months? That's what pisses me off." Mostly he was angry with himself for not pushing for answers earlier, but every time he tried, a pair of blue eyes scrambled his brain circuits.

Dani moved even closer until there was no space at all left between them. "I'm so sorry, Phil, that was mostly me. I was afraid you'd get spooked by all this and run away, and I just can't lose you, not after waiting so long."

"See, that's the main thing that bugs me," Phil said. "It's like everything was already set up, and I walked right into it. Everybody was in on it but me."

She wrapped her arms around his neck and pulled him down even closer to her. "You have to believe me, Phil; all the rest of it doesn't matter. You're all that's important to me."

In spite of his best intentions, it was happening again, his resistance melting away like morning mist. He understood a part of the puzzle, but the critical piece, the one he didn't understand at all, was sitting right next to him, and she was right. The rest of it wasn't really so important.

"What happens now?" Phil asked. "If somebody shot Sy because of his oil rights, what's to stop them from hauling in the heavy equipment now that he's gone?"

"We know he left a will. Probably nothing will happen until that's settled," Earl said.

So, family ties, a repo business, and a big pool of

oil underneath it all waiting to be claimed. That could explain a lot of the weirdness that seemed to be woven into the fabric of the little town where he parked his RV. Phil knew more than he'd known before, but he still had only part of the picture. "Clayton is a weird little town. I guess all of you have noticed," he said.

That broke the ice and brought forth laughter from all.

"You haven't seen anything yet," Earl said.

"That's what I'm afraid of."

"But the people here are really nice. Once you get to know them, you'll like them, I just know it, and they'll like you too." Dani still hadn't released his arm.

"Are we cool, man?" Earl asked. "I don't want to lose you. I mean, you know pretty much everything I know about what's just happened. If I knew more, I'd tell you."

"For now, I guess." He wasn't going to commit one way or the other.

"Enough," Angie said. "If you three are finished solving the world's problems, my ears are still ringing from getting slapped around, and I'm ready for bed. I'll stay in the second bedroom again, okay?"

"That's where I sleep." Dani blushed as she said it, like she'd given her sister more ammunition than she'd intended.

"Oh, come on, sis, you might start there, but I know you don't stay there. Not with this hunk right down the hall. You two have been going at it like rabbits, right?"

"Wrong again," Dani said, turning even redder. She'd already informed her sister that she and Phil had not yet been intimate, but Angie was rubbing it in her face, right in front of them.

"Sorry to disappoint you. You can have the larger bedroom if you two want to double up," Phil said.

"Sleep with my sister? No thanks." Angie got up to go. "Come on, Earl, you have to find me a bed."

After they'd gone, Dani emptied the remaining beer cans and stashed them all in the trash. "You okay?" she asked.

"Yeah, sure, I think I'll turn in early, too. It's been a long day."

Disappointment was spelled out so clearly in Dani's features that it might as well have been written in ink on her forehead. "Good night, then," she mumbled.

He'd had just begun to drift off when he heard the soft tap on the door.

"Just me." She was wearing a black bra and panties. The light from the hallway spread a golden glow around her silhouette. She sat on the edge of the bed and pulled back the sheet. "Scoot over," she said. When he did, she latched onto him with both arms. "You scared me half to death in there," she said. "Promise me you won't leave, please."

"You'll have to treat me like a grownup. Can you manage that?"

"For sure, I was going to tell you, your final divorce papers came through. Your wife's lawyer sent them to me."

"So, I'm a free man," he said.

"Free is about all you got. She got the house, the car, and most of your savings account."

"I guess you'll lose interest now, huh? Nobody wants to get involved with a poor man."

"You don't get off that easy. We'll make do financially. We won't be rich, but we'll be able to eat regular meals and sleep indoors. Now, where were we before you got all distracted?" She ran her fingertips along his thigh. His erection reached vertical in no time at all.

"But…" Any protest he might raise was belied by the growing tumescence from his groin.

"You said to treat you like a grownup, didn't you? That's enough talking. I've been waiting for this for two months, and it's time for you to do your duty."

Her underwear and the top sheet went swoosh, gone so quickly he wondered if it had been there in the first place. She sat astride him, holding him in her hand. It had been a long time since a woman held him like that, and he wasn't entirely sure what she might do next, although he had high hopes.

"That's loaded, you know."

"I'm counting on it." She raised herself and slipped him inside her.

That marked the end of coherent conversation for half an hour or so. Their thrashing about became so violent that he feared for the RV bed. Where would he get a replacement, and how would he ever explain what happened to the first one?

Sometime, shortly before he succumbed to a state of pure ecstasy, he wondered how the stars, which he had admired earlier that same evening, had somehow gotten inside the RV and were now arrayed across the ceiling.

Their synchronized ending, a thunderous event that shook the walls and surprised them both, made him thankful there were no other campers in the area.

"Wow, you really were loaded, but I can't say you didn't warn me." She held his face with both her hands, planting kisses everywhere.

"It's been a while," he said, actually a long time, and never anything as explosive as had just happened.

Later, when they were both breathing in a normal fashion, he moved to shift his weight off her.

"No, wait, stay there, please. I want you right there," she said, holding him tightly.

They kissed again like two drowning people.

"You never answered my question," she said when she came up for air.

"What question was that?"

"You have to promise you won't leave me."

"We have to make some ground rules, you know."

"Anything you want, just tell me. I couldn't bear to lose you." She burrowed into him until they were a single body.

Was he out of the woods yet? Would he really attain adult status, voting rights, and such now that his marital status was resolved? Maybe, maybe not. With Dani, it would be an uphill battle that never ended, but the prize now snuggled against him so closely that there was no space left between them was worth it.

But he wouldn't even have a chance at a morning cuddle; when he woke, she was gone, the morning light came streaming through the window, and her side of the bed had gone cold.

Chapter Thirteen

The way Phil saw it, him being an outsider and Sy Birch being a local institution, he had no business attending the man's memorial service, but Dani had other ideas. The girl, when she had her mind made up, would not be deterred and wore through his puny resistance like morning fog under an August sun. Besides, he'd really developed a liking for Sy, so showing his respects seemed appropriate, just as Dani reminded him.

"But I don't have anything to wear." His protest sounded almost feminine.

"It doesn't matter, not around here," she said. "The only man wearing a tie will be the funeral director. You'll be fine so long as you're wearing long pants."

So, on a Tuesday morning in early July, they drove, Dani at the wheel of the car, to the Burgermeister, an expansive brick structure of one floor that could pass as a high school gymnasium or an American Legion Hall, but in this case hosted the memorial service for Seymour Birch. When Phil had asked about what seemed to him to be an unusual name, Dani explained that the Burgermeister family was now fourth generation in the area and so qualified as long-term residents.

The parking lot outside the hall was almost full by the time they arrived. "They can handle funerals or weddings," Dani said, "sometimes both at the same time." She pointed out the sliding partition that could separate the hall into equal portions. Phil had to admire the Burgermeisters' entrepreneurial spirit.

The girls, Dani and Angie, looked sharp in matching black outfits, whether by design or accident, he couldn't be sure. From the fact that they managed to stay on opposite sides of the room suggested that an unhappy coincidence had occurred. Phil wisely made no mention of it.

Dani had been pretty much on target with her assessment of the dress code for the event. Some of the women had obviously spent some time and effort making themselves presentable and more, but casual was the word for the male attendees. The only exception, besides the funeral director, was a cohort of men in dark suits who attached themselves to Dani and Angie, moving back and forth between the two. Hands holding business cards were extended, and Phil couldn't imagine what they could be selling, or buying, given the situation. "Who are the gents?" he asked Earl.

"Vultures," Earl said, his scowl so angry he half expected him to spit. "Remember I mentioned developers, real estate people, oil people? I figured they'd be lining up as soon as Sy was in the ground, if not before."

"So, the oil is a big deal?"

"Yeah, Sy fought them off for years. So, the vultures figured they'd just wait him out, then jump on Dani and Angie, hoping to talk them into selling. They must have got tired of waiting."

"Do you think they shot him?"

"Don't know, maybe. But they're part of a pretty

powerful group, and nobody wants to butt heads with them unless it's absolutely necessary."

"What about the girls? Are they in danger? Those guys were rough with Angie, but I swear, I'll kill anybody who lays a hand on Dani."

"I believe you," Earl said. "And I know you can do it. You can bet they know you're around now, after what you did to their two boys out at the RV. Just watch your back. If I hear anything, I'll let you know. Between the two of us, we should be able to handle any trouble they want to start."

"Sounds like a plan to me. So, Sy could have made a lot of money off of the oil."

"He didn't want more money. He had plenty of that. See, what he really loved was Clayton. It was always a special place to him, and all he wanted was for the town to stay exactly as it is. I mean, it's as pretty a little town as you'll find anywhere, but if the developers and oil people get hold of it, it won't be pretty very long."

Phil was surprised at the vehemence of Earl's speech, considering that he'd heard most of it before. Clearly, if he had anything to say about it, there would be no oil rigs disfiguring the village of Clayton. Earl wandered away, and Phil hung around the edges of the throng, hoping for an early exit. As the morning drew on, he attracted a small following of his own. Several apparently unattached women drifted by, patting his arms, shoulders, expressing condolences that seemed altogether inappropriate since he had no family ties to the deceased.

"If you ever need to talk…" he heard that phrase several times, usually followed by a bit of paper with a phone number slipped into his shirt pocket. What a compassionate group, practically dripping with the milk of human kindness. Clayton was indeed a special town. One striking redhead came back for a third extension of comfort and slipped her arm through his. When she leaned into him, the neckline of her summer dress flared, and he might have gasped slightly.

Dani, apparently on the lookout for any such maneuvers, was at his side immediately, establishing ownership in no uncertain terms. The look she gave the redhead would have peeled paint off a wall. The other woman wisely yielded and fled the field. "I can't leave you alone for one minute," Dani said. "Even at a funeral."

"What did I do now?" Amazing how you can get into trouble standing perfectly still.

Sy Birch apparently had quite a following in the area, and before long, the entire Burgermeister building was filled, making for a very warm and very uncomfortable situation that mercifully ended shortly before noon. Dani was noticeably quiet on the drive back to the RV, he reckoned as an expression of her loss.

But he learned soon enough, it wasn't grief that kept her silent. She was pissed. As soon as they got back to the RV, she relieved him of the three phone numbers that had been slipped into his pocket. "Any more?" she asked.

"I didn't even know about those."

"Liar, give me your clothes. I can see right now I'm going to have to go through all of your pockets."

"My pockets? What about your pockets? You had a group of guys following you around all morning, if I remember correctly. If I'm giving up my clothes, you're going to have to do likewise. How do I know you don't have phone numbers stashed somewhere too?"

Her expression changed from mock anger to mischievous. "Ooh, I like this new jealous Phil." She reached behind her neck and tugged at her zipper, and in no time, neither of them had places to hide phone numbers or anything else.

****

Phil had just poured his first cup of the morning when the sheriff's patrol car pulled up outside. The sheriff didn't bother with his hat as he got out. He was completely bald except for a little rim of hair that ran above his ears.

"I got fresh coffee," Phil said, opening the door.

"Thanks, but I'm trying to cut back. Wife says it makes me too edgy." He passed a hand over his bald pate as if trying to smooth down hair that was no longer there. "Reason I came out is, they're reading Seymour Birch's will tomorrow, and his attorney said you should be there. His lawyer's name is Newton, on Main Street, and you need to be there at eleven."

"But I'm not family, barely knew him."

"Just be there, okay? On second thought, just a half cup shouldn't hurt, and I can use a little boost. Didn't sleep so good last night."

Phil made toast and came up with a jar of strawberry jam, but other than his news about Sy's will, the sheriff didn't have much to say.

"Any progress on Sy's murder?"

"It's slow, like swimming through molasses. I'll get there, though. I promise you that."

Amazing how the old man had seemingly passed

from memory, as if he'd never been there. And this business about the will had to be somebody's mistake, couldn't possibly involve Phil. Maybe he'd go, maybe not.

Darkness had fallen by the time Dani got in. Momentarily blinded by her headlights, he couldn't see the car she parked back in the trees, only that it was very long, presumably another of the luxury models she almost always turned up in. She practically skipped across the short distance from the car to the RV, a big smile on her face, visible even in the dim light.

"Looks like you had a good day," he said.

"Easy as pie. Here, this is for you." She held out a bag that, from the aroma, could only be fried chicken. "You set out the plates while I wash up."

Moments later, they assumed their customary seating at the small table, her chair pulled up close beside his, never across from him.

They talked over paper plates laden with crispy fried chicken. In spite of MaryBeth's constant admonitions about the health hazards of fast food, Phil always had a soft spot for crispy fried chicken.

"You look like you're enjoying that," she said.

"I am, thanks. Oh, I had a little visit from the sheriff today. Sy's lawyer is reading his will tomorrow, and I'm supposed to be there."

"And the attorney wants you there? Really?"

"I have no idea why. Not like Sy and I were old friends. We had a few beers together, went fishing a couple of times. Maybe he's leaving me that old boat. We could go for moonlight cruises on the pond, just you and me."

"We can do that right now if you'd invite me."

"Maybe later. Now, about tomorrow, I'm supposed to find law offices of a guy named Newton."

"I know the place. It's easy to find, like everything else in Clayton. Just drive into town, make a left at the first intersection, and you're on Main Street. Newton's office is right next to the courthouse. She's been here a long time, and I think she's done pretty well for herself."

"She?"

"Sure, a female lawyer. You have a problem with that?"

"Of course not. One saved my bacon back in Wakefield. I wouldn't be here now if she hadn't done such a good job. You don't want to come along?"

"No, definitely not. Don't worry, I'm sure it will be a quick trip," she said. "And you can take Milly."

****

If the late morning temperature was any indication, the day would be another scorcher, but what else should you expect for July in a Great Plains state? Searing summers and brutal winters…what a choice.

Dani's driving instructions were spot on, small town in the middle of nowhere, hard to miss, although, from what Sy had told him earlier, most people drove right by unaware of its existence. The Clayton County Courthouse, complete with columns rising up two stories, stood out among the more modest buildings on the street. Phil wondered why such an otherwise puny town needed such an impressive building, but a lot of things about Clayton didn't add up right, so he would just add this to the list. He parked across the street, giving himself a short walk to stretch his legs after the drive.

The lobby, yes, the building had a lobby, was cavernous, so much wasted space just to create an impression. Seated at the far wall, behind a polished mahogany desk, a blonde receptionist smiled at him.

"I'm Phil Claussen, here to see Ms. Newton."

"She's expecting you, if you'll follow me."

He followed the blonde's swaying hips. Could that really be her normal walk, or did she just use it when a man followed behind her? She knocked on a side door then turned the handle. "Mr. Claussen is here," she said through a crack in the door.

Sandra Newton, Attorney at Law, walked with a slight limp. She stood almost as tall as Phil but was so thin as to raise questions about her health. Even so, her handshake was firm and businesslike.

One entire wall of her office was taken up with bookcases, every shelf filled. From the rather austere and uniform bindings, he'd guess law books. The other walls were bare, no diplomas, certificates, licenses, or other forms of documentation he would expect in any professional office. The only photo in the entire room sat at the left corner of her desk, and Phil, seated alongside, had a direct view of it. A young woman, an earlier Sandra Newton, no doubt, wearing a strapless sundress, with her arms around the neck of the man sitting beside her, who had his own arm wrapped around her waist. They were seated in what appeared to be a field of wildflowers, and Phil thought he'd never seen a happier couple.

"My husband," Newton said softly. "He passed away six months after that photo was taken."

Even if the photo had been taken a hundred years ago, there was no mistaking the pain in her voice, pain that probably would last as long as she drew breath. "I'm sorry," he said. It wasn't much, but what else could he say that might measure up to the moment?

"We have things to discuss," she said.

"Are the others coming?" Surely the reading of a will would involve several parties, family most of all.

"No, just you," she said.

Just him? What the hell? "Now I'm really confused…why am I here?"

"That will become apparent shortly. Would you like coffee before we begin?"

"No thanks." This could not end well; legal entanglements never did. Only lawyers seemed to come out on top. The smart move now would be to dash back to the campground, fire up the RV, and leave the entire state of Oklahoma far in his rear-view mirror. In fact, he found himself gripping the edges of his chair lest he do just that.

"I'll skip through the preliminaries." Newton had on her stern lawyer face, half grimace, but all business. "You are Mr. Birch's sole beneficiary."

"No, there must be some mistake," he said, thankful he wasn't holding a coffee cup, which he surely would have dropped. Was he about to inherit a load of unpaid bills?

"Mr. Birch has left you his entire estate, debt-free, I might add. The estate includes the campground and just over one thousand acres of land, including a lake. I have a map for you showing you the exact extent of the grounds. It includes his house, which may or may not be good news, considering the recent unfortunate circumstances of his death there. There is also an account at the First National Bank of three hundred thousand dollars. There are other holdings, stocks, and bonds. By rough estimate, the value of the entire estate will run in the neighborhood of three million dollars. Congratulations, Mr. Claussen."

The feeling of unreality that he'd experienced a number of times since his arrival in Clayton now enclosed him like a heavy fog. "No, no, I can't do that. I mean, I liked Sy, we had a few beers, went fishing together, but I only knew him for a few months. I can't possibly be his beneficiary. This all has to be a big mistake."

"Well, you made a very favorable impression on him in that short time. I'm afraid the property passes to you, in spite of your reservations. I'm sure you're concerned about some hidden financial liability, but let me assure you, Mr. Birch's accounts are all in order. He was as clean of debt as anyone can be."

"Wait, what you don't understand, see Sy and me, we talked about the campground, just casual stuff. We never had any agreement about the rest of his property or even the campground, for that matter. So maybe he got confused and thought I wanted it, but I don't, absolutely not. If you can straighten it all out, I'll be on my way."

If eyes could turn hard as flint, then hers did. "I repeat, Mr. Claussen, this is not a mistake. Three weeks ago, Mr. Birch sat right where you're sitting now, and we spent an entire morning and most of an afternoon on a new draft of his will. He was quite specific about what he wanted, and I'll tell you again, there is no mistake here."

"You think maybe there's another Phil Claussen somewhere in the area?"

"I won't even dignify that with an answer."

From her expression, he thought better of raising further protests, even though he remained quite certain that somewhere another Phil Claussen was waiting on an inheritance that had been delivered to the wrong address. If not in this office, elsewhere in the cosmos, wires had gotten crossed.

Several deep breaths failed to clear his head. A few minutes before, he'd been a free man, completely unencumbered and living on wheels. Now everything was upside down. He walked over to the window that faced the street, looked out, wishing he were out there instead of where he was. "Becoming a property owner in Oklahoma was never part of my plan. If I'd ever had even a hint that something like this might have happened, I would have headed in another direction when I left Wakefield, north, south, anywhere but here."

"This is a lot to take in, I'm sure," Newton said. "But I questioned Mr. Birch quite extensively when he came by to change his will, and he was certain and specific about naming you to receive his estate." She came over and stood beside him. "Sy knew this would change your life completely, that you'd be getting more than a pile of money, you'd be inheriting a big responsibility too. It wasn't an easy decision for him either."

"Why didn't he ever mention it before he died, you know, give me a choice about it?"

"We talked about that. I know Sy agonized over it before he decided, but in the end, he said it had to be you. He had his reasons, some of them he shared with me, a lot of them he didn't. But, for better or worse, he chose you, and nothing could change his mind."

"No, I can't do it," Phil said. Stepping into the huge estate and legacy of a murdered man right out of the blue was pure lunacy. He was sure of that much.

"Please, Mr. Claussen, let's not be hasty. Everything is completed and ready for your signature. That's all you have to do, and I'll be ready to help you with anything that comes up."

"I'm sorry. I'm sure you have everything in order, but no."

"Maybe you need a few days to think it over. That will be fine. Let's do that then. Have you come back next week and sign the papers." She was speaking more rapidly now, a hint of desperation in her voice.

He shook his head in what he hoped was a final gesture.

"Please, Mr. Claussen, you don't understand how important this is."

"No, Ms. Newton, *you* don't understand. I'm just passing through. I never meant to stay in Clayton."

He was afraid she might drop to her knees, pleading, in which case he'd jump through the nearest window. She seemed to shrink in front of his eyes.

"If that's the case, everybody loses," she said as though she'd just failed at some very important task.

Phil almost knocked over a chair getting out of the room. He needed air, space. He drove ten miles out of town with the accelerator on the floor all the way. Then he stopped, pulled off the road, got out, and walked into an open field. What the fuck was going on? Every direction he turned was weirder than the last one.

Cy, Dani, and God knows who else, they were all just waiting for him to arrive in Clayton? In what universe does that make sense? Worst of all, he'd begun to feel it, pulling him back like a big magnet and him with a steel plate stuck to his ass. But whatever inspiration or resolution you're supposed to draw from blue skies and open prairie wasn't there for him.

He drove back to the little village with its wooden sidewalks and gingerbread houses, its storefronts so dated they looked like enlarged pieces from an old set of children's toys. Time must have slipped past on the interstate leaving Clayton untouched over the years. Was that what they expected him to do? Hold back time? Good luck with that.

He parked—no parking meters—and strolled down Cherry Street. Every town he'd ever seen had a Cherry Street, but this one was different—no traffic lights. In fact, he hadn't seen a single traffic light since he'd driven in.

He'd taken a brief tour of Clayton that first day after Dani bolted out of the RV in pursuit of the car her ex- had stolen from her, leaving Phil high and dry. It all seemed appealingly quaint then, but now, on closer inspection, it wasn't just a small town dressed up in pioneer clothing to attract tourists; it was the real deal. Why did he get the feeling that if he'd been standing in that same spot ten, twenty, or fifty years ago, things would look the same as now?

Sure, there was another side to the town, a street with bars and restaurants, a tire shop, and a couple of used car lots, but the effect had not yet spilled over into quaint Clayton, which still remained pristine and rustic. Somehow the two areas coexisted without blending.

So, this was where he'd been heading all along? Right from that first day he left Wakefield, he was aiming for Clayton, OK, but didn't know it? No way, people who thought like that wound up heavily medicated in locked wards.

Chapter Fourteen

What now, Phil? Decision time stared him squarely in the face. He could always drive the car back to the campsite, switch into his man-cave-on-wheels, his big RV, and make a run for it. But that idea was *dead on arrival*. Besides, the entry to his RV was blocked; Dani had got there first. If he wasn't mistaken, she wore the same shorts and top as on that first day he'd picked her up from the side of the road. But while that encounter was very pleasant, he didn't think this one would be.

She stood blocking the doorway of the RV, arms folded across her chest and a scowl on her face.

"You turned it down, didn't you?"

"Dani, I just couldn't do it. It was too much, a thousand acres from a man I'd only known for a few weeks." He had no idea how she'd found out so quickly, but it didn't seem the best time to ask that question.

"So, you planned to stop by, enjoy the scenery, catch a few fish, maybe screw some of the local girls, then leave the area, is that it?"

"Not exactly, but I never really intended to stay, you know that."

"If you think you're going to just walk away after I've waited for you so long, you're crazy."

"There you go again. You're not making sense. Until a few weeks ago, you'd never even met me." At least rational Phil was still in the game.

"And in the mind of Phil Claussen, you can't possibly fall in love with somebody you've never met. Is that what you're telling me?"

But rational Phil was about to take a beating. He could feel it coming. If there was a correct answer to that question, he had no idea what it might be. "That's about right, I guess."

"Then you really are an idiot."

"MaryBeth called me an idiot too. I'm beginning to think she was right."

"I agree with her." Dani walked to the front of the RV and sat in the driver's seat. "All that time, all that waiting, and when the guy shows up, he turns out to be a fool. Just my luck."

Phil made it to the first step of the RV and went no further. "So, you're part of the package, are you?"

"What do you mean?"

"A thousand acres plus you?"

"I'm part of the estate. Is that what you're saying?"

He shouldn't have said it. It was mean and stupid, and when she slapped him, he knew he deserved it. But it was one hell of a slap. His head jerked back and banged against the door frame. He ran his tongue over his teeth to see if they were all still there.

"How dare you? I waited and waited for you, then you treat me like dirt." She whimpered. "You hurt my hand."

"My jaw doesn't feel so great either."

He reached for her, but she jerked her arm away. "Don't touch me. You have some serious decisions to make, and they involve a lot of people. Honestly, I don't expect much from you. Remember your last big decision, how you ran away? Maybe you have a chance to make up for that, call it redemption or whatever. But I'm not going to get my hopes up. Maybe I'll come back over tomorrow, maybe not. If you're gone, we'll just have to make do without you."

"Who's we?"

She didn't answer.

****

A half hour or so later, Angie drove up in Earl's truck. She wasted no time in launching herself at him. *"You blockhead."*

"So, you drove all the way over here just to yell at me." Why not? Everybody else was. Why should she be different?

"Actually, I came over here to kick your ass for what you did to my sister."

"How about what she did to me?"

"Your stupid face will get better. What you did to Dani won't. You broke her heart, you bastard." She took a step forward, fists clenched.

He held up his hands. "Stop right where you are. I've had just about enough getting smacked and yelled at for one day."

"What, you'd punch me out, tough guy?"

"I didn't say that, but don't push me."

"I never figured you for such a low down snake, but I guess I was wrong. In all the years I've known her—and that's all her life—I've never seen her so broken up. If I had a gun, I'd shoot your balls off."

"Fuck it. I should pack up and get out of here."

"Yeah, that's the thing to do. The great Phil Claussen, every time things get tough, you run away, right? You must have been a hell of a soldier. When the shooting started, you turned tail and ran, did you?"

"That's enough, Angie."

"You know what that makes you? A coward, that's what. And around here, a coward is no better than roadkill."

"I'm warning you, keep it up, and I won't be responsible for what happens."

"I'm supposed to be afraid, am I? It'll be a cold day in hell when I'm afraid of somebody like you. See, no matter how bad you might think it is, it's worse. It's not just Dani you'll be letting down. It's our whole community. But that never stopped you before, did it?"

"Christ, you're starting to sound like MaryBeth."

"I don't know who that is, but whoever, she's got you pegged just right. So, why don't you pack up and run along, Phil? You might want to wait until after dark. Then you can creep away like one of those small animals that rummages through the garbage then runs away before the sun comes up."

He thought she was going to smack him, but she just took a step back and shook her head slowly, like he was the biggest disappointment she'd ever come across. He'd rather get smacked.

Then Angie tore out in a cloud of dust. Just him now. He looked for comfort in the only place he could think of, his refrigerator. One beer, one lousy beer, not enough to even get started. Getting run out of town was becoming a habit, one he didn't like at all. But he was still a free man, wasn't he? He could still fire up the RV and leave Clayton, OK in the dust, a weird memory, nothing more. That illusion lasted until he actually tried it until he took his seat behind the wheel and found he couldn't turn the ignition key and his foot poised above the accelerator but wouldn't actually make contact. No, he wasn't going anywhere soon.

He walked down to the pond. Early evening now, a few frogs getting tuned up for their evening chorus. He took off his shoes and waded along the shoreline until darkness set in. Only then did he go back to the RV to begin what would be a sleepless night.

****

Dani didn't show up until the middle of the afternoon the following day. By then, he must have walked from the RV to the road and back a dozen times, afraid she wouldn't come. He waited beside the RV. She drove up alongside and rolled down her window. "You're still here," she said. He'd never seen her eyes red like that, still brimming with tears, and it was all his fault.

He didn't plan to say it, didn't even think about it. It just popped out as natural as the sun coming up, and he was completely, totally sure it was the right thing to do. "I can't lose you. I love you. I'll do anything you say." Now it was all perfectly clear. So long as he could hold her close, everything else was a distant second.

"I'm glad you finally figured that out." She got out of the car and wrapped her arms around his waist. "Does your face still hurt?"

"Why, are you going to hit me again?"

"Not unless you start talking crazy." She pulled him closer. "What made you change your mind?"

"It seems like it changed itself when I realized that the most important thing in the world to me is you. Everything else is just so much stuff. It doesn't really matter. You are what's important, nothing else."

"Thank God," she said.

"Let's go for a swim," he said.

"A swim? You really are crazy after all."

"It's your fault," he said. "Let's go."

A light mist was forming along the shoreline. They stripped down and swam out toward the middle of the pond. She wrapped her legs around his waist, her arms around his neck. "Tell me again that you love me."

"I love you. I'll say it a thousand times if you want me to. Of course, I'll probably drown in the process."

"You won't drown. I know CPR."

"I was counting on that," he said.

"Anyway, you'd better get started. You have a long way to go."

****

He got in to see Sandra Newton the next day without an appointment. Her secretary said the magic words: "She's been waiting for you." Wasn't everybody?

"Mr. Claussen, I can't tell you how glad I am to see you again. I hope you're bringing good news."

"I'm ready to sign the papers."

She smiled like he'd just handed her a million bucks, although, from what she told him earlier, he'd still have plenty to spare. Then she walked over and wrapped her arms around him. He'd never been hugged by a lawyer before.

"I have everything ready here in this folder," she said. "Why don't you take my chair, then you can sign right on the desk. I'll walk you through them."

He gave up trying to follow her explanations. Lawyer-speak was way above his pay grade, so he signed wherever she pointed.

Some twenty or thirty minutes later, she said,

"There, all done. There will be some other stuff later. Sy had some out-of-state holdings, and the paperwork isn't all in yet. As soon as I have it, I'll let you know."

"Thank you," he said. "You've made this relatively painless."

"I should thank you. You've taken a huge load off my mind."

"Then maybe you can take a load off mine too. I don't know why it was so urgent for me to sign the papers, and I don't know why it couldn't be one of the family members instead."

"There are things you should know, Mr. Claussen, about Sy and his family.

"So, he did have other family besides his two nieces. Why on earth am I the beneficiary and not a family member?"

"That's what I'm going to tell you. Sy has a brother named Fletcher Birch. He lives right here in town. He and Sy were business partners for years and did very well for themselves, but some eight years ago, they split up, very acrimonious, several lawsuits. It seems that Mr. Fletcher Birch was skimming funds from their repo company, and Sy found out. They were sworn enemies ever since, so there is no way Sy was going to let Fletcher get his hands on the business."

"Any other family?"

"Two nieces, Fletcher's daughters. You've met them. There are rumors of an illegitimate son, but I've checked into this, and there's no proof whatever. The two nieces were never close to Fletcher. Stories circulated about Fletcher beating their mother. Put her in the hospital several times. After their mother's death, the girls took up with Sy, became like surrogate daughters. Needless to say, this left Fletcher Birch a very unhappy man."

"Why didn't Sy leave everything to them? They were his only remaining family, right?"

"Sy was as good a man as you'll ever meet, a real true gentleman. But I don't think he believed his nieces would be able to keep Fletcher from grabbing up the business and the estate. He needed a man, and only one man would do…you."

"Still doesn't make sense to me. Ms. Newton, all I know about the repo business can be written on the back of a postage stamp. You can grab any guy off the street, and, chances are, he'll know more about repo than I do."

"Knowing about the repo business was not Sy's main concern. His nieces know plenty about that, and I'm not sure how long that will last now that Sy is gone. He was mainly interested in character, a man he could trust. Seymour Birch cut a very large figure in this area and, in his own way, left a substantial legacy, much more than just money. Perhaps even more than his property, he chose you to carry on that legacy for the sake of his community."

"This is too much," Phil said. "I don't know what to say."

"Give things a little while to settle in. Then we can talk more if you wish. I'll be happy to help you any way I can."

"I'm sure I'll need lots of help. I have no idea how to manage a place as big as Sy's. And there's still one great big question. When he got shot, why didn't he put up a fight?"

"I can answer part of that. Sy was dying…cancer.

He saw a doctor in Oklahoma City, so I don't think anybody else around here knew about the diagnosis. He told me several times, the thing he dreaded most was not being able to take care of himself. That terrified him, becoming dependent. He might have thought that whoever pulled the trigger was doing him a big favor."

He could almost imagine Sy smiling at his assassin. How do you shoot a guy who's smiling back at you?

"So, that's why he was in such a big hurry to find somebody to take over."

"Exactly, you came along at just the right time. I look forward to seeing you again, Mr. Claussen, and I should tell you, a warning, if you will, some people are going to be very unhappy that Sy named you as his heir."

"So, it's a good news, bad news kind of deal. I should have guessed as much."

"These things often are. If I hear of any signs of trouble, I'll let you know immediately. Just be aware that there are powerful people who covet what you have inherited. I don't think they'll try anything directly at you. Word has already gotten out about how you took care of the thugs who came out to your RV. I expect they'll try something different like contesting the will, but I promise you, I worked long and hard to make it absolutely airtight."

****

When he got back to the RV, Dani was making a sandwich in the kitchen. She was wearing a hot pink bikini, and her hair was wet, skin glistening. "I just went for another swim in the pond. I'd have waited if I knew you'd be back so soon. I really like swimming with you."

She winked at him, and there was no helping what happened next. He had more news to share, but it would have to wait. He lifted her off the floor and carried her back to the bedroom, back to the poor battered bed, already subjected to abuse the likes of which the builder never intended, where they bounced around like a pair of otters at play. Once, during a particularly vigorous surge, she burst into laughter, bubbly laughter, like a kid who'd just found twenty bucks on the sidewalk.

"What's funny?" he gasped, laughter not being a sound a guy usually heard in the bedroom, at least, not in a complimentary way.

"I'm just happy," she said.

Of course, that was just Dani being Dani. He should have known.

Still breathless, she said, "That must have been a great meeting you had with the attorney. I should send you there more often."

"It was a little bit crazy. How about we get dressed and go out for an early dinner?"

She draped a limp forearm across her brow like a '40s movie heroine. "Oh, no, he's tired of my cooking. Next, he'll be after a younger woman."

He turned her onto her side and gave her a smart smack on the backside. "Your cooking is fine. It's your acting that kills me."

"Just for that, I won't let you go until you kiss it and make it better." She pointed to the cheek he'd just swatted.

"Hey, I left a mark. What do folks around here do to mark their women? I mean, they brand their cattle, don't they? Don't suppose you could do that with ladies, though. Maybe just a little one?"

In a flash, she was astride him, her hands pressing down on his chest. "Phil Claussen, what the hell's got into you? The very idea, branding me."

"Just joking, that's all." But the jostling reignited his penis, which now pressed against her backside.

"Now I guess you want to do me again."

"Seems like a great idea to me," he said.

She slipped him inside her and began a slow, rocking motion.

They had an uncanny ability to reach climax together, which brought a happy groan from Phil and a squeal from Dani. All the other momentous events of that morning, stuff that had caused him to wrinkle his brow and scratch his head and wonder about the ninety-degree turn his life had just taken, didn't matter now, gone away like a puff of smoke. All that mattered were a couple of blue eyes so close to his own that their noses were touching.

Later, as they were getting dressed, she said, "You know, if you can't see a girl's brand until you get her pants off, it's a little too late, don't you reckon?"

"Probably not my best idea."

"There's an easier way." She gave him another wink, just as lascivious as the one that got them started in the first place, but with a quirky little smile, suggesting something new might be on the table. He thought he caught what she had in mind, and if that was the case, they were a lot closer to establishing ownership by a trip to the altar. He was now unencumbered by any matrimonial bonds and free to create his future however he chose.

****

Eddie's Steak House, a modest brick building with

an unlit sign, sat a good fifty yards off the main drag opposite a veterinary clinic. Phil had driven right past it on the way to his meeting with his attorney and would have gone past it again if Dani hadn't pointed it out to him. When he saw the veterinary clinic building, he said, "You've got to be kidding."

"The same guy owns both," Dani said. "He serves up a good steak. You'll see."

"I just want to be sure where he gets his beef."

"The usual place, silly, now behave and enjoy yourself."

Eddie's had no bar. This was the first thing to catch Phil's eye, so perhaps they really were all about the food. White tablecloths were another plus.

Unobtrusive would be the best word to describe their waiter, in addition to being courteous and efficient, of course, and best of all, he wasn't chewing gum. Except for the fact that things appeared and disappeared exactly when they should, you'd hardly know he was there. Where in the world had Eddie's found someone like him?

"I like this place," Dani said. "Thanks for bringing me."

"I should thank you. Otherwise, I would never have known about it. And did I say you look especially lovely this evening?" Yeah, this evening was looking more and more special.

"Thanks, you might just become my favorite dinner date, or at least near the top of the list." This message came with a wink and a grin that might be interpreted any one of a half dozen different ways.

"That's good to know because you're certainly in my top five," he said." But I'm sure you can work your way up the list if you try."

Phil ordered an expensive red burgundy to go with the steaks and immediately offered up a toast. "To a long and happy stay in Clayton, OK, with the most beautiful woman on the planet."

"Oh, wow, we'll definitely have to come back here again," Dani said.

After a dinner of rib eye steaks done up in true medium-rare fashion, just the way he liked, they split a chocolate sundae. He had plans for the cherry on top, but Dani was too quick, and it was gone before he even had his spoon in hand. All he got was a satisfied grin as the cherry disappeared between her lips.

"So, you knew, didn't you, about the will, even before I went to see the attorney the first time?"

"I never laid eyes on his will, honest," she said in complete but unconvincing innocence.

"Maybe you didn't see it, but you knew about it, how he would name me as beneficiary."

"He might have mentioned it. I don't recall." She added a grin that said, *yes, I'm lying, and you know I'm lying, and I know you know I'm lying*. All just a part of the plan. The big surprise for Phil was apparently old news for Dani.

"Anyway, it's a wonderful piece of property, and it will be perfect for you. The part you've seen, the campground, is only a small part of it. There's another lake, a lot larger than the pond, and one corner of the property stretches all the way out to the interstate. That piece is worth a lot of money." She took his hand. "But you still don't seem very happy about it. What's bothering you?"

"I'm still trying to get my head around it. I mean,

going from an RV to a thousand acres is a big jump."

"Of course, it will mean you'll have to stay on here, you know, commitment. Does that scare you?"

"What do you think?"

When they got back to the RV, she opened a bottle of Glenfiddich that she provided herself, her own private stock, apparently, and poured them each a generous shot. "You never told me, did you enjoy your steak?"

"It was a great steak, thank you." A great steak and a beautiful woman sitting across from him, most men would kill for such an evening.

That night Phil got a perfunctory kiss on the cheek. "I'll let you sleep alone tonight, don't want to rush you or anything. I know you have a lot to think about, including me, and I'm worth more than a thousand acres, even if it does come with a lake." With that, she adjourned to her separate bedroom.

Chapter Fifteen

Since Dani had left earlier with no word of where she was going, what she would be doing, or when she would return, all as usual, he phoned Earl. "You know your way around Sy's place?"

"Your place, you mean, from what I hear. Congratulations."

"Word gets around quick," Phil said.

"It does around here, yeah. Big changes for you. How do you feel?"

"Shell-shocked. It still doesn't make any sense. I keep expecting the lawyer to call and tell me it was all a big mistake, or maybe Sy was crazy after all."

"Crazy like a fox, they say. Sy never was one for making rash decisions. He would have thought this through from every angle, believe me."

"He could have warned me; to go from an RV to a thousand acres in one afternoon, that's too much to handle. I'm already worried I'll screw everything up, make a big mess out of it all."

"That won't happen. He had a lot of confidence in you. If you want to get a look at the property, I've got just the thing. I can be there in about twenty minutes." Earl said. A half-hour later, his big truck pulled up next to Sy's house. "Help me pull this ramp down."

In the back of his truck sat a vehicle that looked like a turbocharged golf cart.

"This thing will take us anywhere you want to go." He slowly backed the dark blue ATV down the ramp and motioned for Phil to take the seat beside him. "She's all gassed up and ready to roll."

"Where did you get it?" Phil asked.

"Repo. Not all of the repo deals work out. If they don't, we still got the merchandise until somebody pays. I can get one for you if you want it."

The ATV dwarfed the Peerless mower that had originally gotten Phil in hot water, but now, if he wanted the bigger rig, he wouldn't have to ask anybody's permission, and he could park it wherever he damned well pleased.

Earl drove down the lane past Phil's RV, which, if RVs could express emotion, looked unhappy and abandoned, then turned left into the pines. There was no track here as the pines got thicker, but Earl seemed to know where he was going. "Lots of timber back here," he said.

They climbed a small hill, ringed by pines but clear on top except for knee-deep growth of prairie grass. "Maybe somebody thought about building a house up here, but it never happened," Earl said.

On and on they went, from forest to clearing and back again. Phil glanced at his watch. At least thirty minutes had passed since they set out, and while the ATV wasn't exactly tearing along, they'd come a considerable distance.

"How far, Earl? We must have come a couple of miles, maybe three?"

"Close to it. See, the property is pie-shaped, and we're nearing the pointy end. On a map, looks like somebody took a big bite off of it."

"My God, is that traffic I hear, like interstate?" Phil said.

"You hear right, my friend. Your new estate fronts over a quarter mile on the interstate. Give you any ideas?" Earl asked.

"Nothing but makes me wonder more at why Sy did what he did."

"He always had a reason, always. Anyway, we haven't seen the lake yet," Earl turned back in the general direction they'd come from.

"Dani mentioned something about a lake, said it was big."

"Oh, yeah, makes the pond look like…a pond."

They meandered along, crossing ground that, while undulating, seemed primarily flat. The wooded areas consisted mainly of pine trees with the occasional hardwood thrown in, but it was mostly new-growth timber. They crossed a treeless rise.

"Get ready," Earl said.

In front of them lay a broad lake, much of the shoreline ringed with low shrubs, but some cleared beach areas as well.

In spite of himself, Phil uttered a short gasp.

"Something, ain't it?" Earl said. "Almost fifteen acres, as pretty a lake as you'll find anywhere."

"Does anybody know it's back here?" Phil asked.

"Yeah, some of the local kids do. When we get a little closer, you'll see some beer cans, rubbers, the usual stuff. I came back here with Sy a few times, but it's hard to get a boat through here," Earl said. "Be easy enough to cut a road through, then you could come and go as you pleased."

"Fish?"

"Damned lake is full of large-mouthed bass. They'll bite anything you throw in. It's almost too easy. See, you clear out some of the brush along here, and you'll have a first-rate beach. I know a guy who'll cut it out for you cheap." Earl drove slowly around the lake. "I think you're going to enjoy it here. Of course, once you get your boat, I expect you to take me fishing on a regular basis."

"For sure," Phil said. "How did Sy go about accumulating all of this? He win the lottery?"

"You'd never know it to look at him, before he got shot, of course, but he was a big deal for a lot of years. You could call him the godfather of the repo business. Back then, he covered three states. Anybody needed their stuff recovered, their paperwork came to Sy. He was into other things too, but Dani will tell you all about that."

****

Dinner for two became dinner for one when Dani called shortly after six. "I won't be back tonight. Had some complications."

"Are you in trouble?" Phil asked.

"No, just a few things to straighten out. I'm fine. So, where will you sleep tonight?"

"RV," he said.

"Not ready to make the leap yet, huh?"

"Got some thinking to do first."

"Don't start thinking without me, you hear me? I have something to say, too, where you're concerned."

"I don't suppose you could tell me now," he said.

"No, I have to run. But I mean it, no thinking, no decisions without me. Just get drunk if you have to, but do not think."

He returned Dani's steak to the freezer then dropped his own over the smoking grill. The sizzle sent his salivary glands into overdrive. He'd promised himself he would cut back on red meat consumption, but not tonight. Tonight he would tear into that steak like something primal.

He had strung up an overhead light that would have illuminated the entire campsite, but he left it off. Instead, he would enjoy the twilight. A candle on the table was all he needed. This was becoming his favorite time of day, the quiet as darkness crept in, noises as small animals—he hoped they were small—scurried about in the bushes.

But something else crept in too. He caught the movement out of the corner of his eye. His hand went instinctively to the gun, which he now carried in a holster, *like a real cowboy*. As his domestic situation became more and more weird, he became more and more cautious. The gun would be a last resort, but it was there if needed.

He pointed the weapon in the direction of the movement. "You'd better come on out. I'm not likely to miss at this distance." An empty threat because, due to his incompetence with firearms, he was quite likely to miss at almost any distance.

A medium-sized dog crept into the dim circle of light cast by the candle. When the beast got a bit closer, Phil could see its ribs protruding. This dog was starving.

"Get out of here. I know what you want, and you're not getting any of my steak," he said, but he knew that wouldn't hold up. He couldn't very well stuff himself with a hungry animal watching him. He flipped the steak over onto the uncooked side. "You probably don't care whether it's cooked or not, do you? I'll share, but you're going to have to wait for a minute while it cools off."

He set aside the piece he'd cut away from the steak. It wasn't going to be nearly enough to quell the poor dog's hunger, but dammit, he was hungry himself, and he'd paid good money for this steak.

"Should have chased you off in the first place." The dog caught the morsel he tossed in mid-air. It disappeared in nothing flat. The mongrel crept closer, tail wagging even more furiously.

Phil placed his steak on a plate and began to eat as quickly as he could, but savoring this piece of beef was not in the cards, not tonight. How could he enjoy his meal with big eyes staring at him from an emaciated face?

He finished about half of the steak. The rest he cut up into several pieces, hoping the dog would have to slow down and eat them one at a time. Wrong. Two quick passes over the plate by a broad, pink tongue, and it was wiped clean.

"You shouldn't eat so damned fast. It's bad for your digestion. And that's all. I got nothing else for you, so take off."

But the dog stayed put, and its tail didn't stop wagging, and its hopeful gaze never left Phil's face.

This would not do. Phil Claussen had a soft spot, a big one, and the damned, emaciated dog had jumped right into it, all four feet at once. He checked the freezer. Dani's steak was not yet frozen. Maybe she wouldn't notice if he cut off a small piece.

He tossed the uncooked meat on the grill and

waited. The dog's tail looked like a windshield wiper at high speed.

The aroma of sizzling beef revived his own appetite, and as he carved the meat into smaller chunks, he remembered that he'd already given the dog a sizeable portion of his own steak. Now he wanted more…for himself.

He brought out the rest of Dani's steak. He could replace it with a quick trip to the market. When he placed it on the grill, the dog began dancing in close circles.

"Forget about it. You've already had plenty." The dog kept on dancing.

Between the two of them, they made quick work of the remaining beef. "You ever tell anybody about this, and you're history, understand?" Phil's attempt at a gruff tone either missed its mark, or the dog decided to ignore it. It lay down at Phil's feet and gazed upward with a look of pure adoration.

"Oh no, I see what you're up to, and you're not staying around here. Get up. Go away." He nudged the dog with his foot, but the dog, apparently mistaking this for a sign of affection, licked his shoe. A kick would have been more effective, but he couldn't bring himself to do it. "You'd better be gone in the morning." It was the best he could do. His was a hollow threat, and man and dog, one of nature's more basic units, sat beside a charcoal grill while the coals grew dim in the darkness.

****

His warning apparently worked because, when he looked out the door of the RV the next morning…no dog. Yes, the dog had moved, but not very far, only to the chair where Phil sat the night before. It was, at the moment, lying on its back, feet in the air, while Dani gave it a belly rub.

"I see you've found a new friend," she said.

The dog confirmed it by running over to Phil, looking up with that look of pure, unreserved love and affection. "He's not my friend. He just walked up last night."

"Well, for sure, he has a big crush on you."

"I just need to know how to get rid of him."

"I don't think you're going to." She walked over and gave Phil a kiss. "You're stuck with both of us. Now, I need coffee, and some breakfast would be nice. And something for your new friend, too."

"I didn't expect you back so early," he said as they climbed back into the RV.

"It was the middle of the night, and I didn't want to wake you, so I slept in the car."

"Where's the car?"

"Back in the trees."

"The old hidden vehicle trick, eh?"

"Yeah, now stop talking and start cooking, or I'll have to get rough with you." She poured her own coffee. "What's on your agenda for today?"

"I have to go back to the attorney. She has more papers for me to sign, insurance forms, and such."

"You're getting in deeper and deeper," she said.

"Yeah." Getting out from underneath it all would be difficult now and getting more difficult every day. Was he past the point of no return? Damned close, for sure. Dani sat watching him, that little Cheshire Cat grin of hers playing above the rim of her coffee cup like she knew exactly what he was thinking.

He managed to put together a passable breakfast of

bacon and scrambled eggs with toast on the side. Dani finished half of hers then took her plate outside to the dog. "We're never going to get rid of him if you keep feeding him," he said.

"I know," she said. "I plan to use the same trick on you."

****

It must have been a day for wicked grins. He got another one from the receptionist in the attorney's office, the same one who'd brushed up against him on his last visit. She didn't look old enough to vote, but she felt confident enough to shoot a come-hither look at a man almost twice her age.

It was just a game, risky, but still a game. He used to get similar looks from a few of his high school students. For them, it was just practice, a warm-up for the times they would send out the signal for real. In a few years, his own daughter would be old enough to play that game if she wasn't doing it already. The thought twisted his gut into tiny knots.

"Are you okay, Mr. Claussen?" The receptionist looked more disappointed than concerned. "You look a little green."

"Something I had for breakfast. No problem," he said.

No grin from the attorney, though, just another stack of forms that he signed without reading.

"We should plan to meet on a regular basis, so I can update you on your out-of-state holdings."

"Out-of-state?" He must have sounded like a complete idiot, blurting out like that.

"It gets a bit complicated. There are a couple of smaller properties in Texas you need to be aware of. It won't take up much of your time. Are you getting adjusted to your new estate?" she asked.

"I'm still living in my RV. One thing I don't understand," Phil said, "Why didn't Sy just write it into the contract that the oil reserves would never be developed? I mean, if he wanted to keep things the same forever, why not put it in writing and be sure?"

"Sy asked me that same question. The problem is that sort of restriction would never hold up. Sooner or later, some smart attorney would find a way around it, then game over. Clayton becomes just another oil field. Sy knew what he wanted, but the final choice about the property had to be yours. When you've been here for a while and get to know Clayton people and their ways, I think you'll understand why he left that choice up to you."

"But he'd only known me for a few weeks," Phil said. "How could he know I wouldn't sell out and leave town?"

His attorney walked over to her window and stood looking at the light traffic in the street below. The tension in her shoulders was obvious across the room. "Sy had this uncanny ability to read people. I don't know how he did it, but I never knew him to be wrong. He was absolutely sure about you, and that's good enough for me," she said.

"Something else I thought about on the way over. My divorce papers have come through, so that shouldn't be a problem. I should have mentioned it before, but that shouldn't complicate things, should it?" he asked.

"I knew about that when I wrote up the original papers for Sy. I need to see your divorce decree to make sure everything is in order."

"Okay, Dani has the papers. I'll bring them over."

"Well, then, the sooner things are settled, the better. Let me know what you want to do and when you want to do it. I can tell you that Sy would not have wanted his legacy split up."

Added to the weight of ownership of a huge estate that seemed to get bigger every time he visited Sandra Newton's office, Phil now felt the responsibility of preservation of the property in its present condition. If he understood correctly, he'd just become the *keeper of the flame*, the man who would fend off those wanting to transform that same estate into an oil-producing, money-making enterprise. And the choice supposedly was his, but there was no choice, was there? Signing on the dotted line, as he'd done so many times in this office, was a promise, a pledge to preserve and protect Clayton, OK, from all comers. Seymour Birch had done him no favors by naming him as heir.

****

When he got back to the campsite, Dani was giving the dog a bath. Somehow she'd coaxed him into a large aluminum tub, and he was so covered in lather that he looked like a very large ice cream cone with lots of whipped cream and legs, of course. As soon as the dog spotted Phil, his tail began wagging briskly, showering Dani with suds.

She wiped the soap off her face. "I should make you finish this."

"Whatever gave you the idea of giving that beast a bath?"

"Fleas," she said. "He's covered in them. This soap is supposed to kill them off. Once I get him cleaned up, we can take him to the vet, get him checked out. His name is Alfie, now."

"Alfie? Why did you name him Alfie?" *Yeah, out of the thousands of names she could pin on a dog, why that one?* The hair on the back of his neck began to prickle again.

"It's a cute name." All smiles, she was, as if she was very proud of herself. "You don't like it?" But she knew he did, had to.

"It's just that, when I was a kid, I had a dog named Alfie, looked a lot like this mutt."

Alfie responded with more vigorous tail wagging, showering Dani with more soap suds. Damn, was the dog in on it too?

"So, maybe your Alfie has come back," she said. The look she gave him, the left eyebrow arched, that mysterious grin suggested that the dog's return from wherever was exactly what had just happened.

"No way," Phil said, hoping he sounded more convincing than he felt. "That was over twenty years ago, and my poor Alfie was hit by a truck. I saw it happen."

"Then, this is your new Alfie."

"This is too weird," he said, "you picking that name out of the blue."

"It's a cute name, and you like it too, so that's all there is to it."

"It's fine, but it sure looks like you're planning some permanent arrangement here. What if he turns out to be someone else's dog?"

"I'll ask the vet if anyone has reported a lost dog. If not, he's ours, right Alfie?"

Ours, Phil caught that quickly enough, not yours or

mine…ours.

He emptied Alfie's bath water in the woods while Dani dried him with a towel. Next, she produced a new leather collar that she buckled around the dog's neck. "See, I made a little tag with his name on it."

Alfie bounded over to Phil's side as if presenting himself for inspection. "Yeah, you look pretty sharp now, and for certain, you smell a lot better. How did you get the name tags made so fast?"

Her deep, knowing laugh made him tingle in the damndest places but did not answer his question.

"I've got connections," she said, winking at him. "Don't complicate everything, sweetie. Just take it as it comes and enjoy it. That's the best advice I can give you."

Basically the same advice he'd gotten from Earl and from everybody else: *just sit there and smile, and we'll tell you what you need to know when you need to know it, not before.*

She ended the discussion with a kiss, after which his mind always became a hopeless muddle, but she knew, dammit, he was sure of it. She knew about Alfie, the rangy dog that had been his constant companion through his grammar school days, right up until his sophomore year in high school, when the poor animal dashed across the road to greet him and wound up crushed beneath the wheels of a construction vehicle. The driver didn't even slow down.

Phil dragged the bloodied carcass home and buried it in the backyard. Alfie's eyes were still open, not yet clouded over with death, and Phil closed them gently before easing the body into the hole he'd dug.

But was there any way under heaven that Dani

could have known about that? No, absolutely not, this was craziness, looney thinking, but somehow she did; he'd bet his life on it. He groaned, a drowning man in way over his head, and lost, hopelessly lost.

Chapter Sixteen

"And I have another surprise for you, too," Dani said. "Follow me." She led him back into the trees where she usually stashed her luxury autos.

There, parked between two large pines, sat a huge, gleaming pickup, much like Earl's, except this one was bright red and had a standard bumper rather than a steel girder. "Do you like it?" she asked.

"It's gorgeous, but where did you get it?"

"It's a repo, only seven thousand miles on it. I've been looking for one for you. You're more a big truck guy, I think. Our little sedan doesn't do you justice."

He climbed into the cab where he sat up high like in the RV, but that's where the similarity ended. She handed him the keys, and when he fired it up, the engine sounded like a large hungry animal.

But the fantasy was short-lived. "This is too much, Dani. This thing is worth a lot of money."

"You deserve it."

"No, I don't. I haven't done one damned thing to deserve this, or Sy's estate, or you. It's all been dumped into my lap. I have to do something. I need a job."

"A job? Why do you need a job?"

"A man has to work, Dani. Otherwise, he's a bum."

"But then you won't be here. You'll be off doing stuff. I like having you here when I come back." A little girl pout that he hadn't seen before. "You've ruined my surprise." She seemed to have an endless repertoire, all of it effective at making his knees go weak.

"I didn't mean to do that. This is such a sweet, gorgeous thing you've done, and it means more to me than I can tell you. But I need a job. I need to work." He wasn't really sure where the job thing had come from, just popped up, but now that it was on the table, he had to follow through. The only thing worse than being jobless was talking about it and not even looking for one.

When he climbed out of the truck, she wrapped her arms around his neck and pressed her face against his chest. She spoke in a whisper. "I want to be close to you almost all the time. Even when I'm away, I'm thinking about you. Remember that when you're out job hunting, and don't sign up for anything until you hear what I have to offer."

Yeah, a job, he got that far, at least. But the next day, when Dani was out working, repossessing vehicles if that's what she really did when she was away, he sat staring at the big truck, thinking how limited his job prospects might be. After his stint in the military, he'd spent his entire working life in education, most of it at the high school level. But what were the chances he could land a similar job after he'd made such a mess of the last one? What would happen when the local school board called back to Wakefield: "What kind of man is Phil Claussen?" Well, up until recently, a pretty good one, until he ran off the rails, got tossed in jail. Nope, a return to the education field didn't look too promising.

After half a day of dreaming up ideas for employment he would be unlikely to get, he ambled down to his pond and pushed the skiff out on the water.

He drifted there for a while, watching clouds, trying to concentrate on jobs, but instead, thinking about how much fun he would have boating on the larger lake. Of course, he would need a bigger boat. Perhaps Dani could work another repo deal for him. Big truck, big boat, might as well go out in style.

When he got back to the RV, she was waiting for him, standing beside a gleaming vehicle that he recognized only from photos in upscale magazines. "Is that what I think it is?

"Yep, Silver Streak." She posed beside it like a big game hunter who had just bagged an elephant.

"Where did you get it?"

"Don't ask. This is our top repo for the year, maybe ever. How someone could miss payments on a car like this is beyond me."

"Closest I've ever been to one of these…Silver Streak."

"Don't get too attached," Dani said. "I'll be moving it out tomorrow, or the next day at the latest. Hey, I brought a pizza. It's inside."

A pizza delivered in a Silver Streak, just too much. But one of the best things about pizza, almost no cleanup. He took care of what little there was to do, including giving Alfie the two slices they'd saved for him.

"If you don't mind, I think I'll take a nap. Rescuing a car like this can take it out of a girl. You can join me if you like."

"You won't get much sleep if I do," he said. "Maybe I'll walk off some of that pizza." Alfie ran rings around him, always ready for a walk, and he now had a thousand acres for his hikes. This could get to be routine very quickly, and not a bad one at that.

The hike stretched into a marathon since Alfie seemed to be having so much fun exploring, and it was late when they got back. In spite of the warm evening, he built a fire in the fire pit, as much for the dog as for himself. Alfie stretched out just beyond the glowing embers, staring into them as if deep in thought, which, for all anyone knew, he might be.

By the time her long nap was finished and Dani rejoined him, a new moon was just above the horizon. She brought out her bottle of single malt scotch and two glasses. "Join me? If I can't get you into bed the regular way, maybe I'll get you drunk, see if that will increase my chances."

She pulled her chair closer to the fire and appeared to be inhaling the smoky output from the flames. "Alfie seems to be enjoying himself."

"Yeah, but don't go giving him any scotch. Next, he'll want his own set of keys to the RV."

"I can tell from your expression that you've been thinking again, even though I asked you not to do it. What is it now?"

Phil told her about his afternoon thinking about jobs and how he wished he hadn't left his previous position under such bad circumstances. "They could be a big help to me, so long as they don't all hate me. A nice letter of recommendation could go a long way when I'm out looking for work."

She peered into the glowing coals. "You can still get a letter of recommendation if you want it. The charges against you were reduced to a misdemeanor, and the people at your school still think highly of you."

"How would you know about that? You're

guessing."

"I have a law degree," she said, "and friends."

"Whoa, you've investigated me, too?"

"Who else?" she asked.

"Sandra Newton said Sy had run a background check on me, and you say you did one. People back in Wakefield must wonder what the hell I've been up to. Why? I could have told you anything you wanted to know about me."

"You're important to me." She stopped the sentence abruptly, as if she wanted to say more, but, for some reason, did not or could not.

"What else did you dig up?"

She walked a short distance from the fire, came back, and knelt beside his chair. "I know your school hasn't filled your old position."

"So, I could go back to my old life if I wanted to."

She wouldn't meet his gaze. "Yes, you could, but you're supposed to stay here with me. Remember, you promised."

"Yeah, I remember." He pulled her onto his lap, and the spindly camp chair groaned, then collapsed, spilling them both onto the ground. They lay there laughing. "Are you hurt?" she asked.

He shook his head. "You?"

"I'm good. I landed on you."

Alfie obviously thought this was all a new game and tried to join the pile of bodies before Dani chased him away.

"Let's take a walk down to the pond," he said.

"I thought you'd just taken a long hike."

"I did, but the moon is up, and it should be pretty," he said.

"Ah, you're going all romantic on me. I like it."

They held hands along the way, like a couple of infatuated teenagers, and no more was said about Phil returning to his old life. His new world, the one walking alongside him, looked better every day.

The new moon had already climbed high into the sky, casting a surprising amount of brightness for such a slim crescent. She wrapped her arms around his waist. "I want it to be like this, always."

"I just remembered, months ago, when I first started on this trip, I met a lady with a dog at a campground. We talked a little, I told her more about my troubles than I ever intended to, but she was a good listener, her dog too. After I finished babbling, she said that even though I seemed to be running away from a bad situation, it might be the other way around. That I was running toward something that I didn't even know about yet. That didn't make sense then, but now, maybe it does. Maybe this is it, has been all along."

"Well, finally at long last, you've figured it out," Dani said. "And your campground lady was absolutely right."

She moved her arms from his waist to his neck, moved her face up close to his. He could feel her breath, taste it, like some intoxicating fruit that seemed to lift him ever so slightly off the ground. "You don't really need me to explain anything. You figured it out all by yourself, but if you want to, you can always ask more questions."

"But I'm not going to get answers, right?"

"Not exactly, now kiss me, then get undressed, unless you plan to swim with your clothes on.

She was much quicker. In no time at all, she stood

there before him, a naked vision bathed in moonlight. As she slid his shorts down, his semi-erect penis emerged. She took it in her hand, kissed it, and it immediately went on full alert. "We'll have to do something about this later," she said. "Now, come on, everybody in the pond."

Alfie apparently did not find adult swimming games to his liking and lay down on the beach waiting for them to finish with their foolishness.

"Odd," Phil said, looking down at the dog, "my other Alfie didn't care for swimming either."

Chapter Seventeen

"I've been thinking," he said the next morning as they had their coffee out by the picnic table.

"No thinking, Phil, we talked about that several times."

"Hear me out first," he said. "I'm thinking that nobody is going to hire a guy who lives in an RV. I need a permanent address. So I thought more about moving into Sy's house, establish residence."

She closed and opened her eyes a few times as if she wasn't sure what she was hearing. "Moving in? For real?"

"Yeah, I won't take long to move. I don't have that much stuff. I'll be in before noon. We can bring your things over whenever you like."

"You're going to love it here. I know you will. And don't worry too much about the job. If you find a good one, okay, but if you don't, that's okay too. We'll get along just great either way." And the way she looked at him, all the promise in her eyes, somehow made everything seem just fine.

So, it began, the next stage in his life. Moving in took longer than he expected because before he could move his stuff in, he had to move Sy's stuff out. Phil had a chance to check out the labels; Sy's three suits were worn at the elbows, but all were from Brooks Brothers. His shirts bore the name of a local tailor.

"Old Sy dressed well when he dressed," Phil said. "I never saw him in anything but T-shirts."

"He cut quite a figure in his younger days, lots of lady friends. Of course, you are restricted to just one…me. Remember that."

The morning's work ran into the early afternoon before they had all of Sy's belongings bagged and sitting on the front porch. "I guess that's about all of his stuff. I'm ready to move mine in," Phil said. "This part shouldn't take very long. I can just back the RV up to the front door and carry it right in."

"No, first we clean."

"Clean? Place looks pretty good to me," Phil said.

She ran a finger along the top of the dresser, then held it up to Phil's face. "See this?"

"What?"

"I'm beginning to think what they say about dirt being invisible to men is true. See, this is dust, and it has to be removed. Now, you start in here, dust and vacuum. Then clean the windows. I'll do the bathrooms and the kitchen."

"That's going to take the rest of the day."

"Maybe, but it has to be done. Now, the sooner you get started, the sooner it will be over and done with."

She stripped down to a skimpy pair of shorts and an even skimpier tank top, and his mind wandered to something much more fun than cleaning.

She must have guessed his intentions—not exactly transparent, was he? "Clean now, play later."

"How much later?"

Her expression registered somewhere between disdain and disgust. "If you don't get started right now, later is going to be sometime next week."

And so it went. House cleaning was light work, something that didn't require much effort, so he thought, but after a couple of hours at it, he was beginning to ache in several new places. Cleaning the windows was his biggest challenge. The more he rubbed, the more streaks he left behind.

"Beer break." Dani brought in a couple of cold ones. "Come along with me. I have another surprise for you."

He wasn't aware of the gleam in his eye, but she must have caught it. "No, that's not the surprise, not what you're thinking." She stopped him with a stern look and a finger poked into his chest. "We have more work to do."

So, he would have to make do with the image of Dani, slightly sweaty, slightly smudged, swaying in front of him, leading him back inside, and that was enough distraction to make him stumble over a chair.

Phil hadn't seen the basement yet, so everything from the time Dani opened the door and flicked on the lights revealing a carpeted staircase was a surprise, just like she promised.

The rest of the finished basement included an office space complete with a fireplace on the far wall and an upright safe at the edge of the seating area. "That's where Sy kept his guns," Dani said. "But I don't know the combination."

"Sandra Newton gave me the combination. Let's take a quick look."

Two more nine-millimeter semi-automatics similar to the one Phil now carried on a regular basis, without really knowing why. Also, a .357 magnum, six-inch barrel, and a shorter version of the same with a two-inch barrel. Sy had been well-stocked with long guns too, three shotguns, twelve-gauge, a 30/30 lever-action rifle, and a military sniper rifle.

"Haven't seen one of these for a while." Phil lifted the sniper rifle out of the case. Why did Sy have it?

"You've fired one of these?" Dani asked.

"A few times. Never could hit anything, though." He returned the rifle to its place. "I have just one question, do we have to clean in here too?"

Dani laughed. "I think you've had your fill of cleaning today. I'll get a cleaning lady to finish up, and she can come in once a week. You won't have to worry about becoming a full-time house cleaner. This was just sort of a test, you know, check out your domestic side, see how well you've been trained."

"I'm not taking any review courses if that's what you're thinking."

"You're going to be just fine, so long as you do exactly as I say." She laughed again and gave him a kiss. "If you're okay here, I'll go get a load of my stuff. It will take a couple of trips."

"I'll come along. We can take the truck, lots more room, get everything at once."

"No, I got it," she said.

"I don't even know where you live."

"Right here with you. That's all you need to know. Be back in no time." Then she was gone.

****

Dani returned with a carload of her belongings, much of which Phil had never seen before. All of the extra closet space was filled quickly, but his previous experience with married life prepared him for that. No matter how much space there seemed to be, it was never enough, and the lady's stuff always took precedence.

"I have to make a quick trip to the market before dinner," Dani said. "Your cupboard is bare. Any special requests?"

"You mean our cupboard, don't you? I guess we need everything. I have a few things in the RV I can bring over. Maybe you could get a bag of chow for the damned dog. I don't think we're going to get rid of him."

"If you're talking about Alfie, he's family now. I officially adopted him, and you're the daddy. Congratulations."

"Great, just what I needed to hear. Hey, what about his fleas?"

"I cured him, so he doesn't have any now unless he catches some from you. I'm going to check with Angie, see if she wants to go shopping with me. See you later."

The breezy front porch seemed a place where a busy mind might tune out, so that's where he headed next, followed closely by Alfie, who could relax almost anywhere.

About a half hour later, Earl parked his big rig on the street out front and joined Phil on the porch. "Danged women have deserted us," he said.

"Just as well," Phil said. "Unless you wanted to go shopping with them."

"Think I'd rather have my fingernails pulled out. You got any more beer?"

Phil passed him a cold one from the cooler he'd brought out to the porch.

"So, you're moving in?" Earl popped the top, flipped the cap into Phil's lap, then took a long swig followed by a thunderous belch.

"Guess so."

"You don't sound too happy about it."

"I don't know. Life got so complicated all of a sudden. I always felt responsible for my own life, like I controlled my destiny, but lately, it seems like things just happen."

Earl laughed so hard beer ran out of his nose. "Destiny? Let me tell you about destiny. See, destiny always gets a bum rap. We think we control it. We all want to be that strong guy who grabs destiny by the throat, slams it up against the wall, then pokes a boney finger in its chest. "Okay, destiny, here's how it's gonna be. And if I ever find out you've been screwing with me, I'll come back here and kick your ass all over the landscape."

Earl was on a roll, and there was nothing to do but sit back and wait for him to finish his speech.

"So, you spell it out, how you want to be President of the United States, but poor destiny can't do a damned thing about it. The book is already written. So, you can rant and rave and bust down doors, but you won't change a thing. Sorry."

That said, another long swig followed by another booming belch woke Alfie from his sleeping spot by Phil's rocking chair. The dog, apparently finding Earl's behavior intolerable, walked to the other side of the porch and resumed his nap.

"Am I supposed to make sense out of what you just said?" Phil asked.

"Don't matter one way or the other. You know, a lot of folks would love to be sitting where you're sitting right now. Let me give you some advice, my friend.

Don't give yourself a headache trying to figure things out. Just take them as they come. Sometimes things will clear up, sometimes they won't. Either way, you won't change anything by cogitating over it."

Earl drained his bottle in one long gulp, then handed the empty to Phil in exchange for a fresh cold one. Phil's hope that Earl's philosophical discourse was over was a false hope as Earl plunged right ahead.

"See, I'm a diehard fatalist, everything being set out in advance. That day when you first picked Dani up on the road—she told me about that—you're still wondering about that, right? Like, what was she doing out there in the middle of nowhere, and you just happened to come along? Well, let me tell you, that was fate asserting itself. Chance had nothing to do with it.

"It wasn't like she caused it to happen; it was going to happen anyway, sort of like you were both following universal orders. She understands that, see? She knew why she was there and why you were there too. It all happened just the way it was supposed to. Oh, I know you came up with a dozen good reasons for doing what you did, but that was all just rationalization, making up reasons for doing what you were going to do all along. Like I said, fate asserting itself. There's no other explanation."

"You're so full of shit."

"Probably, but I'm right, think about it. Now, I need another beer."

"I just gave you one," Phil said.

"Must not have been a full bottle."

Phil had just fished another beer out of the cooler when Dani pulled the car into the driveway alongside the house. Angie sat in the front seat beside her. Dani yelled at them through the open window. "Okay, you two, get off your lazy butts and help us carry this stuff inside."

They both staggered slightly as they walked over to the car.

"I'm warning you, if you drop anything, there's going to be trouble," she said.

There were four boxes in the trunk, and bags of groceries filled the back seat.

"What you got in these boxes?" Earl asked. "Bricks?"

"Just some of my stuff and be careful with it." She shot Phil a withering glance as he passed lugging one of the boxes. "How come every time I leave you two alone, you get drunk?"

After they'd carried the boxes to the bedroom and groceries to the kitchen, Phil and Earl retreated to the porch. Alfie, the traitorous cur, stayed in the kitchen with the girls and the food. "You think we ought to get off at a safer distance?" Earl asked. "Maybe walk over to the pond where it's more peaceful."

"I'm not sure I can walk that far," Phil said. "Besides, I'm hungry."

So, the two men sat side by side on the porch as the evening shadows grew longer. The beer cooler was empty, but to refill it would require a trip to the kitchen, now hostile territory.

Their mutual reverie ended when Angie burst out onto the porch. "Let's go, Earl. I need to get to Stinson's before they close."

"I thought you just went shopping."

"That was different. I need shoes."

"Dang, woman, you got a closet full of shoes

already."

The look she gave him said, in no uncertain terms, the discussion was over. Earl wisely, and with head bowed, followed her out to the truck.

Dani came out as they drove away. "Are they a couple now?" Phil asked, nodding toward the truck."

Dani wagged her hand back and forth. "Just friends, Earl is sort of like a big brother to both of us." She moved in closer to his chair, her hip pressed against his shoulder. "The more important question is, are we a couple?"

The wrong answer here would bring down no end of misery upon his poor head, so he pulled her into his lap and said, sincerely, "Yes, we are, and I want it to stay that way forever."

The correct answer got him a big kiss. When she pulled him to his feet, he wavered ever so slightly. She grabbed him around the waist and towed him toward the door. "I'd better feed you something before you keel over."

There was a small table with seating for two in the corner of the kitchen. She dragged out a chair. "Sit here so I don't have to worry about you falling. Dinner is going to be pretty basic, okay? Just a tuna melt and cream of tomato soup."

"Sounds great to me."

She stayed by his chair for a moment, then knelt beside him. "Look, I have a confession to make. With this great kitchen, all these appliances, and everything, you probably thought you'd be getting a lot of great home-cooked meals."

"Never gave it much thought."

"Well, the truth, I'm not much of a cook. My mom

seldom cooked, so I just never learned. I'm sorry. Maybe you spoke too soon when you said we were a couple."

The correct move—he was batting one thousand so far—which he did without thinking was to lift her up onto his lap again and cover her with kisses. "I meant it. We're a couple. If you cook, that's fine, if you don't cook at all, that's fine too, no problem. So long as you're with me like this, cooking doesn't matter."

"You're sweet," she said. Then he got a bevy of kisses in return. Slowly but surely, he was getting his priorities in order, and whether the arrangement was something of his own choosing or whether he was stumbling along doing what was going to happen anyway made little difference.

Chapter Eighteen

For Sale RV, like new, only 4057 miles. Call for details. He cut little tear-off tabs with his phone number on the bottom of the sheet. Even at three years old, the RV was still pristine. The main bed had had some heavy use, but otherwise, very little wear and tear on the interior. Someone would get a good deal without having to pay showroom prices.

"What are you up to?" Dani pulled a chair up to the kitchen table beside him.

"Making a for sale sign for the RV. Thought I'd post it in the window at the market. Don't know anybody looking for a nice RV, do you?"

"I'll ask around," she said. She didn't seem at all surprised. This was the way things were supposed to be, according to her.

"Think I'll drive over to the market then, stick this in the window, get some bread, milk, and beer. Anything else you need?"

****

He never expected such a quick response, but late that same afternoon, he got a call; Ed and Jenny Winston wanted to come out to look at the RV

The next day, shortly after ten, the Winstons arrived in a small, oval-shaped yellow car, the likes of which Phil hadn't seen for years. They were small people themselves, both about five-seven, maybe one hundred forty pounds each, and looked more like fraternal twins than man and wife. He thought at first, they were kids until, on closer inspection, their facial creases and Ed's thinning hair revealed otherwise. Still, a very pleasant pair, Ed's twinkling eyes reminding him of a smaller version of Sy Birch, God rest his soul.

Introductions completed, they got right to business. "Just two thousand miles?" Ed asked.

"Yeah, I bought it in eastern North Carolina and drove it this far, decided to stay."

"How's she handle?" Ed again.

"No problem at all. Mileage isn't so great, but all of these big rigs are gas guzzlers." Given the diminutive size of the Winston pair, might they require some additional support, a booster seat, a couple of pillows, perhaps, to bring their eye level up to a suitable height in the driver's seat? Nope, Jenny climbed right in, assumed control of the wheel, and pronounced it "just right."

By then, Alfie, apparently assuming his nap was to be irretrievably interrupted, ambled off the front porch and took a seat on the grass beside Ed Winston's left foot.

"Why, hello there, pal." Ed knelt on one knee and scratched Alfie's ears, which produced a flurry of tail-wagging. "I think he likes that," Ed said. "Does he ride around in the RV with you?"

"No, he's a recent acquisition, just wandered up one evening and stayed. Never seemed to want to get into the RV."

"We have a pair of Welsh Corgis," Jenny said. "They go almost everywhere with us. I guess we should have brought them along, make sure they approve of the RV."

"They'll love it," Ed said. "Lots of room to run around, way better than our little car."

Phil spent the next half hour or so demonstrating the various features of the RV, most of which he'd picked up himself since his attention span at the original dealer's in Wakefield had been brief and unfocused.

"She's in beautiful shape," Ed said repeatedly. "Like new, just like your ad said."

Eventually, they gathered at the kitchen table to review the paperwork on the transaction.

"Me and Jenny spent the summer getting our house ready to put on the market, and it sold in the first week. Our plan was to buy a big unit like yours and see the country. We've got grandkids in Denver and a brand new one in Seattle."

"And we were ready to downsize," Jenny said. "Time to make our lives a little less complicated. We're both teachers, just retired at the end of the last term, and we're ready to hit the road."

Downsizing, an uncomplicated life, the freedom of the open road, all of which sounded great, but Phil was headed in the opposite direction on all counts. Did they know something he didn't?

By mid-afternoon, with a very warm September sun just past the zenith, it was all over. The RV was history, as was that brief interlude of freedom in Phil's life. He stood on the porch looking at the now empty space where the RV had sat, trying to wash down his pangs of loss with a beer. Now the Winstons would be taking flight in his home-on-wheels, watching sunsets through his windshield, finding new campgrounds, then moving on to others.

Maybe to prove to himself that he still possessed some degree of mobility, he grabbed the keys to his big pickup from the kitchen counter. Alfie followed him out to the truck.

"You wanna go for a ride?" Phil asked.

The phrase *want to go for a ride?* must be part of some universal dog vocabulary. Alfie ran to the rear of the truck and waited, tail wagging, for Phil to let down the tailgate. The dog bounded into the truck's spacious bed as if this was something he did every day. Phil thought he might opt for the cushy seat inside the vehicle, but no, Alfie seemed to think the open space was the best of all possible worlds, giving him free rein to run around and bark at anything that caught his attention. More truck rides for Alfie went on Phil's list of things to do.

He drove around county roads past vast open spaces containing far more cattle than people but saw nothing to compare to the oasis Sy had left to him. He drove out the same road he'd taken on that first day when he'd picked up a blonde hitchhiker who promptly flipped his life upside down but could not be sure he recognized the exact spot. That encounter still had a dream-like effect in his memory. Had he imagined it?

It was already dark by the time Dani got back. She offered no excuse for her lateness and made no mention of the absent RV. Instead, she hugged him hard, desperately. Alfie, apparently sensing that something was amiss, pressed tightly against them both.

****

His attorney, Sandra Newton, only called him for important things, and in this case, to inform him that Sy

Birch's will was, as she expected, being contested.

"Who's doing the contesting?" he asked from the now-familiar chair beside her desk.

"Officially, it's a big firm in Oklahoma City, so probably one of the big oil firms is involved and maybe somebody local too."

"Damn, and I just sold the RV," he said suddenly, considering that as quickly as the thousand acres had dropped into his lap, it probably could disappear just as fast. And he'd sold his only means of escape, his home-on-wheels.

"Don't look so glum." She patted him on the forearm the way his dentist used to do just before he started drilling. All she had to add was, "This won't hurt a bit," to complete an alarming scenario.

"I promise you, the will is airtight. Sy Birch sat right where you're sitting now, and we spent days going over every possible angle, making sure there were no loose ends. So, you have nothing to worry about."

"If you say so. The legal stuff is way above my pay grade anyway."

"Has anybody contacted you about selling off any of the land?" she asked.

"Not a word. Wouldn't make any difference because the answer will always be no."

"That's just the way Sy wanted it. I know he picked the right man." She patted him again.

****

The weird stuff began around three a.m. on a Thursday morning about two weeks after he and Dani moved in, when Alfie began growling. Phil didn't want the dog sleeping in the house, but after Dani bought a nice cushy dog bed and placed it alongside their bed, he knew he'd been outvoted. In the darkest hour of night, Alfie, with his early warning growl, proved his worth. Phil slipped out of bed, pulled on his trousers, and grabbed the loaded semi-automatic from his nightstand.

He took a flashlight with him but left all the lights off and crept out to the front porch in the dark. Alfie remained at his side. The dog didn't bark, just a low rumble in his throat to show that he meant business.

A dark sedan was parked on the road in front of their house. The headlights were off, but the engine was running. Phil approached the car from the rear. He lit up the license plate with his flashlight, then fired three shots into the air. The car lurched forward and sped off down the road.

"Phil, what happened?" A near hysterical Dani stood on the front porch with all the lights on.

"You should put some clothes on before you run out like that," he said.

"Come back inside right now, you too, Alfie."

Phil grabbed a pen from the desk and wrote down the license number. "I'll call this into the sheriff in the morning."

"But what happened? Tell me what happened." She had a firm grip on his forearm. God, but these Birch women had strong hands.

"Nothing, really. There was a car parked out front, and Alfie and I chased them off."

"How did you know they were there? You must have ears like a cat."

"Better, good old Alfie woke me up." He knelt down and scratched the dog's head. "Maybe we should keep you after all."

"You didn't get a look at them?"

"No, the inside of the car was dark, but I understand there might be people who don't want me here. I need to know who I can count on if the brown stuff hits the fan. The sheriff, is he a straight shooter?"

"Yes, for sure. He was friends with my mother, and when Dad used to beat on her, the sheriff threw him in jail. You can depend on him."

"Then that brings us around to you. I don't think it's safe for you to be running around and stealing cars in the middle of the night. From what I can tell, you've been lucky so far, but if there are bad guys out there looking to make trouble, you could be in danger."

"I'll be okay. I know what I'm doing," she said. "Besides, repo isn't stealing. I told you before, it's just retrieving property when somebody doesn't make payments, so don't you dare call me a car thief."

"Okay, okay, but you're not the only one involved here." He placed his hands on her shoulders, gripping her a bit more tightly than he meant to. "I need to know you're safe. I get crazy when I think about you running around in the dark of the night when you should be safe in bed…with me."

"Show me," she said.

"Show you what?"

"Show me you're crazy about me."

And he did. It seemed a little weird doing it right after he'd chased off intruders with gunshots from their front yard, but her moods could change in a heartbeat.

With her frolicking around on top of him like an over-excited puppy, he could think of no better way to defuse a stressful situation.

The next morning, a tired but elated Phil gave a sleeping Dani a kiss on the cheek, and to Alfie, apparently still groggy after his night's exertions, a pat on the head, then drove over to see the sheriff. He gave him the license plate number of the vehicle and watched the scowl spread over the sheriff's face like storm clouds brewing on the horizon.

"I think I recognize this number, but I'll check it out to be sure. Did you see who was in the car?"

"No, too dark, no moon last night," Phil said. "Their headlights were off, but the engine was running. When I fired off a couple of rounds, they took off like a bat out of hell."

"You shot at them?" The sheriff's scowl got uglier.

"Oh, hell no, I just fired into the air. I wasn't out to hurt anybody."

"Listen, no more shooting, you hear me? Anybody else gets shot around here, and the state cops will be all over the place, sticking their noses into everything, and that, believe me, is something we don't need. That's why I chased off that state fellow the night Sy got shot."

"Why? Is there something to hide?" It made him uncomfortable, the way the sheriff looked out, his eyes half closed.

The sheriff didn't answer his question. "No more shooting," was all he said.

"What if they come back?"

"If it's who I think it is, they won't be coming back. You look like you need some coffee."

"I would really appreciate a cup."

The sheriff spoke into an intercom, and in a moment, a highly perfumed lady brought in two cups on a tray. Even after she left the room, her scent hung there like a fog.

The sheriff opened a window behind his desk. "I've asked her to tone down that perfume bit, but it doesn't do much good. You getting settled in here now? I hear you're planning to stay around."

"Looks that way," Phil said. "That reminds me, there's something else. I'm looking for a job. Do you know of anything around?" It just popped out again, the job thing. He wasn't thinking about it, really had no good idea as to why he brought it up. It seemed a little creepy, like one of those events Earl, the drunken fatalist, said was already set to happen, then just happened.

"A job? Are you crazy? Good God, man, you're sitting on a thousand acres, got money in the bank, and a beautiful girl who's head over heels in love with you. Why in hell would you want a job?"

"I've always worked. I feel sort of lost without a job, like a bum." Just so much rationalization now, doing something that was going to happen anyway, so much for fucking free will. Earl would be pleased.

The sheriff laughed. His chair creaked as he leaned back. "You're the richest bum I've ever seen."

"If you hear of anything, let me know. I'd appreciate it."

"Okay, but if I'm gonna recommend you to somebody, I need to know something about you. Service?"

"Army, honorable discharge as a lieutenant."

"That's good to hear. What did you do back in North Carolina?"

"I was in education, only job I've ever had. I taught math in high school, and I coached some, football mostly, wherever they needed me."

"Ever been arrested?

"Yeah, that's why I left North Carolina. It sounds so stupid. I'm embarrassed to tell you about it. I fell off a barstool—I wasn't drunk, just lost my balance, taking medication too—landed on a woman. She went berserk, beat me over the head with her purse, and pressed charges against me for assault. Judge knocked it down to a misdemeanor, drunk and disorderly, and I got off with a fine."

"And if I run a check on you, that's all I'll find?"

"That's all, not even a parking ticket.

"Don't seem like enough to run you out of town."

"Mostly, that was my wife. She was big into appearances, social stuff, and she said I'd ruined her reputation in the community, brought shame and disgrace on the family. I guess she was right. It seemed easier to take off and let her do her innocent victim bit. She was good at that. If you want more, Sandra Newton has a file on me."

" I guess that must have been Sy's doing. For sure, he would have checked you out before making you his heir."

"Yeah, sometimes I think Sandra Newton knows more about me than I know myself."

"So, you packed up the RV and took off. God, do you know how many times I've wanted to do that? Probably any man you ask has wanted to do the same thing, but very few have done it. Man, you're living out my fantasy."

"I think maybe those days are over for me. I'm getting dug in here pretty deep." It sounded like somebody else was talking, putting words in his mouth he hadn't thought of himself.

The sheriff slid a manual about one inch thick over to Phil. "In that case, look this over."

"Law Enforcement?"

"Just think about it. I'm tired of running all over the county. I need a deputy. I've had a couple, but they were more trouble than they were worth. So, think it over and let me know."

Holy shit. Phil Claussen, a deputy sheriff. Craziest, damndest thing he'd ever heard of. What was it, just over five months ago, he'd been arrested and spent a night in jail in Wakefield. Now he was being sized up as Deputy Sheriff. Could be, he thought, could be. He was used to working in a uniform, and he'd be able to carry his gun right out in plain sight, even if he couldn't shoot worth a damn.

Since Dani wasn't home when he got back, Phil made a practice run with Alfie, discussing the pros and cons of the sheriff's job proposal. The dog was a very good, nonjudgmental listener and waited patiently while Phil laid out what he felt to be the most important considerations in a life of law enforcement. Whether Alfie agreed or disagreed or didn't care was hard to tell from the puzzled look on his face. Of course, the dog expected a treat for the effort.

Thinking perhaps he'd not made his point clearly enough for the dog, Phil was about to go through the entire presentation again, but Dani drove up, saving Alfie from what probably would be a confusing, boring episode, worthwhile only for the treat at the end.

"Come help me with the groceries. I thought I'd make a big pot of spaghetti sauce. We can eat part of it tonight and freeze some for later."

He retrieved two heavy bags from the back seat of

the car. "You know, for a woman who doesn't cook, you buy a lot of ingredients."

"I'm trying to learn. I just hope I don't poison you in the process. What have you been doing to poor Alfie? He looks upset."

"We were discussing business."

"You were discussing business with our dog? Why don't you try it on me? I might like to hear it too unless you think it's too complicated for me."

"I was planning all along to go over it with you. Alfie was just a rehearsal, so I could get my thoughts straight."

"This sounds serious. Can we talk while I fix dinner? I'm starved."

While she browned ground beef and onions in a large pot, and the luscious aroma filled the kitchen, Phil poured wine for them. "I went to see the sheriff today about the car out front last night. He thought he recognized the license number but said he'd run it through the system to be sure. He wasn't real happy about me shooting, even though I didn't aim at the car. He seems to be afraid that if anybody else gets shot, the state police will come snooping around, and he didn't want that, like some big secret he doesn't want them to find out. You know anything about that?"

"Not a clue." But she looked away when she said it. She stirred the sauce, sipped from her wine glass, and scratched Alfie's back with her toe all at the same time, an impressive display of balance and dexterity. "Is this what you were discussing with Alfie? No wonder he looked confused."

"No, Alfie and I were talking about something else. The sheriff needs a deputy. He asked me to think about it."

"Oh, my gosh." She stopped scratching Alfie, set her glass down, and dropped the spoon into the pot.

"Well, what do you think?"

"Oh, my gosh."

"You just said that, but I don't know what it means. Do you like the idea or not? He hasn't made an official offer, but I think the job is mine if I want it."

She turned back the flame under the pot to a low simmer. "Let's go out on the porch. I can't think in here."

They took their seats in their neighboring rocking chairs as if they'd been doing it for years.

"I think I like it," she said, sounding as though, while she was leaning in favor, still not one hundred percent on board. "Taking a job like that says you're becoming a part of the community…a real commitment, imagine that."

"At least it's a job. I don't know much about law enforcement, but I should be able to pick it up pretty quick."

"And you can take care of yourself. Nobody's going to push you around. Yeah, that just might work. What did Alfie think about it?"

"He wagged his tail, so I think he's okay with the idea."

"Good, it's settled. Now, I need to check the sauce." He got a kiss and a wall-to-wall grin as she breezed past.

When she returned, she brought the bottle along. "So, I can't talk you into the repo business," she said.

He shook his head as he refilled his glass. "You might tell me how Sy made it so profitable. Even with luxury cars, I can't see how you can make real money."

"I'll let you in on a secret; Sy didn't make his money in repo. Oh, he made it into a big business, and he made enough to keep it interesting, but he had a lot of other things on the side. And, just so you know, he set up trust funds for Angie and me. We're both taken care of, although the way Angie spends money, she'll probably blow right through hers. He took care of Earl too."

"Please, please, tell me this whole sheriff's deputy bit isn't just another part of Sy's big plan."

Dani said nothing, but that Cheshire Cat smile danced across her face. "You've got that worried look on your face again. I thought we were all past that," she said.

"Why do I get the feeling sometimes that none of this is real, like it's too good to be true?"

"Phil Claussen, what am I going to do with you? You're a really smart guy, but you don't know everything. It's all real, and it's just the way it should be, believe me."

She cupped his face in her hands, then the long, slow kiss, everything going fuzzy, his brain turning to mayonnaise. Then she went back inside.

Dammit, just not fair, how she did this to him, treating him like a potted plant. *Open wide, Phil, a little water, a little fertilizer, plenty of sunshine, and you're good to go. That's all you need to know.*

She was feeding her reality to him a spoonful at a time, and he might sputter and protest, but his was only a token effort, having glimpsed the wonder that was Dani's world, as impossible as it seemed, he wanted in, to stay.

Chapter Nineteen

"I'm thinking I should meet your father now that we're living together." He tugged on the oars, moving the skiff into the gentle breeze blowing across the pond. Since the mid-September sun was not so brutal as it had been in the summer, they'd been taking short boat trips several times a week. Their brief cruises followed the same format, Phil paddling, while Dani lay back on cushions, her feet in his lap, trailing her fingers in the water.

"Why now?" she asked, her eyes hidden behind dark glasses.

"Just seems like the right thing to do, given our circumstances. What about your ex? For sure you introduced him to your father."

"What ex?" she asked.

"The ex you mentioned right after we started traveling together, the guy you said left you by the side of the road."

"Oh, that ex. My father never met him, and we were never married anyway. That part was a lie, a little one. Well, maybe not so little. You see, there never was an ex. I made him up. I didn't want you to think I was a girl who couldn't attract a man."

"You've never been married?"

She slipped her sunglasses up onto her forehead. "No, but I'm available if the right guy asks me."

He took her outstretched legs behind each knee and half-lifted, half-pulled her onto his lap, her legs wrapped around his waist.

"You're going to do me right here in the boat?" Her grin said she was up for it if he was.

He shook his head. "The way we've been going at it lately, we'd both wind up in the water."

"Nothing bad about that. I'm kinda warm anyway."

"Now, about your father, unless you're ashamed of me and don't want him to meet me."

"You know that's not true." She squeezed her legs together, causing him to emit a little gasp. "It's just not a good idea to be messing with him right now."

"Yeah, you told me he and Sy didn't get along."

"It goes way back, a long way." Lifting herself to her seat on the stacked cushions, she stared into space as if she could see back in time. "See, Sy had a thing with my mom. I even walked in on them once; I was six or seven, and since I didn't really understand what was going on—looked like a wrestling match—I never mentioned it to anybody. But Dad knew what was happening. He and Sy had several big fights over it until Mom threatened to leave Dad if he didn't stop.

"But if that wasn't enough to drive him over the edge, there was the land, your thousand acres. It originally belonged to my mom, passed down from her father. Since she was married, it should have become Dad's in the event of her death. But she worked a deal with Ms. Newton, your attorney now so that she had the deed transferred to Sy while she was still living.

"There's more, you see. Dad was never sure Angie and I were really his daughters. Mom and Sy were carrying on before either of us were born, so Sy might well have been our Daddy. That's the basis of the big feud, why Dad hated Sy and never forgave him."

"Hated him enough to shoot him?" Phil asked.

"Maybe, but I don't think anybody's very eager to open up that can of worms. It involves too many people, and some of them have secrets too." She slid back into the skiff's prow. "Since I'm not going to get any action here, I'm going back to my cushions. Wake me up if you feel frisky."

Drifting along under a deep blue sky decorated with a few wisps of white cloud that looked like they'd been teased from a tuft of cotton, they each adjourned to their separate thoughts.

For Phil, September still brought back memories of starting a new school year in Wakefield, new students wandering about, lost but pretending not to be. In a school as small as Wakefield High, there was no anonymity to hide behind. The newcomers might just as well wear a piece of fresh meat around their necks, marking them instantly as prey.

His heart had ached as he watched the kids stumble and fumble along, trying to find their way into an adult world. Indeed, his own daughter, Addie, would be a member of that group, seeking independence but trying just as hard to fit in, to belong. Exclusion was something akin to death.

This was a big reason why he'd left town like a scared rabbit because he'd lost his membership in the education world, and as hard as it would be for his daughter to find her way with her father as a teacher, it would be impossible if he'd stayed as an ex-jailbird. No, better to give the kid some room, give her a chance, a chance she wouldn't have if he was still around.

****

On Saturday, September 27th, having breezed through his interviews with the local civic leaders, after he received the stamp of approval from the Clayton town council, Phil Claussen was installed as Deputy Sheriff of Clayton County. Sheriff Barnhill stood by, looking pleased and relieved at the same time.

"I have a confession to make," Phil told the sheriff just before he signed on the dotted line. "I can't shoot for beans, never could."

"How can that be? You were in the military, right?"

"Yeah, but it got to be a big joke. Whenever I went to the rifle range, the NCOs would move everybody off the line and ten feet back so I wouldn't shoot any of them by accident. Whenever I hit the target, they'd all laugh and cheer. I did get pretty good at hand-to-hand combat, though."

"I've been on this job for almost eighteen years now, and I've never fired my sidearm, not even once, except for practice," the sheriff said. "With any luck, you won't get into any shooting matches either. There's a shotgun bracket in the front seat, so I'll load it up with birdshot. Even if you don't hit what you're aiming at, you won't do much damage to anything else either."

During his first week on the job, Phil had taken several tours of duty with the sheriff, getting an idea of his new territory, his new "customers."

"Town drunk." Barnhill pointed to a disheveled man sitting on a bench in front of a Laundromat. "I lock him up a couple of times a week, usually after he's got into a fight. Carries a bottle opener in his pocket, likes to rake people across the face with it. You can almost pick out the people he's cut, leaves a ragged scar that never does heal right. Doubt he'd try that on you. If he even looks like he's reaching in his pocket, crack him with your nightstick. He won't try it again.

"Check this place out Friday, Saturday nights." They drove past a shabby building sitting between a hardware store and a drugstore. "Just drive by slow, let them know you're around. Mostly folks blowing off steam, but you'll have to go inside if they get too rowdy. They'll test you the first time, see if you mean business. Pick out the biggest guy in the room, that will be Harvey, he's usually the one starts things. He's big, but he's got a glass jaw. Usually one punch and he's done.

"It's the smaller guys who are harder to take down. You can hit 'em and hit 'em and hit 'em again, and they just keep coming. Won't do much good to try to talk them down. Use your stick; that's why you'll carry it."

None of this was news to Phil, and he probably wouldn't be using his stick as frequently as Sheriff Barnhill suggested. He knew other ways to disable an opponent, large or small.

Barnhill surprised him with several trips that ended up on dirt paths. To call them roads would be a big overstatement. They would creep along until they came to a dwelling; to call them houses would be as much an overstatement as calling the paths that led to them roads. The first stop set the tone for the two that followed, windows either covered over with siding or papered over from the inside, roofs sagging, and a couple of pierced with holes at least a foot in diameter. These hovels couldn't possibly be occupied, but they were.

"Honk your horn before you get out." The sheriff honked three times. "Old Gerald keeps a loaded deer rifle, and if you walk up to the house unannounced, he's liable to shoot right through the door.

"Gerald, this is Sheriff Barnhill. You in there?" The sheriff yelled and waited before he touched the door.

A muffled response from within.

"Don't shoot. I'm coming to the door now. You hear me?" The sheriff stepped inside slowly as if he were walking in slow motion, all the while talking in a low voice. "How you doing, Gerald? Anything we can do for you?"

A negative answer came from what, at first glance, appeared to be a pile of rags in the corner. A bald head with skin as brown as saddle leather emerged from the top of the pile.

"Who's that?" The business end of a rifle poked through the rag pile.

"Don't shoot him," Barnhill said. "He's my new deputy, name's Phil. He's a real nice fella. You'll like him. He'll be out to check on you from time to time."

"Phil," said the rag pile.

"You got enough food?" Barnhill asked.

"Social Services lady brought some a couple of days ago. She's coming back tomorrow."

They chatted for a while, at least the sheriff did; the rag pile mostly grunted.

"How can anybody live like that?" Phil asked when they were back in the car.

"Beats me," the sheriff said. "But whatever you do, don't mention anything to him about moving out or going into a home. That'll get you shot for sure."

More far-out visits, pretty much variations of the same theme. One hovel was occupied by an old woman, bowed with age, the difference being an obvious attempt to improve the appearance of the front yard, free from litter, a few flowers planted by the door. The inside was neater, too. A broom stood in the corner, a clean floor attesting to its use.

Other things she could do nothing about, like the fact that Phil, standing in the middle of the room, could look up at broad daylight coming in through the hole in the roof.

"How you doin', Miss Lilly?" the sheriff asked.

"Getting along just fine," she said, voice all creaky like a hinge that needed oil.

If this was fine, what would really bad be like?

"Are you handy?" the sheriff asked Phil.

"I can do a few things."

"How about roofing, like that hole you're staring at? Miss Lilly would sure appreciate it if you could help me get that patched up before the weather turns cold."

"Ready any time you are," Phil said.

"We'll be back next week," the sheriff said to her. "Get that roof fixed for you."

"Bless you."

They spoke little on the way back to the office. Phil was still overwhelmed, in part at the abject poverty he'd just seen, and more so, by the way the inhabitants of those hovels clung to their space. This, he could imagine, was the same strength of will that enabled early settlers of the region to hang on when it would have been so much easier and safer to pack up and return home. His opinion of Sheriff Barnhill rose several notches.

To celebrate his new status, no longer unemployed, now a man with a job, Phil took Dani to lunch. She picked a drugstore on Main Street, one with stools at the counter and an old-fashioned soda fountain, still in operation, along the back wall. They had hot roast beef sandwiches and shared a chocolate milkshake, two straws. He distracted Dani with a motion toward the front door, then pinched her straw shut. She was not amused. "Right back to your old high school tricks?"

"Sorry, couldn't resist it."

"If you didn't look so sharp in your new uniform, I'd get mad at you," she said.

They finished up their lunch and were at the door when Dani grabbed his arm and pulled him back inside. "What's up?" he asked.

"My father." She pointed out a large man dressed in a brown suit with a broad stripe that must have been out of style for fifty years. If he was Dani's father, the infamous Fletcher Birch, then he was also brother to the deceased Seymour Birch, and perhaps, sometime in the future, Phil's own new father-in-law.

In spite of Dani's protestations, Phil moved forward, dragging her with him.

"Doogie, my precious daughter, how have you been?" The big, talkative man ignored Phil and wrapped Dani in a bear hug that she did not appear to enjoy. "Angie's been around, but I haven't seen you for a long time."

"Work has been crazy busy," she said.

"I see you're with a sheriff," he said. "Hope she's not in custody," he said to Phil.

"Nothing like that, sir. We were just having lunch. I'm Phil Claussen, Sheriff Barnhill's new deputy. Sorry for your recent loss, sir."

"Loss?"

"Your brother, Seymour."

"Oh, yes, that." With the mention of Sy's name, Fletcher seemed to lose any interest in more conversation and waddled off without another word.

"So that's dear old Dad," Phil said.

"Yeah, you just never know with him. Sometimes he's all talkative, and others, you can't get ten words out of him. I don't know which one I prefer, neither of them actually."

"Is there something wrong with him?"

"We think he's bipolar, the way he cycles up and down. He won't go to a doctor, so we don't know for sure. We gave him medication for a while, but he won't take it unless Angie slips it in with his food."

"What kind of medication do you get without a doctor's prescription?"

"We give him lithium. We get it from a friend of Angie's whose mother is taking it, but she refuses it too, so we try it on Dad. Sometimes it seems to help, usually not."

"Tell me, who is Doogie?"

"Damn, that's a nickname Angie gave me when we were kids. Dad still calls me that."

"Doogie…I like it. Maybe I'll call you Doogie, too," he said.

"Don't you dare. I hate that name. Call me Doogie just once, and I'll do something bad to you when you're asleep at night, like shave off your eyebrows. Do you want to take that chance?"

"I guess not unless it just slips out some time. You can't very well hold that against me."

Chapter Twenty

Phil had an office now, small, room for him, a small desk and two chairs, one for him and one for anyone else who happened to be there. He also had a receptionist/dispatcher. Technically, of course, she worked for the sheriff, but Claudia took an immediate shine to Phil and filled his office with the pungent scent of her perfume, the same aroma that had left him gasping during his first meeting with the sheriff. The only window in his office was painted shut, so he had no way to get rid of the odor.

Claudia made several seemingly unnecessary trips into his office, hanging around his desk, "Anything you need, anything at all, you just let me know."

Even after he left the office, there remained the problem of the scent permeating his clothes, a problem for which he had no solution. When he got home that evening, he hung his uniform on a chair by an open window and hoped for the best.

Not good enough. Dani walked out of the bedroom, a scowl on her face and his uniform shirt held out at arm's length. "Who's your new friend?

Her stare burned right into his soul. A woman could do with a look what a group of men could not with beating, sleep deprivation, and assorted torture techniques.

The classic guilty male response was all he had.

"What friend?"

"This one." She shoved the shirt in his face. "First day on the job, and some tart has been rubbing herself all over you. They just couldn't resist the uniform. I should have known."

"Wrong, nobody laid a hand on me."

"Unless you've started wearing perfume, cheap perfume, at that, you better come up with a story, and quick."

He held the shirt to his face, inhaled deeply. Yeah, even he could smell it. "Claudia, she works in the office, dispatcher. She must put the stuff on with a paintbrush. Stinks up the whole place."

"When were you going to tell me about her?"

"Tell you what? There's nothing to tell. She's worked with Sheriff Barnhill for years. It has nothing to do with me."

She circled him, and he wondered for a moment whether she might attack. The top of her head barely reached his shoulder, but if she ever decided to kick his ass, then his ass would be kicked, plain and simple; his only hope was that she wouldn't kick too hard.

"We're having spaghetti again unless you've made other plans." She spun around on her heels and marched back into the kitchen. He was off the hook for now.

"The only plan I have right now is I'm going for a boat ride," he said.

"You want company?"

He shook his head. "Just me."

A little spat, he wouldn't call it a fight because he'd ducked and run away before it got that far. Didn't matter, though. The little ones counted just as much as the big ones. He didn't know much about the mysterious female psyche, but he knew they kept score. He could be a saint for three hundred and sixty-four days a year, but if on that three hundred and sixty-fifth, he screwed up, that would go in the book, nothing about the good days, just the one black mark, alongside all the other black marks.

He pushed the skiff away from the bank. The pond's surface was like polished glass. A waxing crescent moon had risen early in the eastern sky and was reflected perfectly in the still waters of the pond. Two moons at once must be some sort of an astrological record.

He kept the oars inside the boat, not wanting to disturb the glassy surface on which he hung suspended. For a while, time didn't matter. It didn't exist. Just sky and moon and still water, all good stuff. Better than a man cave, it had no walls, no ceiling, and a floor that he could swim in if he chose. And best of all, it never required dusting.

As he drifted along, he could feel himself a part of all around him, no separation between Phil Claussen and the universe, all part of one great cosmic stew that, for the moment, was as calm as calm could be. He felt transcendent. He didn't know exactly what that meant, but he was pretty sure that was what he felt.

He was Icarus, but instead of the sun, he soared toward the moon and passed it. With no heat to melt his wings, he could go as far as he wanted. From far above, he could see himself in a small boat on a tiny pond, a speck in something so vast as to have no beginning and no end.

"Are you all right? I came to check on you."

He jumped at the sound of her voice. Her head and

bare shoulders were above the gunnels. He looked behind her, where ripples should mark the path of her swim, but saw none.

"How did you get here?" In other words, how had she made it from the shoreline to his boat, over two hundred feet, without leaving any trace on the surface?

"How do you think?"

"You didn't swim, did you?"

"Not exactly." She hoisted herself over the side of the boat. Sometimes she wore a bathing suit, sometimes she didn't, tonight she didn't, and she was luminous, brighter than the moon. She must have been visible from some distance, radiant and naked as she was.

"I'm cold. You have to get me warm."

He wrapped his arms around her, and she folded into him every nook and cranny of his body. He ran his fingers through her hair...perfectly dry. How in hell?

Even dragging his fingertips across the surface of the water left a trail of ripples, but she'd left no trace. "Can you fly?" he asked, and he got the answer he should have expected.

"Not exactly."

A woman who could cross open water without leaving a trace—no way, but it spooked him right down to his toenails. So, he let it drop, just another Dani mystery that he wouldn't understand even if she explained it to him, which she certainly would not.

They drifted back to the shoreline, and he helped her out of the boat. "Dani, where are your clothes?"

"Back at the house."

"You mean you came all the way over here completely bare-assed?"

"Don't make it sound so awful. I was careful.

Nobody saw me."

"Woman, you just can't do that."

"Don't you dare go all grumpy now."

"I ought to turn you over my knee and give you a good spanking."

She threw her arms around his neck and bounced up and down against him. "Go ahead, do it, I dare you. I double-dog dare you."

Her bouncing against him had the inevitable effect, as she apparently discovered when she pressed against him. "Well, guess I won't be getting a spanking tonight after all."

"Guess not, but you gotta stop running around naked."

"You're going to have to come up with something, you know. I didn't come all the way over here like this just to talk."

"There's too many rocks on the ground," he said, "and I don't think standing up will work."

"The boat," she said. Her smile lit up her entire face and probably his as well.

After a token protest on his part, he rowed them back out into the middle of the pond, and there beneath the moon and stars took place an event that convinced him, if he wasn't convinced before, that Dani Birch was no ordinary woman.

****

In spite of her almost supernatural appearance on the lake and all the magic that happened afterward, there remained a small (to Phil) issue on the table…the perfumed shirt. His promise that Claudia was just some woman from the office in whom he had no interest whatever meant little. No man ever came home from his first day on a new job reeking of a strange new perfume to confess, "Hot damn, got it on with my new receptionist."

No, as sure as the sun rising in the east, Dani would turn up at the office very soon to scope out any possible competition. And she wasted no time. Late the next morning, after Phil had made his rounds, basically driving around to show that local law enforcement was up and about, he'd just settled in at his desk when he heard her in the outer office, apparently introducing herself to Claudia. "Hi, I'm Dani, Phil and I are...." Her voice trailed off, and he couldn't catch the last part of her sentence, but he could guess. It would be a carefully worded statement of ownership, a veiled warning that, while subtle, made it perfectly clear that Phil Claussen was out of bounds.

Apparel would be an important part of such a scouting expedition, and he wondered what she might have chosen. As usual, she surprised him, conservative gray slacks, a pale blue blouse, and low heels. Business casual? Maybe for the woman who has come to take care of business. Even conservatively dressed, she looked sharp as hell. But the topper was on her left hand, a large diamond sparkling and impossible to miss.

She didn't wait for Claudia to show her in. She marched right into his tiny office, kissed him, and branded him with no more than that. "Good morning, sweetheart, thought I'd take you out to lunch." Now the aroma of lilacs filled his office, overpowering Claudia's scent. Nothing subtle about her entry. This was war.

If military campaigns were conducted with half as much forethought and precision, battles would be won in minutes instead of weeks. In less time than it took him to push his chair away from the desk, she'd arrived, completed the assault, and now stood in complete control of her objective. Poor Claudia was probably trying to figure out what the hell had just happened.

"What's this?" He pointed to the flashing ring.

"Oh, that belonged to my mom. She gave it to me in case I got engaged. I wear it from time to time, hoping I'll get an offer. Do you like it?"

"Beautiful. Must have cost your dad a mint."

"Dad didn't give it to her. She got it from Uncle Sy."

"Run this past me again. You're sure your mother wasn't secretly married to Sy?"

"Might as well have been. From the time I was old enough to notice, they were together all the time."

"Did she move in with Sy?"

"No, it didn't sit too well with folks around here that she was carrying on with somebody besides her husband. If she had moved in with him, they would both have been run out of the county. Now, are you up for lunch?" Dani asked again.

"It's a little early, just past ten, and I have to drive out and check on one of the sheriff's shut-ins."

"Can I come along?"

"Not this time. The old man I'm going to visit shoots people he doesn't know. I just hope he'll remember me from before. What are you looking at?"

"You do look good in that uniform, really good. I'll have to keep my eye on you." She gave him another peck on the cheek, branding him good and proper, mission accomplished.

****

By eleven o'clock on a warm September morning,

Phil was on his way to one of the shacks Sheriff Barnhill had shown him a few days before. The department had two vehicles, both big department cruisers with V-8 engines. Just outside of town, Phil pushed the accelerator to the floor, and the cruiser jumped as it picked up speed. He laughed as the speedometer passed one hundred miles an hour, a long, long time since he'd driven so fast. And he didn't need to watch for speed traps; he was the law, by God. He could drive as fast as he pleased.

He slowed to a crawl as he turned onto the pathway that led up to the shack. The last thing he wanted to do was startle the old man inside and risk getting plugged by a deer slug. He didn't know why he was visiting the old fellow, only that Sheriff Barnhill said the social worker asked him to check him out, so he passed it along to Phil.

Barnhill had also said, of the social worker, "That woman is a saint." Phil couldn't remember meeting a saint before.

As he neared the shack, he found another car blocking the drive. The vehicle had Social Services of Clayton County on both front doors. He remembered too late that he'd forgotten Sheriff Barnhill's rule about tooting the horn a couple of times to alert the man inside. Oh, well, too late now. Nothing left to do but continue on.

The sound he caught at the door brought him up short—laughter. There was the old man's cackle, accompanied by the unmistakable sound of a woman's laughter. A woman's laughter was always a special event, and out here, radiating unexpectedly from a hovel that looked as if it could be blown over by a stiff breeze, it sounded very special indeed.

He tapped lightly on the door, and the laughing woman opened it. "Please, come in, Deputy. I believe you've met Mr. Hennessey." He took her extended hand and felt a grip as strong as that of many men he'd met.

"Phil Claussen, ma'am."

More laughter. It seemed to bubble up from someplace deep inside. Please, don't 'ma'am' me. I'm Regina. I asked you to come because I've finally convinced Mr. Hennessey to come in for a medical check-up. I can't quite manage him myself—she held up her left arm, which was enclosed in a cast from wrist to elbow. "Sheriff Barnhill has always been so kind, helping out whenever he could. I hope you won't mind the imposition."

"Not a bit, but wouldn't an ambulance be better?"

At the sound of the word, the old man lifted his deer rifle from the corner. Regina stepped in front of him. "No ambulance, Mr. Hennessey, I promised you. Now, put your gun away."

Turning back to Phil, she said, "Please, don't use that word. It upsets him."

Phil nodded. Message received.

"If you can help him out to my car, that would be a great help. I can't do it by myself."

As Phil approached the pile of rags, with the deer rifle in the corner, the stench caused him to gag. Regina, standing right beside him, didn't seem to mind at all.

He took a moment, trying to locate the various parts of the man's body before he attempted to pick him up. When he finally got the man's arm over his shoulder, he found that the old fellow couldn't stand, much less walk. Phil grabbed him under the knees, lifted him off the floor, and gently carried the foulest-smelling mass of living, breathing humanity he'd ever encountered. If Dani gave his uniform the sniff test tonight, there was no chance she would smell perfume.

It took a few moments to situate the man in Regina's car. Phil could only imagine how rank the interior would smell later, but she seemed not the least bit concerned.

Standing beside the door of her car, she extended her hand to him once more, the same firm grip by which she held onto him a moment longer than he expected. "Thank you for your help," she said. "Sheriff Barnhill said you would be nice."

He pulled his cruiser over to the side to let her pass. She smiled as she drove by, like she was off to a picnic, instead of transporting a man who could overpower a skunk in a stinking contest.

He didn't have long to ponder because Claudia called in a fight on Church Street, which joined Main two blocks west of a 7-Eleven in a section of Clayton that would never, ever attract tourists. That it was called Church Street was a town joke, a little local irony, because there were no churches, but rather several bars that usually required attention by law enforcement at some time or another.

Claudia's message was terse; apparently, Dani's intervention had quenched any plans the dispatcher had for Phil. She gave him the location, the participants, the Cowdray brothers, and a warning: "Be careful."

He knew a bit about the Cowdray pair from the sheriff. Employed and sober, they posed no problems.

Drunk and jobless, their usual form of entertainment was to double-team some lone bar patron, start a fight, and beat the crap out of him. "Don't bother talking to them," the sheriff said, "Use your stick. That's why you carry it."

True to form, in the street outside Grogan's Bar, were the two Cowdrays, Al, the heavier and dumber, and Pete, smaller and smarter, bouncing a bloodied unidentifiable victim between them. Phil hit his flasher and slid to a stop just inches from the larger Cowdray. Time for a demonstration.

Big Al Cowdray, as Phil planned, took exception to Phil's driving, particularly since the cruiser came so close to hitting him. He was immediately in Phil's face, spewing off a stream of expletives, also as Phil planned. With all the provocation he needed, Phil brought his nightstick down on top of Al's head, and the big man was down and out.

Often, the smaller, smarter participant would take the hint and cease hostilities. Instead, Pete came at Phil, both arms flailing. Phil caught him with an elbow across the bridge of his nose. Enough, Pete dropped to his knees, his nose gushing.

Since this was his first big street brawl, Phil came with two objectives, stop the fight and send a message: *Don't fuck with the deputy.* Now the regulars on Church Street knew what to expect if they stepped out of line.

More arrivals, more flashing lights. The sheriff pulled his cruiser alongside Phil's, followed closely by the EMT truck. "Looks like you've taken care of everything," the sheriff said. He didn't seem displeased in the least.

"No problem. Who's the guy they were pounding

on?" He pointed to the bloody victim, already under the care of the EMTs.

"I know him," Barnhill said. "Name's Lassiter, probably just stopped in for a beer, wrong place, wrong time." He prodded the fallen Al Cowdray with his foot. "As soon as the EMT guys have a look at these two, we can run them in. Better take them in separately."

The sheriff's nose twitched as he sniffed the air close to Phil. "What the hell have you got into?"

"I went out to Gerald Hennessey's place to help the social worker get him into her car. I can only hope she gives him a bath. Which one of these guys do you want to take?"

Drunk and disorderly, plus or minus assault, depending on whether Lassiter wanted to press charges. Phil knew a thing or two about this category, having been jailed himself under the same label. He was thankful, of course, that the police officer who had presided at his own arrest months ago had not broken his nose or cracked him with his stick.

Back at the station, he got a wink and a thumbs up from Claudia, but she kept her distance, apparently respecting Dani's prior claim. Not a bad move on her part, Phil thought, since he still reeked from lugging poor old Mr. Hennessey around. All things considered, he'd had a pretty good day at work, certainly not boring, which was one of his worst fears. Aside from smelling bad, really bad, he'd handled most of what he'd encountered successfully so far.

Home sweet home, Dani met him at the door, with a kiss, then a sniff. "Oh, God, Phil, what have you been rolling around in, a stable? If it isn't perfume, you come home smelling like horse poop. I think I liked the perfume better."

"No, just out to see one of the sheriff's orphans. I don't think a stable could smell that bad." This was their routine, then a kiss followed by an exploratory sniff. Although had she sniffed first, on this occasion, there likely would have been no kiss.

"Strip off that smelly uniform and get into the shower. Dinner is almost ready."

"You're not going to strip with me?" he asked.

"Strip with a guy who smells like you? Never...now, go."

Chapter Twenty-One

Dinner was, by her own designation, Dani's Famous Fried Chicken, which Phil attacked with great gusto and all manner of approving noises. But famous though it might have been, juicy and tender, it was not. Nonetheless, Phil chewed with vigor and a smile, his jaw muscles fatigued, fearing some misstep that might bring down upon him the righteous wrath of a woman whose cooking had been scorned.

Even Alfie, instead of taking up his usual station beside Phil's chair, ready to gobble up any morsel that might fall from his plate, stayed in his bed, feigning sleep. Phil knew better. Damned dog, just when he needed him.

But he loved her for trying. This shift into domestic mode was seismic, and these early attempts, well, he couldn't recall many things he'd done perfectly right out of the gate, so anticipating improvement with practice, he would dive right into whatever she prepared for them a happy smile on his face. Besides, sometimes it wasn't the food itself so much as the way it was presented, like the time she cooked lasagna and served it up to him wearing a frilly white apron, black bra, and panties, and nothing else except glossy black stilettos, an appetizer, entrée, and dessert all rolled into one beautiful dish. Any man who could complain about that was a world-class fool.

After dinner, they took a walk, taking advantage of the unseasonably warm weather. Alfie ran off ahead of them, scouting out the area. "Indian Summer," Phil said. "Is that what you call this?"

"Close enough."

"How are your winters?"

"Brutal, but you'll keep me warm and toasty, right?" She slid her hands up his arm, pulled him close.

Whether by default or by some choice he made at a level beneath his own awareness, he was slipping into a routine. He had a full-time job, visibility in the community, a house, a full-time, live-in girl-friend, who he would, now that the ink was dry on his divorce papers, ask to marry him. He couldn't recall exactly where or when he'd made that decision, just that he had and felt good about it, mostly.

****

With the fall season creeping in and the nights turning cooler, they needed a blanket for the bed, although, with a very warm Dani snuggled close against him, Phil was just as warm as he wanted to be, maybe warmer.

"Is it okay if I order a few things for the house, maybe a new carpet for the living room, some new curtains?" She whispered into his ear.

"Sure, whatever you want, you don't need my permission."

"Don't you even care?" Her tone was a bit sharper.

"Of course, I care, but I couldn't decorate a doghouse, much less our home." He laid extra emphasis on *our home*. "Your taste is much better than mine, so go ahead. I'm sure I'll love whatever you pick out."

"Men," she said with an exasperated sigh. "Just as well, because I already did it."

"Oh? When?"

"Yesterday, I didn't tell you because I didn't know what you would say."

Of course, the reason he was sure he had no taste when it came to home furnishings was MaryBeth's constant reminders when they first set up housekeeping. His ideas about what went into a kitchen were one hundred and ten percent wrong. Okay, he didn't put up too much of a fight there because a kitchen was a woman's domain. Everybody knew that.

MaryBeth let him have two spaces for his own: the basement—too dark and dingy—and the garage. He got the garage because he told her there were rats. He set out traps, that from time to time, he tripped himself just to reinforce the likelihood of rodent infestation. She said no more about it. In fact, refused to get in the car if it was parked in the garage. Phil had to back it out before she would climb in, one of his better moves.

****

At two o'clock on the second Sunday morning in October, having made two more trips to Church Street bars, after separating six noisy drunks, jailing four of them, having his supper interrupted by a call about a missing person who turned up drunk an hour later, Phil got roused out again.

"Barnhill here." His voice was soft, almost a whisper. "Got a situation over at the Birch place. Dani doesn't need to know tonight. Tomorrow will be soon enough for her."

"What was that?" Dani asked in a slurred voice.

"Domestic disturbance. Go back to sleep." He got

dressed in the dark, and, as he was tying his shoes, Dani turned the bedroom lights on. She was fully dressed. "I'm going with you."

"No need, nothing you should get involved in."

"That's a lie. It's Angie and my dad's. I knew this would happen."

He wanted to ask how she knew since there was no way she could have overheard Sheriff Barnhill, but his queries always got him an impatient look, like he was an inquisitive four-year-old pestering his mother with endless questions. Still, he had to wonder, if she had truly foreseen her father's killing, had she foreseen Sy's as well? The thought chilled him through and through. How could anyone foresee a killing, or any tragic event, for that matter, and do nothing to prevent it?

Short of handcuffing her to the bed, and he considered doing it, there was no way he could keep her out of his cruiser, so she rode alongside him.

It was a twenty-minute drive along county roads, mostly unmarked, on a dark night with no moon to obscure the uncountable pinpoints of light from stars so many millions of light years away.

"Do you know what happened?" he asked. He would not have been the least surprised if she'd given him chapter and verse about the situation that lay just ahead of them.

"Not exactly," she said. "I know Angie's there. She moved back in with Dad to take care of him. She said his house was a pigsty, and he wasn't eating properly. I told her to hire somebody to help him, but she wouldn't hear of it. Had to take care of it herself."

"That doesn't sound so bad," he said. In fact, it sounded commendable, moving back home to care for a man who couldn't or wouldn't take care of himself.

They rode in a tense silence, one of them knowing only a little, the other knowing too much.

"Turn left here," she said after a few miles.

"Good thing you're along. I would have missed it." Since her warning about how her father's anger toward Sy might be redirected toward him, Phil had avoided the place completely. Now, in the total darkness, he might never have found it at all. The road leading to the house was covered in gravel, and ahead, through the trees, he could see the flashing lights of the EMT truck. Somehow they always got the message as soon as he did, if not sooner. Clairvoyance must be a common trait in Clayton.

Sheriff Barnhill's cruiser was already there too, parked just in front of the house, but his flashers were off. Phil took the hint and extinguished his own.

The EMTs were wheeling a gurney toward the front entrance, struggling through the gravel. They seemed in no rush. Whatever had happened inside was over and done with.

Phil waited for the EMTs to make their entry. He thought Dani might dash in ahead of him—this was her only remaining family except her sister—but she stayed at his side, clinging to his arm as if knowing already what they would find inside.

A body, barefoot and wearing only pajama bottoms and a stained T-shirt, lay sprawled beside a chair. In the brightly lit room, the single bloodstain in the center of the chest was clearly visible.

"Dad." Dani's gasp was a deep, guttural sound overflowing with pain. There seemed to be no sense of resolution of difficulties past, only dismay. She clung tightly to Phil's arm as if fearing to let go, lest she fall into some dark place.

She released him when he knelt to get a closer look at the single clean entry wound centered in the chest, similar to those in Sy's chest, except Sy had been shot several times. He wanted to talk to the sheriff, but as soon as he stood, Dani latched onto him again, holding him so tightly he would have to drag her to move at all. The sheriff was similarly bound; Angie had her face buried in his chest, arms clasped around his neck. Any exchange of information with Sheriff Barnhill would have to wait until the girls were over their shock.

"We should look around for a weapon," Barnhill said after he'd pried himself loose from Angie's grip. "Doubt we'll find one, though. Looks like the slug went right through him and into the floor. If we can dig it out, we can check ballistics against the bullets that killed Sy."

"Was anything taken?" Phil asked.

Angie shook her head. "I don't think they had time. I was reading in my bedroom when I heard the shot, and I came right out."

"See anybody?"

"The screen door slammed, but I didn't see anybody. There was a car. I wrote down part of the license number."

"This looks familiar," Phil said. "Maybe the same bunch that paid us a visit not long ago."

He wondered about Angie's reading habits; three o'clock on a Sunday morning seemed a bit extreme. Why had she come running when she heard a shot when most people would hide under the bed? And the look that passed between the two sisters, neither shock nor surprise, more like knowing that this whole arrangement, two brothers, one their father, the other their uncle, both shot dead, was all understandable, to them.

The question of how the deed was done posed no problem, a bullet in the man's chest. That left the other issue—motive, and why was he killed on this particular night?

The sheriff looked directly at Phil, both understanding that their lives had just become more complicated.

****

Complication arrived officially two mornings later wearing a black funeral suit worn shiny at the elbows and a bolo tie held in place by a small silver horseshoe clip. The nametag dangling from the breast pocket identified the complication as coming from the State Bureau of Investigation.

He sat at Sheriff Barnhill's desk with two files open in front of him. His cadaverous appearance and deep-set eyes made Phil want to check for a pulse.

"Is this all?" he asked the sheriff. His voice came out as a rumble as though he were speaking through a hollow tube.

"Until we get ballistics back."

"Fingerprints?" the black suit asked without looking up.

"None, our crime scene people have gone through both places."

"Both of these shootings took place in private homes. How could there have been no prints?" Now the black suit looked up.

"What I meant was, all the prints belonged to the

occupants."

"So, they were both suicides? Is that what you're saying?"

"No, of course not. Maybe the shooter wiped the place clean or wore gloves."

The SBI dick was goading the sheriff, not necessarily trying to trip him up, just trying to make his life miserable, and from the expression on Barnhill's face, it was working.

The event the sheriff dreaded, and had told Phil as much, was unfolding right in his office. A small town might get away with one homicide, but two in the space of a couple of months would surely draw attention, as was happening now.

"I want to speak to your deputy if you'll excuse us. I'll call you when we're through."

Phil expected the interview to take place in his own small office, where the state dick would be far less comfortable, making for a shorter interview, but he'd taken over Barnhill's space, made it his own.

"Take a seat, deputy." The dick thumbed through the folders, again focusing his gaze on the desk. The room was quiet enough that the ticking wall clock sounded loud and grating.

Phil recognized standard interrogation technique when he saw it. Most law enforcement people probably became uncomfortable when the tables were turned, when they had to answer questions instead of asking them, but this reversal didn't bother Phil. Years ago, when he wore another uniform, he'd been grilled by experts. Let the state dick have his fun if he thought he could do any better.

"You came to town about six months ago," the

dick said.

Phil nodded.

"Answer yes or no."

Phil hesitated just long enough to be annoying, then answered, "yes."

"Everything has happened since you arrived."

Not put as a question, so Phil didn't answer.

"Is that correct, deputy?"

"Depends on what you're asking."

"I'm talking about two shootings two months apart in a town that hasn't had anybody shot in almost ten years. Seems odd, don't it, that you come in, people start getting shot?"

"Not particularly, since we don't know who the shooters are."

The dick shifted gears. He glanced at Phil with those deep-set eyes. Yeah, Phil had seen this trick before, too, but instead of the silent treatment going on for a minute or so, he'd endured it for hours, blindfolded sometimes. So, once again, the dick was in over his head.

"Do I look stupid to you, deputy?"

Phil took his time as if considering the question carefully, long enough for the veins on the dick's forehead to stand out.

"I asked you a question." Now the dick's voice went up a notch, almost shouting. He was fast running out of ammunition.

"I don't really know you that well," Phil said.

"You play me for a fool, I'll make you sorry you ever set foot in Oklahoma, you understand me?"

"I hear you, but I don't understand why you're so upset." By now, Phil was enjoying himself.

"Why don't you explain how, a few months after you drove up in an RV trailer, you inherit a thousand acres, a house, and a pot full of money, all from a man you just met, and that same man winds up shot, his brother, too."

"Your guess is as good as mine. To this day, I don't know why Sy Birch made me his heir or why he was shot."

"This sounds crooked. See, Deputy, I don't believe in coincidence. When a man ends up shot and leaves everything he owns to a total stranger, something smells bad. I aim to find out exactly what happened."

"That would be a big help to us. We haven't made much progress so far."

The dick made a grunting sound like he might throw up. "We'll talk again. See if you're such a smartass next time."

"I'll look forward to it." Without waiting for the dick to dismiss him, Phil left.

He met the sheriff in the hallway. Barnhill looked to be on the verge of panic. "How did it go?"

"No problem. We had a nice chat."

"Bullshit, you be careful with him. He's a real SOB."

"So am I." Phil walked into his office.

Chapter Twenty-Two

The next morning, a grumpy Phil Claussen, troubled by some vague premonition, got up on the wrong side of the bed, dressed, then went into the kitchen where he snapped at Dani before he realized her sister was sitting in the kitchen with her. It was the first time he'd seen Angie in the house in a while and the first time he'd ever noticed her carrying a purse. Still, there was no excuse for being short with Dani, and he couldn't understand himself why he'd done it, but something had shifted. *Something wicked this way comes* if it hadn't already arrived.

"Where's my damned gun?" he asked. "I always leave it on the nightstand."

"It's your gun. You're supposed to keep up with it, not my problem," Dani said, an unusual edge in her voice.

"Good morning to you, too," Angie said, none too sweetly.

The sisters exchanged a cryptic look, probably about him and not a song of praise, not exactly. Even the dog kept its distance.

"Yeah, hi." Phil spotted his gun on the kitchen counter. The safety was off, and there was a round in the chamber, a decidedly unsafe situation that, while it might be appropriate for a combat zone, definitely had no place in a domestic kitchen. "Has anybody handled this?" he asked.

"It's your gun and your responsibility, Phil," Dani said.

His hands shook slightly as he ejected the round from the chamber and returned the gun to its proper on-safe position. Could he have been so careless? He'd never left his weapon lying around like that before, but he hadn't been grilled by the state dick about two murders before, murders in which he seemed to be the common denominator. He left without saying goodbye, which was probably fine with the girls. Nobody wants a grouch in the house.

The dick had touched a nerve when he made the obvious association, how Phil's arrival in Clayton seemed to set things in motion, ending up with two dead bodies, because Phil, like the state dick, didn't believe in coincidence either. The other possibility caused his stomach to twist and turn…what if he'd been set up? What if he'd been placed under suspicion on purpose? Fuck, no, sometimes shit happened, for no good reason. He'd seen enough to know that.

Still, being the fall guy, a poor dumbass led along by a beautiful woman…wouldn't be the first time that had happened. But he was covered, right? He had solid alibis that placed him somewhere else when both men were shot.

He shuffled papers in the office until he'd had enough of sitting still. "Where are you off to?" Claudia asked as he walked past her desk.

"I'll be in my car if you need to reach me." Right now, he needed to be somewhere else, anywhere else. What he was considering, being set up was crazy as hell, but it wouldn't go away, and it left him in a crappy mood. Quietly thinking things over would not get him through this mess. He needed action. He needed to hit something or someone.

He drove down Church Street, hoping for a fight but found nothing. Eleven o'clock on a weekday morning was not prime time for drunken brawls unless he started one of his own. How he'd love to encounter one, or better still, both of the Cowdray brothers now, preferably drunk and belligerent and looking for a fight. But his luck seemed to have run out, for the day, at least, and the street remained empty. He needed some real action.

He fired up the cruiser. He'd given it a good run once before. Time now to see whether the big V-8 was all it was cracked up to be. He picked a long straight stretch leading out of town, plenty of visibility to avoid any creeping farm machinery before he crashed into it.

When he floored it, the big engine gave a happy roar, as if its mood matched Phil's perfectly. This was what it was made for, speed, not creeping along Clayton's streets at thirty miles an hour. As the speedometer climbed, the fence posts along the road became a blur, and he didn't back off until he'd reached his goal of triple digits on the speedometer, enough thrill to chase away the goblins of doubt clouding up his mind. He ended up in a high-speed U-turn, the kind you only see at the end of NASCAR events, the kind that left black rubber all over the road, the kind that made a statement: *You don't like it, go fuck yourself.* Besides, they weren't his tires he was burning up. He could always get a new set from the county.

About a mile out of town, along a stretch much like where he'd picked up Dani months ago, Claudia's voice crackled over the car radio. "Where are you?" Always her first question. Then, "That attorney, Newton, called looking for you. Wanted to know if you'd stop by her office this afternoon."

"Roger."

"What?"

"Roger means yeah, I'll do it." Apparently, Sheriff Barnhill didn't use the term.

He drove by Newton's office, and, in keeping with his new motto, *you don't like it, go fuck yourself*, he parked the cruiser in a restricted zone marked with diagonal yellow lines. Sure, there were other spaces available, but he was in a belligerent mood, half hoping someone would confront him.

Newton's receptionist looked ready for a confrontation of a different kind. "She's ready for you," adding a clear but subliminal message, *I am too.* As he walked into Newton's office, he heard a whispered, "Some men are born to wear a uniform."

A subdued Newton, shoulders slumped, worry lines across her forehead, said, "Good, you're here. I need a drink."

"You too?" There, at least one other person felt like this might be world-going-to-hell-in-a-handbag day. "It's just that things have been a little weird lately."

"Coming from you, that's saying a lot, seeing as how weirdness seems to follow you around. Now, about that drink, maybe you'd better drive," she said. "I wouldn't want some smartass deputy sheriff picking me up on a DUI."

"So this way, I'm aiding and abetting a miscreant, and I thought you meant one drink. Sounds like you're thinking more than that."

"Could be," she said. "Could well be. Now, come on." She linked her arm in his and led him past the receptionist's desk like a hunting trophy she'd just bagged. "We'll be back sometime," she said to the scowling receptionist.

Out on the sidewalk, she released his arm. "Sorry about that. I was just trying to piss Dolly off. She's had the hots for you since the first day you came into the office."

"Who's Dolly?"

"My receptionist, and don't tell me you didn't notice the way she looked at you. I've heard of men undressing women with their eyes, so I guess turnabout is fair play, and believe me, Dolly just stripped you down to your watchband."

"I thought I felt a draft."

"Hah. I think I'm going to enjoy this drink."

Second time that day he'd made a woman laugh. Sooner or later, his turn would come, had to, didn't it?

"We can walk over if you'd like. Church Street is just a couple of blocks."

"Church Street?" he asked, although he'd been there before. He was just surprised that was where his attorney did her drinking.

"Sure, that's where they keep the liquor, in case you haven't noticed. I usually go to Kerrigan's. It's quieter there, and if I have one too many, Mike—he's the bartender—shuts me down. He's sort of my own personal babysitter."

He stopped and turned, so he was facing her. "You and public intoxication, I never would have thought."

"It's safer than drinking alone. That's where you

can get into real trouble. In fact, I don't even keep liquor in the house, well, just one bottle of scotch, for emergencies."

"Should I be scared?" he asked. "You manage everything I own. If you get drunk and mess up, I'm in the poorhouse."

"Makes you think, doesn't it? Just remember, it was an episode of public intoxication that brought you here in the first place."

"Don't remind me." He didn't need reminding. In fact, at that very moment, he was thinking back to that fateful day in Wakefield when he'd sabotaged his marriage, his job, and life in general. Was he was about to do the same thing all over again? Phil Claussen, self-demolition expert, all part of some big cosmic plan with him caught in the middle. He felt like a hockey puck just dropped onto the ice, and a bunch of ugly guys with sticks ready to whack him.

"Your vehicle is parked in a restricted zone. I should make a citizen's arrest or at least complain to the sheriff," she said.

Now came his turn for a chuckle.

"Why, you rascal." She punched him on the shoulder, a light tap that didn't even disturb the crease in his sleeve. "You parked here on purpose, just hoping somebody would make a big deal out of it. This is a whole new side of you, out looking for trouble. Is there some evil twin Phil Claussen who only comes out during the full moon?"

Once inside, Kerrigan's was indistinguishable from any of the other bars on the street, a long bar polished over the years by many elbows, booths along the wall, and a half dozen tables scattered in the middle of the room. "I'm probably going to catch hell for drinking on duty," Phil said.

"Hi, Mike," his attorney said to the bartender, who waved, revealing a perspiration stain under his arm. She led Phil to a booth in the back of the room, dark enough that he bumped into a chair before his eyes adjusted.

"It's okay to bump into things on your way in, just don't do it on the way out. People will notice and think you're drunk."

They'd just seated themselves when Mike appeared at the table. "Your usual?" he asked Newton.

"I'm a single malt scotch drinker," she said to Phil. "Is that okay for you too?"

"Perfect."

Mike delivered their drinks promptly; they were, after all, the only customers except for one lone bar patron hunched over his glass as if he wanted to crawl right into it. Phil was beginning to know that feeling.

"Cheers," she said as she raised her glass.

"Likewise."

"Do you mind if I smoke?" she asked.

"Help yourself."

"Scotch and a cigarette, some days this is about as good as it gets," she said.

"Sounds a little, well...desolate, if that's not going overboard."

"Nope, desolate fits, not all the time, mind you, just frequently enough to make me wish I could climb into an RV and take off across the country. Remind you of anybody we know?"

"Yeah, it had its moments, traveling like that. Only time I've really felt free, that I can remember."

"I would love to feel the freedom, but I'm a

coward. I mean, I can talk about it, just letting go, taking off for parts unknown. The closest I ever came was a visit to the RV dealership in Oklahoma City."

She sipped her scotch slowly, obviously enjoying it. "I'm guessing your job hasn't been all peaches and cream lately. You looked like you were ready to crack a few skulls earlier. Anything you want to talk about?"

Phil gazed at his glass and scowled. How had it had become empty so quickly? He ordered another one. "I just got my buttons pushed, is all. A guy from the SBI came to the office and made a big deal about how all the crazy things, Sy and his brother getting shot, me inheriting a big estate, everything went nuts after I got here. Too many coincidences, according to him."

"It does seem a little weird, don't you think? You drive halfway across the country. There must have been hundreds, thousands of places you could have stopped. But you wind up in Clayton, Oklahoma, just in time to inherit Sy Birch's estate."

"Come on, don't you start on me too," he said. "I can see how the state guy came to that conclusion. It don't pass the smell test, as my old sergeant used to say."

"So, how did you wind up in Sy Birch's campground? Why pick his?" she asked.

"Earl Biggers asked me the same question. Seems as if it chose me, the campground, I mean." He told her the story of how he picked Dani up on the roadside, how it was like she was there waiting on him, how all the things that had happened since, including the inheritance, all seemed set in place before he ever arrived.

"I always felt like I made the decisions in my life.

Nobody was telling me what to do, but coming here it was like watching a picture develop on a sheet of photographic paper like I didn't have to do anything. It was all ready and waiting for me. Then Sy got shot, and things really went crazy."

"Crazier than you know. When Sy came to my office that day to discuss his will, he looked as if some great weight had been lifted off him. Something big had happened. He hadn't even taken a seat before he said, "He's here. I found my man, Phil Claussen. He gets all of it, everything.

"I didn't exactly fall off my chair, but I came close enough. I spent at least two hours trying to talk him out of it. Remember how insane it sounded to you when I told you he'd named you as his sole heir? Well, that's just how crazy it sounded to me when he first told me about his decision. I thought he'd lost it for sure, but he never regarded it as a coincidence. To Sy, you were right where you were supposed to be."

"Maybe things would have been better if you'd changed his mind," Phil said. "Maybe he would still be alive, and I wouldn't have the SBI breathing down my neck."

"Believe me, I tried. But you have to understand some things about the Birch family, Sy, and Dani. Dani's mom was the same way. They see things, the future, or say they do. And when that happens, nothing will change their minds. Clairvoyance, or whatever you want to call it, I don't really buy into it. I sat right across from Sy and told him he was nuts, leaving everything to somebody he barely knew, but I might as well have been talking to the wall."

"You can take it all back," Phil said. "I'll sign the

papers right now."

"Sorry, my friend, it doesn't work that way. It's all yours, and remember your thousand acres sits on top of some of the biggest oil deposits in the state."

"Oh, yeah, the oil. As far as I'm concerned, it can stay right where it is. I have no plans for digging it up. That would ruin Sy's plans for Clayton, and I'm not going to be responsible for that."

"He'd be happy to hear you say that. He loved this little town and wanted it to stay exactly as it is, but you know that already," she said.

"I need another drink. There must be some way you can get me out of this."

Her laugh came out as a snort. "There are plenty of people around here who wish that very same thing. If there was a way to get you out of the picture, somebody would have thought of it by now."

"Bring 'em on, first come, first served," he said.

"Be careful what you wish for."

"Then I have just one question for you, all that's happened, am I being set up? Because it's starting to feel pretty strange."

"If I get solid information about anything, I'll let you know immediately. So far, everything's conjecture, and there's always plenty of that. If I hear something, you'll know it too. But just so you know, there are some powerful players involved here, and they think you pulled a fast one and grabbed up what was rightfully theirs."

Phil downed his drink, threw a twenty on the table, and headed for the door. He caught a glimpse of Sandra's pained expression as he left without saying another word. Clearly, she had more to say, but he was in no mood to hear it. Coming out of the darkened room, the afternoon sun blinded him, adding to his feelings of having stumbled into an alternate universe. This one, where he'd spent the last six months, seemed to be spinning out of control.

He drove back to the office. He needed to check in, and maybe a few words with the sheriff could bring back some sense of normalcy.

Barnhill met him at the front entrance. "For God's sake, Phil, you've been drinking."

"Just one, well, two maybe."

"How many doesn't matter. Your whisky breath says you've been drinking on the job. If you walk up to that SBI guy smelling like liquor, you'll get both of us shitcanned. Now get out of here. I don't want to see you or smell you for the rest of the day."

Any thoughts Phil might have had about whether his situation could get any worse were dispelled immediately: it could, and just had.

He wasn't ready to go home yet, so he turned off on the path that led to the campground, his campground now, his own little oasis. Should have come here earlier. This would be the perfect place to clear his head, maybe take the boat out on the pond for a little rest and relaxation. But any thought about finding solace vanished as soon as he turned into the drive. He hadn't been there for almost two weeks, and the drastic changes shocked him. The trail was now rutted as if someone had driven heavy vehicles over it, spinning their wheels. He counted four trash bags alongside, two of which had been ripped apart—raccoons, probably—and the contents scattered all over.

So different now from when he'd first driven down

this lane, the fragrant scent of pine needles carried on the breeze, everything in order, no litter, nothing that hadn't grown there naturally. Then it looked as if someone cared, took time to keep up appearances. But back then, Sy Birch owned it, not Phil Claussen.

He parked his cruiser and headed toward the pond. Along the way, he would walk past the showers and toilets. The stench hit him from twenty yards away. By half that distance, he could only hold his hand over his mouth and nose and run. He didn't bother to look. That odor came from only one possible source. He didn't need to see it to know what it was.

This was as bad as it could get, short of finding a couple of dead bodies lying around. In all the weeks he'd lived in these woods parked nearby in his RV, those facilities were always kept clean and odor-free. He'd taken showers there. Sure, it was rustic, but he never worried about sanitation.

He hurried along the path, putting distance between his nose and the putrid toilets. He'd owned the place for about a month now and look at what had become of it. Better still, smell it to get the full effect. How had things gone to hell so quickly?

Before Sy's death, Phil always assumed that the old man cleaned the place himself, but he never saw him doing it. Surely, if Sy was the caretaker, Phil would have spotted him there, but it never happened. So he really didn't know who looked after the campsite, and Sy never told him, but even after Sy's death, the grounds remained shipshape. All the ruin had happened very recently, on his watch, his ownership.

He continued along the path toward the pond. This little oasis had come to be his refuge, his retreat. But apparently, those days were gone as well. Although not so foul as the toilets, the pond now emitted a rancid aroma of its own, dead fish floating on the surface, the very pond where he and Dani had gone swimming so many times, where Phil had taken the little skiff out alone, just to sit and enjoy the silence. Now the sad little skiff lay overturned on the bank, several large holes in its bottom, and swimming in the polluted pond was out of the question.

It couldn't be this way, but it was. If he believed his own eyes and nose, this little Eden where he had landed months before had, under his ownership, turned into a veritable cesspool. And it wasn't just neglect that had caused this ruin. Simple neglect would have led to a return to wildness, and overgrowth of natural things, trees, and vegetation that were a natural part of this habitat. No, this devastation was a willful act. Only humanity at its basest level, humanity with an aim to destroy what had once been simple and beautiful, could do this.

Now he had to find those perpetrators and encourage them, by breaking as many bones as necessary, to tell him why. Then the wrath of God would descend upon those responsible, and the bastards would know fear experienced only by those about to be thrown into the pit. Phil was pissed.

As he walked back up the path, a flash of white off in the pines caught his eye, an abandoned washing machine. His thousand-acre paradise had become a trash dump. Someone would pay…but who?

He parked the cruiser in front of his house. Home sweet home, at least, appeared intact, spared the ravages of what was now the second worst day of his life. Dani's embrace could smooth over any number of slights, and if he got lucky, could turn a bad day into a holiday. She could also tell him what happened to his big truck, which was suspiciously missing from its usual spot.

She sashayed through the bedroom door, a vision in a little black dress, short, snug, and cut low in front. Given the choice between this goddess and a thousand bucks, most men would choose the goddess. Phil would, for sure.

But she wasn't smiling. Where was that high-voltage grin that could light up a room and make him tingle in all the right places?

He reached for her, but she pushed him away. "I'm going out."

Still, he must have got close enough.

"You've been drinking." A scowl on her face as if he'd just driven his cruiser through a troop of girl scouts. "What the hell, Phil? Drinking on the job, are you trying to get fired?"

"Just one."

"Yeah, right. You'll have to fix your own dinner. There's stuff in the freezer. Use the microwave."

"Where's my truck?" he asked.

"Your truck? And what truck would that be?"

"The one you got for me, I keep it parked right out front."

"That's gone. The truck was a repo, remember? It was never really yours. The people paid their back payments and got their truck back."

"What time will you be home?" he asked. They had a few things to discuss, the truck being one of them, and the list was growing rapidly. The temperature inside the house seemed to have dropped ten degrees at least. What the hell had happened between them?

"Don't wait up." All she left behind was the scent of her perfume, something a lot spicier than her usual lilacs.

The rest of his life seemed to be going to hell. Why should his love life be any different? He watched her walk down the path, stiletto pumps and a short skirt sending out a message that needed no explanation.

Chapter Twenty-Three

Microwave lasagna tasted like cardboard soaked in catsup. At least it wouldn't be wasted. Alfie's requirements were very liberal; the dog was a four-legged garbage disposal. But where was the damned dog? Not like him to miss a meal, not like him at all, and right now, Phil could use his company, doggy grin, and wagging tail in particular.

The big universal conspiracy, if that was what was going on, was turning nasty. He parked himself on the front porch, waiting for Dani to return; it proved to be a long wait and futile. He tried not to think of where she might be or what she might be doing. He went to bed alone.

The next morning reflected his mood perfectly, rain driven by a northeast wind, no Dani, no dog, no truck. Sometime during the past twenty-four hours, he'd become radioactive, someone to be avoided. Was the rain falling on everyone else, or just him?

He stopped for breakfast at the local pancake bistro and indulged himself in a second, then a third cup of coffee. So, he'd be a few minutes late, so what? If they needed him, they could reach him easily enough, not like he was some grammar school kid sitting at his desk waiting for roll call.

But this morning, of all mornings, it did matter that he was late because there was someone at his desk…waiting, a very unhappy SBI agent who checked his watch when Phil walked in. Phil didn't know then but would learn, of the dick's obsession with punctuality, how in his Oklahoma City office, tardiness of even a few minutes got a letter placed in the employee's file. A second offense got a two-day suspension, and a third offense, dismissal.

The other aspect of the dick's work proved more problematic; when he thought he'd found some irregularity, he wouldn't let go. The sheriff described him like a dog with a bone, gnawing and gnawing until there was nothing left. At the moment, his bone consisted of the strange coincidence of Phil's arrival at Sy's campground, with two shooting deaths, and, in the dick's point of view, the common denominator was Phil Claussen.

****

Phil settled into a chair across from the dick. He'd probably have to spend much of the day right here going over and over the most insignificant details with this picky bastard, a situation made worse by a headache that had kicked in an hour earlier…hangover? After only two drinks, or had he lost count?

Just as they were getting started, Barnhill stuck his head in the door. "Need your weapon, Phil. We're checking ballistics on all the sidearms in the office. You'll have it back this afternoon."

Then it began, questions, questions, and more questions. Why had Phil left a good job and family in Wakefield? Was there any evidence of brain damage during his altercation with the woman in the bar? Who would the dick contact for copies of Phil's medical records? By the time the noon hour rolled around, they had gotten no further than Phil's purchase of the RV. At this rate, the inquisition would run on for several days.

Except that it wouldn't. After they sat down for the afternoon session, Phil said the magic words: "I've called my lawyer. She says no more questions unless she's present."

The dick, who held a half-inch stack of pages, presumably having decided to start with Phil's birth and work forward from there, looked as if he'd just swallowed a piece of spoiled meat.

"This is highly irregular," said the dick. "You're a county employee."

"You can't deny me my constitutional right to legal representation," Phil said. Actually, he'd made no calls to his lawyer and had no idea whether it was a constitutional right, but obviously, the dick didn't either because he sat there glaring at Phil as if his entire year was ruined, not just the afternoon.

"Anyway, my attorney isn't available until tomorrow at ten o'clock, so I'll see you then." Phil stood and headed for the door.

"No, no, that won't give me nearly enough time." The dick slapped his stack of pages on the desk, but apparently, nothing in his job description trumped the alleged right to legal counsel.

Phil gave him one last look. "You have a good day now," he said, hoping that would be impossible now that the dick had nobody to push around.

He stopped by Barnhill's office. The sheriff wore that worried look that was becoming standard for him. This was a cause of concern to Phil because his job as deputy was to take some of the load off the sheriff,

"When can I get my gun back?" Phil asked. "I

don't plan to shoot anybody, but I feel better wearing it."

"Come in and close the door." Barnhill motioned Phil to a chair. "There's a problem. When we compared the round fired from your weapon with those that killed Sy and his brother—same gun, mind you—they match up pretty good. Now, I didn't tell the folks in the ballistics lab it was your gun; for the time being, all it has is a number. But if the final report comes back showing a match, we have a big problem. I'll keep the weapon pending the report."

"Not possible," Phil said. "That gun was never out of my possession. No way."

They sat for a few moments, looking everywhere to avoid making eye contact. Neither of them had to say it; the sheriff knew from years of law enforcement, and Phil knew from watching TV crime shows: a ballistics match was definitive. Suspects could be put away based on ballistics. Phil himself could be put away based on ballistics, especially since he insisted the gun was never out of his possession. He had alibis for both killings; he was with Dani, but considering the contentious state of his home life, would that be enough to let him continue life as a free man?

"Take a couple of days off," Barnhill said. "We both need a break. Just keep your phone handy, in case I need to reach you, and don't leave the county."

If you asked Phil what he did after leaving the sheriff's office, there would be a blank space between then and the time he pulled into his driveway. For all he could tell you, he might have driven the entire way in reverse. When conscious thought returned, he found himself sitting in his cruiser, in his driveway, the engine running. How long had he been sitting there, a minute, ten minutes, an hour? He had no idea.

His situation now was not totally unlike that of about six months before when he'd stood before a judge in Wakefield, NC, and, instead of being ordered back in the jail for a long, probably eventful weekend, he got off with a rambling lecture about community standards and role modeling, and how those with children of school age expected much better from their teachers. Somewhere during the judge's harangue, Phil realized he had but one choice...run like hell. For him, life in Wakefield was over.

Even if his life in Clayton, OK, was over now, he couldn't run, not this time, because his situation was much worse. The law did not look kindly upon suspected felons who fled the area.

He went inside to change. For a few days, at least, he would not be a deputy, just a regular citizen with a lot of trouble on his plate.

Early afternoon and Dani was sleeping soundly. He didn't know what time she'd come in. The hot little black dress she wore yesterday was nowhere to be seen but lying on the floor beside the bed lay the skimpy shorts and top set she wore when she wanted to attract attention. Okay, he didn't know whether that was the reason she wore it, only that stares from every man in the general area followed wherever she went.

He changed in the next room, draped his uniform over a hanger, and hung it in the hall closet. He donned jeans and a blue T-shirt. Still no Alfie. Where was that damned dog?

He tossed a few toiletries into a bag, along with a change of underwear, and headed out.

He took the car, leaving Dani with no transportation, but getting around didn't seem to be a problem for her. The car had met with some misfortune since he'd last driven it. The right taillight was smashed as if the driver had backed into something, and there was a newly scraped area on the driver's side door, where the rearview mirror dangled from a few strands of wire and sheared metal. When he got back, Dani would have some explaining to do, but that was never a problem for her, either.

With no specific destination in mind, he drove north toward Enid, a town only slightly larger than Clayton. He stopped several times to call the office, making sure he was always in phone range. For almost ten miles, he noticed a car following, always maintaining the same distance. Since there were so few cars on the road, the vehicle stood out like a sore thumb. He was being tailed. Each time he pulled off the road, the car, a dark gray late-model sedan, drove past, but when he was back on the road, so was his tail. The driver knew what he was doing and was making no great effort to conceal his presence. Apparently, he wanted Phil to know he was being followed.

He pulled into a shopping mall and stopped at an outlet store. The late afternoon was getting chilly, and he'd forgotten to bring a jacket. When he came out of the store, the trailing car was parked on the other side of the lot near the exit. There were two guys in the front seat. Both wore ball caps pulled low over their faces.

Phil walked toward the car, time for a little face-to-face confrontation. But when he closed to about fifty feet, the driver tore out of the parking lot, burning rubber, and Phil didn't see them again.

He called Claudia and asked for Sheriff Barnhill. "I'm being tailed. Any idea who?" He didn't think the sheriff was responsible, but Phil wanted him to know he was aware of the tail.

"No idea," Barnhill said. "You sure you're not imagining this?"

"They weren't trying very hard to keep out of sight. I think they wanted me to know they were following me."

"Did you get a license number?"

"Just the first three letters. It was an Oklahoma plate."

"Okay, I'll run it through, see if I can find anything. I'll let you know, and remember what I said, don't leave the county."

Phil stayed overnight in a motel called the Prairie View and had a dinner of spicy fajitas at a TGIF across the street. Probably an after-school job for the very young redhead who waited on him. She would be about the same age as his own daughter, Addie, who, for all he knew, might be waiting tables this evening too.

The motel room was musty, and the windows would not open. There were water stains on the ceiling. He thought about propping the door open for fresh air, but if he was being followed by parties unknown, a locked door seemed a wiser option. Instead, he turned the AC on high and kept his jacket on.

He lay on the bed, trying without success to interest himself in the evening news on the TV. His own dilemma was much more pressing. How had everything gone to hell so fast? He could understand a little bad luck. Everybody had some, but for just about every aspect of his life to suddenly fall into ruin was too much.

He saw only one explanation: someone had a plan, and he was the fall guy. This wasn't cosmic in scope. It was right here and now. He could reach out and touch it, and when he did, somebody would know real pain. Now, who and why? He thought about it, then thought some more, then went to sleep thinking about it and woke the next morning none the wiser.

He was in no big hurry to get back to Clayton. The SBI dick could wait, served him right for being such an asshole. Phil drove around the area for a while, keeping an eye out for the car that had followed him the day before. Check-out time at the motel was eleven o'clock, so he gathered up his belongings and headed south, back toward trouble.

Dani was standing on the porch when he drove up shortly past noon, no welcoming smile, no hug. "Where have you been?"

"Just needed to get away for a day."

"What have you done to my car?" She walked around it as if seeing the damage for the first time.

"Me? I didn't do anything to it. All the damage was done when I got into it yesterday. Must have been you."

She shook her head. "You'd better watch your drinking, Phil. Bad enough that you might injure yourself, but you might hurt someone else driving around drunk."

"Godammit, I do not drive drunk."

She took a step back, raising her hands as if she feared he might attack her. "You should think about getting some help before this gets out of hand. Now, give me the keys. I'll get it fixed today, but you're going to pay for it."

This was so wrong. He did not have a drinking problem. The two drinks he'd had with his attorney were the first he'd had in several months, so long as he didn't count the occasional beer binges with Earl, which seemed more like harmless fun, anyway.

He had to walk around his cruiser to get to the front door. That's when he found the broad scrape down the right side. He found no other damage, but how had this happened? He had the only set of keys in his pocket; no one else could have driven it. He checked inside the vehicle. At least the interior was spared, but deep inside the central compartment, partly concealed, he found a half-empty bottle of cheap bourbon, the type he might use for a disinfectant but certainly would not drink. Not his, absolutely, not his.

Either somebody was doing a number on him, or he was losing his marbles. Denial, he knew well enough, was a characteristic of the alcoholic, but he could not bring himself to believe he was that deep into the process. No, he wasn't crazy, and he wasn't an alcoholic, not yet, but whoever was out to convince him that he was, was doing a damned good job.

Phil searched the rest of the vehicle, making sure there were no more liquor bottles hidden away. He thought about drugs. Could someone have planted some in the car? Probably no need for that since they were so effective in making him out to be a belligerent drunk. He knew the game now; he just didn't know the players or their motives.

He was standing by the cruiser, wondering how he was going to explain the damage to Sheriff Barnhill when Dani came back driving a shining black convertible. The girl had wasted no time in getting new wheels.

"What have you done to your patrol car?" she asked.

"I didn't do anything to it. There was no damage when I left it here yesterday. Now look at it."

"Honestly, Phil, first the car, now your patrol vehicle, you better get this under control before you kill somebody."

"Dammit, Dani, I told you, I didn't damage either of those cars."

"You don't have to shout. What I'm telling you is the truth. Maybe you don't want to hear about it, but it's the truth."

"And another thing, where's Alfie?"

"Alfie? Who's Alfie?"

"Alfie's our dog, Dani. Don't pretend you don't know about him. What have you done with him?"

She walked backward away from him, eyes wide, hands in the same defensive position as before. "Oh, my God, Phil."

Now he was shouting in spite of himself. "Where is he?"

She stopped when she reached the safety of the porch. "We don't have a dog, Phil. We've never had a dog." She raced inside, slamming the door behind her.

She locked him out. He had a key for the front door, but the deadbolt stopped him cold. He thought about kicking in the door, but that would just give her more ammunition to use in her characterization of him as a violent drunk as if she needed much more. His arrest six months ago, drunk and disorderly, would apparently haunt him forever, and another exhibition, truthful or not, would get him put away for a lot longer than a weekend.

But what could she have done with Alfie? If she was looking for a way to really hurt him, she couldn't have done better than doing away with his dog. She knew how he would react to her little act. Alfie was his pal, and right now, Phil could use a friend, even a non-verbal furry one.

His only option for the night, unless he wanted to sleep in the back seat of the cruiser, was to drive back to the Prairie View where he'd stayed the night before. Might this be the second of many nights he would be spending in motels? But even that would be better than jail.

The next morning, after fortifying himself again at the pancake house—it wasn't alcohol he was hung up on, it was pancakes and sometimes crispy fried chicken—he headed back to the sheriff's office to face the music and explain the damage to the cruiser. On the way, he made up a story about how he'd parked it in the motel lot and found the damage the next morning. It was weak but better than trying to explain how it could have happened in his own driveway.

Nobody jumped for joy when he walked into the office. Claudia, wouldn't look at him, neither would the sheriff.

"Here," Barnhill said. "You've saved me the trouble of serving you."

"What is it?" Phil took the folded paper.

"A restraining order. Judge Driscoll issued it this morning. You are to have no contact with Dani Birch because she fears for her personal safety."

"What? This is fucking ridiculous. She can't keep me out of my own house. It's my name on the deed, not hers. She has no legal right to be there."

"Keep it down, Phil. This is a legal document. I don't know what she told the judge, but if you go near her, I'll have to arrest you. If you want it changed, you'll have to see your attorney.

"At least you caught a break with that SBI guy. He got called back to Oklahoma City. Somebody shot a bank vice-president. But just so you know, you're still probably near the top of his shit list."

"Is there anybody around here that I haven't pissed off?" Phil asked.

Chapter Twenty-Four

"What on earth?" Sandra Newton scanned the restraining order Phil placed on her desk. "I thought you two were close. Maybe I'd be hearing wedding bells, nothing like this. Your life seems to have run off the rails, my friend. Anything you need to talk about?"

"If I knew myself, I'd tell you, but I don't. Things have got a little crazy, for sure, but Dani seems to have changed overnight. I mean, I know her moods are unpredictable, but this really threw me. How did she get this order in the first place? I've never threatened her, never laid a hand on her, not in anger, anyway," he said.

They shared a very uncomfortable silence as if there was a big pile of poop on her desk that they were trying to ignore. "Okay, I don't see a big problem here. The house is legally yours, so if anyone has to leave, it will be Dani. The judge will take a little convincing, and I can manage that, but maybe before rushing into the legal side of it, you should let things cool down a bit."

Phil had been standing by her desk until now, but his knees became shaky, and he opted for the chair. "I just don't understand it. Everywhere I turn, I seem to be Public Enemy Number One. It's like some people around here are playing pin the tail on the donkey, and I'm the donkey."

His remark got a brief smile out of Sandra, but her stern professional look returned quickly. "Dani is a very smart girl. Whatever her reasons might be, I'm sure she made a strong case for the judge, and Judge Driscoll, he's...well, he's just as susceptible to a pair of pretty blue eyes as any man. But I should be able to get the wording changed so you can return to your house."

"I'd appreciate that. I'm getting tired of motels."

"But there's another game here, don't you see? There's a bit of character assassination going on. You're described in this document as a violent alcoholic. That's going to stick, even when we get your house back. Your reputation took a real kick in the ass here, and it wasn't spotless, to begin with."

"I still don't get it. If I'd been like she said, drunk, violent, I could understand it, but I wasn't, never have been."

"What if some sharp District Attorney flew to Wakefield and took a deposition from that lady who tried to crack your skull. What would she have to say about Phil Claussen?"

"She would be the only person in Wakefield who hates me, except maybe my ex-wife. Check that file you got on me if you don't believe me. I lived in that town for seven years, a model citizen, not so much as a parking ticket, then one stupid day I screw up, and that's all anybody will remember, not fair."

"It doesn't have to be fair," she said. "You must have had legal representation then, right?"

"Yeah, her name is Marcia Bishop, a friend of the family. I have her contact information on some papers somewhere."

"Get it for me. I'll contact her, see what kind of

argument she made to the judge to keep you out of jail."

"She used my service record. The judge had a big soft spot for the military, but do you think it will come to that?" he asked.

"We'd better be prepared, in case it does."

"When will I know if I can go back to my house?"

"I'll call you as soon as I get to see the judge. In the meantime, stay away from the place, and whatever you do, stay out of bars."

The post office was only two blocks up the street, so he stopped in to check his mailbox. He'd rented the box only a few months before, and already it was stuffed with junk mail. He was ready to throw the entire stack into the trash until he spotted the letter from Clayton County, complete with the official logo, an oil rig, what else?

An official letter from the county clerk, two pages, informing him, complaints received about the unkempt appearance of his campground property, trash strewn all over, foul-smelling facilities, a public health hazard. Failure to clean up the area would result in a daily fine beginning the second week in November, ten days away. So, the *cover Phil Claussen in crap* campaign was still in full swing. Thank God he had no plans to run for public office. How long would his job as Deputy Sheriff of Clayton County hold up? With the big black cloud following him around, probably not so long.

****

It took two days of hauling trash bags out to the town dump, scrubbing down the toilets, then pouring bleach over everything and into every opening. The acrid aroma of bleach was only a slight improvement over that of human excrement, but there was no other option short of burning the facilities to the ground.

On the third day, bone-tired and reeking, he padlocked the showers and toilets and turned off the water main. He had a ten-foot-wide gate made of two sections of chain-length fence installed the same day and secured it with a padlock. The fence was flanked on either side by mature pines, so vehicular entry from the road was effectively blocked. He threw away the clothes he'd worn during the clean-up.

He took down the sign that advertised the area as a campsite and replaced it with a larger one, *PRIVATE PROPERTY, KEEP OUT*. Then he called Sandra Newton: "I've had enough. I want to sell out, house, land, everything. It's brought me nothing but grief, and I want to get rid of it."

"You can't. After you've maintained residence for one year, then you can sell, not before. You should have read the fine print like I asked you to."

"How about if I just give it away, donate it to the county?"

"Sorry, it's still your responsibility for one year."

"There has to be a way. If I can get past this other mess, I'm going shopping for a new RV. I can't wait to put this place in my rearview mirror, permanently."

"And what is this other mess, something you haven't told me about?"

"Yeah, a little problem with the ballistics tests on the bullets that killed Sy and his brother; they might match my gun."

"Might match?" Her voice went up several notches in both pitch and volume. "Phil, either they do, or they don't. This is damned serious. You should have told me."

"I know, I know."

"Who else has used the gun?"

"Nobody, it has been in my possession all along."

"Whose fingerprints were on the gun?"

"Just mine. Barnhill said there was one partial print, but not enough to get a match. So it's just me. Crazy, huh?"

"The DA is going to have a field day with this. Somebody has served you up on a silver platter."

"How do you know I didn't do it?"

"Because you've already passed the Sy Birch character test, mine too. That doesn't sound like much and wouldn't stand up in court, but it means a lot to me."

"Okay, what do I do, and when do I do it?" he asked.

"My office, nine a.m. tomorrow. Be prepared to spend most of the day. I just hope we're not starting too late. Whoever is after you is way ahead of us."

Yep, Wakefield all over again, only worse.

Somehow, somewhere, he must have pissed off some vengeful deity because the shit that had been raining down on him for the past six months was definitely supernatural. Now he was seeking legal advice again. More likely, he needed an exorcist.

****

Phil arrived early for the meeting, but Sandra was already at her desk waiting for him. "I stopped by the bakery to get some donuts." She pointed to a cardboard box on a table next to her desk. "The coffee's fresh.

"I do have some good news; I got the restraining order lifted, so you can sleep in your own house tonight, but no drinking and stay strictly nonviolent."

"Thanks for taking care of that. I still don't get how I got labeled a mean drunk."

"I had a long talk with Judge Driscoll, and he seemed a little embarrassed by the whole thing. Apparently, Dani put on quite a performance in his chambers, tears, hysterics, like she feared for her life, all aided and abetted by the DA who was cheering her on. It seemed strange that she'd consulted him. Has she had any contact with him before?" she asked.

"None that I know of. Why would she?"

"That's a question we're going to have to answer sooner rather than later. My snoop tells me Dani spent a lot of time during the past week or so in the DA's office. I have no idea what she might have been doing there, and I assume you don't either."

"None," he said. "Who is your snoop?"

"I won't divulge her name. She's a private investigator who does background checks for me. She did yours back when you first came to Clayton. You can bet the DA has a number of his own at work, and by now, he knows just about everything there is to know about you. And she tells me that the DA has hired an acting coach from the university drama department in Norman. I can't wait to see how that turns out."

"I just can't understand the connection between Dani and the DA She never mentioned him before," Phil said.

"Just keep in mind that, if they're working together, they could be splitting up a fortune in oil rights between them once you're out of the way."

"Hard to believe she would turn on me like that." It was a gut punch for Phil, the thought that this mysterious woman who now occupied so much of his life could be sailing under false colors. " You know this DA pretty well, then?"

"Oh, yes, we've butted heads in the courtroom a number of times before."

"Do you trust him?"

"Whether he's trustworthy or not doesn't matter. What I do know is that he's very thorough, and he'll do whatever it takes to bring you down. If he has to bend the rules, he'll do it."

"I don't get it. I never did anything to him," Phil said.

"Oh, but you did, you took his oil, or what he believes to be his. Remember, he claims to be Sy's son, illegitimate, of course, and thinks he should be next in line for the oil rights. But you jumped ahead of him, and that puts you at the top of his shit list. My snoop turned up some more interesting information about him. It seems that the DA owes money to some people who have a short fuse when it comes to repayment, so he probably wants to get you out of the picture as soon as possible.

"So, the word to keep in mind…oil, you're sitting on a lot of it. The DA, among others, has had his eye on it for a long time. Sy Birch didn't do you any favors when he left it all to you."

"Just what I needed to hear."

****

"I pulled the tax records on the Birch repo business," she said when she returned with more coffee. "Even when Sy was alive, they reported only a modest income, so either they were not reporting all of their revenue, or they weren't making as much money as they said they were. From the description of the cars you saw Dani driving, I'd say they were cheating the tax man. Of course, if the cars were stolen, they wouldn't be paying taxes anyway."

"I guess I never asked enough questions. But even when I did, she managed to duck them. She is a hard girl to pin down."

"Income tax evasion is serious. I know some people at the IRS, and I might drop a suggestion that they check out the repo business."

"Do you think Sy was involved?"

"Could be. In the legitimate repo operations, there's a paper trail, and it can be traced all the way along. Of course, if it's done under the table, cash only, that's a different matter. Unless they have a really slick process, luxury vehicles are hard to conceal. At the very least, an investigation will give them something else to think about, so they can't spend all their time smearing you."

"I'm beginning to feel like a first-class idiot here. I just assumed these expensive cars were part of their usual inventory. Didn't even ask where she got them, not that she'd tell me anyway."

"This repo business definitely needs a closer look. Now, tell me about the night Sy got shot."

"Dani and Earl and I were at the RV. We'd had a couple of beers. Angie was there too. Do you want the whole story or just the highlights?"

"Everything," she said. "You might leave out important things, and we can't afford to get careless."

It was not a story he was particularly proud of, how he and Earl had gone fishing on a hot afternoon in a small boat with a cooler full of beer. Since the fish wouldn't cooperate, they drank, eventually winding up stuporous. The girls swam out and somehow got them back to shore, then back to the RV, then onto foldout lawn chairs, where they slept it off. Phil remembered the girls chatting while he feigned sleep, hoping to pick up some information because, at that point, he knew almost nothing about Dani, past, present, or future.

"I think it was early evening, just after dark, when we heard the first shot, then two more, coming from the direction of Sy's cabin. I got up to investigate, but Dani and Earl got in his truck and drove away. Before she left, Dani gave me a handgun; I just remembered that. She told me to stash it in the RV. And she took some money that I'd hidden in the fridge."

"Where was the money from?"

"From one of her repo sales, I guess, about twenty thousand dollars. She got it from Earl."

"That's a lot of money to keep lying around. How about the gun? Where did she get it, and what did you do with it?"

"I don't know where she got it, but I stashed it in the RV like she asked. Then Angie and I went to Sy's cabin and found him shot dead. We didn't go any farther than the front door. The sheriff and a state trooper got there a few minutes later."

"Who called them?" she asked.

"Don't know."

"Seems strange that they arrived so soon after the shots were fired, don't you think?"

"Yeah, almost like they knew about it beforehand. The sheriff was all in my face, implying that I was a suspect."

"Why did he think that? You weren't carrying the

weapon, were you?"

"No."

"Did you touch the body?"

He shook his head.

"So, you don't know whether it was still warm or not. The EMTs should have made a note of it. I'll check."

"Why?"

"Because we don't know for sure the shots you heard were the same shots that killed Sy, do we? Let me see if I have this straight; you wake up out of a drunken stupor, hear three shots, Dani and Earl leave in his truck, not before she gives you a handgun and takes money out of your freezer, you and Angie find Sy shot to death, and moments later the sheriff and a state trooper arrive."

"Yeah, that's pretty much it," he said. "I'll ask the sheriff how he got to the house so fast, him and the state trooper both. I'm still his deputy now, so he should tell me that, at least."

"You were supposed to make my list shorter," she said, "but you've added a third sheet. And the gun Dani gave you, what became of it?"

"I kept it. Tried to give it back to her, but she wanted me to keep it, so I did."

"Did she tell you why you should keep it?"

"No, I did fire a couple of shots in the air one night when a car parked in front of the house. I told the sheriff about it. One more thing, when I moved into Sy's house, I opened his gun safe. There were two more semiautomatics inside, along with some other revolvers. Handguns seem to be popular around here, never would have guessed. Why are you laughing?"

"This story might make a great romance novel. Just taking the high points, a guy comes to a small town in Oklahoma, picks up a girl alongside the road, falls in love, her father and uncle are shot to death, and the guy winds up inheriting a thousand acres with a lake of oil underneath. Now, does this sound believable?" she asked.

"No, not even close. I know it sounds weird, but how do we present my side of the story unless I tell it?"

"You won't. You can't. If this comes to trial—and I think it will—you won't go anywhere near a witness stand. The DA would destroy your credibility in a heartbeat. Whoever has set you up has done a very good job."

She refilled their coffee cups. "I was thinking, it's been a long time since one person kicked up such a fuss around here in such a short time."

"It wasn't just me," he said. "I've had lots of help."

"That you have, Phil Claussen, that you have."

Chapter Twenty-Five

Sheriff Barnhill sounded like he was a million miles away, but his telephone voice always sounded that way. "Bad news, Phil, the ballistics match."

Fortunately, Phil was sitting down. Otherwise, he might have wound up on the floor. The impossible had just happened. "Who else knows?"

"The D.A. for sure and the bastard from the SBI. First time I've seen him smile since he got here. You should let your attorney know, too. Do you want to come in, or should I come and get you?"

"I'll call Sandra Newton. She's probably expecting this. I'll drive in since I have to bring the cruiser back anyway. This afternoon okay?"

"That's good. The sooner you get here, the better. And just so you know, I'm just as unhappy about this as you are. Sandra Newton is a sharp lady, so hopefully, she can make some sense out of this because I sure as hell can't."

****

Sandra Newton was sharp, all right, and she was also stern. "Do not say anything to anybody about this case until I get there. Do you understand?"

"Yeah, I get it."

"No, you don't. We're not talking about a night in the county jail here, Phil. This is damned serious. You could spend a long, long time, maybe the rest of your life behind bars if this doesn't go well."

"I understand." No, she was right...he didn't. He didn't understand because it all seemed unreal. The woman he'd planned to spend the rest of his life with had suddenly turned on him without, so far as he could see, any cause whatsoever. Meanwhile, the powers in a small town in Oklahoma had drawn a big target on his back, apparently intending to grind him into mush. So, no, he didn't get it, unless Earl with his rant on fatalism was right, and this was all part of some big cosmic plan. In which case, he didn't stand a snowball's chance in hell, never had.

****

No surprises with the process at the sheriff's office. He'd been through the same steps about six months before, courtesy of the Wakefield Police Department. He handed in his badge to Sheriff Barnhill, who looked quite sheepish when he took it. Then the fingerprinting, then sitting for the photo ID, same as when he'd posed earlier in that same office, except that one was part of his deputy sheriff identification, and the current one was for incarceration.

"I feel pretty shitty about this, Phil," Sheriff Barnhill said as he led Phil back to his cell, "but I got no choice. Have to treat you the same as everybody else."

"Something I forgot," Phil said. "I never asked you about that night Sy was shot, how you got there so fast. Couldn't have been more than ten, fifteen minutes since we heard the shots before me and Angie were at his house."

"You didn't touch the body, did you?" the sheriff asked.

"No."

"It was stone cold. The shots you heard were not the shots that killed Sy. I got an anonymous phone call about twenty minutes earlier about a shooting at Sy's place. I never found out who placed the call. I had a pretty good idea but couldn't prove anything. They must have notified the state troopers too."

"It doesn't make sense at all," Phil said.

"Nope, it doesn't unless whoever is pulling the strings here started off with a plan, and Sy naming you as his heir kicked everything into motion."

"I knew it. I should have climbed back into the RV and hauled ass out of here as soon as I heard about that." Now it was way too late. "Do you think Sy knew this would happen?"

"I've asked myself that a number of times. I don't believe he did, but he must have known the shit would hit the fan after he turned everything over to you."

"I feel like a world-class fool," Phil said.

Sandra Newton arrived shortly past three o'clock, and Sheriff Barnhill let her into Phil's cell. He didn't bother to close the door.

"I'd forgotten how bad it smells back here," she said after Barnhill left.

"You get used to it," Phil said.

"I have some information about how the DA will come after you. You're in for a few surprises, but for the first two days, you'll just have to sit there and take it. It's his job to make you sound like Public Enemy Number One, and he's pretty good at his job. Whatever you do, don't react. Leave that to me."

"I asked the sheriff about the night Sy was shot. He said he was tipped off by an anonymous phone call, so

Sy was dead long before Angie and I got there."

"That makes a lot more sense but still doesn't answer who did it and why," she said.

"The sheriff thought this might be part of a plan that started months ago, right after Sy's will was read. Ever since, I've been walking around with a target on my back."

The color drained from Sandra's face, and, for a moment, Phil thought she might cry. "Dammit, I should have looked after your interests better. Part of this is my fault. I knew there would be people coming after what you inherited, but I didn't think they would go so far as cold-blooded murder."

"Not your fault," he said. "I went along for the ride when I should have been asking questions. I've acted like everybody's puppet and have nobody to blame but myself unless Earl Biggers was right."

"What do you mean?"

"He'd say it was all going to happen anyway no matter what anybody did to prevent it."

"I don't think that argument will carry much weight with the jury. Now, where are your other clothes, the ones you'll wear on Monday in court?"

"This is it," he said, holding up his arms.

"You don't even have a proper suit of clothes?" Sandra Newton looked at Phil as if he'd been running around in his underwear.

"Didn't have any use for one, so I left them in Wakefield," he said.

"What about the ones you wore to Sy's funeral?"

"That was pretty casual, just sports coat and slacks," he said. "Nobody seemed to get very dressed up."

"Well, this is different. Your appearance in court matters a lot, and you can't very well show up dressed casual. Do you understand me, Phil? This is not casual." She slid a sheet of paper across to him. "Write down your sizes, all of them."

"You shouldn't have to do my shopping," he said.

"Don't worry, you'll pay for it."

****

So, there he stood for the arraignment, his second in six months. Judge Driscoll denied Sandra's request for bail because the DA made a better case for Phil being a flight risk. "He came into town in an RV, your honor, from out of nowhere. Who knows where he might go next?" the DA said.

Sandra's argument that Phil was a deputy sheriff and that he should be released on bail out of respect for his position fell short.

Based on the ballistics analysis, he would be charged with both homicides, but the two would be tried separately. The DA, Sandra said, was trying to squeeze as much publicity out of the trial as possible, and two convictions would be much bigger than one, even if it was the same man who pulled the trigger…Phil. It was possible as well that the DA didn't feel quite as confident about the second case involving Fletcher Birch as he did the first because the sheriff was already at the crime scene when Phil arrived.

For Phil, the state of mindlessness that began when he first heard about the ballistics test persisted and had grown even more profound. He just wasn't there. He was floating someplace above it all, watching himself and everybody else scurry about, without really being a part of it.

He floated as Judge Driscoll, heavy, ponderous, simian, with a hairline that extended down almost to meet his eyebrows, asked, "How do you plead?"

He floated, mute, while Sandra Newton spoke up: "My client pleads not guilty.

"Phil, is something wrong with you?" She asked when she'd taken her seat beside him. She leaned in toward him as if trying to come up with a diagnosis. "You seem so distant, almost detached, and this is no time to be detached. This is serious. I need you to focus."

"It still doesn't seem real to me, like it's happening to somebody else."

"It's you, Phil, just you, and you'd better start to pay attention quick." She made a few more notes. "Monday morning, they'll start with your little friend, Dani Birch. I'm still not sure about her angle...love or money usually, sometimes hate. But I don't think she hates you, and she sure isn't acting like she loves you. So that leaves money."

"I don't know what she'll say." There had been a time in the recent past when he'd have been sure of her love and support, but not now.

"I expect she'll say plenty. She's the only one called to testify that day, so the DA probably has big plans for her."

"Poor girl," he said. "Hope they're not too rough on her."

"Phil, listen to me, she's a witness for the prosecution, and she's been carefully coached. She's not there on your behalf. Her testimony might send you to prison, or worse. Do you understand that?"

Then the cloud drifted in again, and he was back

with Dani, buying curtains for the house they would share together, laughing when Alfie turned up his canine nose at her fried chicken. This couldn't be real, so it must be a mistake. That's it, a mistake.

Sandra slapped her hands together. "Look at me. Either you wake up and work with me, or I'm going to ask Judge Driscoll to appoint another attorney, somebody who can make you understand you're in serious trouble."

Maybe that's what woke him up, the look on her face, his attorney, his friend. She'd been with him all along. Now she looked defeated, lost. He was letting her down, and he would not do this. "I'm sorry, no more fucking around, whatever you need, I'm ready now."

****

Saturday afternoon, she brought a gray suit with a muted pinstripe, two white dress shirts, and a couple of ties, one navy blue and one with diagonal stripes. "Try these on," she said. "I still have time to get back to the shop if they don't fit."

He changed in his cell, under the watchful eyes of Sheriff Barnhill, who looked thoroughly embarrassed. The suit was a bit snug in the shoulders, but it was not something he would be wearing for very long, and it was a big improvement over the orange jumpsuit he'd worn at his court appearance in Wakefield six months before.

"You look good," Barnhill said.

Sandra agreed when she came back to inspect him but said, "Oh, shit, shoes. Please tell me you have a decent pair of shoes somewhere. Those hiking boots will not do."

"In my closet back at the house. Look, you can't be running all over fetching stuff for me. Nobody is going to look at my shoes."

"You never know," she said.

"I'll drive him out," Barnhill said. "Go home and get some rest. You're both in for a long week."

He led Phil out the back door to his own personal vehicle, a white sedan with a small crack in the windshield on the passenger side. The interior smelled like cooking spices. The sheriff handed him a baseball cap. "Here, put this on, and try to look inconspicuous. The press vultures have already started to come in. I guess the DA got the word out. He likes to see his picture in the paper."

It was a tense, quiet ride out to Phil's house—he still couldn't bring himself to think of it as his own—where the front door was standing open. "You locked it before you left?" Barnhill asked.

"For sure."

"Who else has a key?"

"Dani."

"Holy shit," said Barnhill when he stepped inside.

Phil following closely behind immediately saw the reason for the sheriff's expletive. Torn apart, that was all he could think of. Even the sofa cushions were slashed open. "I don't think I want to see the bedroom," he said. And quite right he was. The obvious aim was to destroy everything that could be destroyed. Oddly, Sy's artwork and piano were spared, so the destruction took on a more personal note with a new target…Phil Claussen. The pure malice on display there turned his stomach. He thought back to Sandra's list of possible motives: love, money, or hate. Now hate moved to the top of the list. He had enemies he didn't even know about. He could only hope Dani wasn't on the list.

He checked the gun safe in the basement. The marks on the door indicated that someone had made a vigorous but unsuccessful attempt to get inside.

When he looked in the closet, the only thing intact was the shoes he had come for, apparently not worth destroying.

"Any idea who?" asked Barnhill.

"Maybe the same people that trashed the campsite," Phil said. "The only difference is they didn't smear shit over everything here."

"This is definitely a crime scene," Barnhill said. "Go get the yellow tape out of my trunk. I'm going to call the Crime Scene Unit out here. Are you insured?"

"Sandra insisted I get homeowner's insurance when I signed the papers for the property. Guess she was right about that."

"Call them up. Make sure they get lots of photos."

"You took my phone."

"Here, use mine."

The irony of assisting at a crime scene that was all part of his own criminal investigation was not lost on Phil.

After Phil called the insurance company, he called Sandra Newton. "I really hate to bother you, but I thought you ought to see this. Somebody trashed my home."

Twenty minutes later, she walked through the ruin with Phil. The Crime Scene techs were falling over one another, so Phil walked her back outside.

"What on earth?" she asked, her eyes wide.

"Probably the same people who trashed the

campsite. I got a nasty letter from the county, so I cleaned that up myself. Don't think I can handle this job, though."

"Okay, Monday morning, I'm going to take all this to Judge Driscoll in his chambers. We don't know who did this or why, but I think this will throw the DA off his game. He doesn't like surprises." She took a long, penetrating look at Phil. "I hope you're telling me everything because you have some serious enemies. And I don't want any more surprises myself. Look, I have to ask, you don't think Dani could have done this, do you?"

"No way. She just bought most of these new furnishings herself. She wouldn't tear them up like this."

****

"Did you see Judge Driscoll?" he asked his attorney Monday morning while he had breakfast in his cell.

"I did, showed him the photos, told him the sheriff is conducting a criminal investigation."

"What did he make of it?"

"The DA wanted to make it out as vandalism, nothing more, but the judge wouldn't buy that, not after he saw the photos of the damage," she said.

"So, it didn't make much difference."

"I think it did. It added a seed of doubt. Our best shot is making things appear that you've been set up for a murder rap by someone for some reason that isn't clear yet, although oil is number one on the list. The judge will have to give us some leeway there. I won't present this straightaway. We'll hold onto it for now. The judge knows we have it; the DA knows we have it, and, if we get lucky, the sheriff will turn up something in our favor."

"Okay, then, what should I expect this morning?"

"Expect to see your reality, what you've known and seen and heard, all torn up and put back together in a way you've never seen before. That's what the DA does, takes facts and reassembles them until they tell a completely different story, and he's good at it. And remember, you're a good man, no matter what you hear in the courtroom."

Chapter Twenty-Six

He'd drawn a much larger crowd this time compared to his previous courtroom appearance back in Wakefield. Main Street in Clayton must have been deserted since everybody in town was packed into the courtroom. They filled every available seat and lined the back wall. So many bodies, some of them supportive, some of them angry, most of them just curious——all of them packed in together producing heat and an aroma that by midday would resemble an overfilled laundry hamper. So far as he knew, there had never been a public execution in Clayton; would he be their first?

Across the aisle sat the loyal opposition, the guys who wanted to hang him, the DA and his minions, four of them. Seated up front at the small desk with only his attorney for company, Phil felt like a seal on a small ice floe surrounded by hungry polar bears.

He glanced at the jury box, where the twelve sat, comfortable with each other, probably acquainted, maybe old friends. Had they known Sy Birch? Perhaps, he would never know. One thing for sure, they didn't know Phil Claussen. He would be reconstructed, created here in the courtroom from the testimony of others. The Phil Claussen who had driven his RV into the Birchbark Campground six months ago was a blank page, waiting for others to fill in all the empty spaces.

He'd had only the briefest of encounters with the DA, and that was quite enough to form an unfavorable opinion. Although the general physical type was not restricted to the military, that's where Phil had encountered a number of them, men of smaller stature who used every imaginable trick to make themselves larger than life. District Attorney Tommy Thompson fit the mold. He held himself so stiffly erect that Phil wondered whether he must sleep standing up. His major flaw, one which he had not been able to correct, was his voice, high pitched and rasping, so that when he increased the volume, as he often did, the pitch rose even higher, and the raspy quality became a squeak.

The judge gave Thompson considerable flexibility in his opening statement, that is until Sandra began leaping to her feet shouting "Objection," so regularly that he seemed to lose his train of thought.

"Such unsubstantiated conjecture has no place in opening statements," she said several times.

"Arriving in town in an RV is not a crime. Otherwise, we would be arresting half of the tourists who drive through," she said when Thompson tried to depict Phil as a fugitive who abandoned his family, fleeing across the country in the comfortable confines of the RV.

Some of her objections were just as tenuous as the accusations set forth by the DA, drawing the judge's ire on more than one occasion. But the name of the game was upsetting Thompson's rhythm, keeping him off balance, and she appeared to be accomplishing that goal. He still managed to slip in a description of Phil's street brawl with the Cowdrays, all in the line of duty, about how he'd sent both men to the hospital, establishing Phil as a violent character.

The court settled into the business at hand shortly past ten, when the DA called his first witness, Dani Birch. This was the first big shock of the day, even though his attorney had warned Phil in advance, but how bad could it be? They were in love. They had plans. Phil had known her intimately for at least six months. He knew her moods, as changeable as spring weather, volatile and youthful one moment, dark and withdrawn the next. Having seen her in various states of undress, he knew her body more intimately than he had known his former wife's, even after years of marriage.

She could be playing a role, too. He expected that much, but this was one he hadn't seen before. Here was thoroughly demure Dani, wearing a dark suit and a white blouse buttoned at the neck, leaving the skin of her hands, ankles, and face visible, but no more. She kept her hands folded in her lap, gaze focused on them as if she could not trust them to behave unless closely watched.

Would the DA get a straight story from Dani? Presumably, words following a hands-on-the-Bible oath of truth-telling would provide an accurate rendition, but with Dani, who knew?

"How long have you lived in Clayton, Ms. Birch?" The DA positioned himself in front of the jury box, becoming one of them, just another local guy trying to put in a day's work and get the job done right.

"All my life, sir."

"And that would be…?"

"Twenty-six years on December eighth, sir." When she glanced up, her look was shy, like that of a small child, unsure of her way in an adult world.

Fetching, Phil thought, she must have practiced for hours.

"Where did you first meet Mr. Claussen?"

"He gave me a ride into town."

The DA waited, not asking the obvious question about the dire straits that would force a demure young woman to accept a ride from a total stranger, especially a violent alcoholic like Phil Claussen.

Dani did her part as well, hesitant, a bit ashamed, but still brave and plucky enough to step up and take a chance. "I had an argument with my boyfriend, and he made me get out of the car, and left me out in the middle of nowhere, no houses, no people, nothing. It was getting dark, and I was really scared. I've heard awful things about coyotes, how they hunt in packs, and how some of them have mated with wolves."

"Coywolves, I believe they're called, and you were right to be concerned," the DA said. "That must have been a frightening situation. I must ask, how were you dressed then? Do you remember?"

"Jeans and a T-shirt and sneakers, sir."

Only Sandra's firm grip on his arm kept Phil from jumping out of his chair. "That's a damned lie," he said, none too softly. If he hadn't known what to expect before, he knew now, lies, lies, and more lies. How could she?

"Hardly enough to keep you warm through the night. So, Mr. Claussen stopped and offered you a ride?"

"Yes, sir. I felt like I didn't have a choice. I was so scared."

"How did he behave when you got in?"

"He was driving one of those big RVs. All he said

for a while was he was driving across the country, and would I like to go with him? I told him I only wanted to go as far as Clayton. He looked at me sort of funny, and I thought there might be trouble, but nothing happened."

"Did he give you any idea where he was headed that evening?"

"No, sir, but there's only one road into town, so I figured this was where we'd wind up eventually."

"And where did that eventually take you?"

At this point, Sandra was on her feet, raising her objection. "Is there a point to this line of questioning? I fail to see how a detailed account of a trip down route eighty-one, which we've all driven many times, sheds light on the business at hand."

"I agree, Ms. Newton. Mr. Thompson, you need to wind this up now," the judge said.

"Yes, your honor, if you'll just allow me one more question, my reason for pursuing this will become clear. Now, Ms. Birch, please tell us how the trip ended."

"He, Mr. Claussen, pulled off the road and into some woods. It was just light enough to make out the trees. He said he was spending the night there, and I could suit myself."

"Meaning, you could walk out into the woods in the dark or spend the night with him."

"Yes, sir."

"Again, not much of a choice."

Yeah, between sleeping indoors or getting eaten by wolves, what was a girl to do? Phil thought they were pushing the poor girl as helpless victim angle a bit too far, the way she hung her head like she was confessing something she would never want her parents to find out about. This was the same Dani Birch who loved skinny dipping, and who the less she wore, the better she liked it…the better he liked it too. There must have been other locals, maybe some of them sitting in the jury box, who'd seen the wild side of Dani Birch, and who wouldn't, even for a moment, see her as a candidate for religious orders.

"The next morning, when it got light enough to see, I realized where Mr. Claussen was parked. We were right in Uncle Sy's campground, the Birchbark Campground, he called it. It must have been where Mr. Claussen was headed all along."

The judge rapped his gavel a couple of times. "I think this is a good place to stop for lunch. We'll resume sharply at one o'clock. Jurors, you'll have lunch in the jury room, and you are not to discuss any aspect of the case with anyone other than your fellow jurors."

Once again, Sandra grabbed Phil's arm. "Not one word to anybody, you hear me? I have to run back to the office for a moment. I've brought lunch for us. We'll eat in the interview room. It's the only place that doesn't smell bad where we'll have any privacy."

No problem, nobody in the courthouse wanted to talk to a scumbag like him anyway.

****

While Phil devoured the excellent chicken salad sandwich she'd provided, Sandra wrote furiously, barely touching her own lunch. "They're doing a good job," she said. "Thompson has coached her well. So far, it's just she said/he said, and that comes down to who the jury believes."

"But it's all just an act," he said. "Just a pack of lies. It's like I don't know her at all. It didn't seem to matter so much before when she did weird things and never explained them, but it does now, and she's twisted everything around."

"Her word against yours," Sandra said. "With no witnesses to contradict her, it all comes down to believability. Do you know what's become of her sister? I expected to see her here."

"Don't know," he said.

"I'll see if the sheriff can find her."

After the lunch break, Dani was back on the witness stand, the same furtive look as before, as if wondering where a painful blow might come from. It seemed effective, Phil had to admit, and one had to wonder about the source of the poor girl's fear, and if that source was no farther away than the table where he sat beside his lawyer...Phil Claussen, killer from out of town.

Thompson, the DA, took up his favorite spot alongside the jury box. "Ms. Birch, tell us a bit about your uncle, Seymour Birch, his business interests, other than the campground."

"He had a small repo business, just a few cars, an occasional boat. I did the paperwork, but it didn't amount to much."

"By boats, are we talking yachts?" Thompson turned to the jury and grinned, so they wouldn't miss his little joke.

"Oh, no, sir, a few bass boats, but nothing bigger than that."

"And the cars?"

"Mostly used cars, nothing new."

"I see, and did the defendant, Mr. Claussen, show any interest in this repo business?"

"I think he was more interested in Uncle Sy than he was in the business. He asked me to introduce them, and then it seemed every time I went by Uncle Sy's house, Mr. Claussen was there. I didn't like it because he got Uncle Sy drinking again. But they both seemed kind of lonely, so I guess it was for the best."

"How about you? Was the defendant friendly toward you?"

"Yes, sir."

"Would you say you became romantically involved?"

Now she turned the contrition dial up a few notches. She nodded as if she were confessing to capital murder when what she was really doing was sealing the doom of Phil Claussen.

"Please, answer yes or no, Ms. Birch. I know it's hard."

"Yes."

"Could you speak up, please, so the jury can hear you clearly?"

"Yes, sir."

"You went out on dates and such?"

"Yes, sir. Most of the time, he was nice, and he seemed lonely. But he always wanted me to dress, well, sexy. He wanted me to wear clothes that embarrassed me."

"I see. I must ask this, were you intimate?"

Phil thought he'd seen her entire repertoire by now, but he was wrong. Masterful, that's the only way he could describe it, like a deer that's just heard the click of a trigger pull, knowing it's all over.

"Yes, sir. I spent a couple of nights with him in his RV. I knew it was wrong, but like I said, he seemed so lonely."

"Was alcohol involved?"

"Yes, sir."

"And you're not a drinker, are you?"

"No, sir. And he never told me he was married."

"Married, you say?" The DA's eyes grew wide, such a shocking revelation, even more reprehensible than homicide, a married man on the prowl, using his RV to entrap helpless girls before having his way with them. A man like that deserved no mercy at all.

"Yes, sir."

As he watched and listened, his gut churned, breathing required conscious effort, and his palms became so wet that he left an imprint on anything he touched. Who was this woman, and why was she telling such godawful lies? Lies, lies, and more lies. He didn't so much as jump out of his seat, more like he exploded, an involuntary act beyond his control. "Lies, lies," he yelled, "all lies."

Dani drew down into her chair as if she feared imminent attack. The DA might have smiled just a little.

Sandra used a chokehold and wrestled Phil back into his chair. "Sit and stay," she said like she was commanding an errant dog.

The judge pounded his gavel. "Counsellor, the court will not permit such outbursts. If you cannot control your client, I'll have him removed from the courtroom."

"Your Honor, I'm deeply sorry for this disturbance, and I apologize to the court. This will not happen again."

Phil had not seen Sandra Newton's angry face

before, but he saw it now and didn't want to see it again. "So, what do we do now?" he asked.

"Stella is on her way to Norman with a subpoena for that drama coach. At the very least, we can embarrass the hell out of the DA."

"Stella?"

"She's my snoop. I wasn't going to tell you her name, but it doesn't make much difference now. We're still going to need other witnesses to contradict Dani's story. Stella has been trying to locate Dani's sister, Angie, but she seems to have disappeared. Do you have any idea where she might have gone?"

"Earl Biggers might know something. He and Angie are close. I just hope some other thugs like those two that came out to my RV haven't snatched her up."

"You know, for a little town like Clayton, this amounts to a major crime wave," she said.

"Just my luck."

****

In addition to his teaching and administrative duties, Phil occasionally coached the Wakefield High School athletic teams and was acquainted with the so-called mercy rule. When one team was so far superior to another, and the lesser team had no chance of catching up, the coaches could agree to invoke the mercy rule, allowing both teams to leave the field relatively intact. The losers would then be spared the physical and psychological humiliation of continuing a hopeless endeavor.

After watching himself smeared, portrayed as the worst of the worst, knowing anything he tried to do to change it would only make things worse, Phil needed a mercy ruling, for himself.

But mercy wasn't on the DA's agenda. The next day, demure Dani was back on the stand, apparently ready to do more damage.

Chapter Twenty-Seven

"When we left off yesterday, Ms. Birch, you mentioned the defendant's drinking; was this an issue between the two of you?"

"Yes, sir, Mrs. Claussen always had a bottle around, and he was always trying to get me to drink with him."

"Did you?"

She shook her head vigorously. "My mother warned me about drinking over and over. I didn't always do what she said, but I'm thankful she warned me against drinking."

Thompson walked over to where the court recorder sat, then back again, giving everyone time to be suitably impressed with Dani's virtue, holding out in the face of temptation. Wouldn't her mother be proud?

"Weapons and alcohol are a bad combination," he said. "Did you ever see the defendant with a weapon?"

"Yes, sir, sometimes he carried it in a holster. I asked him why, but he never told me."

"So, a man who drank and carried a gun, were you afraid of him ever?"

She nodded her head without looking up.

"Please, speak up, Ms. Birch."

"Yes, sir, sometimes I was very afraid."

"In fact, you had the court issue a restraining order against the defendant, didn't you?"

"Yes, sir."

"What did he do that caused you to be afraid?"

"He did away with my dog." Now, out came the tissues, and down came the tears. "Alfie, that's what I named him, just a little brown stray. He was such a sweet dog. But Mr. Claussen didn't like him. Then one day, I saw him put Alfie into the back seat of his car, said they were going for a ride, but Alfie didn't come back, and I never saw him again." Now came a gusher, complete with sobs, choking on her own tears.

"Your honor, I wonder if we might have a brief recess. Ms. Birch has obviously suffered severe emotional trauma and will need some time to recover."

"Very well," said Judge Driscoll. "Court will reconvene in one hour."

A dog killer, now that's something everyone hates. Judging from the looks that came his way from the jury box, Phil wondered if he'd get out of the courtroom alive. He didn't have to be a mind reader to guess what they were thinking. *String up the dog-killing bastard right now.*

****

When they reconvened, Dani's powers of recuperation seemed to have served her well, and her recovery from her severe emotional trauma appeared to be complete. Such is the resiliency of youth, or so it seemed. Phil had another explanation.

"Now, Ms. Birch, you seem to be portraying the defendant as an angry man, is that correct?"

Instantly, Sandra was on her feet shouting her objection, demanding to see Dani's credentials in the field of psychology before allowing her to make such a characterization.

"Sustained."

"Very well, how did he like Clayton? Did he ever mention anything about this town or this area?"

"Objection," Sandra yelled. "Relevance."

"I'll allow this one. The witness will please answer."

Dani appeared shaken. She'd been given a free ride the past day and a half, and the possibility that she might be challenged appeared to surprise her.

"He didn't seem happy here. He was always badmouthing the town, saying it was the dullest place on the planet, had the stupidest people he'd ever seen."

A buzz ran through the courtroom as if a swarm of bees had just made an entrance. The judge thumped his gavel several times.

Phil glimpsed his attorney, who had fixed a laser-like gaze on Dani. If he ran his hand through her line of sight, might it get burned? He knew, and Dani must too, that she would hear this outrageous prevarication read back to her in the near future, and she would be forced to substantiate it.

"On the twelfth of September, Mr. Seymour Birch was shot three times with a nine-millimeter handgun causing his death. The coroner placed the time of death between two and six o'clock that day. Now, as painful as that recollection must be, I'm asking you to take us back, Ms. Birch, and tell us what you remember of that day."

And painful it must have been; Dani had the tissues out again and was dabbing furiously. For a girl who almost never cried, she was going at it like a pro.

"Earlier that day, Mr. Claussen invited my sister Angie, Earl, and me to a picnic at his RV at the campsite."

"Was this usual?" Thompson asked.

"The first time ever," Dani said. "We got there around four-thirty, but Mr. Claussen wasn't there. We waited, and around five o'clock, Earl thought he heard several gunshots. We didn't know what to do since Mr. Claussen wasn't around, but soon he came running up, all out of breath. I told him about the shots, but he said I must have been mistaken. Then he asked me to hide his gun."

"He had his weapon with him at the time?" Thompson asked.

"Yes, sir, I told him to take the bullets out first because I didn't want to cause an accident. Guns are dangerous."

"Indeed, they are," Thompson said. "And what happened next?"

"Mr. Claussen took the part with the bullets out of the handle."

"The clip," Thompson said.

"I guess so," Dani said. "Then he told Earl and me to leave, but he wanted Angie to come with him."

"Did he say why?" Thompson asked.

"No, sir. The next morning, I found out Uncle Sy had been shot dead." More heavy-duty work with the tissues.

"I have no further questions for the witness at this time." Thompson gave her a big smile. Phil thought tossing her a fish would be more appropriate in view of her bewitching trained seal act.

"No questions for the witness at this time, but I will cross-examine later." Sandra Newton spoke with such calm assurance that Phil had to wonder what she had up her sleeve because she'd given him no real idea of how she would attack Dani's testimony.

Thompson next called the coroner, a rather nervous, balding man who apparently didn't like crowds, especially when they were all looking at him. He gave information about the nature of the wounds that killed Sy, and the approximate time of death, no surprises there.

Sheriff Barnhill, the next witness called by Thompson, seemed equally unenthusiastic about the information he had to impart, but what else could he do? He could only answer the questions put to him, nothing more, nothing less. He read off the damning ballistics report matching fatal bullets with Phil's weapon.

This, Phil figured, was even better for the prosecution than a smoking gun; it proved the bullet had struck the target. And the rest of it, the quote from Phil's own lips, about how the gun had never left his possession, sealed the deal.

"Never left his possession." Thompson seemed quite taken with this phrase and repeated it three times as he walked back and forth in front of the jury box.

Guilty as hell. How could there be any doubt, reasonable or otherwise? Even Phil had begun to doubt his own innocence.

"I have no questions for Sheriff Barnhill at this time," Sandra Newton said, still sounding oh, so confident.

And so ended the second day of Phil's trial with the home team so far ahead as to make recovery seem remote indeed.

"Court is adjourned. We will resume tomorrow

morning at nine." With that, the judge banged his gavel, and the crowd filed out of the courtroom. A swarm of reporters hovered around Dani and the DA, both of whom seemed to be enjoying the attention.

"I'd rather they be over there than over here," Sandra said. "Now, I have lots of phone calls to make, so I'm going back to the office. I'm afraid I'll have to leave you with jailhouse food tonight."

"No problem, remember I lived on army chow for three years."

"No talking to anybody tonight. Remember that if you remember nothing else."

"So, tomorrow will be our turn?" he asked Sandra as they left the courtroom.

"Oh, no, not yet, at least. Maybe later. We'll have to see how it goes."

"But I want to tell my side." He wasn't sure he could sit through much more testimony that made him sound like pond scum, or worse.

"It won't help right now. All you can do is contradict what Dani said, and it will come down to who is more believable. And the jury is just as likely to believe her, maybe more so. Besides, I don't want to give Thompson the chance to cross-examine you. He can make things very hard for you."

"You have an alternate plan? Or do they go right ahead and hang me?"

"You're not going to hang. They've had their fun. Now it's our turn. Just be patient."

"You know what I wish? I wish I knew whether Dani was playing me right from the start or whether something just happened that made her turn on me."

"You still have feelings for her, don't you?" Sandra

asked.

"Yeah, we had some great times together, and I was hoping for a lot more. Hard to believe it was all a big fat lie."

"We're going to find out about that, I promise you."

Without doubt, Sandra was trying to put out positive vibes about the case and its likely outcome. Maybe that was all just part of the process, keep the poor dumb defendant in a delusional state, thinking he had a real solid chance of winning, even when she knew he didn't. Yeah, there was a certain twisted logic there. A man who looked beaten, defeated, couldn't expect a sympathetic response from a jury. Probably they would see him as someone overwhelmed by his own guilt. So, Sandra Newton was just doing her job, and he would have to do his.

Such were his thoughts when Sheriff Barnhill opened the door to his cell and walked in. His appearance, downbeat, a little depressed, didn't inspire much confidence in Phil, not after the little pep talk he'd just given himself.

"Tell me, how did a smart fellow like you get in such a mess?"

"Guess I'm not so smart after all," Phil said. "A smart man would have climbed right back into his RV and driven away a long time ago. Sy might still be alive if I'd done that."

"Maybe, I don't know. Your being here somehow brought things to a boil, but it would have happened sooner or later."

"What do you mean by that? Somebody planned to kill him all along?"

The sheriff slumped back against the wall. "When did you find out about the oil?

"Earl mentioned it months ago at Sy's burial service, and Sandra told me more about it when we were discussing the will. All Sy ever said about it was how much he hated oil rigs. I know he wanted Clayton to stay just as it's always been, and oil rigs would change that permanently."

"A lot of people don't see it that way. It's a beautiful piece of property he left you, but the oil underneath, that's where the real money is. Take the million or so it's worth now and multiply that many times over. People have been killed for less."

"Sy talked a lot about the property, how it would be a great place to settle down. But I thought he was looking for a caretaker, like maybe he was going to offer me a job managing the campground. It wasn't until Sandra read the will that I found out he meant me to be the owner of all of it, and he sure as hell never mentioned the whole place was sitting on a lake of oil."

The sheriff let out a little grunt, whether of approval or disbelief, Phil couldn't tell.

"I never had too much confidence in these courtroom proceedings. I've seen crooks walk out free men, and I've seen good men ruined. I don't aim to see you ruined. Mind you, you're still in a big mess, and the DA wants your scalp, so you and Sandra Newton have to be careful."

Phil and the sheriff exchanged a long, soulful look, no words, just an understanding, a trust, an acknowledgement that the right thing would be done, but that still wouldn't ensure a favorable outcome.

"I'll have another talk with your attorney." The

sheriff got up to leave. He and Phil shook hands, affirming an ancient code that neither would violate on penalty of death, hopefully not Phil's own.

****

The next morning, Sandra was already at the table waiting as the bailiff brought Phil in. She patted Phil's arm. "It's time for the good people of Clayton to meet the real Phil Claussen."

The first witness Sandra called was Regina Philpott, a surprise to Phil. He wouldn't have thought of her as a character witness but was very glad to see her take the stand on his behalf. She looked quite official in her blue suit, maybe worn a bit thin in the lapels and elbows. But since her organization was strictly grass roots with barely resources to do the basics and nothing left over to spend on appearances, this was as it should be. The good people who funded her work with their tax dollars should know their money was being spent appropriately, going directly to those in need, not just lining the pockets of those in charge. As a character witness, she was, in Phil's opinion, pure gold, completely and unassailably truthful.

"Please state your occupation, Ms. Philpott."

"Director of Social Services for Clayton County."

"You sometimes need Sheriff Barnhill's assistance in your work, isn't that true?"

"Yes, the sheriff keeps watch over several shut-ins, people who for one reason or another are unable to leave their homes and have no family to care for them."

"Aren't there facilities available where they can live and receive the care they need?" Sandra asked. These two women appeared locked into each other, and Phil was very thankful they were on his side. Sure,

Dani's testimony, her charade, actually, had done him considerable damage, but the grown-ups were back in charge now.

"Yes, but most of these people have lived in their homes, just shacks, really, their entire lives, and they refuse to leave. So we have to do the best we can where they are."

Thompson with an objection: "I fail to see any connection between Ms. Philpott's testimony and the crimes committed by the defendant."

"Alleged crimes," Sandra said in a loud voice. "And there is a connection, if you'll allow me to continue. Ms. Philpott, would you describe some of the peculiar circumstances you face in caring for these shut-in people?"

"They are very suspicious of outsiders, paranoid, even. They allow me to visit, and Sheriff Barnhill, but no one else. A few of them keep guns, and they will shoot if they feel threatened."

"Deputy Claussen has accompanied you on a few such visits."

"Yes, the sheriff requested that Deputy Claussen go with me."

"And how did that work out?"

"It took some time before they accepted him, but he won them over with his patience and his kindness. In short order, they came to trust him, just as they have Sheriff Barnhill. Deputy Claussen helped me transport a few of them in for medical care, and even helped clean up a few of the shacks, and believe me, that's no task for someone with a weak stomach.

"He and the sheriff repaired the roof on one of the shacks, otherwise I doubt the poor old woman who lived there would make it through the winter. I thought Deputy Claussen one of the kindest men I've ever met."

Hers was a brief testimony, but one that went straight to the heart of the matter, was Phil Claussen a demon or a decent human being?

"Thank you, Ms. Philpott. I'd like to call Sheriff Barnhill."

Barnhill looked far more comfortable than when he was being questioned by the DA That aura of suspicion that Phil guessed most law enforcement personnel must feel when placed on a witness stand was gone, and if Phil could sense it, for sure the DA could too. *Too bad, asshole, you had your chance.*

The Sandra Newton that Phil watched now was an altogether different person than the rather sedate woman who had steered him through stacks of legal documents pertaining to Sy's estate. This new version took control of the courtroom in a way he would never have imagined.

Command, that's the word he was searching for.

The DA didn't have it, never would. His most frequent techniques were probably bullying and trickery, effective sometimes, but when the brown stuff hit the fan, he would find himself all alone.

Sandra Newton had it. Phil watched the eyes in the courtroom, judge, jury, Sheriff Barnhill, all looking exactly where she wanted them to look, seeing exactly what she wanted them to see. And he raised a silent prayer of thanks that she was representing him.

"Sheriff Barnhill, taking on a new deputy is an important step, important to you and to everyone in our community. Could you please tell us about the steps you took prior to appointing Phil Claussen as your

Deputy?"

Barnhill would have known the question was coming, because, without any further prompting from Sandra, he went into great detail about the extensive background check he'd done before offering Phil the job, including information from his military background as well as supportive statements from friends and work associates in Wakefield.

Yes, he was still on the hook for one, maybe two homicides, but at least there were some people in the world who thought Phil Claussen was better than roadkill. So, perhaps Sandra Newton had partially repaired the damage to his reputation, and the jury had an alternative version from a credible source.

"Just one more question, Sheriff, knowing what you know now, would you still offer him the job?"

"Yes, I would." No hesitation.

"In spite of all the evidence, the ballistics test?"

"I know the ballistics work is powerful information, and I do not doubt that it is correct. What I doubt is that Phil Claussen pulled the trigger in either case. I don't believe he did."

The DA was on his feet shouting, "Objection."

Judge Driscoll looked down at him. "Seriously?"

Chapter Twenty-Eight

Sandra's first two witnesses filled the morning session. She had lunch sent to Phil's cell. "I'm not eating jailhouse food," she said. "I draw the line there."

"I was surprised to see Regina up there today," he said.

"The sheriff suggested her. She carries a lot of weight around here, and you made quite an impression on her. Careful, you'll have ladies beating down your door."

"If that happens, I'll buy another RV. Say, I didn't see Dani around. Maybe after she spent two days trashing me, she didn't want to show her face."

"Well, she'll be coming back, whether she wants to or not. She and I have a lot to talk over, under oath. As it turns out, we're very short on witnesses. Stella informs me that the drama coach has left the country. Someone gave her an all-expense paid trip to Paris. I'm sure the DA's fingerprints are all over that ticket, and we haven't located Angie yet either."

When they reconvened for the afternoon session, DA Thompson sat at his table alone, no Dani. The star witness for the prosecution was AWOL, perhaps dreading what certainly would be a withering cross examination by Sandra Newton, perhaps just being impulsive Dani, chasing after something else that caught her fancy. Any and all of these seemed equally possible to Phil. His unconventional former girlfriend was not bound by schedules or structures, so she might be just about anywhere.

Around two o'clock, Sheriff Barnhill entered the courtroom and approached the judge's bench. "No sign of her. I've alerted the boys in Kingfisher and Enid to keep an eye out for her. If nothing else works, I'll call the State Police in to find her."

The sheriff's statement to the judge was clearly audible in the front row where Phil, his attorney, and the prosecutor sat. Thompson, the prosecutor, was obviously agitated over the absence of his star witness, absence that could lead to a judgment of mistrial if she wasn't available for cross-examination by the defense. With the judge glaring down at him, he seemed even smaller than usual.

The thought occurred to Phil that perhaps her unorthodox behavior was not voluntary, that she might be absent against her will. He mentioned this to Sandra.

"Possible," she whispered. "I don't like to think about it. If she's been taken and held somewhere…not good. Not good at all. It wouldn't make sense for Thompson to pull something like that, because it would screw up his case."

But the news that really caught the attention of everyone in the courtroom was when the sheriff added, in a louder voice for all to hear: "There's a storm coming up. Heard about it on the radio driving over. No sirens yet." Sirens would mean a storm—a tornado— was imminent and would send all in earshot scrambling for cover.

Storm systems were never taken lightly in the Midwest. Unlike coastal hurricanes, which could be tracked somewhat effectively for days, even weeks before their arrival, allowing time to prepare, even though so few actually did, tornadoes were helter-skelter events, unpredictable and deadly. One house might be reduced to matchsticks, while another, only a short distance away might sustain only minor damage. There might be some advance warning, such as the sheriff had just provided, or there might be none at all.

In an instant, Phil and all his troubles were forgotten, displaced by a clear and present danger to the community. People were on their feet, ready to dash out to their cars when, a moment after the sheriff's words, rain droplets began pecking at the windows, followed soon by a flash of lightning. Then the rainfall became a steady drumming, and those standing closest to the windows could hear the clicking of hailstones as well. The storm was coming on strong.

"Better stay put, folks, and move away from the windows," the sheriff said. "Too dangerous outside."

When the doors of the courtroom burst open, and the wind blew stacks of official papers around like so much confetti, its occupants feared for their lives, for it was indeed a tornado, but only a small one, about five feet two inches tall. Dani Birch, her shy, demure persona washed away by the storm, stood there dripping all over the threshold, her hair plastered to her head, her clothing soaked through, and, as on that first day months ago when Phil had picked her up from the side of the road, shoeless.

She stormed into the courtroom, right up to the table where Phil sat alongside his attorney, leaving a trail of wet footprints behind her. "They tore up our house," she cried to Phil, because somewhere in that sheen of raindrops were real tears as well. "Have you seen it? Everything, ruined, all our furniture, our new curtains, all gone."

She redirected her attention to the other side of the courtroom where the DA cowered. "Did you do that? You bastard, I'm going to break your neck."

And she might very well have, had not Sheriff Barnhill grabbed her around the waist and dragged her into the jury room. Instantly, Phil went charging after her.

"Wait, stay right where you are," Sandra yelled.

"No way, she needs me," Phil said. Gone was any consideration of the character assassination game she'd played for the past two days. His feelings for her proved far stronger than all that had just happened. When the bailiff, not a small man, blocked his way, Phil picked him up and moved him several feet away from the door. The bailiff wisely stayed where he'd been put.

Chaos outside the courtroom where the storm raged, chaos inside the courtroom where another storm raged, and the judge had no control over either. He banged his gavel so hard the head came off and rolled onto the floor. His shouts for "Order," amounted to so much wasted breath.

Inside the jury room, Phil held Dani, rocking her gently, while she dripped all over his new suit. "It's okay, it's okay," he said.

"I reckon I'd best leave you folks alone for a bit," the sheriff said. "Phil, don't leave the county until we get this all wrapped up."

"It's not okay," Dani wailed. "It's all my fault. I lied and lied and lied. Everything I said...lies. I lied with my hand on the Bible, and now I'm going to hell for sure. But I don't care. You hate me, and I don't care what happens to me."

"No, no, no, I don't hate you. You did what you did for a reason, I'm sure. Sandra will fix everything." He pulled her head down onto his shoulder and continued rocking until she stopped shaking.

"I'm going to kill him," she said.

"No, there's been too much killing already. Let Sandra take care of him. You stay right here with me."

Everything he did, everything he said came as a complete surprise to Phil. If his rational side were still in control, he'd be sitting at the table alongside his attorney, waiting for her to carve Dani's testimony into tiny pieces. But where Dani Birch was concerned, reason flew right out the window. All that had happened during the past few days, all that would come after, mattered little, because he held his universe, his sun, moon, and stars, dripping wet, in his arms, and the rest of it…just details, small stuff.

Sandra made a quiet entrance, then stood looking down at the two of them in a motherly sort of way, as if her offspring had done something remarkable, only she wasn't quite sure what it was. "Now I've seen everything," she said.

"Was there a tornado?" Phil asked.

"Just a little one, and she's sitting right beside you."

"Will I have to stay in jail tonight?"

"I don't think so, but if your house is too torn up to live in, both of you are welcome to stay in my spare bedroom until you get things fixed up."

"Thank you," Dani said. "What happens now? I

lied in court. That's bad."

"Yes, that's bad, but I think there were extenuating circumstances. If your testimony was coerced, you can't be held accountable. Poor Judge Driscoll will need a few days to recover from this, so I doubt we'll start up again until the first of the week. I'm sure he'll call this a mistrial, so we'll have to begin again. Dani, I'd like to have a nice long talk with you before then."

"I want to be there too," Phil said.

"You should," Sandra said. "Besides, keeping the two of you apart might not be possible."

What had been obvious to Phil for months now, was also obvious to his attorney, for better or worse, for richer or poorer, etc., etc., he and Dani were a bonded pair. Weeks before his life spun out of control, late one night, after all the TV sports channels had closed up shop, and the news stations were rerunning the same spiel they'd been serving up all day, Phil caught a wildlife documentary that included a brief section on possums, not his favorite animal, but what stuck with him was the way the baby possums clung to their mom's back. Wherever she went, six tiny appendages stuck to her like they were sutured in place.

Same with Dani. From the moment she latched onto him in the courtroom, all during the drive to Sandra's house, she clung to him, possum-style. Twice he had to make her switch arms, because her grip was making his fingers go numb.

****

Dinner at Sandra's was scrambled eggs and toasted English muffins. Phil tried to help out, but even with the preparation of such simple fare, mostly got in the way.

Dani had dry clothes, at least, a T-shirt from Phil's bag he brought to jail with him, and a pair of Sandra's sweatpants with Missouri State Track printed down the right leg.

"I ran track in college," she said. "Not half bad. Collected a few trophies in my day."

"Guess you weren't a smoker back then," Phil said.

"Oh, yes, I was. Smoking never seemed to hurt my running, so I kept right on doing it. The only vice I've added is single malt Scotch...couldn't afford that in college."

This was about the tone of the conversation that evening, light, superficial, everyone avoiding the very large subject waiting for them, because it was so very, very important. Sandra had a legal morass to sort through. Phil, while probably off the hook for the two homicides, had taken some very painful hits during Dani's testimony. His standing in the community, if he stayed, would require some serious repair work.

Soon enough, the scotch worked its mellow magic, and the necessity of sleep caught up with all three of them. Sandra provided them with extra blankets to cover an antique brass bed. Phil was not surprised when Dani stripped off her dry clothing and crawled naked into bed with him. And, as usual, she pressed every inch of herself tightly against him, still trying to crawl into his skin. Ah, just like old times, he thought, except that it wasn't, not yet, and maybe never would be. But he wanted it to be like before; he wanted her back in the worst possible way. Who knew? Maybe what came after might be even better. Was that too much to hope for?

The stress of the past week, seeing part of his life

story being rewritten, drove him into a deep sleep, then, sometime later, he was climbing, or being dragged, out of that deep place because someone was shaking him, speaking in a loud voice directly into his ear.

"Phil, wake up, we have to talk."

"Huh? What time is it?"

"I don't know, but we have to talk right now." A naked Dani sat astride him, pushing against his chest.

A bedside clock glowed faintly. "Dani, it's three o'clock."

"Now, Phil, please."

"Everything okay in there?" Sandra's voice came through the door.

"Please, Sandra, I have to say this right now."

Classic Dani, he thought, clocks, sunrise, daylight, her internal timekeeper was totally out of sync or just didn't matter in the first place, another of her quirks that frustrated the hell out of him and made her all the more irresistible. He drew her to him.

"What are you doing?"

"Hugging you."

"Why?" she asked.

"Because I want to."

"Okay, but we still have to talk."

"I know, and you still have to put your clothes on. I wanted to get in a quick squeeze before you got covered up. It's been a while."

"I love you."

"I love you, too.

"Now, talk," she said. "I have to say this right now."

A bit later they gathered around Sandra's kitchen table while the coffee pot did its thing on the counter.

Sandra, looking drugged but functional, had a notepad and several pens set out in front of her. On the witness stand, being questioned by the DA, Dani had followed a well-rehearsed script. Now everything was in play at once, gushing forth like water from an open hydrant, and Sandra must have realized that, unless she kept Dani on track, she would spend the next few hours listening to a rambling rendition that left her no more well informed than when she started.

"Dani, work with me, who approached you first?"

"The DA, Thompson, I was out on a repo job, and it was past midnight. I was by myself, and Earl always got bent out of shape when I worked alone, but this one looked easy. Anyway, two guys grabbed me. They blindfolded me, and drove me to a building or something, someplace I'd never been before, at least I think. I was scared to death. I was sure I was going to be raped or killed or both."

Phil put his arm around her. "Your repo career is history."

"Yes, well, Thompson was inside waiting. He said he had some news for me, that he knew who had killed Uncle Sy and my father. He said you did it, Phil. I told him that was bullshit, because I knew you had done no such thing. You were with me when both of them were shot. He said he could prove you did it, because the ballistics test matched the bullets with your gun."

"When was that, Dani?" Sandra asked.

"Friday, October seventh, I remember because the sixth would have been Uncle Sy's birthday, if he'd lived.

"That was almost two weeks before Sheriff Barnhill had the lab report. There's no way Thompson could have known that soon," Phil said. "Unless he had my gun, which he did not. I always kept it with me."

"But he did have your gun, Phil. That's what he told me. He had it, because Angie pulled a switch on you. She took yours and left another gun in your holster."

"No, she could not have done that, unless she got into the house."

"She got into the house and made the switch, right after Thompson or whoever shot my father. You carried the wrong gun around for weeks. Think about it, how could you have known the difference? Whoever shot Uncle Sy and my father shot them with the gun Angie planted on you, my own sister, so Thompson knew how the ballistics would turn out even before the test was ever run."

"Dani, what did Thompson want from you?" Sandra asked.

"He wanted Phil convicted for the killing. He said he could do it with the ballistics alone. If I helped him convict Phil with my testimony, he would only go for a manslaughter conviction, but if I didn't help him, he would press for a murder charge and the death penalty, and he was sure he could make it stick, or so he said."

"So, he told you what to say," Sandra said.

"Over and over and over, until I got the answers exactly the way he wanted them. They had this acting coach from the University. She was a total bitch. They both kept after me hour after hour. He told me how to act around Phil, made me get the restraining order claiming Phil was drunk and violent." By now Dani was sobbing again. "I did some awful things, but I was trying to save your life. He promised you would be out of jail in ten years. That's a long time, but it's better than the death penalty, and I would have waited for you, no matter how long it took."

Phil didn't have much to say now, because his mind was made up; Tommy Thompson just got the death penalty...for himself. For what he'd done, he was going to die.

"Phil, look at me." Sandra moved around the table closer to him. "I can tell what you're thinking, and it's not the right way. If you kill him, you will go away for a long, long time, and I won't be able to help you."

Now Dani was in his face too. "You don't get to kill him. If anybody gets to kill him, it will be me."

"Enough, you two, nobody's going to do any killing. Obviously, Thompson wasn't sure he could make the conviction stick with ballistics alone, not with Sheriff Barnhill's testimony so that's why he went after you, Dani," Sandra said.

"But why pin it on me?" Phil asked. "What did I ever do to him?"

Sandra poured coffee for the three of them. "That's the easiest question of all...oil. When they couldn't get the will overturned...because your attorney, yours truly, did such a good job writing it up...you were next in line, so, they had to get rid of you.

"Thompson still claimed to be Sy's son, illegitimate, of course. There was never any definitive proof one way or the other. His mother was a dancer in Oklahoma City. Sy never acknowledged him, even denied he was the father. I knew about it from talking with Sy, but neither of us expected it to amount to much since Thompson couldn't prove anything. But when Sy left his estate to you, Phil, I guess Thompson hit the roof. He figured all the land, all the money rightfully belonged to him, but he'd have to get rid of you first."

"What about Sy's murder. Did you figure that one out too?"

"I talked a lot with Sheriff Barnhill about it. Most likely Sy goaded Thompson into shooting him. Taking out Fletcher Birch was the next logical step, then, unfortunately, you were next."

"Can you prove any of that?" Phil asked.

"Of course, Thompson will deny it all. The ballistics study is the main thing here, so we'll need someone else to verify Dani's story about your gun. Where's your sister?"

Phil felt Dani stiffen in his arms. "I found her, but she's scared, really scared. She believes Thompson will have her killed if she tells about any of this."

"Where is she?"

"She's hiding out at our father's house. There's a basement nobody knows about, and she hid out there when Sheriff Barnhill came looking for her. You have to promise me you'll protect her."

"I'll take care of that personally," Phil said. "Does she have our dog?"

"Yes, she does. I feel worse about that than anything else, because I know how much you love Alfie. He's safe and sound. Let's go get him today. He'll be so glad to see you."

Chapter Twenty-Nine

They stopped by their house to take another look at the damage, and to pick up what remained of Dani's wardrobe. The yellow tape was gone, and the front door was closed, but the devastation inside drove Dani into another crying jag, and it took some time for her to settle down. The poor girl probably had shed more tears in the past twenty-four hours than in the preceding twenty-six years.

"Just look at what they've done." She said it sadly, in between sniffles, because so much of what was torn apart were new furnishings she had selected herself. "They tore up all our things, but left Uncle Sy's artwork. Maybe Thompson wanted that for himself; with you out of the way, it would have been his. I guess that's something to be thankful for. We could never have replaced any of that."

"I have insurance," Phil said. "We can get new stuff."

"Our first real home together and look what happened." She clung to him, still sniffling in little bursts.

"I thought the RV was our first home."

"I mean a home without wheels, one where I didn't have to worry you would drive away and leave me."

"That would never happen, and you know it."

"What makes it all so mean is how personal it was,

351

just our things, like they wanted to erase any trace of us."

"Well, it didn't work," Phil said. "We're here to stay." All of his prior ambivalence was gone now. They would start over again, this time with all of the skeletons out of the closet, and all of the family secrets clear and transparent, most of them, anyway.

Then it was on to the pancake house to indulge Phil's new passion, blueberry pancakes.

"This cannot become a habit," Dani said as she poured on the blueberry syrup. "We'll both become tubbies, and fat guys just don't do it for me."

"Yeah, like ugly old women don't turn me on either."

"What, if I went to prison for lying in court, you wouldn't want me anymore? Where was I to turn when I got out? Some old ladies' home?" Her attempt at an angry scowl fell flat in comic fashion, leaving them both laughing.

"You were never going to prison in the first place. Now if you're not going to finish your pancakes, slide them over."

They picked up a double order of bacon for Alfie.

****

They found the door to her father's house open. Angie hadn't locked it, but she didn't answer when they knocked, either, so they let themselves in. Alfie was indeed overjoyed to see them both, Angie, not so much. Dani had to coax her out of her hiding place in the basement. When she crept forth, eyes wide and blinking, hair uncombed, clothes wrinkled and dirty as if she'd slept in them for several days, she cowered behind large pieces of furniture, chairs, sofas, in case she needed physical protection, as if unsure whether Phil might extract revenge for what she'd done.

"That was a pretty rotten trick you pulled on me," Phil said. "I'm not going to forget it."

"I was scared half to death," she said, voice quavering like she was ready to burst into tears, and Phil had already seen enough crying women to last him for a long time. "Thompson brought his big ugly guys out, and I can't even repeat what they said they would do to me if I didn't play along. Gives me nightmares even thinking about it."

Dani embraced her sister. "Phil, she's suffered enough. This ends right here, all of it."

"You're not going to have any more trouble from those guys or from Thompson. I guarantee it," Phil said. "But you have to tell your story to my attorney and the judge."

"Okay, whatever you say, so long as you'll protect me."

Alfie took up a position close by Phil and refused to budge until Phil passed over his bacon treat. "Miss me, did you, pal? I sure as hell missed you."

"Do you know who tore up our house?" Dani asked.

"Thompson's goons," Angie said.

"Why?"

"Trying to run Phil off is what they said."

"Well, it didn't work."

****

After a long conference in Judge Driscoll's chambers, with Angie corroborating Dani's story about the gun, the authorities convened a second trial in Enid, the next town over, because, as the judge put it, they needed a new prosecutor to prosecute the old prosecutor. Tommy Thompson turned out to be the big loser, not so big, of course, as the Birch brothers, who had lost totally.

Sandra Newton chuckled as she told Phil the story. "A little bit of irony," she said. "In the end, Thompson made the same deal with the prosecutors he was trying to pin on you; they agreed not to seek the death penalty if they were guaranteed a conviction, so he confessed. Poor guy will likely never see the sun rise again as a free man."

"That poor guy is the same sonofabitch who tried to hang me for something I never did. Spare him the sympathy. He doesn't deserve it."

****

Wrangling with the insurance company about due compensation for the destruction of their household goods seemed to go on forever, even though most of the inventory was brand new. But Phil and Dani restored order to their home by mid-November, just in time for the first serious storm of the season. She had insisted on a big shopping spree in Oklahoma City to replace what they'd lost, and, although he balked at first, he caved soon enough. She could be ever so convincing when she put her mind to it. He thoroughly enjoyed having her put the pressure on him, using her own special tactics that no man with a pulse could withstand. It was a win-win situation; she got what she wanted, and he definitely got what he wanted.

When the last delivery van pulled away, their new home had a very cozy feel, a nice place to come home to at the end of the day.

By now, with the Midwest winter settling in, his

reputation at least partially restored, and life spinning in smoother circles, he was becoming more fully invested in his job as Deputy Sheriff. Barnhill began dropping more hints about retirement, indicating the sheriff's job would be Phil's if he wanted it. Dani had turned the repo business over to Earl, but not without a struggle. "What if I just do a little, part-time?" she asked.

"No way, too risky. Running around in the middle of the night in someone else's luxury automobile is over and done with. Besides, that business was not exactly legal. There was the little issue of taxes that weren't filed. If you started it up again, I'd have to bust you."

"You wouldn't, would you, over a little thing like taxes?" She gave him the full treatment with her blue eyes, something that invariably worked on Phil the civilian, but would not hold on Phil the law enforcement officer.

"No choice, sworn to uphold the law."

"But I'll get bored without something to do."

"Take up a hobby, motorcycle racing, sky diving, something safer."

"How about rodeo? I'm a pretty good rider," she said.

"That is definitely not in the picture. I like your bones just the way they are now…intact."

"You want me sitting around the house, painting my toenails, reading movie magazines, waiting for you to come home. I'll get into trouble, I just know it."

Phil knew it too. Dani with time on her hands was not a long-term solution, and, in a way, it was the flip side of his own argument in favor of finding a job for himself. He couldn't very well deny her the same options he claimed, so long as he had a say in what those options might be. "Did you ever read a book called *The Stepford Wives*?"

She shook her head

"Probably wouldn't help," he said, "bad idea, don't read it."

"You don't know what to do with me, do you?"

"Not exactly." He'd failed to anticipate this problem. If he'd ever been able to find out how she spent her time, he might have been able to make some arrangement, but she'd always been so secretive that he had no real clue what he'd be replacing.

One afternoon he returned home, the wind howling so fiercely that the blowing snow obscured his vision, to find Dani sitting at the kitchen table, a blank stare on her face. She didn't even look up when he walked into the room. Trouble, for sure.

He kissed her, then pulled a chair alongside. "Is something wrong?"

"I'm bored." It was a plaintive sound, scary too.

Without giving it a second thought, he knew exactly what to do, something he'd been considering for the past couple of weeks, but the situation was now well past the point of mere consideration; this required an urgent remedy. She squealed when he hoisted her over his shoulder and carried her into the bedroom, where a few moments later with clothing thrown all around the room, he positioned himself above her, ready to carry out his mission.

"But you're not using any protection," she said, her breathing already labored.

"I know."

"But I might get, you know, pregnant."

"That's the idea, woman. Stop wiggling around so much so I can do my duty."

"You snake." She laughed out loud. "You were planning this all along."

"Not exactly, but it'll do. Now, will you please hold still?"

****

On that and many subsequent occasions, Dani met him at the door and had him stripped and bedded before he even got the snow dusted off his jacket. His pleas for a reprieve of even one evening got him nowhere.

"You promised," she said.

"Not a promise exactly, more like a suggestion, me and my big mouth."

"I don't need your big mouth, not yet anyway. What I need now is right here in my hand, so no backing out, Mr. Deputy Sheriff." She had hold of him by a delicate body part that left him no choice but to follow wherever she might lead.

It should have become routine after a while, come home, take off the uniform, jump on his house-mate for a few minutes of vigorous love-making, then have dinner. Except that routine did not seem to be part of Dani's vocabulary. The act itself was straightforward enough, but what might happen before and after was something he could never anticipate. One night they wound up in the middle of the kitchen floor, three chairs from the breakfast nook lying upside down, a naked Dani sitting astride him, her happy laughter bouncing off the walls while Alfie licked his face. What man, in this or any other universe ever enjoyed such an evening?

After all that vigorous, purposeful sex, he wasn't

quite sure of her intentions on that cold winter evening when she pounced on him, arms around his neck, legs wrapped around his waist, as soon as he'd shut the door behind him, but things became clear quickly enough.

"We did it," she announced so loudly that a frightened Alfie ran out of the room. "Well, say something." She tightened her grip on his neck and shook him. "This was all your idea, remember?"

As usual, at moments of high intensity, his voice failed him. She did her little trick of touching her nose to his so there was no space between them, and they shared the same breath. "Phil, are you in there?"

Then it came to him, verbal salvation: "I love you, and I want to spend the rest of my life with you. Will you marry me?"

"Finally, took you long enough." Her smile raised his body temperature by several degrees.

"I was working my way up to it. How did you find out about the pregnancy?" he asked.

"The pharmacy has these little kits where you can test your urine. Mine went positive this afternoon. I was going to call you at work but decided to wait until you got home so I could see your expression."

"Yeah? How do I look?"

"Like a guy who just got conked on the head with a beer bottle." She laughed, he laughed, and Alfie crept back into the room.

"Hey, you didn't answer my question. Are you going to make an honest man of me?"

"I think you have that turned around. You're supposed to make an honest woman of me."

"Same difference," he said.

"If you say so. Now, take me to bed."

"We have to keep on doing this? I mean, you're already pregnant, right?"

"Yeah, we're okay there. This one is just for fun, and yes, I will marry you."

****

Phil and Dani made things legal in early December, right between their two birthdays, in the First Baptist Church on the outskirts of Clayton. Sheriff Barnhill was Phil's best man. The couple expected a quiet event, just family and a few friends, but that wasn't how it turned out. The church was full, standing room only, and the reception went on into the early evening hours.

"Who are all these people?" Phil, who recognized only a half dozen of them, asked Dani during their few moments alone.

"Mostly friends of Uncle Sy's," she said.

"Are they friends of ours too?"

"If you want them to be. I think some of them are a little bit intimidated, you being a big old deputy sheriff and all. Just give them some time. They'll warm up to you."

So, he would be patient, remembering that a lot of the people at his wedding reception had also been present for his day in court where he'd been depicted, by his blushing bride, no less, as the worst of the worst. Such a complete turnaround would require time, and that's just what he would give them. But they gave in return, the good people of Clayton did, wedding presents, so many that Phil had to make a separate trip with the truck to cart them all back to the house.

He insisted on carrying Dani across the threshold, the same threshold they'd crossed so many times already, but this was a different situation altogether, crossing it as man and pregnant wife. She was a bit hesitant, aware that Phil had had several drinks during the festivities. "Don't you dare drop me. I'm carrying our child, remember?"

"No power on earth could cause me to drop you, now or ever." He carried her through the house and set her gently on their bed, where he knelt before her trying to find the right words to tell her how much he loved her and how if a guy could feel, just for a moment out of an entire lifetime, how he felt with her, he should consider himself luckier than any man alive, but he kept getting the words mixed up until finally, he hung his head in her lap. She lifted him up, kissed him, and pulled him on top of her, and somehow, in spite of a suit and a long dress, they consummated that happiest of moments.

After they'd shed their disordered and wrinkled official attire and slipped into more comfortable clothes, he reminded her that they hadn't made any plans for a honeymoon trip. "Nowhere else I want to go," she said. "I'm completely happy right here with you." Yeah, the luckiest man alive, for sure.

Chapter Thirty

Since they'd been practically living together for a number of months, they eased into the routine of married life with only a few minor bumps and adjustments. The first challenge of any magnitude was Dani's insistence on throwing a big Christmas party.

"A party for who?" Phil asked. "I only know a few people here, and that makes for a very small party."

"Uncle Sy always had a big Christmas party, invited the whole community. It's a Clayton tradition. Angie and I always helped him set it up, so I know where all his decorations are. Your job is to get us a tree, a big one that reaches all the way up to the ceiling." She'd started to walk away but turned back to him. "And you have to be more patient with the folks around here, give them a chance to get to know you better. You'll see."

What he saw was himself, Phil Claussen, becoming the new Uncle Sy, dead man's house, dead man's legacy, dead man's traditions. Far from starting over with a clean slate, he'd stepped into a life in which the broad strokes, and probably some of the finer points as well, were already sketched out. But he was in for the full ride now, wherever it took him. He'd bought into the Clayton mystique without reservation.

Dani, already familiar with the planning process, went into frenzy mode in the days leading up to the party. Phil stretched his workday out an hour or so because the household, at least during the earlier days of preparation, was pure carnage. He managed to escape some of the chaos, but not the traditional male role of stringing colored lights, which took up an entire weekend.

He'd anticipated the usual tangled web of lines and lights that strikes fear into the heart of every home-owning male, but instead, Sy had left behind neatly coiled cords, the only problem being there were so many of them. They stretched all across the front of the house and down the sides, with additional strands looping around the front dormer windows. He called Earl to come over and help out, but Earl refused, saying, "Only a crazy man would hang around with something like that going on," and advised Phil to leave town for a week.

Angie, still treading lightly around Phil, was on hand to help out, and between them, the two ladies transformed the house into a holiday wonderland, leaving Phil slack-jawed over the transfiguration. Wreaths, garland, strands of twinkling lights, all placed by Phil under Dani's strict supervision.

"I'll need your truck tomorrow," Dani said. "Angie and I need to run over to Oklahoma City."

"What on earth for?" Phil asked. Part of the restitution, once his good name had been restored, had been the return of his big truck, this time complete with all the paperwork.

"There will be kids," Dani said. "They need presents." She kissed him and drew his face down close to hers. "And you are now officially Santa."

Then there was food; the few days just before the

big event, they came, like ants bringing treasures back to the colony, the Clayton Neighbor Lady Brigade arrived in cars, trucks, a few vans, all laden with homemade treats. So, this was what tradition looked like. Phil felt his jaw drop so many times he feared it might become a permanent position.

****

His first ever Sy Birch Christmas party, the big community event for the holiday, took place on Friday evening. He'd seen military operations carried out far less smoothly. Would it ever become the Phil Claussen Christmas party? It didn't matter, and he was savvy enough not to tamper with tradition.

The responsibility for donning the Santa suit, a task he greatly feared Dani would force upon him, turned out to be part of the tradition in the form of the local postmaster, Don Lincoln, whose own expansive girth needed no extra padding. What Don did need was someone to clear a way for him among the room full of kids that seemed to have appeared from out of nowhere. An ever-so-slightly-pregnant Dani, stunning in a short red velvet dress with fluffy white trim, was supposedly Santa's helper, but she drew much more attention from the adult males in the room than from the kids.

Whether from an effusion of holiday spirit, the antics of the kids besieging Santa Claus, or just plain old body heat—the first floor of the house was spacious but packed to capacity with holiday guests—Phil was aware of unusual warmth. He found signs that at least some of this might be due to the good people of Clayton finally accepting him in his new role.

They introduced themselves, golfers inviting him to join them when the weather turned warmer, runners inviting him to join their morning outings, fishermen, who, he guessed, were mostly interested in an invitation to have at the large-mouthed bass in his big lake. And slowly but surely, he was catching onto what he thought of as the *lingua franca*. For instance, the answer to the casual query, "Bad winter, you think?" was always, "Never seen a good one." And there were others, many others, but he would learn.

All of this was tumbling through his mind when he felt a tug at his arm. "Merry Christmas, Phil." Angie stood close by, holding onto his forearm. When he didn't respond immediately, she said, "Congratulations on impregnating my sister. I've never seen her look so happy."

"I think it's the dress," he said. "She likes playing dress-up." But he had to admit, his new bride was radiant.

"So, can we be friends?" she asked.

"What do you mean?"

"Forgive and forget what a dirty trick I did to you, switching your gun then lying about it. That was awful."

"It could have been worse. You know what happens to law enforcement officials who get thrown in prison? They don't last very long."

"I would never have let that happen. Please, believe me. I was all set to tell your attorney about what I did, even go into witness protection if I had to. It's a lot to forgive, I know, but will you please try?"

He wrapped his arm around her shoulders and kissed her on the cheek. "We're family now, so let's forget about that stuff."

"Thank God," she said. "Now, that brings me to

my next official act. I'm your escort until Dani gets through playing Santa's helper."

"Escort? You think I might get lost?"

"I'm supposed to keep you out of trouble."

"What kind of trouble could I possibly get into here? You're wasting your time."

"Definitely not. See that redhead over there, the one wearing the tight white dress with no underpants?"

"How the hell can you see that?"

"Believe me, I know. Anyway, she's been checking you out for the last half hour, and I'm afraid she's finally got up the courage to make a move on you." Angie moved closer to his side. "So that's why I'm here, to run interference for you because there are a few others I'm watching too."

"And I thought they were just being friendly."

Angie laughed out loud. "How Dani ever keeps you in line is a mystery."

He spotted Sandra Newton standing by the punch bowl, went over, and gave her a vigorous holiday hug. "Thanks again for saving my bacon," he said. "I've seen the inside of enough jail cells to last me for a long time."

"My pleasure," she said. "I am so glad you've kept up Sy's tradition. This party means so much to people around here."

****

By any measure he could think of, the party was a huge success. The curtain came down shortly past nine, a bit earlier than he expected, probably because those families with kids had to leave earlier. Angie stayed around to help Dani tidy up, but there was very little clean up to do. The neighbor ladies, as organized and effective a group as he'd ever seen, had things mostly under control.

Dani, who was still a bit flushed, as she had been all evening, wrapped her arms around his neck. "I'm so proud of you," she said.

"Why? I didn't do anything. It was all about you and Santa."

"You must have done something good because I got all manner of favorable comments about you, especially from the ladies. Angie must not have been a very good chaperone."

"I don't remember meeting any ladies at all. The guys were nice, though. But you know, I don't remember seeing the social worker, Regina. Did you see her?"

Dani shook her head, then left to say goodbye to Angie. Phil slipped into the bedroom to check the pockets of his jacket. Sure as hell, two slips of paper with names and phone numbers, and he had no clue how they got there. He carefully ripped both of them into tiny shreds then flushed them down the toilet.

He was already down to his jockey shorts when Dani came into the bedroom. "Help me off with my boots," she said.

"How often do you wear these?" he asked.

"Once a year, same with the dress, so you can help me with the zipper."

"You looked so cute in that dress, flouncing around, showing your butt."

"What?" Her voice was shrill. "I did not show my butt, did I?"

"No, just kidding."

"I'm a married woman now, pregnant, at that, so I

can't very well go around flashing my butt."

"Not like you used to, huh?"

"Careful, big boy, or I'll have to hurt you."

"Like I said, just kidding. Now, come here." With one motion, he stripped off her pantyhose and underpants, then listened over her abdomen. "Are you sure there's somebody in here?" he asked.

"Positive, but it's too early to hear anything yet."

He planted kisses all across her abdomen, ending up in the golden fleece between her thighs. He pulled her onto the bed, pushed her knees apart, and got down to business. "Merry Christmas to all of us," he said.

****

The storm that had roared in on Saturday night with wind, snow, and temperatures in the single digits, still raged Monday morning as Phil was finishing breakfast and trying to think of some way to avoid heading out into the tempest. But like most of the other residents of Clayton, OK, he had a job to do, and it started when the call came from the social services office.

Regina Philpott had not returned to the office Friday night and still hadn't turned up. Her last appointment on Friday was a visit to one of the shut-ins, Mr. Gerald Hennessey, a man known to Phil because of his habit of shooting at strangers, but he'd been out to Hennessey's place with Regina before, and she seemed to be on a very friendly basis with the man. He gave Dani a quick peck on the cheek, grabbed his coat and hat, and headed for the door.

He didn't want to surprise old Gerald, but he didn't have time to waste either, so about fifty yards from the cabin, he turned on his flashers and continued on up the drive. The social services sedan was parked in front of the shack, and Regina's body, partially covered with snow and probably frozen stiff by now, lay just in front of it.

Phil approached cautiously, his weapon drawn, the time for haste long gone by now. She had fallen on her side, knees drawn upward toward her chest, perhaps a final agonal movement. Small animals, coyotes probably, had been at her face, making recognition difficult. The bullet entry wound remained clearly visible at the base of her neck. Hopefully, death was instantaneous, but he couldn't be sure.

Remnants of white wrapping paper lay strewn around the area, and, just a few feet from the door of the shack, lay a bow and a strip of red ribbon. A small cardboard box ripped open with just enough of its contents remaining to be identified as what was once a fruitcake, had been dragged off to the side. She had been out delivering Christmas presents to her shut-in clients when she was shot.

He slipped off his jacket and draped it over her face, then he staggered behind her car and vomited up his breakfast. "Fuck," he screamed at a universe that didn't give a damn where it set down its big ugly foot, crushing the good and precious along with everything else in the area. Such a lonely death for a woman the sheriff had called a saint. She deserved better.

He didn't know whether Gerald waited inside his cabin with his rifle trained on the door, and at the moment, it didn't matter. He kicked the flimsy entryway to pieces, stormed inside with his weapon pointed at the pile of rags in the corner. The rifle lay on the floor. He secured the weapon, ejected the chambered round, and threw it across the room.

The rag pile made no movement, no sound. When Phil finally got to the body, Gerald was just as frozen and dead as Regina.

He got back into his vehicle and waited until his hands stopped shaking so he could punch in the numbers to the EMTs and Sheriff Barnhill, and, for the first time in many years, he wept. The thought kept washing over him that while they'd all been enjoying the grand Christmas party, Regina had been lying here dead, freezing solid. When he'd tried to move her body inside his vehicle, the arrangement of her frozen limbs prevented him, so all he could do was wait.

The cleanup crew rolled up in the EMT vehicle, preceded by Sheriff Barnhill's cruiser. He nodded at Phil but said nothing. Indeed, what was there to say? Phil stared off into the frozen wasteland, having seen before the problems with recovering bodies with limbs akimbo, limbs that no longer moved into convenient positions.

Barnhill handed over Phil's coat. "You'll freeze out here like that."

"Couldn't just leave her lying there."

"I know. Somehow, she must have spooked old Gerald, probably fired right through the door. Doubt he ever saw who or what he was shooting at."

"Makes no sense at all," Phil said.

"Never does."

Neither of them was a stranger to violent death, but Regina's killing rocked both men. For Phil, it unleashed an unhinged, free-floating rage, the kind that could and would lash out in any direction without provocation.

Barnhill, apparently picking up on Phil's mood,

moved in close. "Look at me, Phil. Dammit, I said, look at me." He grabbed Phil shoulders and pulled him around until their faces were inches apart. "You're on the verge of doing something crazy. We both know it. What you're going to do instead is go home to your wife and stay there. If I have to, I'll throw your ass in jail until you cool off. You hear me?"

Phil nodded without really understanding his own feelings.

"I'm going to call Dani when I get back to the station, and if you're not home by then, I'm coming after you," Barnhill said.

"I hear you," Phil said. He spent the rest of the day at home, sitting by a window, looking out at blowing snow and creeping darkness, although the darkness inside him had come hours before. Several times during that evening, when the pressure inside him rose to a dangerous level, he'd grabbed his coat and started for the door, only to find his path blocked by Dani, reinforced by Alfie.

"Phil, listen to me. Everybody around here loved Regina, and most of us are hurting just as much as you are. But you going out and doing something crazy isn't going to help anything." She placed her hands on his chest, not pushing against him, just letting him know his pain was shared, and she was right there with him, and he was going nowhere.

****

There are no good times for funerals, but some are most certainly worse than others. Smart folks would stay indoors on a day like that on which Regina Philpott was buried, a day with a vicious wind snarling unimpeded across the plain, searing anything and everything it touched. But they came out anyway, trudging along, stronger arms supporting those less strong. They parked so far along the street that the most distant vehicles were lost in blowing snow. Still, they came.

The site was completely unprotected because no tent could withstand the fury of the gale, so they stood in the open, clinging to hats, scarves, anything that might afford even a little bit of protection. Phil had suggested to Dani that perhaps she should wait in the car since the weather was so bad. The look she gave him would have broken glass. She would crawl if she had to, but then, so would he, and so would most of the people who made that difficult trek.

When it was over, and Regina Philpott's earthly remains lay deep in partially frozen ground, Phil and Sheriff Barnhill patrolled the area, making sure everyone made it safely back to their vehicles. Then the snow covered the area as if nothing at all had happened there.

Chapter Thirty-One

Given the foul and dangerous weather that prevailed for most of the next two months or so, Phil expected most of Clayton to go into hibernation. Of course, those with animals to tend to did not have that option, nor did those with law enforcement duties to carry out. Surprisingly, the bar business remained brisk, but the alcohol-associated hostilities tapered off, so Phil's nightstick remained on the seat of his cruiser.

He made more trips out to the shut-ins who'd been in Regina's care and found that others visited them as well, apparently taking up the slack left when Regina was killed. He drove his truck out with a load of wood for the lady still known to him as Miss Lily because that's what Sheriff Barnhill called her. Even keeping her woodburning stove going full blast, he didn't see how she would survive the winter, but somehow she managed. On one such trip, he found her decked out in a relatively new down jacket that, given her small stature, extended down to floor level. "Neighbor lady," she said. Phil wanted to know more but didn't ask. He knew of no neighbors within a radius of several miles, but clearly, the Clayton Neighbor Lady Brigade was still at work and taking care of business.

****

The weeks flew by, becoming months, and as Dani's pregnancy gained traction and her abdomen grew, he worried about her isolation too. He'd never seen her with girlfriends before, but most days of the week, he found fresh tire tracks in the driveway when he got home, and one evening walked into a boisterous baby shower, the front room of the house packed with women and littered with gifts and wrapping paper. Dani had given him no warning about the event, and after retrieving his dinner from the oven, he and Alfie were banished to the basement. Apparently, the Clayton community had a safety net that extended to ladies in need, whether the need was wood for the stove or a knowing shoulder to lean on during a first pregnancy.

He still was allowed to participate in outdoor activities, and on a Sunday afternoon in February with a crystal blue sky and, for a welcome change, no wind, Earl pulled up in front of their house towing his ATV on a trailer behind his truck. With Dani and Angie safely bundled up in the back seat, passing a thermos of hot chocolate back and forth between them, they all set out for a horseless sleigh ride, covering much of the thousand-acre spread in an hour or so, before the cold temperatures began to take their toll. Earl insisted on leaving the ATV with Phil, so they could take little jaunts whenever the weather permitted.

The Clayton social net also ensnared Phil when a luncheon with several members of the local Rotary Club ended up with Phil as a new member.

****

On a wind-swept morning in late February, complete with flying needles of sleet mixed with freezing rain, after he'd untangled a fender-bender between a pickup truck and a white van, almost becoming a participant in the accident himself owing to the icy roads, and after he'd finally settled in at his desk with a cup of coffee, Sandra Newton called to tell him a letter had arrived for him addressed to her law office. "The name on the return address is Addie—she spelled it out for him—no last name."

His daughter, had to be. Phil's gut tied itself into tight little knots as he remembered his rapid exodus from Wakefield, how he'd had only the briefest conversation with his wife, MaryBeth—most of that taken up with her screaming at him—and none at all with his thirteen-year-old daughter, Addie. At the time, he'd blended them into a single entity, mother and daughter, both halves of which were imperiled by his toxic presence, giving him adequate reason to flee and not look back.

Now that past seemed to have caught up with him, and he had no choice but to stand up and face the music, whatever the tune might be. "I'll come right over and pick it up," he said. Waiting would just make it tougher.

Not long after, Sandra met him in the foyer of her office and paraded him past her leering receptionist like a hunting trophy she'd bagged and was not about to share. "How are things on the home front?" she asked after they were seated, and she had poured coffee for both of them.

"Chaos, mostly," he said. "I spend most of my home time hiding out in the basement with the dog."

"A wise move. Is Dani getting help with the household stuff?"

"She's got me." It was meant as a joke, but then, his delivery never was the greatest.

"If you were able to step into the role of

homemaker, you'd be the first man I've ever seen do it." She laughed.

"Well, the neighborhood ladies have taken over, like a small army. I call them the Clayton Neighbor Lady Brigade. They clean, they cook, they do the laundry, amazing to watch. I just try to stay out of the way."

"You know, I'd have been happy to forward the letter to you, save you a trip over here, although I have to say, it's always fun watching Dolly drool when you walk by."

"I wanted to read it myself before I showed it to Dani."

"You sounded a bit hesitant about it when we talked on the phone."

He stared at a spot on the wall for a moment. "Don't know what to expect," he said. "Haven't had any contact with Addie since I left Wakefield, and, to be honest, we never were really close when I was there." He didn't mention he'd forgotten her birthday, although this thought began to gnaw at him like a wound that hadn't healed properly.

"She's still your daughter." Sandra passed a fat envelope across her desk to him, and he immediately recognized Addie's looping cursive. "And you owe me for the extra postage."

He took the envelope back to his office, closed the door before he broke the seal, his hands trembling ever so slightly.

"*Dear Dad*" sent little shock waves through him. For his last few years in Wakefield, she'd barely addressed him at all. Now, out of the blue, he was Dear Dad.

I miss you. You probably know by now, Mom has remarried a guy named Larry Lemmings.

Larry Lemmings? Phil had suspected some sort of shenanigans for some time but never believed she would select him for a husband. Talk about scraping the bottom of the barrel. She couldn't have done any worse if she'd put a sign on the front lawn inviting homeless men in for marital interviews. It shouldn't have upset him so much, but it did, for Addie's sake if nothing else, and besides, being replaced by Larry Lemmings really stung.

I don't like him. Smart girl. *He claims to be real religious and makes me go to church in the middle of the week for some Bible study group, but I think it's just a place to dump me for the evening.*

There were three more pages of chatty items, including some stuff from school where a number of people, faculty, and students as well, had expressed regrets about her father's abrupt departure. *You were the best teacher ever.*

A new warmth flooded through him as he considered that perhaps he hadn't left his family in a state of complete disgrace after all, that his years of exemplary behavior and contributions to his school and his community counted for something. Best of all, his daughter didn't have to hang her head in shame whenever his name came up.

Addie had included several photos (*Send me your email address, and I'll mail more to you*), Addie playing on the Wakefield Junior High basketball team—something new—all those years he'd tried to get her involved in something athletic, now he left town, and she started playing basketball. Go figure.

Addie at the beach with friends, Addie wearing a skimpy bikini. What the hell? His daughter wasn't old enough to wear stuff like that, except she was, along with her friends. Fourteen now, if he was counting correctly since he'd blown right past her last birthday. She signed the letter in big block print: *All my love, Addie*.

He realized as he thumbed through the pages and photos for a second, then a third time, that reading her letter had taken more time than any conversation he'd had with his daughter in recent memory. He had faced some emotional twists and turns during the past eighteen months, but this one caught him by a particularly tender spot and would not let go.

A seemingly insurmountable wall had grown between himself and his daughter. Now, with a letter and a few photos, she had smashed it into very small bits. Biting his lip did not prevent a tear from escaping the corner of his eye and rolling down his cheek, followed by others. Now he would have to explain all this to Sheriff Barnhill, who had just entered his office and stood watching the Claussen waterworks.

"Phil, deputies don't cry. We talked about this. Are you okay?"

"Yeah, fine, no problem."

"*No problem* is making you cry. Is that what you're telling me?"

"Just got a letter from my daughter."

"Good letter? Is she all right?"

"Yeah, she's fine, great, actually."

"I guess we've never talked much about your family back in Wakefield." The sheriff looked almost fatherly, the way he folded his arms across his abdomen, nodding, a faint but warm smile.

"It was hard," Phil said, "considering the circumstances when I left them. They weren't exactly showering me with rose petals when I drove away."

"Maybe a good time to mend some fences, you think?"

"Could be," Phil said.

****

He didn't mention the letter to Dani until they had cleared away the dinner dishes because he wasn't sure how she would react to a reminder of his former life, pregnant as she was. As usual, she surprised him.

"Phil, that's wonderful news. When were you going to tell me? That's your first contact with her since you've been here unless you've been holding out on me."

"No, you're right, first time."

"Well, let's have it. What did she say?"

"Oh, just some stuff about school," he said.

"You'll have to let me see it. I should have known you'd leave out all the important things."

"It's in the pocket of my jacket." He retrieved the letter and handed it over to Dani as they both settled onto the sofa, and Alfie curled up on the carpet for his nap.

"Oh, there's all sorts of stuff in here." Dani spread the contents over the sofa cushion. "Your ex remarried...Larry Lemmings? Sounds like a rodent."

"Looks like one too. She could have done a lot better."

"And she sent photos. Is this Addie?"

He nodded.

"Phil, she's a beautiful girl. It must have broken

your heart to leave, hers too."

"It didn't seem like it at the time, more like they were glad to get rid of me."

"Okay if I read the letter?"

"Sure, go ahead."

After the first page, she was practically bouncing on the sofa cushion. "Oh, Phil, this is a wonderful letter. She says so many sweet things about you."

"Sure surprised me," he said.

"And she says she would love to see you. Well, that settles it. As soon as I get this baby of ours delivered and get back on my feet, we're going to fly Addie out for a visit."

"What will she do here?" he asked. The thought of entertaining a teenaged girl terrified him.

"You leave that to me. We'll have a blast. I can find plenty of things for her to do."

"Such as?"

"Maybe I'll teach her to hotwire a car."

"No way, you will not turn my daughter into a car thief. Anyway, you're joking, right?"

"Maybe."

****

He hadn't heard Dani come into the kitchen where he sat working at the table. He quickly put his arm over the page, hoping she couldn't see the pile of crumpled sheets he'd begun, then discarded.

"What's this, some big secret?" she asked.

"No, no, it's just a letter to Addie."

"Phil, you poor thing, that should be the easiest thing in the world to write."

"Well, it isn't. I know what I want to say, but I'm not sure how to say it."

She put her hands on his shoulders and began a gentle massage. "She's just a fourteen-year-old girl. You saw hundreds of them when you were teaching. You know what they're like."

"But none of them was my daughter. I messed up last time, and I don't want to mess up again."

"You won't, no chance. She's going to be so glad to hear from you it won't matter what you write. Let me know when you're ready to send it off. I have a couple of pages to add."

"What did you write?" he asked.

"Just girl stuff, things you don't need to know about."

It was well into the evening hours when he finally stacked three pages together. His fingers trembled as he folded the sheets. He had no idea what Dani had written, only that she insisted on tucking her own pages into the envelope, so he couldn't peek.

"I'm so happy about this, Phil." She wrapped her arms around his neck.

"If you're happy, I'm happy." And if the letter made his daughter happy too, he'd be ecstatic.

****

In early April, after he'd made it through most of his first Midwest winter, Phil, with Earl's help and equipment, began work clearing a roadway to the big lake on his property, ending up with a boat ramp from which he could launch a sizeable craft. The lake and ramp required that he buy a bass boat, so he did, a twenty-four-foot screamer with a one hundred horsepower outboard engine that pushed the boat across the lake in nothing flat. And just as Earl had promised, the large-mouth bass were thick in the lake, but he found no sport in boating bass that insisted on being caught.

Needless to say, the thrill wore off soon enough. Roaring across the lake was fine at first, but what then? Turn around and roar right back again? Alfie was the first to see the futility in it all. After a few rides, he simply refused to get back in a boat that was going nowhere fast and making all manner of noise while it did. How could a dog sleep with such a racket?

And Dani put the lid on the whole adventure. "You're not bringing those smelly fish into my house."

Phil sold the bass boat. What else could he do?

What he really missed were those magical days and evenings spent with Dani on the small pond, and, since Sy's old boat was no longer seaworthy, he ordered a skiff from a boat builder in Wakefield. The builder was renown in the coastal area for his craftsmanship and for the beauty of the skiffs he turned out, one at a time. His was a one-man operation, and getting in touch with him involved the luck of the draw. The builder answered his phone only when he felt like it, and he accepted orders from customers only if he liked them. He liked Phil.

The trim, graceful little boat he made for Phil was the last he ever made for anyone because the elderly craftsman died at his bench in mid-June, the week after Phil's boat left his shop.

Shipping the skiff from North Carolina to Oklahoma cost almost as much as the skiff itself, but when Phil got his first look at the sleek, one-of-a-kind beauty, it was love at first sight. The little craft got Alfie's approval first thing; the dog jumped right in and stood there, tail wagging contentedly, waiting for Phil and Earl to join him. Enough said.

There was no champagne bottle broken over the bow. Phil wouldn't risk any dings in the perfect hull, which would hopefully have a long and gentle life, drifting along on sunny afternoons, ferrying two adults, a baby, and a comatose dog wherever the breeze might carry them. And who knew, maybe his daughter from Wakefield could come along for a ride.

Chapter Thirty-Two

In early May, some nineteen weeks into her pregnancy, Dani prepared to report to the hospital for an ultrasound, a routine procedure, as she described it. "And we'll be able to find out whether it's a boy or a girl," she said.

"As if you didn't know," Phil said because the nursery was already decked out floor to ceiling, and all spaces in between in pink.

"We can always change it if I'm wrong."

"Are you ever wrong?" Like many of his jokes, this one fell flat, and the look she gave him warned him to change course before he got into real trouble.

Phil missed out on the ultrasound procedure because he had to attend to a head-on collision just south of the Interstate, between a mammoth SUV and a much smaller sedan. How vehicles could collide on a straight stretch of road with wide shoulders on either side would remain a mystery to him, but it happened. In this case, the SUV was the clear victor in the collision, collapsing the front end of the sedan like a sheet of crumpled aluminum foil.

The young couple in the front seats of the sedan were both dead, the woman with a look of surprise on her face, the driver with hardly any face at all. But their child, strapped securely into its car seat, appeared unharmed and in possession of an excellent set of lungs.

The young female EMT, tears in her eyes, unbuckled the child and carried it away from the wreckage, probably knowing that for the child, the trouble had just begun.

Sheriff Barnhill walked up alongside Phil. "Drunk," he said. "The guy driving the SUV is drunk as a skunk, got a little bruise on his nose where the airbag hit him, otherwise not a scratch. Seems like drunks never get hurt. They just hurt other people."

By late afternoon, when all that remained of the two vehicles was an oil stain and the sun glittering off tiny fragments of glass that littered the shoulder of the road. After Phil had picked up the drunken driver at the emergency room and transported him to jail, he made his way back home, where he found his wife and her sister huddled together giggling like a pair of successful thieves.

"I didn't know ultrasounds were funny," he said. "What did I miss?"

"Are you going to tell him, or should I?" Angie asked.

"Go ahead, you're the one who thought it was so funny," Dani said.

"Well, Dr. Polhill was checking Dani over, and he was concerned because her ankles were swollen a little, and he said she should keep them propped up. And she said lying around with her legs in the air was how she got like this in the first place. And the funniest part, the doctor didn't crack a smile. His nurse laughed so hard she dropped the urine sample, and they had to wait for Dani to pee again. You should have been there."

"Yeah, sorry I missed that." Phil got the joke, but the tragic event out on the highway had pulled the plug on his sense of humor. "You checked out okay?" he asked.

"Just the ankle thing." She pushed herself up and came over to where he was standing, still wearing his uniform jacket. "Rough day?" She wrapped her arms around his neck.

"You could say that. You haven't told me yet, boy or girl?"

"You can have as many guesses as you want."

"So, it is a girl," he said.

"Of course, and she looks just like her handsome father."

"Oh, no," he said. "She has to look exactly like you. Besides, no way you could tell that from an ultrasound, not at nineteen weeks."

"I'll leave you two to sort things out," Angie said. "Dinner's in the oven."

"Please, stay and eat with us," Phil said.

"You two lovebirds need some time alone. Besides, I made Earl promise to take me out."

After they'd seen Angie off, Phil and Dani cuddled on the sofa, Dani's feet propped up on cushions.

"That was kinda funny, that bit about having your feet up in the air," Phil said. "Never guessed you were such a comedian."

"You don't get most of my jokes," she said. "There's something else we have to decide, a name for our daughter. I have one in mind if you agree."

"I'll bet it's the same one I'm thinking."

"Regina," she said.

"Yeah."

The buzzer on the oven timer went off, adding an exclamation point.

****

Phil had played no part in MaryBeth's pregnancy from her previous marriage—Addie was already six when they were married—so Dani's travails in the scorching summer months were his first experience of what a woman had to endure as her pregnancy wore on. Dr. Polhill placed her on a diuretic to decrease her ankle swelling, requiring numerous nighttime bathroom trips and adding sleep deprivation to her list of problems.

Phil did what he could to boost her sagging spirits. "Before you know it, we'll be taking rides in our new boat, just the three of us, well, four if you count Alfie." She seemed to like the idea.

She surprised him when, early on a Sunday morning in late July, she walked into the living room wearing a new dress that left her shoulders mostly bare but was cut to accommodate a full-blown pregnancy. "How do I look?" she asked.

"Gorgeous, but you're going to need shoes if you plan on going out. What's the occasion?"

"Church, I want us to go to church services today at First Baptist. I want Regina to grow up in our community, and the local church is a good place to start. That way she'll be sure to meet nice people."

"Sweetheart, she hasn't been born yet. Why start so early unless you have other reasons."

"Now is a good time to start. You don't need to wear your dark suit, but dress nice," she said.

Preparations went smoothly enough until Dani began trying on shoes. When none of them fit her swollen feet, she began crying. "I can't go to church without shoes."

Actually, she could, he thought, without too many eyebrows being raised. The townsfolk were probably even more used to unconventional Dani than conventional Dani. "Do you and Angie wear the same size?" he asked.

"That's a great idea. She might have something that fits."

He won a few points with that suggestion. "So long as she's home," he said.

"She probably will be, and if she isn't, I'll pick the lock."

"You pick locks too?" he asked.

"It comes in handy sometimes. I can teach you if you want. Maybe I'll teach Addie when she comes out for a visit."

"Don't even think about it."

With Dani hobbling along in her sister's shoes, she and Phil caused a bit of an uproar when they entered the church while so many of those in attendance gathered round to greet the new mother-to-be. But all of the attention seemed to sap Dani's energy reserves, and the preacher was only halfway through the sermon before she asked Phil to take her home. She spent the rest of the day in bed.

****

By the end of the third week in July, when Dani began to complain more and more of her feet swelling—"I can hardly walk to the bathroom,"— Angie, her attendant-in-chief, called in Dr. Polhill's visiting nurse, who soon after called Phil's office. This message that Dani was on her way to Clayton County Memorial Hospital by ambulance was relayed by Claudia from the office to Phil's patrol car, causing him to execute a one-hundred-and-eighty degree turn in the middle of state road Number 63 and tear back toward the hospital, roof lights flashing, siren blaring, all in violation of department policy, but then, he didn't care, did he?

Phil skidded to a halt in the spot for emergency vehicles and tossed the keys to his cruiser to the attendant as he ran past the desk: "Move it if you need the space."

A nurse with no visible neck, broad shoulders, and biceps bigger than Phil's own, all encased in a uniform stretched so tightly it appeared ready to give up the struggle, grabbed Phil's arm. "This way, Mr. Claussen." The uniform gave her more freedom of movement than Phil would have expected because he had to trot to keep up with her.

Clayton County Memorial, a one-hundred-and-twenty-bed hospital, had a six-bed intensive care unit, where, for the moment, Dani was the only customer. Her face was partly concealed behind an oxygen mask, and her EKG and blood pressure readings spilled out onto a screen above her bed. The number jumped off the screen, 215/120. Angie, who had insisted on riding in the ambulance with her sister, stood beside the bed, her hands in prayer pose, and, Phil guessed, that was exactly what she was doing.

"I'm Dr. Pennington. Dr. Polhill is on his way. I've spoken to him about Mrs. Claussen's blood pressure, and we've started treatment with intravenous medication."

Such a tiny little thing she was, this doctor. Even Dani, a small woman herself, would tower over this medical person who, for the moment, was running the show. But her handshake was firm, even though her hand felt like a child's held in his own, and she maintained direct eye contact with him throughout their brief conversation. The feeling he got was that of confidence that Dr. Pennington knew her stuff and would get the job done.

"Thank you," he said. "But the blood pressure is still way high."

"Yes, but we only started the treatment a short while ago, and we have to proceed with caution. Don't want to drop the pressure too fast or too far."

He edged closer to the bed and took Dani's hand. He said her name softly. No response.

"She's on a sedative," Dr. Pennington said. "She has what we call pre-eclampsia, a syndrome with high blood pressure and protein in the urine, more common in first pregnancies. Until we get the blood pressure under control, there's a risk of convulsions, which would be dangerous for her and the baby as well. Dr. Polhill will be here shortly, and he'll tell you more about it."

Convulsions…Phil didn't like the sound of that word, not one bit.

Pennington motioned toward the monitor above the bed. "Her blood pressure seems to be responding to the medication, systolic down to one-seventy now."

"When will she be out of danger?" Phil asked.

"I want her systolic pressure no higher than one-forty. With it decreasing like this, she should be there soon. Then Dr. Polhill can decide whether to stop the sedative. I'll be out at the nurses' station if you need me."

Angie crossed over to Phil's side of the bed and,

wrapping her arms around him, proceeded to cry all over his shirt. "I should have done something sooner," she said.

"It would have been hard to get her to come in. She hates hospitals. I'm just thankful you got her here when you did." He didn't mention that he hated hospitals too, waiting patiently not being something he did easily or very well.

They both focused on the blood pressure monitor as if forcing the numbers to decrease by sheer power of will. If the monitor had betrayed them and the numbers risen, Phil might very well have smashed it with his fist. Angie, with her arms around him, was obviously aware of his tension. "Breathe with me," she said.

"Huh?"

"You're all tense, and you're holding your breath. Just breathe with me nicely and slow. It'll help you relax." She moved around until her upturned face was just inches below his.

"I don't want to relax."

"You have to. Listen to me. I bet if we hooked you up to that blood pressure machine, you'd break it. Now, breathe with me before you have a stroke or do something stupid."

He did, and she was right. Only when his tension eased did overwhelming fatigue set in like a damp, heavy blanket. Angie pulled up chairs for both of them, and Phil all but fell into his. Yeah, he had to remind himself to breathe, because the shock of seeing Dani lying unwell, unresponsive, with an intravenous line and an oxygen mask blasted his autonomic circuits and what was supposed to come naturally became erratic, requiring conscious effort as he tried to cope with this new world order where he could only wait and watch as her life flitted across a dark screen in bright yellow lines and numbers.

Dr. Pennington moved so quietly that he hadn't heard her reenter the room. "Mrs. Claussen's blood pressure is almost where we want it," she said. "Dr. Polhill just pulled into the parking lot, and I'm sure you'll have lots of questions for him."

"Thank you for taking care of Dani." Phil wanted to hug the tiny doctor, but, if he did so too vigorously, altogether possible in his current state, he might injure her, so he gave her his best and warmest smile.

Phil had met Dr. Leon Polhill, Dani's obstetrician, before at one of the more and more frequent town meetings he was expected to attend as official representative of the sheriff's office. He guessed by now that his increased visibility in the community was all a part of Sheriff Barnhill's retirement plan in which he, Phil, would take over the duties of sheriff. He had also been to Dr. Polhill's home one evening to investigate an attempted burglary, an attempt foiled earlier by the family's ninety-pound German Shepherd.

Polhill greeted Phil warmly and gave Angie a hug. "I see Dr. Pennington has everything under control here," he said, peering over the wire rims of his glasses. He listened over her chest with his stethoscope, then examined her swollen ankles. "Shall we step out into the hallway where we can talk more freely?"

"Can she hear me?" Phil asked before he left the bedside.

"Quite possibly," Polhill said.

With that, Phil leaned in close and whispered, "I love you," in Dani's ear.

Dr. Polhill seemed to have found a comfortable place to rest his backside, the edge of the circular desk that surrounded the nurses' habitat, and proceeded to deliver his monologue on pre-eclampsia and its occasional disastrous sequel, full-blown eclampsia, in lecture mode, apparently for the benefit of anyone in hearing distance.

Phil tuned out on most of Polhill's sermon, picking up only a few points about continuing light sedation through the night and waking Dani up tomorrow, keeping her in the ICU for a couple of days because only those beds were equipped with the necessary monitors, and, best of all, anticipating a full and complete recovery. All the while, Angie was scribbling notes furiously on a tablet she'd pulled from her purse.

"Any questions?" Dr. Polhill concluded his oration with a slight nod of his head, not unlike a bow.

"What caused this?" Angie asked.

"We don't know," Polhill said. "It isn't all that uncommon, maybe in ten percent of first pregnancies. Most go on to complete recovery and a successful delivery."

Neither Phil nor Angie asked about the unfortunate few who didn't do well because the question was irrelevant, right? Dani was going to recover, go home and return in about five weeks to drop off a healthy newborn, and that's all there was to it.

"Do you have any questions, Phil?" Angie nudged him with her elbow.

"Just when can I take her home?"

"Plan on about four days here, so we can be sure we have things under control. Don't want to take any chances."

"We sure don't," Phil said.

They returned to the same two bedside chairs they had vacated earlier, narrow, uncomfortable chairs that required the sitting body to conform to an exact ninety-degree angle. Phil began to fidget. Then he began to pace, back and forth, back and forth.

Angie jumped out of her chair and grabbed his arm. "Phil, will you stop it, please?"

"Stop what?"

"Prowling around like an old bear. You're driving me crazy. You should go home. Feed your dog and get something to eat for yourself."

"I want to be here in case she needs me."

"She'll be fine. The doctors and nurses will take good care of her. I'll get them to bring in a cot, so I can stay tonight. Now, go home so I can rest."

Helpless and useless was a bad combination, but there was nothing else he could do about it. Angie was right, and good soldier that he was, he would follow orders. His reluctance to leave was, of course, based in part on his wish to remain with Dani, but even more so on knowing what he would find when he got home because it wouldn't be home, would it? Without Dani, it was just a house, a very nice house, mind you, but its heart and soul would be elsewhere, lying in a hospital bed.

His drive home was a slow, mournful trek, and when he arrived, the house looked dark, empty, just as he knew it would. Alfie had been cooped up inside all day, and, as soon as Phil opened the door, the dog bolted past him, barely clearing the front porch before releasing a steam of urine that formed a glittering arc in the moonlight.

"Poor guy," Phil said as he refilled Alfie's water dish. "I'll find you something special for dinner tonight." Consumption of his own meal—-cornflakes— was a purely mechanical process, something to quiet the pangs in his stomach.

He called Sheriff Barnhill with an update on Dani's situation. "Take as much time as you need," the sheriff said. "You're both in our prayers." Phil was quite sure he meant exactly that.

Next, having tried without success to ignore its persistent flashing red light, he turned to his answering machine...twenty-eight messages. Must be a mistake because he couldn't think of twenty-eight people he knew in the area, and besides, how would word of Dani's hospitalization have spread so quickly? Yeah, must be a mistake, stupid machine.

But whether or not he recognized the twenty-eight callers, they knew Dani, and they knew him, and while they all sent condolences, the messages were more specific than the standard Hallmark lines, "...get well soon," or "...best wishes for a speedy recovery." They offered assistance, help with everything from cleaning the house to running errands to feeding the dog (how did they all know he even had a dog?), and food, so many offers of food, including delivery, "...we'll bring it right over." Later, when he mentioned the calls to Angie, she shrugged. "That's the way things work around here, always has been."

The night was much as he expected, long and empty like the rest of the house, only worse because the bed was where their togetherness mattered most. He clung to her pillow through the night like a child clutching a beloved teddy bear. Eventually, finding no comfort in their bed, he gave up on the idea of sleep and went out to sit on the front porch, awaiting a dawn that could not come soon enough. Alfie followed him out, apparently not liking being alone any more than Phil did.

He must have dozed off because when he woke, the sun had already climbed above the low rim of the pine tops and was shining straight into his face. His first movement after spending much of the night sitting in the rocking chair brought a jolt of pain through his back and shoulders. When the world came back into focus, he saw Earl Biggers sitting on his front porch drinking a beer.

"A little early for that, isn't it?" Phil said.

"Never too early for a beer." Earl let out a prolonged, satisfied belch. "Actually, this one is a bit on the late side, seeing as how I never really stopped last night. Got a few more cold ones in the trunk if you want one."

"No, thanks, coffee is what I need. How long you been sitting there?"

"Don't know for sure, an hour or so, I guess. Figured you might be up," Earl said. "You dog is getting fat."

"Dani feeds him too many snacks."

"Sorry about your trouble. Anything I can do?"

Phil shook his head. "Doc says she'll be in the hospital a few more days. She'll have to take it easy when she comes home, bed rest mostly. She won't like that."

"Baby okay?"

"Yeah, they say everything looks good. She's on medication to keep her blood pressure down. I'm just glad they didn't have to do anything else. Dani's only eight months along."

Earl rose, emitted one more belch, clapped Phil on the shoulder. "You need anything. You know where to find me." And then he was gone.

Since it was still too early to go back to the hospital, Phil opted for a walk. "Come on, Alfie, we both need some exercise." They walked along at a fairly rapid pace down the road to the campground entrance, still blocked by the gate Phil had put up to keep out whoever had decided to turn it into a trash dump. The area, at last, more closely resembled the oasis Sy Birch had managed and left in Phil's care. A refreshing northerly breeze had sprung up, and Phil felt his spirits lift a little. Of course, his elation was incomplete because Dani wasn't by his side. It was like having only half a body, half a soul.

"Been a while since I've been over here," Phil said aloud to no one in particular. Aside from a few weeds encroaching on the path, the area looked much as he'd left it. Should he think about reopening it? Maybe he would mention it to Earl, see if he'd like to take on the job as campground caretaker. Alfie was nowhere in sight, having run on ahead, apparently chasing some small game he had zero chance of catching.

The pond was a welcome sight, its tranquil surface once again golden in the morning sun. Lots of good memories here, but he didn't want memories. He wanted the real thing, his adorable little blonde wife, who by now would probably have stripped off her clothes and gone for a swim. With a heart suddenly grown even heavier, he turned and headed back home.

Later, on his way to the hospital, Phil stopped at a

small eatery called Shakee's, which served up its best fare in the early morning—great coffee and glazed doughnuts made on site. After waiting through a lengthy line that had extended out the front door, he bought large coffees for himself and Angie, a dozen doughnuts for the nurses, and a few for his personal use.

"Oh, thank heavens," Angie said when she saw the coffee. "I tried a cup from the cafeteria, but it tasted like muddy water. I poured most of it down the sink."

"Did you get any sleep?" Phil asked.

"Not bad." She pointed to a fold-up bed sitting in the corner. "I kept an eye on Dani's blood pressure, and it stayed around one-thirty to one-forty all night."

"Thanks for staying with her. If you want to run home, shower, whatever, take the car." He handed her the keys.

"I smell bad? Is that what you're saying?"

"No worse than usual," he said.

"If I weren't enjoying this doughnut so much, I'd throw it at you. Look, while you're in such a good mood, how about when Dani goes home? I move a few of my things into your spare bedroom for a while. Dani's going to need some help, and you'll be working unless you plan early retirement. Sit around on your fat ass all day."

"That's the last time I bring you coffee but staying over sounds like a good idea. She'll like having company, even if it's only her sister."

As Angie left, she punched him on the shoulder. "I don't know how she puts up with you." Then she kissed his cheek. "Take good care of our girl."

Sometime later, while Phil was still trying to find a

comfortable position in a chair apparently designed for something other than sitting, a place to stack books, perhaps, a nurse with hair almost the same shade as Dani's came in and adjusted the IV. "Thanks for the doughnuts, Mr. Claussen. We really enjoyed them."

"You bet." He stood beside her as she turned a dial, watching the digital reading on the machine.

"Dr. Polhill wants the sedation reduced, so don't be surprised if she wakes up soon."

"Thank God," Phil said. "I can't wait to hear her voice."

His gaze flicked from Dani's face to the wall clock to the blood pressure monitor, then started the same sequence all over again. He tried to look away, thinking that by watching so closely he caused things to slow down, like a closely watched kettle that refused to come to a boil, but he couldn't.

Then, at last, it happened; her eyes opened, and just that quickly, she seemed to be wide awake, none of the post-anesthesia drowsiness. With her free hand, she pulled the oxygen mask from her face. "Hi, handsome, give us a kiss, will you?"

Just as quickly, Phil's world filled with sunlight, storm clouds rolled away, roses bloomed, and children laughed. He wanted to fall on his knees and give thanks, but first, he wanted to kiss her, over and over again.

Then the nurse was tapping him on the shoulder, gently at first, then more forcefully. "Mr. Claussen, you're making her blood pressure go up again."

Chapter Thirty-Three

On the fourth day, Dr. Polhill came by shortly after the breakfast trays had been taken away, changeover time for Angie and Phil, who had been trading twelve-hour shifts at Dani's bedside. "Since she's been perfectly stable for the last couple of days, I think we can move her out of the ICU today. Lots more space for you in the regular rooms."

Dani gave him a thumbs-up and a big smile.

"Okay, if I leave you at the mercy of your loving sister for a while?" Phil asked.

"Only if you give me a big kiss before you leave. Look, you guys don't have to watch me all the time. I love having you around, but the nurses take great care of me."

"Wait until we get you home again," Phil said. "I'm going to ignore you completely. Stay out late partying every night."

"You do that, and I'll have all the locks changed, and you can sleep in the garage." She grabbed his nose and pulled him down to kissing distance. It was a long kiss.

****

At the end of the third week in July, after a brief thunderstorm had cooled temperatures slightly, Dani was sent home in an EMT vehicle, but not without a struggle. "It's humiliating, getting hauled around in that." Only after Phil threatened to handcuff her to the gurney did she submit.

"And my house had better be spotless," she said.

"Earl and me had a few parties while you were gone, so there might be a few beer cans lying around."

"If I find even one, I'll murder you in your sleep. Now, give me a big kiss before they shut me up in here."

Keeping Dani on bed rest was even more difficult than getting her into the EMT truck. That task fell to Angie, and she carried it out with moderate success. She moved into the spare bedroom so she could keep an eye on her rebellious sister.

During most of the daylight hours, Phil and Alfie were kicked to the curb, having too little to contribute and taking up too much space while doing it. Only at night was he allowed into the bedroom to cuddle. "I'm sorry to be so much trouble," she said as she pulled him as close as her massively distended abdomen would allow."

"You're no trouble," he said.

"But women have been doing this forever, most of them with no help at all, and I have to get driven around in an ambulance, waited on hand in foot."

"I hope you don't expect this kind of treatment after you've delivered our daughter."

"Oh, I'll be even worse. I'll keep a little bell beside the bed to ring for you."

"I expect I'll be putting in a lot of overtime at work."

****

In mid-August, Dani put an end to all the bickering. She was rushed to the hospital in Phil's cruiser, red and blue lights flashing, and, after three-and one-half hours of labor, brought into the world seven pounds and two ounces of beet-red, screaming fury, Regina Elizabeth Claussen. Her piercing protests continued until she was placed in Phil's arms, where she became strangely quiet.

"What have I done?" he asked, even more frightened by the quiet than he had been by the screaming.

"Looks like she's going to be daddy's girl," said Dr. Polhill's nurse."

****

The Clayton Neighbor Lady Brigade, that small, effective, and unobtrusive troop of women who came and went, rain or shine, each day, doing whatever needed doing, came and took care of all that needed taking care of, then left as quietly as if they'd never been there. Their number quickly dwindled, though, as Dani became more active. Angie moved out of the spare bedroom by the end of the second week but continued with frequent visits.

"Amazing how close the girls have gotten," Earl said one Sunday afternoon as he and Phil, banished to the front porch, drank their beer in relative quiet. "You're a real family man now."

"It's easy enough. Most of the time, they just want me out of the way. What are you doing with yourself these days?"

"Nothing much. Hardly any repo work to do. What I need is a real cushy job like yours, just drive around all day, crack a few skulls with my nightstick...all legal, of course."

"Maybe I'll mention it to Angie, see if she's got

401

any ideas for you."

"No, please, man, don't do that to me."

****

The transition from summer to fall was gentle and seamless that year. The days becoming shorter, the temperatures moderating, was hardly noticeable. On these balmy evenings, the Claussen family, baby Regina in a carrying pack that left her staring out at the world from the height of her father's chest, had begun taking walks, usually ending up at the campground. Phil had left the gate unlocked now since the motivation for someone to trash the place seemed to have disappeared when the primary culprit, the DA, entered prison.

"This will always be such a special place for us," Dani said, pressing close against Phil's side. They walked to the campsite where, not quite a year ago, an RV had sat, their first home. The new skiff sat on a trailer that Phil could manage by hand. "You have to start taking us for boat rides when it gets a little warmer," she said.

Dani poked a stick into remnants of blackened wood in a circle of stones. "We had so many fun campfires here, remember?"

They walked on hand-in-hand down the path to the pond where an early-rising crescent moon had already climbed above the rim of pines. "Lots of memories here, too," he said.

"How do you think Regina would feel about her mom and dad skinny dipping in the pond?" She stopped for a moment, staring at him. "Did I say something wrong?"

"No, I was just remembering seeing you standing naked in the water one night, all golden and glowing in

402

the moonlight, the most beautiful thing I'd ever seen and something I'll never forget."

"I'll do it again for you right now. Just say the word."

"Don't you dare," he said. "Your days of running around naked are over."

"Rats, you're no fun." She slipped an arm around his waist.

"I've been thinking," he said as they ambled back up the path.

"I thought I'd cured you of that."

"Almost, but consider this for a minute. It seems like a big waste, all those nice campsites going unused. I don't want to open it up to the general public, too much trouble, but maybe Boy Scouts, Girl Scouts, church groups, and such. I could fix up some more campsites. There are fourteen now. What do you think?"

"Holy cow."

"Holy cow good or holy cow bad?"

"Holy cow, that's a wonderful idea," she said.

"Okay, here's the part I need your help with. What do you think of asking Earl to be like a manager?"

"Earl Biggers herding a bunch of kids? That's something I'd pay to see," she said.

"He wouldn't have to do much, I mean, any group would have to bring their own responsible adults. Only problem is, I can't pay him very much."

"Don't worry about Earl. Uncle Sy left something behind for him."

"Earl too? How many people did Sy set up?"

"Uncle Sy had a lot of money. He set up annuities for Dani, me, and Earl. Besides, Earl has been grumbling about wanting out of the repo business. He might jump at the chance to do something else, especially something where he wouldn't have to do much work."

"I'll talk to Sandra Newton, see if I have a green light with the property."

****

Phil set up a meeting with his attorney to discuss the legal aspects of the campground proposal. She greeted him with open arms, then she held him at arm's length and looked him up and down. "You've lost weight, and you need a haircut."

"I think I can manage that," Phil said. Then he laid out his campground proposal. Sandra's eyes lit up as she listened.

"A wonderful idea," she said when he'd finished. "Whatever made you think of it?"

"I was walking through it a few days ago, and it seemed like a shame to leave it sitting empty when somebody could be enjoying it. It's such a beautiful spot."

"I see no reason why you can't move right along with it," she said. "Sy had all the permits and insurance set up, so I'll just dig out the paperwork and bring everything up to date. You might think about some security on-site, just in case."

"Earl Biggers will take over security."

"I can't tell you how happy I am to see you doing this. Once you get it set up, you'll probably be getting a call from the Clayton Civic League."

"What, more paperwork?" he asked.

"No, membership, Sy was a member, and I'm sure they'll want to recruit you. So, does Clayton feel more

404

like home now that you've become an integral part of the community?"

"Yeah, just so long as I don't get arrested and thrown in jail again…twice in the last two years. That's too much, don't want to start a trend."

"I know it isn't funny," she said, still laughing, "But for a man who never even got a parking ticket before, you've led a very exciting life lately."

A moment passed, the soft ticking of the wall clock the only sound.

"You remember when I told you once that I felt like everything was all prepared and set out for me before I got here like I was just following a script?"

"I do remember, yes, the big cosmic plot. You still think that?" she asked.

"I think I have an alternative explanation, something much closer to home."

"Tell me, I'm dying to hear this."

"Our old friend and benefactor, Sy Birch, I think he understood human nature a lot better than I realized. I think he knew what he was setting in motion all along. It wasn't a cosmic plan. It was the Sy Birch plan."

"Including getting himself shot to death?" She looked incredulous, eyebrows arched, head shaking slightly.

"Including getting himself shot. I don't know if I ever told you, but when I found his body, he was smiling. He knew the old bastard knew what he'd set in motion, maybe not down to the smallest detail, but the bigger picture. I think he saw that clearly because he'd planned it that way."

"I think I like your cosmic plot idea better," she said.

"You knew better than anyone how smart he was. I can see him pulling all the strings like some puppet master."

"Phil, we should keep your theory to ourselves, okay? Maybe you're right, but if you go telling people what you've just told me, they'll put you in jail again, and remember, three strikes and you're out, or in, as the case may be."

"I guess I didn't really expect you to buy it. I just wanted to say it out loud, see how it sounded."

"I'll say again, Sy Birch picked the right man. I'm glad you're here, Phil, really glad." She pushed her chair away from the desk. "Now, when can I come out to see the baby?"

****

The warm days of autumn ended officially as December roared in with wind and rain and skies so dark that AM and PM seemed only slightly different. The deluge continued for four days, flooding roadways and washing away a few bridges. Phil drove the new social worker, a tall, rather gaunt woman who reminded him of Sandra Newton, out with some emergency supplies for the local shut-ins.

"I can't understand how they live like this," she said several times as they skidded up the boggy paths to the individual shacks. Phil lugged in boxes of food and other needed items, and, in each case, the social worker pleaded with the occupant to come back into town with them where they could be safe and warm and dry...to no avail. She would learn. Those to whom a hovel and a small plot of ground were all they had left would leave only when they had taken their last breath, not before.

Creek beds that had contained only a trickle, if any

stream at all, now overflowed their banks, threatening homes and families. The sheriff, laid up with a severe ankle sprain, issued a temporary evacuation order, ineffective, since the residents refused to leave. By the time the storm weakened, Phil had been on the road continuously for four days, including a good part of the nighttime hours. Still, there were those who fared worse, such as the poor ranchers who somehow had to keep livestock fed and safe from drowning.

Late in that fourth evening, a drenched, exhausted Phil staggered through his back porch door, tripped over his dog, and fell to his knees. Dani was by his side in a flash, tugging on his arm. She pulled him into a chair, took off his waterlogged shoes, and peeled off his jacket, now pasted to him like a second skin. Then she pulled him toward the bathroom.

"Where are we going?" he asked.

"Hot shower for you, very hot."

"I don't need to get any wetter," he said.

"First, we get you warmed up—you're shivering— then we'll dry you off."

Sometime later, a much warmer, much drier Phil sat at the kitchen table, sipping a hot cup of coffee as if it were the best he'd ever tasted. "Much better," he said.

"Have you eaten today?" Dani asked.

"I think so, can't remember for sure."

She sat a steaming bowl of beef stew in front of him along with several hot, golden-brown biscuits on a side dish. "It's probably not as good as Angie's, but it will fill you up, and it's hot."

Phil said nothing else until the stew was gone, every last morsel.

"I guess you liked it," she said.

"I guess I did. Thanks."

He crept by the nursery for a quick peek at Regina. Instead of sleeping, she was wide awake and smiling. He gathered her up in his arms, the first time he'd held her in four days. "You're supposed to be asleep, young lady."

"She was waiting for you." Dani had followed him in so silently he didn't know she was standing beside him. "That seems to be the way with women around here, all of us waiting for you."

****

It seemed as if he'd just drifted off to sleep when the phone rang. Ten-thirty, an elderly man driving home from the market had apparently abandoned his truck when it stalled out in a flooded section of the road. The neighbor who found the truck said the groceries were still in the front seat of the vehicle, but the driver was nowhere to be found.

As Phil walked out of the bedroom door, Dani met him in the hallway. "Don't go back out, Phil. Can't it wait until morning?"

He shook his head. "I'll be back before you know it." The thought of not going out never entered his mind. This was his job, his community now, and when the call came, he would go, simple as that.

Phil pulled up behind the stalled truck, its tires half-submerged in water, moments before the EMS vehicle arrived. He waded into the flooded area and found the man, incoherent and shaking uncontrollably, trapped on a rocky outcropping, not fifty yards from his truck. Phil and the taller of the EMS crew struggled through thigh-deep icy water, tripping over stones they could not see, loaded the man onto a stretcher, and carried him to safety.

"What about my groceries?" the man said after they'd moved him into the warmth of the EMS van.

"I'll get them," Phil said.

For the second time that night, Dani helped him out of soaked clothing and hustled him into a hot shower.

"This is the last time," she said, "because you don't have any more dry clothes."

His labors did not go unnoticed. The following Saturday, under an innocent blue sky that showed no remorse for the tons of water it had dumped on the town of Clayton, endangering life and property, causing misery and chaos, most of the seats in the county courthouse were filled as Phil, and the EMS crew were called up to receive citations for bravery and service to the community. Dani and Regina had front row seats, alongside the sheriff whose ankle was in a cast: the sprain had turned out to be a fracture.

****

The relative calm that followed the storm lasted about two weeks, ending when preparation for the next annual Christmas party kicked into high gear. Phil and Dani had had a brief discussion about the event, both agreeing that community traditions had to be upheld. Dani and the Neighbor Lady Brigade bustled about doing all manner of mysterious things, while Phil, as instructed, stayed out of the way. He and Alfie kept up their daily walk, leaving and returning via the back door. Weather permitting, he took Regina along in her carrier. He'd had little experience with babies, but this one seemed much happier than he would have expected. She occasionally fussed, almost as if to show she could, then quickly returned to her cheerful self.

In the third week of the month, a large Christmas tree appeared, carried by two strapping young men who brought it into the living room. When set into its base, it reached almost to the ceiling, leaving just enough room for the star that would be placed on its top. Other than carrying in boxes and boxes of decorations, Dani informed Phil that his help with ornaments and such would not be needed. She and her friends could handle it. Just as well, he had a dog to walk and a baby to carry.

The transformation from living area to holiday wonderland, which had seemed magical to him the year before, left him just as mystified now, all a tribute to Dani's efforts and Sy's organizational plan, honed and refined over the years.

The evening before the big event, he gathered Alfie and Regina, now bundled up so thoroughly that she barely fit into her carrier, for their evening stroll. "You can come along if you want, beautiful night out," he said to Dani, who was stretched out in his recliner with a drink in her hand and a frazzled look on her face.

"Thanks, but I need some time off my feet, and this drink, most of all."

"You've done an incredible job," he said.

"As Uncle Sy used to say, it's all in the planning."

"Back soon," he said.

Later that evening, with Regina down for the night and Alfie banned to the back porch, Dani gave him a preview of the rooms with all the colored lights twinkling away. "Stunning," he said. "You've done a fantastic job."

"I had lots of help," she said, holding his hand.

"Now, all we need is food and people."

"No problem," she said.

No problem at all. By noon on December 24, food began arriving in vans, family cars, in the back of pickup trucks, continuing until every available surface was covered with edibles.

"Who's going to eat all this?" Phil asked, having forgotten about the hordes that descended on them the year before, and probably many years before that as well.

****

Dani had just given him his pre-party inspection. "I want you to look good, but not too good." She straightened his tie for the third time.

"Whatever, I thought you'd be wearing that little red Santa's helper dress," he said.

"Oh, no, Amy Pendergast is wearing that. She's just turned eighteen, and she's cute as a button in it, sexy too. She'll be a real treat for the guys, except you, that is. If I catch you gawking at her, there'll be trouble."

****

Phil felt as if he'd just blinked, and a room that was almost empty was suddenly filled with people, shaking hands, hugging, laughing, chatting. Dani brought Regina out for her grand debut, and the little show-off charmed everybody in sight. Now, just short of five months old, she was beginning to form words, sounds, actually, because so far these gurgles lacked specificity; "Da-da" might be directed at Phil or the dog with equal enthusiasm.

Tall Jack Penfield, local pharmacist and chairman of the Clayton Chamber of Commerce, whistled, drawing everybody's attention to where he stood with his hand on Phil's shoulder. "I want to take a moment to express my deep personal thanks to Phil and Dani for carrying on the tradition of this great party. It just wouldn't seem like Christmas without it."

He was interrupted by an enthusiastic round of applause.

"To Phil, I want to say that Sy Birch made a good choice when he chose you to carry on his legacy. We all know this has been a hard year for you, as hard as they come, and it means a lot to us that you've seen fit to carry on with this fine shindig. I want to add something that some of you might not have heard. Phil and Dani have plans to develop the Birchbark Campground into a recreational area for local youth groups." More applause, louder this time.

The ball was in his court now. Time to step up. Phil took a deep breath and hoped the right words would come out. "First things first," he said, "and that is to give credit where it's really due. Dani, come over here."

She came, holding Regina in her arms and blushing furiously.

"Dani told me early on that as far as party planning went, my job was to stay out of the way while she and her friends took care of business. I did just as I was told, and you can see how things turned out. Thank you, Dani, and thanks to all of you who worked so hard to make this happen. Sy would be pleased."

More applause. Regina beamed since obviously, all this commotion must be about her. But her patience soon wore out, and she began to fuss. "Someone needs to go to bed," Dani said.

"Let me take her." As soon as she was folded in Phil's arms, she settled down and went to sleep.

****

With his daughter bedded down after he'd covered her with kisses, he rejoined the festivities. Dani pushed her way through the crowd tugging Angie along behind her. As soon as they reached Phil, Dani took her sister's left hand and shoved it into Phil's face. "Would you look at that?" she said.

The diamond on Angie's ring finger reflected the multicolored lights on the tree.

"Congratulations." He wrapped her in a vigorous hug.

"Earl said you convinced him," Dani said.

"Me? I never said anything."

"Well, something you did or something you said put him in a marrying frame of mind because he proposed with roses and down on one knee. He was so nervous and cute he could hardly get the words out," Angie said.

"Oh, man, I'm going to give him so much grief about that. Down on his knees, you say?"

In unison, both women jammed forefingers into Phil's chest. "Don't you dare say anything about that. It took him long enough, and I don't want him to change his mind."

"Okay, okay, where is the lucky man?" Phil asked.

"He caught a cold and didn't want to spread it around, so he stayed home," Angie said.

"Come to think of it, I never got an official proposal," Dani said, "Certainly not one with roses and a guy on his knees."

"We were just celebrating the news about your pregnancy," Phil said. "It didn't seem like the right time."

"You're not going to get off that easy, Phil Claussen. As soon as we get the party stuff put away, I want a real proposal, one with romance and roses and you down on both knees."

"If that's what you want, that's what you'll get," he said. "But I don't know where I'll find roses in December."

"Ask Earl. He found some."

****

"What an incredible evening." Much later, Phil looked around at a room that, despite having been packed with people a short time before, now was amazingly neat and tidy and contained just the two of them.

"You looked as if you were enjoying yourself," Dani said. "Now, carry me to bed like you carried our daughter."

The logical course of action after a long, strenuous day would be a good night's sleep, but that was not to be, not yet. Dani wanted to talk, and Phil, wiser man he had become, would listen.

"I do wish Addie could have been here for the party," she said.

"Yeah, but her mom had other plans, or so she said. At least she'll be here next week."

"I can't wait to meet her," Dani said. "She'll get to meet her new baby sister. Aren't you excited?"

"Yeah, I wonder if she's changed much."

"She's a grown-up girl now, probably thinking about college."

"She'd better be. I just hope I can keep her entertained while she's here."

"I'll take care of that, don't you worry," Dani said.

With that, Phil thought perhaps it was time for sleep, but no, Dani switched on the bedside lamp and pulled off her nightgown. "I have another job for you. Regina will need a playmate."

"But she's got me and Alfie too."

"She'll need someone her own size. Besides, you're *my* playmate. She'll need one of her own. So, now that you know how to make babies, this would be a good time to get started on another one, don't you think?" She flipped the sheet off him, then climbed astride, beginning a gentle rocking motion that had his full attention in no time at all.

"Oh, God, do we have to start this all over again?" he said through a grimace so obviously fraudulent as to be laughable.

"That's right, Mr. Phil Claussen. I waited a long time for you, so get busy." She leaned down, so their faces were close, that old trick where noses touched, and they breathed the same breath, and the magic in her eyes was all he could see or wanted to.

Later that night, as Dani, snoring softly, lay so close to him it was as if her own bare body was fused to his own, he whispered softly into the golden pillow of her hair. "You know, I finally figured it out. That first time on the road when I picked you up, and you said you'd been waiting for me, and I said that was crazy. I get it now. All along, I'd been waiting for you too."

"Took you long enough," she mumbled, still groggy. "Now, kiss me and go to sleep."

A word about the author…

A native Tar Heel, Mike Owens obtained his undergraduate and medical degrees from the University of North Carolina, Chapel Hill, NC, and later, an MFA in creative writing from Old Dominion University in Norfolk, VA, where he now resides. His topics in fiction vary widely, ranging from science themes to end-of-life issues to erotica…go figure! His new release, *IT HAD TO BE YOU*, follows a man whose self-destructive behavior leads him into a romantic adventure with a young woman who appears to have been waiting for him all along.

https://www.mikeowens42.com
https://www.twitter.com/mikeowens42
https://www.facebook.com/mikeowenswriter
https://www.goodreads.com/author/show/1701
5032.Mike_Owens

Thank you for purchasing
this publication of The Wild Rose Press, Inc.

For questions or more information
contact us at
info@thewildrosepress.com.

The Wild Rose Press, Inc.
www.thewildrosepress.com